"You can relax now. It's secured here."

"So I can see, *chouchou*." Ja— —'s not every day I see sh——— —ready and pointir— —rded her for a r— —hers. "You could— —lone something c— —men down?"

Vivi had thought about it, but for some inexplicable reason, she had decided not to. He was supposed to be this hotshot SEAL, so . . . Okay, she admitted to wanting to test the man. She had omitted telling him the people here worked for her.

"And what good would that do, Lieutenant? I'd be dead and so would you. I figured you'd be smart enough not to do anything."

"Don't test me, Vivi," he murmured, still looking around. "I'm very unpredictable when I'm nervous."

She doubted that; she had seen him in a few situations that told her the man didn't get jittery very often. She hid a smile. "Don't be," she said. "I'm here to protect you from bad people."

"I feel better already."

By Gennita Low

THE PROTECTOR
FACING FEAR
INTO DANGER

Gennita Low

THE PROTECTOR

AVON BOOKS

An Imprint of HarperCollinsPublishers

Low

AVON BOOKS
An Imprint of HarperCollins*Publishers*
10 East 53rd Street
New York, New York 10022-5299

Copyright © 2005 by Jenny Low
ISBN: 0-06-059110-2
www.avonromance.com

First Avon Books paperback printing: January 2005

Avon Trademark Reg. U.S. Pat. Off. and in Other Countries, Marca Registrada, Hecho en U.S.A.
HarperCollins® is a registered trademark of HarperCollins Publishers Inc.

Printed in the U.S.A.

10 9 8 7 6 5 4 3 2

To Mother and Father;
to my Stash, my Knight,
and Mike, my Ranger Buddy,
the ultimate protector

Acknowledgments

Special thanks to Maria "HoF" Hammon and Melissa Copeland, two special gems; the sea mammals whose smart mouths were a bad influence; Erika Tsang, my editor, and Liz Trupin-Pulli, my agent. They are all my special protectors.

And always, the ladies at Delphi TDD, my shadow warriors, who read for me, especially Sandy "Sadista" Still, Mirmie Caraway, Karen King, Angela Swanson, Teena Weena Smith, and Katherine Lazo.

Thank you RBL Romantica for all your support!

Please support ECPAT (End Child Prostitution in Asia) and TWMAEW (Third World Movement Against Exploitation of Women).

CHAPTER
1

Beer in hand, Jazz leaned back against the sticky wooden counter and surveyed his men and a bunch of other military outfits having their version of civilized fun. Who cared that half the guys here had dried blood on their clothes? Or that some had weapons out in the open?

After a week toting submachine guns and C-4 around in a hot jungle in Southeast Asia, his team had netted twenty-two kills without a single casualty. Twenty-two lives gone and three government hostages freed. They had disappeared back into the darkness when the expected "aid" had arrived to clean up. Such was the nature of covert operations. All the fighting and none of the glory. Now, as they relaxed in this little bar, it wasn't easy putting back the thin veneer of humanity. Most of the boys didn't even bother. Who cared in a noisy, flashy bar this side of civilization?

Jazz crossed his legs and took a long swig from his bottle. He was tired, but this was as good a place as any to hang out until their ride arrived. He and his team had just finished a bloody battle with a gang of drug lords who were holding some local officials hostage. The drug lords, however, were revered as rebels by the locals, and the government didn't want to be the ones to get their own.

So let's send in those crazy Americans, thought Jazz cynically as he took another swig. Those stupid commandos would go in where no other governing body would. Operation Kum Quat. The little golden fruits. He had no idea why it was called that until he saw the "lords." He shook his head and finished his beer, setting the bottle on the bar counter. A fresh ice-cold one appeared immediately, and he twisted the cap open.

He shook his head again, trying to clear the image of the two little boys with fat cigars in their mouths, carrying small Uzis like pros. They had been sitting on some sort of double throne, passing judgment on the captives when Jazz and his men surrounded their hideout.

Unfuckingbelievable, Cucumber had whispered into his radio mouthpiece. Jazz couldn't have agreed more. Here they were—eight SEALs, trained to operate in the deadliest of situations—and they had to deal with two kids who didn't look older than ten or eleven. Except they weren't two ordinary kids. One of them had pointed his weapon casually at the first prisoner, and before anyone could move, the captive was dead.

That was when Jazz put aside the thought that those were kids. Their operation was to extract the hostages, and one of them had just been eliminated. No time. The command had come over his helmet intercom and the battle began . . .

Jazz finished his second beer, looking around again to check on his men. Cucumber and Mink were relaxing by the piano. Crazy guys had their Hollywood sunglasses on. They had gone to D.C. to do some unkoshered favor for Hawk and his cousin Steve McMillan, and Steve's girlfriend had given them to the boys later. They even got a pair for him. Hawk was talking to some chick in the corner. Of course, no surprise there; he was a chick magnet.

As if he knew he was being watched, Hawk turned his head to meet his eyes, a silent question between cocommanders. Jazz shrugged. Everything was A-OK. Hawk shrugged back and returned his attention to the female.

His other men were sitting quietly conversing by the door.

Two of them had volunteered not to drink tonight—their job was to sit by the entrance and to be alert for anything. They were in a strange land, after all, and not everyone was friendly to Westerners here, only to the almighty American Dollar.

There were other soldiers around, mostly Americans, and they had given Jazz and his men little attention since they'd strolled in separate small groups into the bar. Their mission was completed, they had no need to draw attention to themselves, except as regular military personnel out having a good time . . . with blood on their clothes.

Jazz downed his beer. Another one slid down the counter. He didn't even glance at the bartender as he caught the beer bottle with one hand. What he needed was a good buzz. He wanted to wipe out the jungle scene in his head. Maybe they would have a few days of down time before the next job. Just . . . him and his dog, if possible.

"Yo, Jazz, we need some tunes!" Cucumber yelled out.

"Yeah, come over here and give us some of your blues, man!" Mink encouraged, waving his beer bottle in the air.

Jazz grinned. The two men looked ridiculous in their sunglasses as they executed a series of Blues Brothers moves. These were his brothers-in-arms, celebrating the fact that they were still alive. He uncrossed his leg and sauntered to the corner of the dark bar. The guy at the piano stood up, waving him the rights to the seat. Obviously, Cucumber and Mink had told him that Jazz was the entertainment tonight.

Jazz sat down and looked at the yellowed keys of the piano, automatically testing some chords. Someone at the bar liked music, obviously. The piano had been recently tuned.

He took another long swallow of beer and smacked his lips. A big smile surfaced as he glanced at the expectant faces of the men standing around the piano. Boys would be boys. And military boys, fresh from combat, the smell of jungle still in their hair and clothes, in need of a shave and a hot shower, always needed entertainment.

He cracked his fingers exaggeratedly and waggled his eyebrows. "Blues, eh?" he asked. "My specialty, as you know."

Cucumber leaned a big arm on Mink's shoulder and pretended to play a harmonica, giving the standard beginning chords of a blues tune. "That's right, Jazz-man . . . we wanna hear the bluuuuueeeeeees . . ." he howled the last note out. Mink joined in.

Jazz repeated the beginning blue chords and sang without prompting. Blues had always been his favorite kind of music, right from the soul. The words came naturally.

"I was wearing a pair of white shoes,
I said, I was wearing a pair of white shoes . . .
Now they're bloody black and sooooo uncool
You don't track in the jungle in no white shoes
You stupid bloody fool . . .
Bloody black and sooooo uncool
And that's why I'm siiinging the bluuuues. . . . yeah . . ."

Used to singing and making up silly songs from their years together in training and field work, Cucumber and Mink dutifully repeated the refrain and added their own dirtier versions, about women and white shoes, about drinking and white shoes, about anything and white shoes. None of them brought up the reason, which were what those kids in the jungle were wearing.

As Cucumber and Mink jived, heads bobbing to the rhythm, sunglasses sliding down their noses, a commotion in the far corner of the room caught Jazz's attention. He continued pounding the keys as he gazed across the bar.

Two men had a woman cornered against the dirty wall. There was another man holding her arm, stopping her as she backed away. She shook her head vigorously, and the man who had her captive smacked the side of her head. She immediately stopped struggling, standing there passively as the other two men started touching her.

Jazz stopped playing. Pushed back his chair. Stood up.

As he approached the group, he noticed three other women cowering on a bench against the far wall. He hadn't noticed them before since his back was to them and they sat out of sight behind the wooden bar. There was a doorway next to the bench, with a dirty flowery plastic curtain partially open. Every bar had such a side entrance. They led into dark hallways with small cubicles that contained nothing more than a mattress and an oil-lamp.

"What's the matter, babe? Let me take care of you!" one of the two men crooned.

Jazz didn't need an explanation of what was going on. It was always the same. Soldiers, professional or mercenaries, attracted certain types of businesses at the edge of civilization. There were always alcohol and gambling. And there were always women.

It was the uncivilized part of being a soldier that no one actually talked about. One could boast of how many kills one had gotten in the field. One could tell the story of all the blood and gore he'd seen. But other than among themselves, most soldiers left out the chapters and verses of the dirty fights and drinking bouts, the lack of humanity and manners, and the use of female flesh, when they went home. They were things soldiers just didn't tell their girlfriends and wives.

Jazz walked around a table, passing Hawk and his girl nearby. Hawk made a gesture with two fingers, a secret signal to tell him he would back him, if needed. Jazz nodded slightly. Hawk seldom interfered with anything unless he had to, but he was usually the one to drop everything to help his buddies out.

Jazz stared at the two men wearing camouflage clothes, still oblivious to his approach. They weren't SEALs and didn't look as if they belonged to any special operations from any military branch. He could usually spot the highly trained ones, Americans or foreigners alike. He visually checked them for weapons, lengthening his strides now that he was nearer.

"Come on, baby, don't be shy. See? GI give you money to buy pretty clothes." The man, with a slurred speech, had an American accent.

It never failed to disgust Jazz, though, no matter how many times he'd witnessed it. Girls—barely women—being used by drunken men who had no right to touch them. Most of them caught in a life of poverty, sold by their parents, and unable to escape. From the beginning, he had been briefed about this horror, that some countries allowed this, and had been ordered not to interfere with the cultural aspects of any foreign countries unless directed by his superiors.

Most of the time, he had learned to ignore it. His unit consisted of men trained by Admiral Madison, commander of STAR Force, the "black operations" SEAL team, and they had never caroused with women too young for them, or Jazz would have something to say about that. But this week he had seen too many children playing grown-ups. He didn't care about protocol anymore. Hell, he was going to break the arm of the asshole who cuffed that girl.

He was close enough to see the fear in the girl's eyes as she stared at the two tall men groping her. She was also obviously afraid of the man who'd hit her—a local, probably one of the bar owners—lowering her eyes when he barked sharply at her again in her native tongue. He was small, slightly a bit over five feet tall, but he had a strong build and big fists.

One of the men—sleazebags, Jazz corrected as he noted the girl's youth—reached out to touch the girl's face, and she backed into the wall, shaking her head. The man holding her pulled her back, at the same time lifting his hand.

"I don't think so." Jazz easily grabbed the short man's wrist. Despite his height disadvantage, the other man's arm was hard and strong.

The little man's beady eyes looked him over. "GI want this one, too?" He waved at the other three girls in the corner. "Lots of women, no need to fight!"

They were all too young to be women. One of them didn't seem afraid as she posed in an incongruously adult manner and smiled seductively up at him. Her eyes were bright and bold, studying Jazz's body as if he was naked already. "GI, take me. Me number one," she said in broken English, meaning she was the best. She glanced dismissively at the cowering girl between the two men, and added, "She number ten, no good, not know how to please GI."

Jazz barely paid attention to the second girl. He had met many like her, young girls who had given themselves to prostitution, and had accepted the way of life as a means to buying material things. In spite of her age, there was nothing innocent or youthful about her attitude. In this world, she could take care of herself.

He was here to make sure the first girl wasn't forced to do anything she didn't want. Tears ran down her cheeks as she stood there, watching the two men and him.

"Listen man, we saw her first. You pick somebody else."

"Yes, GI," said the local man, tugging at the wrist Jazz still held. "No need to fight."

Jazz released him. Leaning forward, he tipped up the girl's face so she had to look at him. "Do you want to go with them?" he asked softly.

There was surprise and panic in her big brown eyes, and then she shook her head. She flinched away from the man holding her arm, expecting another blow, but Jazz had already warned him with his eyes. He straightened, turned to the two men.

"Sorry, boys. The young lady said no," he informed them.

"This is none of your business, man. We're paying extra for a cherry, so fuck off," the bigger of the two said. He stepped forward and gave Jazz a push.

"No fight! No fight!" the diminutive owner yelled. "You fight, you get out."

"Aww shit, Rob, just pay for another and let's get some girlie action," the other soldier said, his speech slurred from alcohol. "Don't need no cherry, man. Let's take that babe who's all hot over there. And that other one."

He gestured at the girl who had spoken up, and she imme-

diately stood up and tugged at the hand of one her compan-
ions. Jazz was sickened at her eager smile as she almost ran
to them, pulling along the very young girl. They reminded
him of the kids from last night.

"Yes, yes, GI number one. My sister and me, number one,
number one!"

The men waved dollar bills at the owner. The pimp nodded. "Pay inside and girl show you room," he said. After
they went through the curtained door, he turned to Jazz, a
crafty look in his eyes. "You take this one?"

Jazz didn't want to, but he knew the girl would be going
with the next customer. In his heart he knew he couldn't
save her from her fate, but he was damned if he didn't save
her now. Tonight. Maybe even tomorrow, if he had enough
money. A reprieve was a reprieve.

"Name the price," he said.

The asking price for a virgin was higher but with the exchange rate as it was, every soldier was equivalent to a mil-
lionaire in these parts.

"Hawk?" he called softly, not wanting to cause any more
attention than necessary. After last night's bloody battle, he
wanted to help a real child.

"Yeah."

"Give me some money."

Hawk stuffed some notes into his open hand. Jazz pulled
out what he had in his breast pocket. There was enough to
keep the girl out of sight for forty hours, at most, but he had
to do this. Showing the cash he had, he lifted an inquiring
eyebrow. "Two days," he bargained.

The little man released the girl. "Oh yah. Pay inside. Then
take room," he said, all businesslike and polite now that he
saw cash was available. He placed the girl's hand in Jazz's.
"Rose, you be good to GI, or no money!"

The girl had been looking at the wads of cash with wide
eyes. She blinked and nodded dazedly, not taking her eyes
off the money. Jazz could see she was already imagining all
the things she could afford, and his heart sank a little.

"Hey, man, you sure you know what you're doing?" Hawk asked.

Jazz glanced at him sideways. "I'm doing nothing," he said.

"I know that, but where are you taking her? You can't keep her. We're going as soon as our ride is here. What'll happen to her then?"

"I'm going to go in there, pay for her and leave her in that room. Then I'll wait outside." Jazz didn't want to be in the bar anymore. His smile softened when he turned back to the waiting girl, who stood passively beside him. "I promise, no one is going to hurt you for a while, okay?"

She frowned, not really understanding. Her brown eyes were still frightened, but her mouth pursed determinedly, as if she was trying to be brave. Jazz sighed inwardly. It was always the same dilemma for him. Coming to the aid of women in distress was his weakness. He would leave her in that room with the rest of the money, or tell her to go home, if she had one. Hawk would be mocking him after this. He always did.

"You can marry every one of them and send them back to your mama," he would deadpan. "With the way we travel, no one would be able to keep up with your polygamy habit. This way, you get to save all of the women, and I get to save my money."

Jazz's lips twisted. Oh yeah. Sending home an underage bride once a week to Louisiana. He could just see his maman's expression now.

"Pay inside," the girl said, pointing at the door.

Jazz followed her and had to bend his head to clear the doorway. He was about to step across the threshold when a leg, resting against the doorjamb, effectively blocked his path. He couldn't straighten up without risking hitting the back of his head against the frame.

"GI go home," a weak female voice said from the shadows.

She was sitting right inside the doorway, hidden from view. From his angle, Jazz could see only the top of her head, which had streaks of white in it. A cash box lay on the floor by her feet. There was a large ring with keys by the box.

"I paid," he said, thinking that the woman hadn't seen the girl. He thumbed behind his shoulder. "I paid for the girl."

The girl peeked over his side. There was a pause, then the reedy voice said again, this time more firmly. "GI go home."

The leg barring his entrance didn't budge. Not sure what the usual procedure was, Jazz waved his cash at the old woman. "Here, take this and let me pass, old lady."

There was another short pause. "You not drunk, so listen. The young should always listen to the old," she said.

Oh great. He had Grandma Confucius advising him. Maybe she was related to this girl? "It's okay, Grandma-masan," he said, trying to keep things simple. "I'm just going to pay and then make sure Rose is safe in the room and I'll be right out. See here? I'm paying for her to be in there for two days with food. You make sure she gets fed, okay? Now where is the room?"

"I take her. You go now," the old woman insisted.

She had gotten his curiosity up now. He hadn't noticed the other two soldiers before him having any problems getting inside this place. What was back there? "No, I'll take Rose myself." He climbed over the extended leg, bent down, and took the woman's hand in his. Opening her palms, he placed the dollar bills in her hand and closed it. "Now, which room?"

The bad lighting revealed a wizened face staring back at him, but he was surprised by the charged anger in her eyes. The woman didn't like him.

"The young is stupid," she told him. "Go back to bad singing, GI."

Bad singing? This old lady just called him stupid and insulted his singing. Jazz didn't quite know whether to be amused or pissed. All he wanted to do was to see this girl safely into her room and get out of there, and he couldn't even get past some pain-in-the-butt old lady.

"Room number," he said firmly. He repeated, "Room number, Grandmamasan."

The old lady bent, revealing osteoporosis in her humped back, and retrieved the big ring of keys. With trembling fingers, she pulled out one and handed it over. "GI number ten," she said loudly, "so room number ten."

Jazz shook his head in disbelief. He could hear Hawk's laughter from outside the room, which meant he had heard every word of the exchange. He took the key and walked past the old woman. She must be mad at him because she knew the girl was a virgin. That was the only reason he could think why she was angry. He sought to soothe her fears again.

"Don't worry," he said, as he followed Rose down the corridor. "I'm not going to do anything. I'll be out before you know it, Grandmamasan."

Room number ten was easy to find. It was in back, and as he passed each doorway, he heard sounds and grunts coming from inside. There were no doors, Jazz noted in disgust. He clenched his hand, resisting the urge to punch something, as he continued until he reached the one with a big red number ten painted on the plastic curtain. He wasn't sure whether he wanted to leave Rose here without a door between her and the outside.

He pushed aside the curtain, and Rose went inside first. The room was a little brighter, barely furnished, and musty smelling. She seemed to know what to do because she immediately sat on the mattress and began to unbutton her blouse.

"Oh no," Jazz said, coming forward. "No, no, don't do that."

She stopped, confusion in her eyes. Her blouse was open partway, revealing her young bosom. Jazz coughed and bent down to pull together the gap.

Suddenly the curtain behind him swished opened. Jazz pulled the girl behind him, protecting her from the intruders. There were two men, and their weapons were pointed at him. One of them flashed a badge at him.

"Interpol." The French accent was strong. "Please come with us, soldier."

"Why?" Jazz asked politely.

"We're under orders to seize all military personnel in the act of committing a sex crime against a child, per the UN directive. You will be placed under arrest until your commander or someone from your base comes for you."

"And if I say that I wasn't doing what you thought I was doing?" Jazz asked.

"You can say everything to your commander. This is a sting operation. The UN directive mandates all military personnel caught with underage prostitutes be returned to their base of command and face the appropriate laws pertaining to their own countries. Would you come with us peacefully, please?"

They were the most courteous captors Jazz had ever had. He might as well let them take him in. A fight, especially with Interpol soldiers, would get him into more trouble than he was already in.

Jazz lifted his hands in surrender. He hadn't wanted to stay in the bar anyway.

The old woman cocked her head, listening intently. The music stopped out in the bar. A lot of arguing in between sounds of chairs and tables being knocked about. It should be over in five, four, three, two . . . now. Interpol had done this exercise enough times to have it down to the exact second—confusion, badges, explanation of rights. Most of the time it was a bloodless affair. The soldiers treated it as a joke because most of the authorities didn't enforce it, shipping out suspects to avoid prosecution or embarrassment to their respective countries. The mercenaries just disappeared.

The old woman by the door sniffed angrily as she bent to pick up the cash box at her feet. Before she could retrieve it, a big pair of army boots appeared beside it. She froze, then looked up slowly. It was a long way up for a little woman. The man before her was tall and commanding. He stayed silent as he waited for her to respond.

The old woman squinted her eyes, trying to make his face

out in the dim light. "What you want?" she asked in broken English.

"Where's my friend?" He sounded calm, unhurried. He was the one who didn't sing along with the others.

"GI number ten?" she asked, tilting her head sideways to get a better look at him. Like the other man, he looked as if he needed a long bath, but the dirt and leftover streaks of camouflage makeup didn't hide the glitter in those strange golden eyes.

"That's the one, Grandmamasan," he said. "You tried to stop him from going in there. So save me some time. Where is he now?"

"Are you his big boss?" Her neck hurt from looking up. "You squat down, golden-eye GI. My back not good. I no like talk to big man's shoes."

He complied and went on his haunches so she could comfortably look down at him. Having seen so many men in this environment, she was good at judging faces. She leaned a little closer, blinking her eyes. "GI gonna listen to old woman? Not like GI number ten?"

The man nodded. "You tell me, Grandmamasan. I'll listen."

She cackled, showing her rotted teeth. "You GI number one." She bent even closer. "They have big lorry out back for all bad GIs. Take them away."

"Where will they take them?"

She shook her head. "If I tell you, you go play cowboy, right? Bang, bang, take him out of prison."

She smiled knowingly as Hawk settled back on his haunches and studied her for a moment. "You seem to know a lot, Grandmamasan." He cocked his head. "How much they pay you to do this?"

Her smile widened, pleased that she had been right. This young man was smarter than most of them. "Me old lady. No GI want old lady. Got to eat. Got to pay government." She counted off her obligations, her fingers trembling as she folded them into her hand. "Got to pay landowner. Got to pay doctor for medicine. This old back . . . it hurt when rain outside—"

She stopped when he grabbed one of her hands. "Grand-mamasan," he said quietly, calmly. "My friend is not a bad guy. I know you know this because you tried to stop him from going in there. Those Interpol men won't tell me anything, and I need him back very quickly."

She wasn't afraid of him, though he could easily crush her hand. She sensed he was a dangerous man, but then there were plenty of dangerous men in these parts. "Do not interrupt," she scolded. "I keep you waiting because you GI number one. You go after your friend, those others outside go with you. You stay here with me, they wait out in bar like good boys, yes?"

He drew in his breath sharply. "Why keep me and my men here?"

"Because you don't want to be all in prison, yes? Those guys outside powerful. Big guns. You are five, six men?" She shook her head. "They have more. They take you all in easy, and then you all in prison many days. You don't want, no?"

The young man was cocky. He grinned at her as she told him her fears. He shook his head. "No, you're right, wouldn't want that, Grandmamasan, but they won't be taking us that easily, so don't you worry about us. Tell me where they took Jazz."

"Jazz?" She frowned. "Oh, GI number ten."

"Yes."

She pointed to the cash box at her feet. "Open that." He picked it up and flipped open the lid. "See card? They give me phone number to call them."

He drew the card out and studied it. "Why did they give you the number?"

She smiled. "Young man, we all do business. Old lady not tell everything. But you call that number and you ask them where GI number ten is. I know they let go many, many GIs after phone call." Her smile turned unpleasant. "But only if they have friends who have number. No number, long long time inside waiting for their big boss."

"How do you know this?" His eyes were curious. He put the card back into the box.

She shrugged. "Old lady listen. Old lady see. You listen to old lady and so you get number. You don't listen, you go with GI number ten."

He grinned again. "Very good, Grandmamasan. I'll remember your advice. I'll call this number and if I get my friend back, I'll come back here and give you money."

"Not a kiss?" She showed him her mouth full of bad teeth, then cackled at her own humor. "Long time since old lady got kiss."

He laughed softly. "Grandmamasan, you wicked lady." He gave her the cash box, then stood up. "Tell you what. When I get Jazz out, I'll tell him he owes you a kiss."

"Two," she told him firmly.

"Two?"

"One for your thank-you. One for his thank-you."

He shook his head. "You drive a hard bargain."

She nodded in agreement. "Old lady not same with those young girls. You tell Jazz that. Now go. Old lady go bathroom."

She watched as he saluted her and walked out of the dim hallway, back into the bar to his waiting men. She knew they were a group when she first saw them wandering in. Something about them was different from the others around.

Peering out from between the curtain flaps, she waited as she watched him speak briefly to those men. They got up and left. Aha. She had been right again. That young man was the big boss. She frowned. So was GI number ten. She remembered the way he'd talked to this one, who paid attention to an old lady. Very like friends and equals.

"Jazz," she repeated in the dark. Stupid name for stupid GI.

She slowly got on her feet, and carrying the box and keys in her hands, she shuffled into the back, past all the cubicles with the ugly numbers painted on the plastic curtains. When she turned the corner, her steps lengthened. Her back straightened. By the time she reached the back room where the owner of the bar waited with an Interpol agent, she had gained several inches in height, her stoop was gone, and her movements were unhurriedly assured.

She bared her ugly teeth at the angry little man who started calling her obscenities. "You shouldn't make me angrier than I am already," she replied in his language. She came forward and backhanded him before the Interpol operative could do anything. "That's for hitting Rose."

"Got some rest?"

Jazz grinned at Hawk's question. This was his first time being confined in an Interpol facility. He knew his friend would get him out of there sooner or later. He had been surprised that the team hadn't stormed the army truck that transported him here and rescued him, but he'd guessed that was probably a bad idea. If this whole thing was a UN directive, it was better to have one SEAL in prison, rather than eight. Anyhow, if they'd taken down the Interpol team, there would have been more charges.

One of the guards had brought him to this small office, saying someone was there to meet him. Jazz guessed it was Hawk. He looked around. The room had a noisy fan in the corner. The old table, with paperwork strewn all over, inkstains and cigarette burns scarring its shellac veneer, revealed more about the situation before Hawk told him anything. Probably the office of some low-ranking personnel, and the fact that there weren't any guards outside or inside the room implied that he wasn't regarded as a prisoner who might flee.

"My roommate snores," Jazz complained.

"What's the cell like?"

"Regular. Ten by ten. One window to the outside. They change guards every four hours." Jazz sat back, eyed Hawk quizzically. "Is there a problem getting me out?"

Hawk scratched his stubble. "Yes and no."

Jazz raised a brow. "It's not like you to be undecided, pal." There were two options. Regular channels, which meant paperwork. But a covert SEAL team from the black operations group wasn't on any paperwork. If someone checked on their military "backgrounds," they weren't supposed to be anywhere near here. The other option was more unconventional.

"Do you know there's really nothing they could do except hole you up in here till your base or someone in charge calls up and gets you out?" Hawk asked. "Technically, you didn't break any local law, but since this is a UN directive, they go around pulling in military personnel because they're easier to stop."

"To stop what, soldiers from buying kids for sex?" Jazz leaned back in his chair, crossing his arms. "And are you suggesting that I sit in the cell a little longer?"

"Yeah, to both questions."

"If I didn't break any local law, and they had technically stopped me, then why am I still here? Why not just let me go?"

"It's not that simple. Interpol has a team that tracks global child sex trends, and certain individuals in there also support an organization called United Third World Against Exploitation of Women. They take the data collected by Interpol and use it for their cause."

Jazz raised his eyebrows. "Trends? Is that what they're calling it?"

"For the study, yeah." Hawk shrugged. "We both know criminal acts when we see them, but I don't think Interpol can actually call them crimes unless every UN country agrees. So anyway, you just participated in a study, buddy."

"Let me guess. A public list of military personnel in the kind of sex scandal that would horrify Westerners. That, in turn, might embarrass a government into a more active role to help fight child prostitution." Jazz rocked his chair as he thought about it. "Good tactic. But not good for us."

"Nope."

"So why aren't you busting me out?"

"Because the admiral knows where you are. Normally, getting you out would be a snap, but it would still have taken a few days for me to locate you because Interpol doesn't release information to anyone except the proper governing authorities. And since we don't exactly want the authorities to know where we are . . ." Hawk trailed off and shrugged.

Jazz shook his head. "You know, you're lucky I'm not your wife. You'd drive me insane with the way you give nonanswers."

Hawk's lips quirked. "You're lucky? I'm lucky you're not my wife. It'd be disconcerting to wake up hugging a snoring Cajun son of a bitch, to say the least." He looked around the room. "You don't think they'd just grant me access to you so easily, do you? And let me use one of their offices for a quiet chat?"

Jazz gave an exaggerated sigh. "There you go again. Are you suggesting you told them that I was your wife?" He was used to Hawk baiting him. They were coleaders in this team, and often challenged each other physically and mentally. "Don't you think they might be a bit skeptical about the relationship?"

"Unfortunately, they were. You're a bit too ugly for the part, so I had to call Admiral Madison for help."

Calling Mad Dog before debriefing was not good. It was almost admitting that they'd failed their mission. Jazz frowned. "You didn't." When Hawk shrugged, he added, "Okay, you did, and that's why you can talk to me without guards. But you aren't getting me out immediately, so I'm assuming that Mad Dog has a plan."

"Yeah. Remember that old lady that tried to stop you from going in there?"

"Yeah."

Hawk rubbed his stubble again. "She gave me the number to Interpol's UN sector. If she hadn't told me, I wouldn't have gotten through to you so quickly."

"And you wouldn't have found out that they don't release any apprehended military personnel to anyone but their commanding officer," Jazz said, his mind going through the possibilities. "So you called Mad Dog to see how to avoid the paperwork and still get them to release me without any covert activities. Who was that old woman?"

Hawk shrugged. "Some local lady who's being paid for the sting operations, I'm guessing." He gave a sly smile. "But she fancied you. I had to promise her two kisses from you to get her to talk."

Jazz stopped rocking the chair. "If she were some young chick, you would have offered your own lips instead of mine," he said dryly.

Hawk's smile widened. "Hey, you were the one who insisted on entering that backroom." His expression turned serious. "As far as Interpol's concerned, the moment you handed the money over, you bought the services of an underage female. Didn't matter what your intentions were, buddy."

"So this old lady . . . she was trying to help me all along," Jazz said thoughtfully. "Okay, what now?"

"Admiral Madison is calling our UN liaison to see how to extricate you out of this without hardware."

Hardware meant the use of force. Jazz could see the potential problems of busting a soldier out of jail when so many international organizations were involved.

"Okay, I guess I could use more sleep."

Hawk nodded. "It'll take a few more days. The liaison happens to be on vacation. You can imagine she isn't going to be too happy to get a call from Mad Dog about helping out a stupid SEAL boy in trouble for buying an underage prostitute."

"I'll have to apologize to Admiral Madison for my mistake," Jazz said quietly. "And to the team."

Hawk shrugged again. "You didn't know. Any of us would have stepped in to help that girl. For what it's worth, that part of it wasn't staged. I did some checking and found out that the stings are independent, without warning to the bartenders or the local pimps. The object of the UN directive is to take action against the soldiers, not the locals, especially those from nations that signed the Human Rights Treaty."

Jazz never did like politics. To him, it was mumbo-jumbo territory, making sense only to the people who played that game. He could see the political intentions were always good, as in this case, trying to stop the trafficking of children as sex slaves. However, he could never understand the long-winded way they took to reach that objective. He was a soldier, and the simple solution was to attack the problem head on.

"Okay, teacher," Jazz said. "Tell me why they don't just arrest the bartenders and the local pimps along with the customers? They're the ones trafficking these girls. You just said that what we saw wasn't staged, so those girls are back out on the street again, right?"

He didn't like that at all. What was the use of any directive that was only a temporary stopgap? How did that protect Rose, or kids like her?

Hawk was silent for a few moments. Jazz studied him as he waited. He'd known Hawk for ten years, from the wild days of gung-ho youth to the cynical realization of experience. Their job had always been to complete missions, and not question the politics behind them. They had celebrated and sacrificed together, and he was closer to Hawk than to his own brother. Yet sometimes he could feel Hawk distancing himself, as he was now, as if he didn't want to say aloud what was on his mind.

"The system can only do so much. In this instance, the locals don't care and their culture might seem a bit barbaric to us." He looked straight at Jazz, his clear golden eyes glittering. "I could easily kill every one of the bastards, but they're replaced immediately by others. I suppose the UN thinks taking away a source of their income is better than nothing."

"Sucks," Jazz said.

Hawk stood up. End of discussion. "You can spend the next few days writing a UN treatise if you have a better solution. I'm going to find out how this delayed our timetable." A corner of his lips curled up. "I'll make sure Grandmamasan knows you're coming to thank her."

Jazz narrowed his eyes. "I'm not kissing that mean old woman," he said, as Hawk left the room.

Hawk turned and gave his usual nonchalant salute. "A deal's a deal," he said.

CHAPTER
2

Vivi's back hurt. It wasn't easy to hunch with the extra weight of padding. Her lips twisted into a wry smile. Next time she would have to use a less strenuous disguise. Her smile turned bitter. If she were successful, she wouldn't need any of these disguises any longer.

She sat on a stool near the doorway, hidden in the semi-darkness, listening to the activities outside. Another bar. God, she was getting so tired of these dives. Another day, another bar. There were the familiar sounds of clanking glass and macho chortlings, the odd camaraderie that men found so easy whenever they gathered together.

Women would never clasp strangers around the shoulders and sing dirty ditties, with glasses of beer in their hands. But then women would never go to a bar without a little bit of perfume. These men definitely needed something. There were manly smells, and there were . . . manly smells.

She sniffed, peering out from between the plastic curtain. The girls were sitting at their corner and she frowned at the sight of a familiar face among them. Damn, it was that one who hated her. The last time she had "interfered" in her liveli-hood, the kid had gone after her with her nails, missing Vivi's eyes by mere inches.

Kid. She was barely fourteen, but there was no kid left in

that girl. She had a "business," and hated what Interpol was doing, refusing everyone's help. Her language was specific. "Fuck off," the young girl had screamed. "*Bookoo* fuck off!"

Vivi shifted in her seat, looking at the men. They would be coming over soon and she'd click the remote to signal the agents. She'd picked out the most likely to move over to the corner first; they were often already drunk and rowdy, waving their cash like kings. When they handed over their cash to her, she'd give the second signal.

Her eyes narrowed at the sight of a loner sitting in the corner. It was the grunt she'd talked to the other day . . . Hawk, that was what the men in his group had called him. What the hell was he doing here now? He was quietly drinking his beer, but his eyes were watchful.

She didn't think he was there to just drink beer. There was something dangerous about him. Same with his buddy, Jazz. She had been told he had paid Jazz a visit that morning, and was easily given access to his friend. That was interesting by itself. No one had ever gotten access so quickly before; obviously someone with a lot of power had called in ahead of time.

Even more interesting was the email she'd received this afternoon. It was from her operations chief, T., and after decrypting it, she had sat and pondered her instructions. It had to do, of all things, with the two men she'd met—Mr. Jazz and Mr. Hawk. *Bookoo, bookoo* interesting, as the local lingo went. She started at her own use of the corrupted form of *beaucoup*. God, she'd avoided using that for decades, and now it had slipped back into her vocabulary like some thief.

Her frown deepened as she continued studying Hawk at his table. Her orders were clear but it would have been nice to have an explanation. Who the hell was countermanding over and above her contract? Sure, Jazz hadn't deserved to be taken in. He'd told her he was just escorting Rose to the back and leaving, but—she shrugged—words meant nothing. The Interpol agents said they caught him unbuttoning her blouse. Besides, it wasn't *her* job to prove his innocence. Where was his commander or operations chief?

Instead, somehow, she was now responsible for that dumb GI who wouldn't listen to her warning. She didn't have time to go through all the paperwork to get him out. Who was he, anyway? The email told her to leave her fax line open, so she should have some answers soon.

She watched three party-hearty males in uniform staggering over to the corner. Right now, it was time to focus on her job. Once they handed over their cash in exchange for services, she had the evidence necessary to call in the operatives outside. After that—she gave Hawk a last peek—she would handle that one.

It didn't take long before he wandered over. She gave him good marks for waiting until after Interpol had taken away the new detainees.

"Grandmamasan."

She feigned surprise as she looked up from the cash box. "Oho, you! Golden eye. What the soldiers say? Whazz-up?" She cackled in amusement as she imitated the American slang, then coughed feebly as she peered up at the tall soldier.

The man really had remarkably pretty eyes. They glittered back with amusement. "You funny, Grandmamasan," he commented and squatted down in front of her without her asking. She stared straight into his eyes, knowing the semi-darkness protected her. "I'm still waiting for my friend to be released."

"GI number ten," she reminded him, suppressing a cheeky grin.

"Yes, GI number ten. I was wondering, since you've done this with Interpol so many times, how the operation works. First, you get the bar owner to agree to all this operation, then when the men pay you and go back there, Interpol comes in and does their part. Like clockwork. Everything very practiced. What do you do after this happens, Grandmamasan?"

She paused a few seconds, half tempted to tell him the truth. "Why you want to know?" she countered in her broken English.

"To help my friend."

She shook her head. "Oh, he in big trouble. I tell Interpol people he give me money and say he want room. I sign papers. Interpol agents also sign papers, tell what they see in room."

"Okay, that makes sense. Have you ever been told not to sign any papers?"

She smiled slyly. "Of course," she replied. Hell, if she had to release the guy, she might as well have some fun. "Old woman smart. Never give things for free."

"How much?"

She leaned close and whispered *sotto voce*, "I always ask for kiss. Some GI, no problem. Some GI, they rather go to jail." She cackled.

Hawk laughed aloud. "That's the price?" he asked, his eyes thoughtful.

"That's only for all GI number ten. For all GI number one, I have special offer," she told him airily, enjoying herself now, wondering how far she dared to push this. She wanted to test these two grunts who were so important that their leader had managed to contact her operations chief.

"And what is that?"

"You have to give time. Old woman thinks slow."

"No problem, but I have a favor to ask."

"What?"

"You find me that girl Rose, the one Jazz took to the back room. I want to give her more cash to help her out."

Now that was unexpected. She was intrigued. These two men seemed genuinely concerned about Rose.

Later that day, after getting out of her disguise, Vivi went to the Interpol office to start the usual paperwork. As Hawk had said, everything was done in clockwork fashion, down to the part where many of the prisoners would be released without being punished. Their commanding officers always assured that the men would face punishment in their respective military courts but Vivi knew very little was done.

She felt disgusted at the system, and helpless. But her employer was satisfied for now—the crimes were stopped and they had data for evidence, important facts that would help them get the UN recognition and funding they desperately needed. The big picture was more important, they'd told her.

Not today. She had new orders from her own agency.

Pushing the authorization papers aside, Vivi gestured to the girl waiting patiently on the nearby sofa. She pressed the intercom. "Send the comptroller in," she said. "Rose, come with me to the window."

Rose obediently got off the sofa and followed her. The "detainees" were given a little time in the small courtyard for fresh air. As usual, the UN had special terms—the men weren't "prisoners" because they hadn't broken any local law. Only their own countries could charge and bring them to trial.

Vivi could recite the UN directive by heart, all ten paragraphs of weaving passages that had nothing to do with the crime. Instead, the whole process was slowed down by paperwork that didn't do a thing to end the purpose of the directive—to curtail the encouragement of prostitution of minor children in Third World countries by citizens from developed countries. As far as she was concerned, people who traveled to poor countries to prey on children should be the targets. Instead, she had these men down there in the courtyard, most of them young and stupid, like kids driving drunk for the first time.

It didn't excuse what they did or had planned to do. She understood the corruption that went along with the business of war. Someone who started walking down a tainted path would most likely continue, and soldiers who treated children like pieces of meat should be punished.

But she also knew they weren't. Not by their governments, anyhow. They would be whisked away as soon as their superiors found out what had happened, with no one the wiser. Unless there was a major fuck-up, like the couple of soldiers raping a teenager in Japan, there wouldn't be any black marks in these men's records. In the Japanese case, all eyes had been watching and the soldiers were taken through the system.

Vivi studied the men from behind the tinted glass window, knowing they couldn't see her. She didn't want to be here, looking at them in their uniforms. Murder was okay to men like them. Sometimes rape. Or, if they were just friendly peacekeepers, a couple of visits to the local young girls went unquestioned. Uniforms were like political words, used to commit crimes.

Her eyes were drawn to the only man who was shirtless at the moment. Unlike the others, who were talking in small groups or smoking cigarettes, he was alone, hanging on the hoop of the rusty iron basketball post. His body gleamed with perspiration in the sun as he used the post, which was buried in concrete, to exercise. She had watched as he shimmied up the post and, dangling from the hoop, did pull-ups, his powerful muscles straining as he kept going.

He was impressive to watch. He hadn't stopped since . . . she'd lost count a few minutes ago as she'd stood there admiring his physique. Up and down he went, apparently unaware of how his chest expanded as he pulled up and his stomach muscles contracted as he lowered himself down. She wanted to run her hand down that hard wall of muscles to test its strength.

He suddenly paused in mid-pull and looked in her direction, as if aware of her thoughts. Vivi blinked and almost took a step back. He couldn't see her, but that didn't stop her heart from beating a tad faster. She watched as he resumed his exercise, pulling up till he was chin level with the hoop, the muscles in his arms rippling in the sunlight. Strength. The kind that could hold a girl down. Damn that man. Why did she have to be responsible for his release?

"Come in," Vivi said, at the knock on the door. It was the comptroller. "Ready?"

"Yes, Miss Verreau."

Vivi put her hand on Rose's shoulder. The girl had been

standing quietly beside her, looking out at the scene. At her touch, she turned her attention to Vivi.

"He cannot see you," Vivi assured. "Everything you have told me is the truth, right? Are you sure he never touched you anywhere?"

Rose looked back at Jazz in the courtyard and shook her head. "No touch me," she said softly. "He no want me."

Vivi looked over Rose's head at the comptroller, who was taking notes as well as handling the tape recorder. He nodded when she arched a brow at him, answering her silent question that he was recording Rose's words.

"He never touched you intimately?"

Rose nodded in agreement. "No touch me," she repeated.

Vivi looked at the comptroller again. "Will they okay his release after I sign the papers? I don't want them protesting later because they didn't have enough figures and facts."

"They" were the members of the United Third World Against Exploitation of Women, a group that was writing a report for the UN and that was also the watchdog for the directive. They had asked the UN for an independent contract agent to facilitate part of the operation and to authenticate the study, as well as be responsible for future references. GEM had been chosen because of one very important factor. It was an agency made up of eighty percent female operatives. Perfect for the group. They even approved the GEM candidate—a woman who came from the region, who could communicate in several languages.

Vivi had wanted the job. It was a chance to return home. A way to personally find out what had happened . . .

"They won't like it," the comptroller said.

"They don't have to like it," she said. "The man's innocent, and surely they don't want the wrong people to be charged."

She said the last sentence with barely hidden cynicism. She had worked in projects where numbers were more important than truth, especially those that brought funding for the all-important bolstered figures. There were always radicals in every organization, even her own. The last thing she wanted was to come between a group and its cause, but—she glanced again at the object of her thoughts—if her operations chief wanted him out of here, there must be a good reason. T. had never done anything without one. Vivi might not trust this man's seemingly good morals and his superhuman stamina, but she trusted her operations chief implicitly.

She abruptly turned away from the window. "Give them the report, Monsieur Comptroller. Tell them I stand by it. I'll personally conduct another interview with the man and they can watch and review on their own."

"Yes, I'll set it up."

Vivi affectionately squeezed Rose's shoulder. "We have a few more things to do, Rose, then I'll take you home, okay?"

"I not want to go home," the young girl said.

Vivi sighed inwardly. That was the other problem. Stopping soldiers didn't stop the parents from pushing their daughters toward an awful fate. Poverty was pervasive in these areas, and daughters were considered useless, with their need for dowries. And she had only so much cash to give away, to stall for time.

"I'll see what I can do, Rose," she told the girl, without a single idea how to solve her problem long-term.

A couple of days of R and R—albeit behind bars—Jazz found himself in a standard interview room, with a nice clean table for a change, and a fake mirror. Just like a regular TV show. He sat there and waited. If he were a prisoner of war, all he would be required to do was give his name, rank, and serial number. But they'd assured him that he was just being "detained" by the UN police. That was the problem with politics. Too many ways to explain a situation. Either he was a prisoner or he wasn't.

The door opened and a woman walked in. She was about five-foot-seven, wearing a white short-sleeved blouse and fashionable long pants. Her dark hair was tied back tightly. She looked to be in her mid-twenties. Definitely French, he thought, as he looked into her disapproving eyes behind her small glasses. Her lips, pale pink, were unsmiling. She had a slight overbite, which gave her the stern expression of a schoolteacher.

She was probably one of the volunteers for that organization Hawk told him about. He didn't think she was there to help him, not with that glare that told him she thought he was the scum of the earth.

Jazz couldn't help it. He gave her his best smile.

Vivi almost stopped in her tracks. That cat smile was so male and assessing, for a moment, she thought he'd seen through her disguise and recognized her. She was surprised at how self-conscious she felt, walking the short distance to the table with his eyes on her under the bright, glaring lighting.

She placed the folders she was carrying on the table and looked across the four feet to where he was seated. He looked bigger than she'd remembered. Of course, playing the role of a hunched over old woman made everyone automatically look taller. But even now, with a different perspective of her target, she was quite sure *that* expression hadn't been on his face. She pulled out the chair and sat down.

"Pardon me, ma'am," he drawled, "for not getting the chair for you, but the guard did inform me to stay put in my seat and not move."

Vivi nodded. "Yes, that's the right thing to do." She pointed to a small tape recorder. "This session will be taped as soon as we begin."

Jazz liked the sound of her voice. It had a husky undertone, like a slow bluesy melody. Her French accent wasn't thick, and she spoke without hesitating, as if she used English often.

She pushed several forms in front of him. "Read these," she said. "The first one explains the directive. The second is the account of the incident by Interpol agents. The third one is a translation of Rose Tham's own account. The fourth is a questionnaire, which is optional on your part. When you're done, you may ask any questions before we begin the tape for the interview."

Jazz picked up the first form. "I have a question."

She arched a brow at him. "Shouldn't you read the forms first?"

"It's personal."

She waited, but when he didn't elaborate, she said, "Go ahead."

"How do I address you? Ma'am? Madam? I don't want to say the wrong thing on tape."

It was a simple enough question, but he made it sound intimate. His voice had the laid-back drawl that she now knew was a Louisiana twang, like velvet, with a smooth and a rough side. It made her wonder about the owner, whether he had these characteristics, too.

"You may call me Miss Verreau."

"Miss Verreau," he repeated slowly, rolling the *r*'s. "Will this interview be conducted in French?"

She cocked her head, looking down her small pert nose at him. "We're speaking in English, aren't we, Lieutenant?"

She knew his rank. What else did she know? "That's good," Jazz said. "You'll laugh at my Cajun French."

She sniffed. "There is no such thing as Cajun French."

"Then you ought to come to Louisiana sometime and listen to my maman and sisters talk. I think they have been living under the wrong impression."

Her eyes were hazel brown behind her glasses and they were looking at him superciliously at the moment. "There is only French. Everyone else speaks nonsense," she said. "But right now, that's the least of your problems, Lieutenant Zola Zeringue."

"Ouch." Jazz winced. The painful truth was out. "Please call me Jazz."

"I'm sorry, there is no Jazz Zeringue in my files. Your commander wrote all the information down himself. Now, can we get back to the papers in front of you?"

He was going to beat up Hawk. He looked down at page one. Mumbo-jumbo. Moved to page two. Okay, Interpol thought he had his hands down the girl's dress. But they were French; the French thought differently from others. Page three. Ah, the girl was on his side. That was a relief. He wasn't sure she'd understood his intentions. Page four. Oh geez.

He glanced up at Miss Verreau. She was studying him like some ugly specimen under a microscope. "Do you frequent brothels," he read aloud. "Is that a trick question?"

"What don't you understand about that question?"

"It's like one of those medical questions they ask when you apply for insurance. Do you have cancer? If I say yes, it's pretty safe to say they aren't going to give me any coverage," Jazz said dryly. He continued reading a few more questions. "How many prostitutes have you ever solicited? Do you use condoms? What countries have you been stationed in?"

"You can always say no to the first question," Miss Verreau suggested quietly. "As I've told you, the questionnaire is optional."

"Then why give it? And wouldn't the information be used against the detainee?"

She marked something down into her file, as if his questions meant something. "Lieutenant, the questionnaire is done anonymously. It's going to an organization called United Third World Against Exploitation of Women for a study."

"And I'm supposed to take your word for this?" he asked gently, and glanced at the telltale mirror to his right.

Vivi liked the way the lieutenant's mind worked. He was smart and quick. A grunt who had brains. She hadn't met that many around here. Most of them were eager to get out, signing anything put in front of them. Their commanders usually had already told them they would be out of the area within twenty-four hours, so they knew the score. Sign, deny, or make up some lame story, and then freedom.

She was tempted to call him Jazz. He didn't look like a Zola; his mother must have had scholarly aspirations for her son. "Lieutenant Zeringue, believe it or not, I'm on your side." She indicated the tape recorder. "That is for your protection. There are two tapes in the machine. You'll get a copy of the interview immediately for future reference."

He looked slightly disbelieving. It irked her, since it should be she who should regard him with dubious contempt. But the faxes she'd received today had very specific instructions.

First, she must ensure his presence not reach investigative status. She wasn't going to lie, so she had to prove to the watching witnesses that the man was innocent and the usual paperwork shouldn't be needed. Second, she was to see him safely to his commanding officer, a Lieutenant Commander Steve McMillan. That was the golden-eyed soldier who called himself Hawk. She didn't think Lieutenant Zeringue needed her to keep him safe, not after watching his exercise routine, but that was her new assignment, and she would do her job.

"Here is a fax from Admiral Jack Madison vouching for me," she continued. "You can agree to this interview, or not, after you've read it. It doesn't matter to me." She gave one of those continental shrugs that could mean anything.

He opened the envelope, and, noticing his long, artistic fingers, she couldn't help but remember his turn on the piano the other night. She had noticed him at the bar, drinking one beer after another before joining his buddies at the piano. She had thought him average, but her opinion of him since then had changed.

The few encrypted pages she had received on the man were impressive. Her operations chief obviously wanted her to know that he was important, giving her more background than usual. Lieutenant Zola Zeringue, SEAL Green Cell of STAR Force, as in Standing and Ready Force, a black operations platoon commandered by Admiral Jack Madison, was not to be taken lightly. He wasn't a run-of-the-mill soldier out for a wild night. Remembering his soiled clothing, she wondered what he had been up to with his team before that.

Jazz looked up as he refolded the fax. Why would the admiral send him a French liaison? he wondered. Hawk would have to explain it all to him . . . after he beat him up for revealing his legal name.

"All right, Miss Verreau," he said. "I've been instructed to follow your advice."

She gave him a slight nod. Did the woman smile at all? He had the urge to tell some silly joke to see whether she had a sense of humor. She turned on the recorder, stated some numbers and the date, then his name, rank, serial number, and platoon.

Jazz didn't say a word as he listened to the fictional background. He doubted Admiral Madison would leave out who he was to this liaison. In any case, he was a SEAL. He knew when to shut up and let someone protect his ass.

CHAPTER
3

Vivi didn't want to be swayed by Lieutenant Zola
Zeringue's file full of recommendations. Nor would those
watching from behind the mirrors. They would be expecting
the usual excuses they had heard so many times before. So it
was up to Jazz to convince them that he had wanted to help
Rose out by buying her.

"I didn't like the way the man was threatening the young
lady," he said calmly. "He hit her and I felt it my duty to intervene. If I recall correctly, I asked the young lady whether
she wanted to go with the two men, and she shook her head."

The man was giving a command performance, oozing lazy
charm like his nickname. Ripe and sensual, like something
one took with cream and sugar. Sweet, hot New Orleans latte
immediately came to mind. Vivi's eyes immediately went to
his mouth. He had a dimple at the corner that deepened every
time those lips quirked, which was often, as if something privately amused him. She gave him a cold direct stare, and it irritated her that he wasn't fazed by it at all. Instead, a hint of
amusement entered his eyes, although his demeanor and answers remained respectful.

"Yet you paid for her services?" she countered. That was
what had gotten him in trouble. "The other two soldiers had
paid and went off by then, isn't that right?"

"Yes, but I wanted to help the young lady out because she obviously didn't want to be there. The owner of that place was threatening to hit her. It was the only way I knew how to get her out of there with the least amount of disruption, Miss Verreau. If I had started a fight in the bar, it wouldn't have solved the situation, which was two drunks forcing themselves on an unwilling woman. I felt it was better to get Rose out of the way. I couldn't take her anywhere else, so I paid for her. The object was to keep the woman safe from harm."

With the comptroller and several volunteers for the women's organization watching, Vivi couldn't afford to be easy on him. She pressed on, trying to corner him.

"You didn't have to take her to the back room. I believe you scolded the old lady there into giving you a room number."

His blue eyes narrowed a fraction. "I didn't scold the old lady. She was a grump."

"A grump?"

"I was very polite to her, Miss Verreau. She didn't understand the situation, that's all."

"But I think she did understand, Lieutenant. She told Interpol that you'd told her to keep the girl in the room for two days. She was very detailed about what happened, giving an exact account of what you said to the two soldiers mishandling Rose. GI number ten, I think she called you. I think you owe her an apology." Vivi hadn't meant to go on and on about the "old lady." That was the point of her disguise, to be dismissed as unimportant. But a grump?

"I didn't know that. I guess she was warning me in her own way."

Vivi couldn't help herself. She knew she was playing with fire. "The young should always listen to the old," she said softly, keeping her expression innocently mild.

Jazz studied the French woman across from him as she noted down his replies. *That was what that old lady said to him.* Were those words some kind of code for him? The letter from the admiral had only two specific instructions. Listen to Miss Verreau. Follow her orders.

"Yes, I owe her an apology," he agreed amiably. "But I won't stand by and allow any man to hit a woman. If the organization doing this study can't understand that, then I have nothing else to say. And if the directive doesn't make allowances for certain scenarios, then it needs to be rewritten."

"That's not your problem now, Lieutenant."

"I know that, Miss Verreau," he said. He decided that it was her lips that caught his interest. The pale pink didn't really suit her coloring. She was what his sister, the cosmetologist, would declare an autumn girl. She needed a warmer color, something darker; then the lower lip would look more generous and her slight overbite would make him want to kiss her more.

He blinked, and almost laughed out loud. He had never redone makeup on a woman before, and God forbid that his sister's female prattling about looks and fashion had somehow invaded his subconscious. It was both ludicrous and horrifying.

"Something about the situation amusing you, Lieutenant Zola Zeringue?"

He winced at his name again. He didn't need her frosty expression, or those primly set pale pink lips, to know that the woman was warning him to pay attention to what he was saying and doing. But must she keep calling him Zola with that sting?

"No, ma'am," he said. "I don't find the charges amusing at all. I come from a large family, with six sisters and a brother. My maman always says, *'Y a pas d'homme plus bien-aimé que celui qui estime les femmes.'* I'm very well-loved."

The pale pink lips curved derisively. "Can you repeat that? Your French needs . . . practice."

Jazz didn't think his Cajun French was that bad, but then, the woman obviously thought everything other than true French barbaric. She looked down her pert little nose, daring him to repeat the sentence and embarrass himself again. He suppressed a grin. Oh, he dared.

"Y a pas d'homme plus bien-aimé que celui qui estime les femmes," he reiterated.

There is no man more well-loved than one who respects his women. Vivi twitched her nose at the sight of the dimple appearing and disappearing at the corner of his mouth. Arrogant man. And too damn confident.

"Par toutes vos femmes?" She asked with slow emphasis, arching her brows. "By all your women?"

"I hope so, Miss Verreau."

She wanted to ask how many there were, besides his many sisters, but this wasn't the time or place. She regarded him for a moment. His dossier showed a good soldier. His actions at the bar proved him to be a gentleman. His answers revealed a keen mind. But she had heard the sensuous lilt in his voice when he sang; she was now being subjected to a wicked gleam in those baby blues. She wasn't fooled. The lieutenant wasn't as perfect as his file or manners would have everyone believe.

"It seems your mother steered you right, Lieutenant. Your creed might have saved your behind in this instance. The young lady's statement supports yours as you can see from the translation in front of you."

Rose was very clear when she gave her version of what had happened. *He showed me respect.* That line and what Lieutenant Zeringue just expressed should be enough to convince the board to release him without further paperwork.

"I'm glad she understood," Jazz said. "I wasn't sure. How is she?"

"Fine."

"I hope all will be well for her."

His concern sounded genuine, as if he cared about the girl's future. Vivi recalled that he had given all his money so the girl would be "free" for two days. It was the reason she tried to stop him from walking into the sting.

As for Rose's prospects, Vivi didn't want to discuss it

now. She didn't want to dwell on how she would have to take the girl back to the shack she called home. She changed the subject abruptly. "Your money will be returned to you upon your release."

"Just give it to Miss Rose."

She met his eyes sharply. First his teammate Hawk had wanted to give the girl money, now him. She had never met men like these two.

"That's very kind of you," she said.

"It's not much. Maybe things will get better with a little money."

Vivi thought of Rose's father, who gambled all the time. She thought of her mother who only cared about Rose's brother.

"It shouldn't be long before you're freed, Lieutenant," she said at the end of the interview. "I'll take you to your commanding officer."

His blue eyes had that gleam again. *"J'espère que oui,"* he said.

I hope so. She hadn't asked whether he was referring to the first statement or the second.

Leaving Jazz with the guard in the interview room, she walked into the observation room and gave a copy of the taped interview and the folder to one of the women. "I signed my statement and stand by it. Release him," she said.

"You seem in a hurry with this one," Juliana observed. A tall, blond woman, she was the public information liaison for the organization. One of her jobs was to review the results of the directive and report back to the UN. She was one of the few who could affect the outcome of any study, so many deferred to her. And she knew it. "Shouldn't we delay his discharge until I finish reading his files?"

Vivi wasn't going to tell her that the files on her desk weren't the same information that had been faxed to her earlier. Juliana Kohl had too many connections with the media, and despite that cool and collected demeanor, she was ruthless when it came to exploiting news to help her cause. Vivi had a cordial relationship with her, mostly because she didn't trust anyone who could manipulate numbers. She didn't have proof that Juliana did anything wrong . . . yet.

"He isn't a prisoner, Juliana. And he hasn't done anything wrong. Would you rather have complaints lodged by his commander or base?"

Juliana crossed her arms. "That would be interesting—the U.S. causing a stir."

Vivi picked up her purse hanging on the hook and slung it over one shoulder. "You misunderstand. I would."

The other woman's eyes narrowed. "Surely that's not part of your job, Vivienne? You were hired to catch the bad guys."

Vivi arched her brows. "I was hired to be the liaison to ensure the directive is doing what it's supposed to do. Making sure you get the right data for your report is part of it, don't you agree?" Juliana shrugged, not answering. The comptroller and the two others in the room shifted uncomfortably, obviously aware of the tension in the air. Before Vivi turned to leave, she added, "He'll muck up the numbers, and you don't want that, do you?"

"Who authorized you to take him?"

Vivi opened the door. "I don't need authorization to drive people around town. If there are any questions, just refer them to me."

"And if there are any problems, are you willing to speak for him?"

Vivi bit back the sarcastic comment at the tip of her tongue. Juliana didn't like a liason who didn't answer to her, so she was pretending there would be more to this. Everyone knew the soldiers would be gone like the sudden daily monsoon storms. She looked through the mirror at the man sitting at the table. Like all the others, Lieutenant Zeringue would disappear into his camouflaged woodwork, but in this case, if his name sprang up in the future in a similar bad light, Juliana Kohl was going to put the blame on Vivi Verreau.

Well, he stuck up for Rose, so it was only fair that she, in turn, stick up for him. "Yes," Vivi said.

"You're very confident about your man, Vivienne. He'd better be as good as you think."

Vivi smiled. *"J'espère que oui."*

Jazz was brought up on hip French novels and dark film noir. His maman never let him forget that the most powerful figures were always female and the mysterious rescuer always spoke with an accent.

"Ready?" He glanced up from his release papers at the woman waiting for him. His rescuer was mysterious and French. He signed the papers and gave the pen back to the clerk.

There was always double entendres in everything the heroine said and did. Jazz showed his hands, indicating that he was all hers.

"Come with me, then," she said.

The film noir heroine also usually seduced the guy and then set him up with murder. Jazz grinned. Maman always enjoyed those parts the best. He followed Miss Verreau, enjoying the way her tight black skirt clung to her behind. Going through the double doors, he found the young girl from the bar sitting on a bench outside. She rose up eagerly at the sight of the woman before recognizing him.

Rose's smile was shy. She gripped Miss Verreau's sleeve tightly. Jazz grinned back, giving her a wink.

"You've met Rose, of course, Lieutenant."

He extended a hand to the young girl. "Nice to see you again, Miss Rose."

She covered her mouth with one hand, then reached out and shyly touched his. "Nice," she replied.

"I have a few errands to run first, Lieutenant. Is that all right with you?"

"Absolutely, Miss Verreau." He was perfectly willing to spend more time with the mysterious French woman. He had lots of things he wanted to find out before he went back to Hawk. Like her first name, for instance.

He walked a little behind the two women, looking around him casually as they stepped from the cool interior of the building into the humid heat. Cars and rickshaws zigzagged in front of the building. "Not quite what I expected."

"And what was that?"

She looked so cool and unruffled in the heat, Jazz felt the sudden urge to loosen the tightly braided hair and muss it up. Would that take away that high-and-mighty look?

"I thought since this is a UN building, there would be more security around," he said. He waved at the traffic. "This isn't very official, is it?"

"It's an Interpol office, Lieutenant. We aren't UN funded. What we do isn't dangerous enough for the media to report. We don't have real arresting powers, unlike CIVPOL."

Jazz noted the cynical bitterness in the tone of her voice. "What's CIVPOL?"

She gave him an impatient sideways glance before crossing the narrow road. Rose followed wordlessly, and they had to stop in the middle to avoid a speeding scooter. A man pulling a watermelon cart yelled out a curse as he maneuvered around them. His French liaison said something back and Rose giggled, covering her mouth.

Jazz didn't think she was commenting about the weather. "What did you say?" he asked.

"Full of questions, aren't you, Lieutenant Zeringue?" she mocked as she continued crossing the road. "Where's the thank you, ma'am, and really appreciate your helping me, ma'am? Didn't your maman teach you good manners?"

"I was hoping to thank you properly later," Jazz told her.

"Oh, and when is that?"

"Over dinner, perhaps?"

She stopped at the side of a parked car and leaned a hip on the hood. "Lieutenant Zeringue," she began.

"Couldn't we be less formal under the circumstances?"

She arched a brow, and he thought he saw a glimpse of

laughter in her eyes. "Very well," she agreed. "Dinner is out of the question, Zola."

Jazz winced noticeably. "Jazz," he said.

"But Zola fits you so well," she mocked.

She might look supercilious and aloof, but there was a mischievous streak to her that fascinated him. It didn't go with the image she projected during the interview.

"I'm Zola only to family and very intimate friends, Miss Verreau," he countered gravely.

The laughing eyes gleamed at his unspoken challenge. "So, if I go out to dinner with you, does that qualify me as an intimate friend?" She pulled out a set of keys from her purse. "So easy?"

He smiled, leaned down, and opened the car door for the women. He waited till Rose had gotten in the backseat before saying softly, "You'll just have to find out for yourself."

Miss Verreau's expressive eyes narrowed a fraction. "I'm not as easy as you, Lieutenant," she said, as she climbed into the car. Jazz closed the door, and she leaned out of the window. "You'll find that your uniform isn't going to get anywhere with me."

She was as cool as those film noir chicks, a combination of fire and ice that never ceased to capture their victims. Jazz could almost hear the music in the background, the slow, sensuous rhythm of a deep bass that echoed the web of intrigue being laid out.

"I can be out of uniform in seconds," he promised, putting both hands on the roof of the small car so he could bend down closer.

Her forefingers tapped the steering wheel. "How many ways do I have to say no before you understand that I'm not going out with you?"

Her change of demeanor was just as challenging as the mischief that had been in her eyes a few moments earlier. There were layers to her that Jazz wished to explore. He lived in a world where time and decisions changed in a heartbeat; he was trained to go after what he wanted.

Jazz grinned. "There is no such word in French when it comes to a romantic dinner."

"Oh? Now our dinner has progressed to something more. Really fast, Lieutenant. A girl likes to savor the chase a little bit."

He would love to savor her, but he didn't say that. Not having talked to Hawk about the team's new plans, he doubted that he would really be able to take her out to dinner anyway.

She arched her brow again, cocking her head to one side. "It's getting hotter out here. Are you going to get in the car or do you intend to hold this conversation all day in the sun?"

He must be losing his touch. The lady had easily evaded his questions without much effort at all. He still didn't know a damn thing about her. Straightening, he moved to the other side of the car and got in. He adjusted the seat back as far as it could go, squeezing his long length into the vehicle. Her eyes glinted at him before she turned her attention to starting the engine and pulling out into the traffic.

"Where are we going?" he asked.

She looked into the rearview mirror. "I have to drop Rose off," she told him quietly.

"No, no, Vivi! No want to go home," Rose said, her voice agitated, leaning forward between the two front seats. "No take me home."

Vivi. Her name was Vivi. Jazz repeated it silently. It suited her. She gave him a brief glance, as if it were his fault for bringing up the subject.

"Rose, I don't know where else to take you," she said slowly, as if she was weighing her answer carefully. "You don't have any other relatives, and the orphanages won't take you in because they know you have parents. Do you have any friends who can help you?"

Rose shook her head. "No. You can take me?"

The hope in her voice was heartbreaking, and Jazz wished he could offer her a place to stay. Seeing that she had almost been sold as a prostitute, he had a fair idea that her parents didn't care one way or another where she was. He looked at the woman driving beside him.

Vivi Verreau was chewing on her lower lip. There was grimness to her profile as she stared ahead. The knuckles of her hands on the steering wheel were white as she made a turn. So much tension suddenly. He wondered at the strength of this woman's emotions.

"I can't take you," she said, and Jazz could hear the tightness in her words, as if saying them was choking her. "I'm sorry, Rose."

Rose's lower lip trembled. "Vivi, I so scared."

"I know you are. I'll think of something."

"You promise?"

"I . . . promise."

Jazz caught the slight hesitation in Vivi's reply. She gave him a brief glance before he said anything.

"No more questions for now, Lieutenant."

In a back room in town

"I don't want any young girls," Stefan said. "I want you."

Without any greeting, she came to him with greedy hands and lips, stripping him where he stood. He knew that she was a woman who liked control, who enjoyed being in power. He drew in a breath when she raked her fingernails down his stomach suggestively and tugged on the buttons of his pants.

She reached inside and drew him out. Still without a word, she went on her knees and wrapped her eager mouth around him, tasting him as he stood there in the dark room. She finally made a throaty approving murmur as he grew big and hard, filling her. Giving him one final lick, she released him and worked at taking his pants off.

Naked, he followed her to the bed in the corner and pushed her down on the soft mattress. She licked her lips as he put on a condom, opening her legs invitingly. The bed creaked as he climbed on top, scooping her legs up with his arms and parting her thighs wider and higher. Without preliminaries, he was inside her. He knew she would already be wet, and he didn't wait as he took her hard and fast. She gasped at his roughness, and then started purring, becoming more agitated, as he pushed her legs higher over his shoulders without losing a beat.

He moved his hand between them, stimulating her as he slid in and out. He watched as she gave a final shriek before succumbing to pleasure, wetting his hand with her essence. He didn't stop. The plan was to satisfy her for an hour, put her in a good mood.

She moaned softly. "No, no more, please, *s'il vous plait*."

He ignored her. It was part of their little game. She liked it rough and demanded it. She pushed against him, struggling, telling him over and over, "No, no . . . stop."

He stopped. Slapped her lightly. There was a moment of silence, and then she laughed and raked her hand down his chest. Then she screamed again as he pounded relentlessly into her. He didn't stop again, no matter how much she begged. He was a master to her slave, fulfilling that fantasy she wanted. Taking her over the edge one final time, he let himself go with a grunt before collapsing on top of her, his body slippery with a sheen of perspiration. She ran her hands up and down his sides, massaging him.

"Hmmm . . . you never disappoint me," she said, flicking her wet hair from her face.

"I don't intend to," he said, turning his face from her shoulder.

"I love your taking me so roughly. It's very liberating."

"Those are two contradictory sentences."

She shrugged. "I don't care. I like it."

"Obviously," he said, a dry note creeping into his voice. "You also make sure your girls know that."

Her laughter echoed in the dark room. "Oh yes, of course. I make sure they're in the next room listening to the best lover a girl could have. They must have me for inspiration."

"If I didn't know you, Lis, I would call you cruel." He turned sideways, resting his head on a crooked elbow.

She turned, licked his chest and bit it. "And you are soooo sweet." She languidly rose to a sitting position, playing with her hair. She turned and studied his naked form. "Don't you know I see you giving some of my girls cash for nothing?"

"Don't forget where the money comes from," he reminded her. "Even a sweet man has to have a means to make money."

"Oh yes. We're two of a kind then, aren't we?" she said as she stood up. "Come on, lover, give me the information you have and I'll see what I can do."

As she reached for a robe hanging by the bed, he pulled on one of her hands and she flew into his arms again. His hand went between her legs.

"Ooooh," she moaned, then kissed him hungrily. "If you're ever in trouble, you *have* to come to me, *cherie*. I'll take you underground with my brothers. Then I can have you for a long, long time."

"You sure they will let me in at your word?" he mocked, as his hand continued its leisurely exploration.

She arched to meet each caress, her eyes half closed. "Honey doll, I'm the favorite sister to the second brother. Do you think he would deny me a favor?" She mewed as his rhythm slowed, controlling her release. "Oh, please, please."

"Don't you mean, 'No, no, stop'?" he mimicked her earlier cries. He slid a long finger in her and felt her tensing, anticipating what he could give her. "So, whatever big sis says, little brother will do, huh?"

She didn't have a chance to answer. Her moans filled the room again.

Finally, after several minutes, she opened her eyes. Her voice was hoarse from the pleasure he had given her. "Honey doll, as long as you keep doing that, you'll always be under my protection. And, don't forget, you're smart and can make us money."

He bent down to kiss her bow-shaped lips. "And don't forget," he added, "I can make you come some more."

He was running late, and there was business to be done, but he had found that one couldn't hurry business in this part of the world. One must make a lot of deals. Without warning he turned and locked the woman's hands above her head. Her eyes widened, and a sultry gleam crept in them when he slowly nudged her thighs apart.

"Some more?" she asked.

"It's part of the deal," he said, and bit her shoulder to mark her.

4

Jazz was a Cajun boy, brought up in the bayou swamps outside Slidell, Louisiana. His grandfather was an alligator catcher the locals called The Raging Cajun, and as a kid, Jazz lived his summers in the deep swamp camps where the very poor eked out a living off the land, supplemented by selling alligator teeth and chicken claw mojos in the local markets.

Since joining the SEALs, he had seen other kinds of slums. The garbage mountain city in Manila where the children dug through trash for food. The slums in Hong Kong where people lived like sardines, arranging bed shifts according to their work schedules. The arid lives of people who owned nothing but a piece of Persian carpet spread in a hand-hewn mountain side cave outside Kabul. He had seen them and had compared the lives of the people with his own childhood. He had grown up in a large, loving family, with a mother who had fiercely protected her brood, and a rascally grandfather who told tall tales and refused to live a normal life. Poverty had never bothered him, since he had been taught to take care of himself and his family. He could do anything.

And being a SEAL reinforced that pride. Except that his deployment overseas and what he had seen was eating at his soul bit by bit, and sometimes he thought he would go a little crazy. He had learned that there were other kinds of poverty in the world, some more horrific than others. Most of the time, he did his job with his SEAL brothers and left quickly. If the team stayed longer, he usually ended up giving most of his cash away. That was why Hawk always joked about his needing to marry every poor girl he'd helped and sending her home to Louisiana.

Jazz looked at the tin huts in the small shantytown Vivi was driving through. People peered out of windows and men stopped whatever they were doing to stare at the vehicle passing by. The ride was bumpy and slowed down by carts and livestock haphazardly blocking their way. They finally stopped in the middle of the dirt path. Children raced over and climbed onto the vehicle, swarming like ants, peering inside at the occupants curiously. They were dirty and bedraggled. Some of them yelled out to Rose.

"Is it safe for you to be out of the vehicle?" Jazz asked. He had experienced the vicious kiddie pickpockets in Rome before.

"I think I can take of myself. What about you?" Vivi didn't wait for his answer, climbing out of the car. She pulled the lever to move her seat forward. "Rose?"

The girl gave Jazz a pleading look, then obeyed Vivi's request. The moment she was outside, the kids started talking to her all at once. She shrugged at them, pushing away some of them rudely. Vivi slammed the door shut.

Jazz opened his and climbed out. He attracted even more attention. Young girls started appearing from nowhere, surrounding him. He looked at Vivi, who stared in contempt.

"It's the uniform, Lieutenant," she informed him in a clipped voice.

He frowned. "What's wrong with my uniform?"

A girl slipped her hand into his. "GI want girl? GI take me out?"

Vivi cocked her head. "Need more explanation?" She turned away, leaving him with the crowd of young women.

Jazz gently unlaced the girl's hand from his, shaking his head. "No, thank you," he told her. She pouted at his reply. He began going after Vivi and Rose, even as the bolder girls kept touching him.

When he caught up with them, Vivi darted him a scathing glance. "Maybe you can marry one of them and take her home to your maman."

"You sound like Hawk," Jazz commented as he unhooked another hand from his belt.

"I hope not," she retorted. "I wouldn't want to be compared to a bunch of drunk soldiers telling each other whom to marry."

"You don't just dislike uniforms, do you?" Jazz asked quizzically. "It's the men, too."

She rubbed her pale pink lips together. "My opinion is formed by observation and experience. Soldiers use their weapons too freely and frequently." She slanted a downward gaze below his belt and added, "And they destroy everything."

So his French film noir heroine had an acid tongue. No wonder he had the feeling all along that she wasn't on his side.

"That's what soldiers do," he agreed. He had always believed that one couldn't win an argument by taking the opposite side immediately. "Are you one of those who believe that there will be no wars if there weren't soldiers?"

Vivi and Rose came to a halt outside one of the huts. The younger girl had been dragging her feet, growing more and more reluctant as they went nearer. The broken wooden door leading into the house was open, and shouts were coming from inside.

"Soldiers count their success by their number of kills, Jazz. I don't think they care whether there's war or not, just where the next battle is to add to the count," Vivi murmured softly as she gazed at the entrance to the hut. "And in between kills, they enjoy the spoils."

She spoke so softly that he must have imagined she called him Jazz. He would have liked to be given a chance to answer the charges she had just made, but the shouting from within the hut didn't seem conducive to further debate. He stepped closer, not liking the tone of voice as it went on and on, almost shrill in its demands.

"What's the shouting about?" he asked.

"Money," Vivi said, and tapped at the old battered door.

There was a pause and then a short little man, no taller than five-feet-one, appeared. Unkempt, with a cigarette hanging from his lips, he stood with his hands on his hips. His eyes narrowed at the sight of Rose standing behind Vivi. He began to speak quickly, angrily, the cigarette dropping ash. Vivi shrugged. His face turned beet-red. He ground out the cigarette and started gesturing wildly as he shouted, his words in broken English.

"I have no interest in your income, Mr. Tham," Vivi finally interrupted. "You refused the food the organization brought here for distribution."

"Food? Who wants your food?" the man sneered, his speech slurred by accent and alcohol. "We want cash, American dollar. You bring food! Gimme money and we be fine."

"You'll be fine, Mr. Tham, but what about your family? I think they'd be happier with food than you gambling and losing all the money."

The man looked as if he was going to explode in fury. He started yelling at Rose in his native tongue, gesturing her to get into the house.

Jazz looked at Vivi. Was she really going to let Rose go? The younger girl cast a quick last glance at Vivi, who nodded to her. Rose disappeared into the dark interior.

Vivi held up an envelope, took out a small wad of cash, and fanned it out in front of Mr. Tham. The change in the man was instantaneous. A smile broke out, showing yellowed teeth. His eyes lost their glare, gleaming now with anticipation.

"Let me make this very clear," Vivi said in a soft voice. "This is not U.S. government money. This is my cash. I expect Rose to be here for a few weeks or you'll answer to me."

Mr. Tham's eyes narrowed. "Woman don't threaten man," he announced.

"I wouldn't dream of threatening a man like you," Vivi said, arching a brow. "This is purely business. If you don't want to do it, I can always negotiate with some of your neighbors for their daughters."

The man scowled and tried to snatch the money away from Vivi. She kept it out of his reach. "Three weeks, Mr. Tham," she pressed.

"Three," he agreed, small eyes following Vivi as she put away the cash.

No sooner had Vivi handed him the envelope than he turned his back to them, pulling out the money to count. He began walking back into the house.

Jazz watched Vivi's expression closely. She was clenching her jaw as she stared stonily at the empty doorway. He felt helpless, not knowing how exactly to help.

"Why negotiate with a man like that?" he asked gently.

The gaze she shot him was heated. "All I can do is buy more time," she said, and turned back toward the path. The kids followed them.

The girls continued to touch Jazz wherever they could. He unhooked a hand from his back pocket. "Is he her father?"

"Yes."

"Do you want me to beat him up?"

Vivi stopped and turned around slowly. She stood there as the girls crowded around him, still hopeful that he would change his mind. One of them said something, and the rest giggled loudly. Jazz didn't want to guess what they were talking about so animatedly.

"Do you think anything would be accomplished if you beat him up?" Vivi asked conversationally. She arched her brows as Jazz disentangled himself from a pair of arms around his waist. "Look at them hanging on to you like leeches. Are you going to beat them up?"

"I don't hit women." He was, however, beginning to

weary of these girls, who didn't seem to want to take no for an answer. He wanted to get out of here soon.

"You see, that's all very good and proper," she said, "but what are you going to do about the situation?"

He frowned at her. "Not sure what you mean."

"Well, soldier, what's the favorite hot phrase these days—think outside the box." Vivi stopped just in front of him. "You can't hit them. So do you run off and ignore the situation? That's what all the soldiers they've met have done, you know. They all took off."

His frown deepened. "Not the same thing," he said, shaking off someone patting his butt. "I'm not taking off that way. I don't even know them."

"They don't know that. They think you're just like the others. They believe one of them will get you sooner or later, and then you will give her money, establish the same pattern of existence she's seen a dozen times."

Jazz stared back into her dark eyes, trying to read her thoughts. She was so angry. Or frustrated. For some reason, she was testing him, or goading him to do something. Fine. Think outside the box. She obviously thought all military men were alike, that they were a group that had established some sort of destructive pattern when it came to women. He looked around at the eager eyes and hands, and wondered which came first—the temptation of money from the men or the temptation of willing flesh from the women. But like many times before, he shook off the need to philosophize too much. In his profession, it was best not to think too deeply.

Right now, he wished to make a point. His eyes met Vivi's mocking ones again. Being a SEAL, he had been trained to think outside the box before the stupid phrase ever existed. His gaze never leaving hers, he pulled out from inside his collar the chain with the pendant his maman had given him. Her eyes narrowed as she watched him take it off, then widened as he stepped closer to her. She didn't move as he slipped the chain over her head, the look in her eyes turning mysterious, like dark chocolate, full of sensual promise. His maman's pendant slipped inside her blouse.

Jazz slid his arm around Vivi's shoulders and curled her unresisting body against his. He grinned cheerfully at the girls who were watching the entire scene. "Mine. Number one girl," he declared, and turned to kiss the top of Vivi's head. He murmured into her hair, sniffing appreciatively at her perfume. "Let's go, shall we, *chouchou*? I bought me some time too."

Now if he could buy some time to understand Vivi Verreau's anger. For some reason, he felt compelled to know more about this woman.

Vivi glared at the girls hanging on to Lieutenant Zeringue, buzzing around him like flies. It upset her. It was an irrational irritation because she understood why they were the way they were. Yet the idea of them and Jazz together made her want to go to each one of the girls and shove her out of the way.

It couldn't have been that long ago, could it? Not to Vivi's mind, which was spinning with angry voices and hushed whispers. Not to her heart, which was thudding painfully at every step she took back to the car.

She had touched a soldier like that once. He had the smile of someone who knew about life. He descended into her village like one of the ancient Asian demigods, bearing good tidings for everyone. And she had touched his sleeve for good luck. She remembered that one time when he turned to look at her, that big smile, and the piece of chocolate he had offered.

But of course, as the years went by, she had grown to understand why there were so many orphans like her around. Abandoned by family. Outcasts. No one wanted half-breeds in the family—too obvious where they came from. Her mouth twisted. There were more enterprising families, of course. Females could be a commodity.

Vivi recaptured her childhood every time she drove into

this kind of neighborhood. It wasn't pleasant, a constant reminder of how she could have turned out. The tangy smell of food and trash. Burning incense from the outside altars permeated the air. The clucking of hens as they moved among the humans. The sight and sounds of days gone by when she was at that desperate stage between fear and trepidation. The fear that she would be trussed out alone in the world with no income. The trepidation from knowing what she had to do to survive.

Vivi didn't want to be here. She felt out of place, unwelcome.

She blamed her bad mood on the frustrating day. She was edgy from her inability to find a solution for Rose. Then she had challenged Juliana Kohl, knowing very well it was going to come back to bite her ass. But her instructions from GEM were specific. She pursed her lips as she darted a quick glance at Jazz again. He was too busy peeling another one of the girls off him.

Jazz's offer to beat up Rose's father gave her an opening to vent her frustration. He was so smart, wasn't he? Just beat up the guys at the bar, give the girl enough money for a couple of nights in the room, and all would be well. Just beat up the father, then life would be blue skies and sunshine. So she had goaded him, questioning his ability to act beyond violence.

What he did next silenced all her inner rage. She could feel his pendant hot and intimate in the valley between her breasts. When he put his arm around her shoulders, drawing her own body against his, it caught her off guard. Then he nuzzled her hair, his breath blowing warmly where he gave her a kiss near her forehead. Through the rush of blood in her head, she heard him call her an endearment.

Had she said there were choices? All alternatives narrowed down to a puddle of female hormones in those five seconds. She had been very conscious of the man's sexual charisma since arguing with him at the bar, had even taken the steps to create a shield of dislike against him. She hadn't been wrong about her instincts. The man was dangerous to a woman's self-preservation, with those sleepy baby blues and that lazy Louisiana drawl. She'd made a mistake coming up so close; now he'd put his arm around her and like one of these girls, she wanted to slip her hand under that shirt, tuck her fingers into those pants, explore the hard body she had seen that morning. Check out and affirm those girls' lewd observations to one another. *Yeah, baby, he was as big as he was tall.*

That line jolted Vivi out of her fantasy. What the hell was wrong with her? Not only was her body flushed with sudden sexual heat, but her imagination had run off with a wet dream. She scowled. When had she lost control of the situation?

"You can at least look more ecstatic at being my number one girl," he murmured.

"I have no intention of being your girl."

"You did say think out of the box. Now you're mad because the girls have stopped."

The girls had indeed stopped touching Jazz, even though they still followed them. They appeared to accept that he had a girl with him already, and so was unable to afford them. Vivi let out a small sigh, following his lead as he maneuvered them back on the dirt path.

There were small kids playing on top of the hood and the trunk of the car, and they made honking noises as Vivi and Jazz approached. They were still too young to care about being poor, to know about choices and alternatives. She smiled at a really tiny kid sucking on his thumb as he sat on his brother's shoulders. He grinned back and waved his wet thumb at her.

"Hi there," she said, wiggling her finger at him.

Jazz removed his arm from her shoulder and took two kids off the roof of the car. They laughed at being swirled high in the air before being set on the ground.

"Little rascals," he said, and laughed as one of them kicked his shoe.

He was good with kids, she had to give him that. In fact, everything about Jazz Zeringue was too good to be true.

Gentleman. Knight. Protective male. There must be something negative she could pin on him.

"Where are their parents?" he asked.

"Some of them don't have any."

He ruffled a child's hair. "Poor kids. Wish I had some more cash to give them."

"Don't train them to beg, Lieutenant. Each generation becomes more and more weakened by this system of dependence."

He regarded her with those blue eyes quietly. "You've given this some thought," he observed. "I was only thinking of a way to help, *chouchou*."

"Easy, isn't it? Throw money at the problem and it should solve itself." Vivi shrugged, taking a last look around at the shantytown. "It's a temporary patch, Lieutenant. You have to understand cultural values and start from there."

"I thought your calling me Jazz earlier was a good start to cultural exchange," he said as he came near again, much too close for comfort. "Maybe you and I can talk more about this over dinner, *chouchou*."

The man was also far too persistent. "Stop calling me that. We aren't exchanging any kind of cultural lessons during dinner or at any time."

He grinned devilishly. "Don't you want to give me some cultural instructions?"

Vivi ignored the challenge. She didn't want to flirt with him. It was far too tempting. She opened her handbag to retrieve the keys to the car. "Get over to the other side, Lieutenant, or they will all be swarming in with us. Then you'll have to send them home to your maman too. What will your poor maman do with your wife and kids?"

His laughter was low and sexy, as if he was very aware of his effect on her. She couldn't remember the last time she was this flustered by male attention, jabbering nonsensically.

She waited as Jazz cut over to the passenger side. He had a kid hanging on to his back. It seemed the children liked him as much as the girls. There was something about watching a big man playing with a small child that made her weak. She watched as he patiently waited for the kid to get off. Then he turned and gave her one of those lazy smiles.

"Ready, ma'am."

Vivi pulled the door handle. Something tugged at her blouse and she looked down. It was the same little kid, barely able to stand without wobbling. He looked at her with round innocent eyes full of wonder. She opened the door and slid into the seat. Slipping her hand into one of the side pockets of her purse, she pulled out a bar of chocolate. The child grabbed the candy as soon as she showed it to him, a smile lighting up his face like bright sunshine.

Vivi smiled sadly. She was now the one handing out the chocolate.

CHAPTER
5

Jazz caught the fleeting sadness in Vivi's expression as she started up the car and turned the vehicle around. It must be tough to have a job like this—saving kids, only to return them back to the system that created them. His job was much easier, he decided.

"Are you going to give money to my commander to keep me safe for a few days?" he joked, hoping to cheer her a little.

He was rewarded with that half-mocking secretive smile, as if the same thought had run through her mind. She refused to answer him, but it was okay. He had achieved his goal.

The heat from the sun had curled the loose tendrils around Vivi's face into ringlets. Jazz wondered whether her hair was naturally curly once it was freed from that braid. He hadn't had time to dwell on why every aspect of her face fascinated him, from those kissable lips to the texture of her hair. He enjoyed women—they were like bursts of laughter and sunshine, the taste of thick vanilla ice cream shakes, and the smell of homemade pie. He treasured them because they were generous creatures, with their loving hands and marvelous ways of making a man feel like a man. But he had never had the urge to get too close. Until now.

"I'm not cheap." He continued his banter. "I assure you ￼e's willing to negotiate."

"You'll let another man negotiate your price?" she coun-￼ered as she slowed down for a farmer and his goats crossing ￼he busy road. "You trust him that much?"

"I trust him with my life," Jazz told her. "He'll drive a ￼ard bargain."

"We'll see whether you're right," she said dryly. "What ￼hould I say I'm keeping you safe from? Those girls in ￼Rose's neighborhood?"

She had the sass of a cocky trumpet interrupting a good ￼piece, creating the interesting reply to the string of back-￼ground harmony.

"Maybe," he replied, looking at his target through half-closed eyes.

Jazz had never looked at a woman and thought of music before. He studied the woman next to him and wondered what she would say if he told her that she was inspiring some pretty cool rhythms in his head. His lips quirked. She would have one of those tart comebacks in that soft French accent that inspired other kinds of rhythms.

"You get amused easily, don't you, Lieutenant? No one even need tell you a joke."

"I can't even smile now?"

She sighed. "You smile too damn much."

He had been told that before. "I can't help it," he told her solemnly. "I was born with a big smile on my pretty face. Maman always said she had to smack me to make sure I knew how to cry."

Vivi gave him a startled glance, then laughed. He liked the way her laughter sounded—full-bodied and mellow. "I'll have to remember to kick your ass a bit then," she said.

"Over dinner?" he persisted.

"Maybe after," she replied very softly.

He grinned. Maman's advice had always been good. To get a date, always make the woman feel like a woman, she had said. And always tell her his maman beat his behind a lot. He had gotten his two wishes—a smile and dinner. He had been around women enough to know not to push his luck. He changed the subject.

"How do you know where to take me?" Jazz asked. He was curious about how Vivi had gotten such information, anyway. He belonged to one of the top covert groups in the United States; very few people knew anything about them. He suspected that Vivi was one of them, and that added a whole layer of intriguing possibilities.

"My boss told me," Vivi said, slanting him a quick glance as she maneuvered the small car through the hodgepodge of traffic down the increasingly busy downtown.

They were back to mysterious film noir heroine leading the man around, Jazz thought in amusement. "And your boss is . . . ?"

Her answering look was telling. "Have I asked any questions about you, your covert activities, or your outfit, Lieutenant Zeringue?" When he smiled lazily at her, her back straightened defensively. "What? Why do you always do that?"

He was getting to her. "Do what?" he asked.

"Don't give me that innocent boy act. You always give me that look whenever you think I'm speaking double entendres."

"Well, you were the one who brought up covert activities and outfit, *chouchou*," he pointed out. "I'd be happy to demonstrate all my covert activities after dinner tonight. I have no outfits in mind."

Vivi answered with a sudden bout of choked coughing. He had a feeling she was trying to disguise her laughter. For some reason, she didn't want him to know she enjoyed his company, but he'd caught the laughter gleaming in her eyes before she turned back to the traffic. He leaned over and whispered wickedly, "Except for my pendant, of course, *chouchou*. I think it'd make the covert activities very exciting."

Her hand came up between her breasts, grasping at the

idden pendant. "You'll have this back as soon as we
eached our destination."

"No, keep it warm for me till after dinner," he told her
wickedly.

Her hand stroked at his necklace absently, and he suddenly wished she were doing the same thing to him somewhere more strategic. "Lieutenant Zola Zeringue," she
warned. "You don't know when to stop pushing your luck."

Whatever had possessed her to even contemplate a dinner
date with this man? Vivi slammed the car door shut. The
subject of her thoughts did likewise, looking around the
neighborhood as he did so. It dawned on her that his lazy perusal was mostly a disguise. She doubted those baby blues
missed much as they took in the deceptively understated
surroundings.

The warehouse nearby looked ordinary enough, with the
rusty fencing and men moving crates onto the lorries and
carts waiting in line. Loud rock and roll music blared from a
nearby radio, mingling with the sounds of hammers and
saws in the background.

Two men watched as Vivi and Jazz picked their way toward the warehouse. One of them approached when she
walked in and rapped on the counter. Jazz stood by the entrance a few feet away, giving him easy access to move in or
out of the building. He was a good soldier, she thought.
Never let his guard down, even when he knew she was taking him to meet his friends.

"Can I help you?" the man asked.

Vivi showed him an order slip. "Are they ready?"

The man inspected the paper, then checked a book behind
the counter. He shook his head. "No, ma'am, not ready.
They're working in the backyard."

"Can I talk to the supervisor?"

"Sure. Go through the side door, turn left, ma'am. Be
careful of the electrical cords."

"Thank you."

Vivi turned to Jazz. "If it helps, this is a secured place."

"So I can see, *chouchou*. It's not every day I see shop-keepers with weapons ready and pointing from under the tables," Jazz said. He regarded her for a moment, his blue eyes probing hers. "You could have warned me. What if I had taken one of those men down?"

Vivi had thought about it, but for some inexplicable reason, she had decided not to. He was supposed to be this hot-shot SEAL, so . . . Okay, she admitted to wanting to test the man. She had omitted telling him that the people here worked for her.

"And what good would that do, Lieutenant? I'd be dead, and so would you," she pointed out. "I figured you'd be smart enough not to do anything, like when you were caught with Rose at that bar."

"How did you know I didn't?" he countered.

She smiled. Almost got caught there. "The report said you didn't struggle, of course. What, did you see me there taking notes?"

He seemed satisfied with her response, taking her last question as a joke. "Don't test me again, Vivi," he murmured, still looking around. "I'm very unpredictable when I'm nervous."

She hid another smile, pointing at the direction she wanted to go. She had seen him in a few situations that told her the man didn't get jittery very often. The sound of male voices and tools being used became louder. Jazz would recognize the voices of his men. "Don't be," she said. "I assure you this is a very safe place and that I'm here to protect you from bad people."

He flashed a returning smile. "I feel better already."

They turned the corner and the men paused in mid-conversation, turning to their visitors. Some of them put down their tools. Vivi surveyed the men with interest. She had met only Jazz and Hawk up close. She remembered the others gathered around the piano that other night, making a lot of jovial noises. They looked a lot cleaner today. She nodded to all of them, her gaze resting a little longer on Hawk McMillan, the mission commander.

"Don't let me interrupt that interesting story, gentlemen," Vivi said, shifting her attention to the big tall man, the one everyone called . . . Cucumber. She didn't want to guess the reason. "You were telling your friends about getting your balls checked out by some doctor."

"You must have excellent concentration, Miss Verreau, talking to Jazz and listening to us at the same time," Hawk said as he approached them. "Jazz, you look well rested."

Vivi felt each man's examination as she stood there. She wondered what their commander had told them about her. Hawk's eyes, intimately assessing, didn't reveal anything.

"Yes, I am," Jazz replied from behind her.

"Then you ought to be ready for some action."

"Always. Did I miss anything important?"

"I'll fill you in later."

The exchange between the two men interested Vivi. She knew they were close friends from their interaction at the bar. Hawk was the unit commander, but her papers told her that Jazz was a Joint Task Force coleader in their covert work, each coordinating their teams of three and two men in the operations. It took a lot of faith between two men to have confidence that the other's timing would be right.

"Miss Verreau," Hawk greeted her, his hand extended. Vivi returned his direct perusal with the same candor.

Hawk McMillan had the face of a poster boy for the military. His eyes, that shimmering color that reminded her of brandy, glittered rakishly. She knew from their last encounter that they missed nothing. His file told her that he played the ladies' man, yet she was very aware that there was nothing soft about the SEAL. She also knew from personal experience that when Hawk wanted information, he was unconventional and persuasive. She still laughed when she recalled the promises he had given to her old lady disguise.

Vivi shook Hawk's hand and was vaguely amused when

he smoothly tucked her hand into the crook of his arm and pivoted her toward the group. The man was also very suave. Behind her, she felt Jazz's gaze boring into her.

"Men, this is going to be a first for you. Meet Miss Vivienne Verreau. Admiral Madison has instructed me to tell you that she will issue the Patrol Leader's Order."

So Hawk McMillan had waited until now to reveal her role. She knew it wouldn't be easy to appear in front of a group of warriors and be told she was going to be their general for the next battle. A challenge had been issued here. She smiled up at Hawk, slipped her hand free, then moved a few steps forward, making sure the men stood in a loose circle around her.

A Patrol Leader's Order was war cry to covert teams to drop everything and listen to orders. At this moment, these men, accustomed to their all-male circle, were being told that the person who was going to give them these orders was . . . a woman.

Vivi remained silent for a long second, unruffled by the undisguised interest in the male eyes. At least none of them looked shocked or disgruntled. Yet. She didn't look at Jazz. He distracted her too much. First, she had to show these men she could handle them. "I'm still waiting for the rest of your story," she addressed Cucumber softly. "Unless, of course, you're too embarrassed to go on."

His story, from what she had caught, was the usual male banter around that thing between their legs. It was a favorite topic of conversation. That, and sex and women. Or, with soldiers, that, and sex and women, with a big smattering of war heroics. Her gaze hardened as she challenged the big SEAL, raising her brows a shade higher.

She noted that Cucumber hesitated long enough to catch the silent go-ahead order from Hawk. Relaxing a little, he never let his eyes leave her face as he continued his tale. "Like I was saying, I was getting a check-up after a field assignment with a different outfit. I won't name the commander but he didn't like my SEAL attitude. I had a slight injury from the assignment and he sent me to the med, with specific instructions."

One of the other men laughed. "Yeah, to have his asshole checked out."

Vivi cocked her head. "Did you bend over, like you were told?"

There were a few low chuckles. "I had trouble unzipping my pants because my hands were the parts of me that were injured," Cucumber informed her with a straight face. His eyes had that glitter of a male being challenged. "So I requested that he aid me."

There was outright laughter now. "Shit, man, you have some ba—gumption."

Cucumber ignored his friend, continuing, "He sat right there between my bloody pants and casually asked, 'What the fuck have you been doing, soldier, cutting up your hands like that?' as he helped me out of my pants. He fucking knew all along that I didn't need my pants down but he was following orders. Stupid bastard couldn't say no to his fuckass arrogant commander, so he had to play dumb. So I said, 'It's some shrapnel and dirt, nothing very serious. Land mines.' He shook his head, and . . ."

Cucumber finally turned to the guys, his lips twitching. ". . . with his fucking head at eye-level to my balls, he said, 'That's a nasty job you have.' Fucking idiot was actually holding my balls while he said that." Cucumber turned back to Vivi. "So I said to him, looking straight into his eyes, 'Not as nasty as yours.' "

The howls of laughter were very male. The joke was funny but Vivi heard the underlying message. "You're a brave one," she commented, amusement in her voice, "saying that to a man holding your balls in his hands."

"He has big balls, ma'am," one of the men chipped in.

"I'll keep that in mind for our operation," Vivi said, deliberately bringing the subject back to her. She knew they were all wondering why she was the one giving the Patrol Leader's Order, and not Hawk.

Her own orders had come with cautionary instruction. This was the first time GEM was working alongside Admiral Madison's top secret SEAL team called STAR Force, the acronym for Standing and Ready Force. She was warned that there might be resistance among the men, who might object to the fairly active role that she would be playing in the forthcoming assignment. Her authority would constantly be challenged. First, she had to convince their leader, a man she suspected didn't always follow rules himself. Then—she thought of the pendant lying heavy and tempting between her breasts—she had to deal with the Joint Task Force leader, Jazz. She didn't know exactly how or what she was going to do with him, but she knew instinctively that working close with him was going to be dangerous for her peace of mind.

Vivi turned back to Hawk. "Perhaps you should talk to your men first."

"They understand what a Patrol Leader's Order is."

"And are SEALs good at following those orders?" Vivi asked.

"Hasn't Lieutenant Zeringue been a good boy?"

She finally darted a glance at Jazz. She had been aware of his quiet observation all along, shoulder leaning against a big barrel nearby. Her heart skipped a beat at the look in his eyes—hard and penetrating, as if he was seeing something new. Of course he was; he hadn't seen the real Vivienne Verreau. He also hadn't known she was going to be working with his team.

"I didn't know that was a prerequisite of being a SEAL," she murmured, eyes still on Jazz. "Are all SEALs good boys, then?"

"We're all good at some skill or another, Miss Verreau. Some are more hidden than others, that's all," Hawk told her. "Right, Jazz?"

"So I'm finding out." Jazz straightened up and came a few steps closer.

"So let's all find out together how we can combine our skills for this new operation, shall we?" Hawk didn't move from his position beside Vivi. "I think we both have our own separate instructions from our agencies. I suggest we exchange the documents privately before we proceed. Jazz, they've set up a war room for us. The boys will lead you there and give you details about the last couple of days while Miss Verreau and I get our game plan together."

The men exchanged the merest eye contact. It was just the barest of pauses, and Vivi was sure no one but she noticed it. Jazz didn't answer as he did as he was ordered.

"From what Admiral Madison told me," Hawk said to her within Jazz's hearing, "I think we'll work well together, Vivienne. I have more to tell you over dinner tonight."

Startled, Vivi gazed straight into the golden eyes of the man beside her. They were filled with amused mockery, and there was a ghost of a smile curving his lips. She darted a quick glance at Jazz's. He hadn't turned around but she imagined that his back was a little straighter. Her eyes returned to Hawk to see that small smile growing into a satisfied and devious grin. Okay, so Commander McMillan was even more observant than she had credited him.

She gave Hawk a sultry smile. "We'll see."

Over his dead body. If there were going to be any combination of dinner and Vivi, it would be with him, not Hawk. But Jazz didn't say anything as he joined his motley crew, most of whom had huge grins painted on their faces. He gave them a shrug as they greeted him.

"That was one way to get free bed and board for a couple days, man!"

"Do I detect a note of jealousy?" Jazz countered lazily.

"Made any new friends in the big house?"

"None with your big balls, sweetheart." That one was met with howls of laughter.

"Who's the Frenchie?"

Jazz glanced back casually at Vivi and Hawk. Damn it. He had her laughing already. It didn't look like they were in deep discussion about a job.

"You know about as much as I do," Jazz answered smoothly as he turned abruptly away. He followed his men as they led him to a wooden door that had seen better days. "Does this go to the 'war' room, or a toolshed?"

"Oh, you need to take a look at this place." Cucumber opened the door, revealing a dark stairway. "It's pretty amazing."

"How did we get to meet here?" Jazz peered down into the darkness. "I thought we were to be picked up at Point Zero."

Point Zero was their original rendezvous place. Of course that was several days ago. Jazz knew it was his fault that they were still in the area. This new development was a surprise, though. He had expected very little delay after his release.

"Don't know how, but Hawk led us here after getting in touch with Mad Dog."

Jazz nodded. Of course Admiral Madison would have contingency plans in case one of his teams had a setback. Failure for a SEAL team wasn't an option, but a setback was always possible. If one of them was injured or captured, Admiral Madison would know it immediately and would be the first to take responsibility. He was that kind of a leader. Jazz also knew that the admiral would try his utmost to save the injured or captured SEAL. No micro-management, with outside people calling in asking for permission to do anything. No bureaucratic B.S. If he had to, Admiral Madison would simply fly down here personally and take charge.

"Let me see what's down there then, and then you can tell me what's going on," he said.

They descended the stairs with the ease of men used to walking in dark tight places. Jazz wondered what was down there that would constitute a war room.

"They told us this place's always activated, no exceptions. There's no light because the whole way has warning sensors for any intruders using flashlights or lanterns," Dirk, who was closest to Jazz, explained quietly. "Anyone planning any sneak attack would have to literally sneak in."

"I'd just throw in a couple of flashbangs and smoke out anyone down there," Jazz pointed out. The use of the pocket-sized CS gas containers was popular for use in extraction activities. The stinging chemical usually incapacitated the enemy, and sooner or later, they would run out of any hole they'd chosen to hide in.

"They have a two-foot-thick metal door down there, Jazz, that would take quite a bit of explosives to break through. Everything here is just a façade. It may look like some kind of crummy factory on the outside but the facility is A-combat ready."

They reached the bottom. Jazz couldn't see much in the darkness.

"Here, put these funky glasses on," Cucumber said, tapping him on the shoulder. "We saved this for last so you would be properly impressed, sir."

"These aren't the ones you got from D.C., I assume?" Jazz asked as he slid them on. Immediately the whole room changed, like a bad photograph brightened digitally. The darkness became opaque and Jazz could see pinpoints of light crisscrossing parts of the small space ahead of them. The glint of some kind of metal door to his left caught his eye.

"Some toy, huh?" Cucumber asked.

"Infrared?" Jazz asked.

"Something like it. Mink thinks it's similar to a PAS-7 infrared viewing system, except that these are glasses."

A PAS-7 had thermal imaging capabilities. Jazz glanced around, checking out how his teammates looked through his glasses.

"Cool, huh, Jazz?"

It was indeed. "Hell, Cumber, I can see your balls," he remarked dryly. "They're glowing red."

The men laughed. Through the special glasses their movements looked like patches of energy masses.

"We need some of these in the field, man," Cucumber told him. "Tell the admiral to get some for us."

"So who are these people and why are we here?" Jazz asked, as he followed the others climbing through, and avoiding, the crisscrossing blue laser beams. He didn't need to be told if he touched those beams, hell's bells would start ringing and he would be one red-faced SEAL. They reached the steel door.

"Some outfit named GEM. Hawk hasn't volunteered much info yet. But he did say they were mostly American."

"So these are government-issued equipment? We're on American property?"

"No idea, Jazz," Dirk answered, as he slipped a keycard into a slot. "It's all in English so I assumed they are American-friendly. But we're definitely preparing some kind of mission with them. Hawk communicated with Mad Dog using their systems, and that amounted to quite a bit of trust on both their parts."

Yeah. Both Hawk's and Mad Dog's trust were very difficult to earn. The two men very rarely used equipment belonging to any team but their own, especially when they worked with foreign agencies. That GEM, or whatever, had their confidence in their communication systems pointed to a lot of respect on both Hawk's and the admiral's parts.

Which brought Jazz's mind back to a certain lady. Who the hell was she? She wasn't just some UN liaison or whatever spiel that clerk told him when he had asked during his release, that was for sure. And the way she had taken charge of his men had been very revealing. She showed the self-assurance of someone who was used to giving orders to guys. Her body language had changed too. And Jazz didn't like the way she and Hawk looked at each other.

Damn Hawk. Jazz knew that his friend would view someone like Vivi as a challenge. He frowned in the darkness just as the steel door slid open and they entered an elevator.

"You can take off the glasses now."

Cucumber keyed in another code and the opposite side

opened with a slow, smooth motion, revealing a well-lit modern room. Jazz stood there as the others went in, a habit of his to go in the rear, as it was his usual role to take in everything and anything as his teammates made their way ahead of him. His mind was still on Vivi as he checked out the massive space. War room. This was what his film noir woman had finally led him to—a secret underground facility that seemed to house some pretty nifty electronic gadgets, from what he could see. A huge electronic screen with zoomed-in aerial and satellite photos dominated the room. Another screen was tracking some kind of electronic movement . . . courtesy of a spy plane, he suspected.

Yeah. Like the unpredictability of his beloved jazz, his film noir woman had just morphed into female operative. Time to change the tune and up the tempo.

CHAPTER
6

Vivi wondered what Jazz was thinking. He had shown neither surprise nor anger as he stood there, although she suspected that he wasn't pleased that he had been left out of the loop. It couldn't be helped. Information was her business, and everything had to be done a certain way or chaos would reign. He should understand that. Military procedures were all about doing things a certain way, right? She frowned. Why the hell should she care?

"Do you want to give the Warning Order as well as the Patrol Leader's Order?" Hawk suddenly asked her in French. His golden eyes glinted with barely suppressed amusement. "If you need any general info on how we execute, I'd be glad to help out."

"Let me guess," Vivi replied, her lips curving mockingly. "Over dinner?"

"I don't like talking work when I'm dining. Bad manners to discuss things with my mouth full."

She cocked her head. "After dinner then?"

He gave her a slight shake of the head. "Bad for digestion."

"Monsieur Lieutenant Commander McMillan, earlier, you did say you have more to tell me over dinner tonight," Vivi said, arching a brow. "What were you planning to tell me if it has nothing to do with our work?"

"You'll have to come to dinner to find out, wouldn't you?"

The man was a smooth operator. What was more, he sounded like his friend. The two of them must have honed their pick-up lines together through the years.

Vivi abruptly changed back to English. "I'm afraid I have other plans." She nodded at the envelope in Hawk's hand. "Shouldn't you read that first before we head down below? As for the Warning Order, I think you should go ahead and issue it. It'll allow me to observe and learn more about how your team works."

Without taking his eyes off her, Hawk tore the top of the envelope off. "Come to dinner," he said softly. "I want to talk about Rose. And help a few other girls her age."

Before Vivi could answer he turned away, walking off toward the underground facility. She stared after him for a moment. These men really wanted to help.

Jazz didn't like it one bit. They had been in the war room for almost an hour now, and while he got caught up with what was happening, Hawk and Vivi appeared to be comparing notes from the papers in their hands as they stood close together. The room had good acoustics; he could hear them talking in bits and pieces. They were speaking in rapid French.

He and Hawk were two of the few SEALs who were trained in foreign internal defense and unconventional warfare, having undergone extensive linguistic training sessions at DLI, the Defense Language Institute in Monterey, California. Hawk could speak a couple of languages like a native. And French was one of them, damn it. Jazz remembered how snooty Vivi had been when she heard his own Cajun accent. She didn't seem to have the same condescending attitude with Hawk.

As usual, sensing his thoughts, Hawk glanced in his direction briefly. Jazz and he always had that mental link. One look was usually enough for both of them to know the next move in any combat situation. Jazz gave Hawk his best inscrutable expression. He wasn't in combat mode . . . yet.

Vivi turned at that moment and caught his eye, too. She was smiling, as if Hawk had just told her a joke. Her expression changed, and that odd, secretive look he had seen before entered her dark eyes. It had been a while since he was so attracted to a woman. She intrigued him, with all these different veneers. What exactly did she do? Giving a Patrol Leader's Order wasn't a small thing. It meant she had experience coordinating teams before.

"Have a seat, men. It's show time," Hawk announced, moving toward the seating area around a big screen.

The seats were arranged in a semicircle, behind long, curved tables. There were notepads and pens for each person. The men picked their seats. Jazz sat in the back, stretching his long legs out under the table as he watched Vivi and Hawk getting ready in front.

Hawk pulled a disk from an envelope and inserted it into the computer mainframe on the front desk. Vivi punched some buttons, and the screen behind her lit up as the lighting in the room dimmed.

"Can you hear me?" she asked, after clipping a small mike to her collar.

"Yes, ma'am." The men's tone was now respectful, anticipating action in the future.

Hawk came to the point, issuing the Warning Order, something Jazz and the others were used to. It was the same old–same old, whereby a selected special operations team was taken to a secured area and the unit commander gave a brief description of the coming mission; general instructions that included weapons, chain of command, schedule, and rehearsals; and specific instructions for individuals. Everything followed a set of standard operating procedures—actions on contact, reaction to ambush, individual activities—that each SEAL team member could execute without a word ever spoken.

No, Jazz was currently only interested in the Patrol Leader's Order, in which all the unique details of the operation would be revealed. He looked forward to listening to Vivi Verreau's French-accented voice telling him and his men about radio frequencies, rendezvous points, routes, and commander's intent. At that moment she looked straight at him again.

Jazz leaned back, one hand playing with a pencil, and gave her a lazy wink. Oh yeah, let's see what else was up her sleeve.

"Merci." Vivi took the glass of water from Hawk. The refreshment was welcome. She had spent most of the day talking people into doing what she wanted. She looked across the room at Jazz sitting at the back. He winked at her. Okay, some of the time was spent trying not to do what she wanted.

She took her time with the drink, deliberately studying the men in front of her. Eight pairs of eyes regarded her with different levels of interest. Eight male psyches and egos to convince to follow her orders. She wasn't nervous because she had done this before, had faced hostile males and amused intimidation during a few of those missions. But these were SEALs, notoriously antifemale in their little male world. They weren't Interpol or CIA operatives used to paper shuffling. She would have to tread carefully.

"I'm Vivienne Verreau," Vivi began in a crisp, businesslike voice. "I have different responsibilities to different organizations. Currently I'm the French liaison for a group called United Third World Against Exploitation of Women. They've hired me to observe and report how the UN is doing with the new directive. You saw part of the function of this particular watchdog group when Lieutenant Zeringue was taken into custody. To CIVPOL, I'm nothing but a useless nuisance because I'm supposedly doing nothing. As of today, to you all, I'll play negotiator/translator in an operation that involves a drug deal. I'm passing down files with relevant information. Please take a few minutes to read through them before I continue."

"What is CIVPOL?" Jazz asked from across the room.

"It's the UN international police force. It has a division called Drug Trafficking and Prostitution Investigation Unit, headed by a man named Sun. He doesn't particularly like the new UN directive."

"Why?"

The man really liked to ask questions, Vivi decided. "The UN directive is like a tracking device," she explained. "The peacekeepers and soldiers who are caught committing sexual crimes against the local women are handed back to their own authorities. There isn't any world court system to put these men on trial, Lieutenant. You saw how you were released almost without paperwork. You were innocent, but those who aren't don't stay too long in there, either. The directive is aimed at stopping the act but not the criminal gangs that perpetuate the crime. Mr. Sun considers it a waste of time."

"Do you agree?"

Jazz's blue gaze was sharp and clear, and Vivi felt as if he could see right through her. She instinctively closed off her emotional response whenever it came to questions too close to home. "My job with the United Third World is as an observer. I have no say over whether the directive is a good one or not," she informed him politely. She didn't add that she also worked as a volunteer for their field program in placing orphans.

"We're straying from the subject at hand," Hawk interrupted quietly. "Let's stick to the file. You can ask other personal questions later."

"Actually, we aren't straying off too far," Vivi countered. "CIVPOL wants the same man you're after. He is just now moving into Asian territory because of the drug business but his main business ID in Eastern Europe is the sex trade."

"We don't care what CIVPOL wants," Hawk said.

"I know that, Lieutenant Commander. Your men know that, but CIVPOL also knows that Dilaver is headed to Asia, and I assure you, Mr. Sun or someone under him, is hot on his heels. It's always good to keep in mind third party interference."

"*Absolument.*" Hawk nodded at her. "Third party duly noted."

Hawk's quiet agreement was deceptive. Vivi was aware that all his men were watching their discussion with interest. He seemed bent on testing her, provoking her into sounding defensive. She, on the other hand, wasn't going to give an inch to this kind of manipulation.

Vivi picked up the video control and clicked the button. Behind her a giant picture of a man appeared on the screen.

"This is your target. Dragan Dilaver, a notorious kingpin in Eastern Europe. Headquarters is in Velesta, Macedonia. As you can see, except for the dark blondish hair, he looks more Asian than European, with Asiatic eyes and high cheekbones. He is in his late thirties or early forties, about five feet, six inches, heavyset, probably one hundred seventy to two hundred pounds depending on the description from sex slaves who escaped his hellholes. He has several brothers who work for him on and off, and they have been expanding the family business beyond Europe these past couple of years."

Vivi looked at each of the men in the eye before continuing. "My outfit is GEM. We've been contracted to stop a certain shipment of these girls crossing the border. Admiral Madison wants Dragan Dilaver. Our operations cross paths because Dilaver himself is bringing these girls. My concern is to get this shipment out of his hands safely. Your own operation will be outlined by your commanding officer."

"Why is Dilaver bringing these girls personally?" Jazz asked.

"There's a rumor that he's meeting with some local Triad members to negotiate territory and expanding drug trade," Vivi replied. "Even criminals have their own politics. Dilaver is bringing some girls as a peace offering."

"Let's blow him up," Cucumber chimed in, his voice full of disgust.

"That would be nice," Vivi agreed readily. Her notes on Dilaver made her retch. "However, my contract's orders are very specific. I'm only to make sure the girls get out of the way and leave Dilaver to the SEALs."

"We can do that ourselves," Dirk chimed in. "We've extracted prisoners before."

Dirk was the quiet one, Vivi mentally noted, the one everyone listened to whenever he spoke. "You have your own mission," she told him. "I think you'll have a clearer idea after Lieutenant McMillan briefs you. Besides, I speak the local dialect, and believe me, you're going to need me in this extraction."

"Since we aren't negotiating, why would we need you?" another one of the men spoke up. "Not arguing here, Miss Verreau, just wanted to understand your role within our group."

"I have no role within your group, save that you will need me where the safety of these girls are concerned," Vivi said.

"Frontline combat is no place for women."

Jazz's quiet comment sliced through the growing edginess. Vivi didn't look at him immediately, choosing to study the others' reactions first. Some of the men hid their surprise well. A few of them had the smiles of cocky males in agreement. Arms folded, Hawk remained impassive, but his eyes were watchful. And all of them were waiting for her eruption.

Vivi leaned a hip against the nearest table in the front, then deliberately crossed her legs. It was all about power, she told herself.

"I'm not going to be shooting and running around with you guys, if that's what you're afraid of, Lieutenant. But if need be, I'm handy with a weapon. I can run the army standard requirement of two miles in seventeen minutes and fifty-five seconds maximum. But, I'm sure you're all faster than that, so let's breathe a sigh of relief that you don't have to worry about my pretty ass out in the field with your big Uzis, hmm?"

That caused a laugh, which was what she wanted. She understood how testy the situation could get if the men had to adjust to someone new, and a woman at that. So she didn't reveal that she was more than qualified, since speed was one of her strong points. No. She would have to prove that to these men. They would only sneer at the five minutes' difference that the army generously gave to female recruits. Men were men, after all.

"Our preferred choice of weapons are either the M16 or the CAR-15, Miss Verreau," Jazz came back. "If need be, which type would you be carrying?"

Vivi cocked her head. "It depends on the situation, Lieutenant."

"Target acquisition, let's say."

"Depends on the duration of the operation."

"On foot, let's say, with the surroundings similar to our environment—mountainous and thick jungles. Then a stake-out and surveillance. Perhaps a firefight ground-combat situation. Then an immediate extraction of target and continual rapid-mobility track back to point zero."

Vivi noted the challenge in Jazz's voice. He was testing her combat knowledge, trying to gauge her experience, especially in extraction procedure. Even though the men might think she wouldn't be out in the field with them, they still needed to know she could analyze situations and make good decisions. She didn't blame him; he was one of the two leaders of these men, and not likely to hand over the reins of command so easily. "Tell me your concerns, Lieutenant."

He paused a second as he scratched down some notes. "There won't be any micro-management, where you have to go up the chain of command to get the next order. Since you're going to be part of this extraction, I think it's important to know how experienced you are and whether you're knowledgeable in field operations, since you just told us your main job is observation and negotiation. Those are passive skills." His eyes were very blue in his tan face. "I need more than your word that you aren't going to end up a liability."

This was a new side of Jazz, Vivi realized, the side that was responsible for his men. Before he had been alternatively wicked and teasing, cajoling and even macho, when it came to protecting women and children, but this was the Jazz Zeringue that she had read of in those files, the one with the ribbons and badges. He was a warrior through and through. She wondered whether this was the real him. Soldiers. Slash and burn. Take and destroy.

"Yes, I do see your apprehension. However, I can try to convince you that I know what is involved and how to operate within the framework of a field operation. Is that fair for now?"

"Fair, yes, but war isn't about fairness."

His curtness grated. He was already assuming that she knew nothing about warfare. Her eyes narrowed slightly, even as she willed herself to relax.

It's all about power, she repeated to herself. It's all about who had the knowledge.

Vivi leaned forward a little, as if she was sharing a secret. "You're right, Lieutenant Zeringue. War isn't fair. The rules we learned go out the window the moment bullets start showering down on you. And yes, women in combat isn't about war but fairness, but the arguments against this issue are moot. There aren't any *known* women in the front lines today. I don't intend to argue it with you or"—she paused and looked around, making eye contact, keeping her voice low and confidential—"anyone here in this room. All I care about is for you to know that I'm in charge of one big part of this operation and under no circumstance can you deviate from my orders there. The extraction is mine and mine alone. Your orders, coming from Hawk or Lieutenant Zeringue, concern your mission outlined by Admiral Madison, and on that I'll count on your skills and all your team knowledge. On that I'll have very little say. I promise to get out of the way when the right moment comes. Now is that fair?"

Some of the men nodded. Vivi turned slightly to her right. Hawk was leaning against a console, a quirk playing on his lips. She knew that he was the one who initiated this test. He hadn't said a word for or against her thus far. She arched a brow at him. His gaze didn't waver. The golden gleam in his eyes was predatory. The silent challenge in them was unmistakable. It was dinner or nothing. She would have to be the first to blink.

Vivi nodded. "Fair, Lieutenant Commander McMillan?"

"Yes," Hawk replied immediately, smoothly.

But there were two different teams in the room. Two different leaders to deal with. She turned to the other one, and her heart skipped a beat at the sight of Jazz sitting in the back, with that lazy deceptive sprawl, playing with the pencil in his big hands.

His silent challenge was just as unmistakable. It was dinner or nothing. Vivi wasn't a GEM operative for nothing. She had been trained to handle men. She gave a slight nod, chin going a little higher at the amusement that suddenly lit up the blue eyes.

"Fair, Lieutenant Zeringue?"

"*Oui*, Mademoiselle Verreau," he drawled, jabbing his pencil playfully at the papers in front of him.

Vivi felt like cracking her knuckles. "Good, then let's get down to business. I plan my operation on the basis of the KISS principle. In short, back to basics. You do what you know best and you let me do what I do best. This is a direct extraction, so timing is very precise. Look at the map and photos behind me, please. This is your terrain. You're going to be transported there at night. Follow SOP."

"Are you going to be making the decisions or will you be radioing back and forth to a phantom command for orders?" one of the men asked.

Vivi decided to counter drollness with drollness. "Do you stand around and wait for orders while attempting a DE?"

Direct extraction was a short-term seize and destroy, damage and capture operation. The members of a team must complete it with exact precision, or they risked failure. Failure could mean loss of opportunity, and probable loss of lives. There wouldn't be any time to consult with anyone while the operation was under way.

At the silence, Vivi nodded and drove the point home. "This is a joint mission and I'm just as unfamiliar with your methods as you are with mine. I need you to put aside your prejudices and get this job done. Believe me, if my side didn't need you, and if the admiral didn't need my cooperation, we wouldn't be in this together. We're mainly contract agents, not very good at following military procedures. We don't play with red tape. We do have military training, please don't misunderstand this point, but we don't"—she paused, noting with satisfaction that she had their full attention for the first time—"have the same culpability."

"Meaning?" Hawk questioned.

Vivi stood up. Power was in letting others think they had it. She smiled grimly. "We like to think we're the best at what we do. If I die, no one outside my agency will give a damn."

7

Jazz wasn't a male chauvinist. Far from it. His maman and sisters made sure of that. He had grown up loving the way the women around him gathered forces in their own little wars and won them by the oddest ways. He and his brother were skilled in the ways women manipulated men. His eyes narrowed as he studied the lone female in this underground room, listening to her words and noting her body language as she gave instructions like a pro.

Vivi Verreau was halfway to winning the wills, if not the hearts, of the men in the room. Including, he noted, his best friend Hawk. He hadn't liked the way she kept calling him by his name while addressing him as Lieutenant Zeringue. He was used to Hawk getting women; Hawk was like catnip to them—they saw him; they had to have him. Jazz pushed the point of the pencil into the pad. Damn it, why must Vivi be seduced by those weird eyes, anyhow?

That Admiral Madison had approved of this joint mission was pretty telling. It meant he had enough confidence in Vivi and her group to allow his own SEALs to be under her command. Jazz hoped she wasn't going to think that she would have total command of the operation. He doubted Hawk would go that far, even to get a woman. He himself wasn't even sure what to think yet. He knew Hawk would fill him in regarding what the admiral had told him, so he would withhold his apprehension until then.

A direct extraction was no easy matter. It involved lives. If it were just some search and destroy mission . . . but they would have no need of Vivi Verreau then. Any SEAL team had the capability of creating a lot of destruction without any female help. He eyed the woman leaning against the table, admiring her long legs. Oh yes, she knew what she was doing—every male in the room was thinking of those same legs running in camouflaged pants with them. She hadn't convinced them that she was capable of being on a mission with them yet, but she had certainly caught their imagination with her very solid knowledge, her sound answers, and those luscious legs.

Jazz jotted down notes for later discussion with Hawk. Dragan Dilaver—what was the SEAL team's main objective with the guy if he weren't the subject of direct extraction?

He looked at the "overhead" imagery, the photographs of all altitudes of the target area. They had plenty of time to do a run-through of the mission, and he looked forward to comparing strategy with Hawk. They had done this before. Only thing different this time would be an additional teammate. A female.

He looked at Vivi again. Not just any female either. This woman was very comfortable working with men, very good at putting the opposite sex at ease. It was this element and the earlier display of her dislike of all things military that intrigued him more and more. She didn't want to go on a date with him, yet he felt she had been very close to actually admitting to liking him. And now she had skillfully gambled and agreed to have dinner with two soldiers just to make a point. How far was she willing to go? And what was she up to anyway?

In film noir, a woman of mystery had a secret arsenal. Jazz was beginning to believe his playful analogy was becoming more and more genuine by the moment.

"I have to leave for another appointment soon. Tomorrow

ve'll brainstorm strategy." Vivi concluded the Orders, giv-
ng them the time of the next meeting. "Your commanders
vill now take over and fill you in on the rest of your opera-
ion. I'll sit in the back and if you hear me leaving, it's not
because you guys are boring me, okay?"

She smiled winningly, and Jazz could almost hear the
dark sexy notes of a lone trumpet following her footsteps towards him. He couldn't help giving her a knowing grin,
partly because he knew that would irritate her.

He had to give Vivi credit. Instead of avoiding confrontation, she slid into the seat right next to him. Most women
would let the poor guy stew and wonder about what was happening next. That must not be her style.

Her hazelnut eyes still held a combative light. She had to
be mad at him for asking those questions. Part of him had
enjoyed the exchange. It was his job to make sure that his
men remained safe, or as safe as possible, in their kind of
work. The addition of someone unknown needed careful
analysis. Again, he needed to talk to Hawk. Hear what Mad
Dog had instructed.

Strange how a woman's presence a couple of feet away
could bring sudden awareness when his body was used to
tossing around with other bodies in small spaces. But of
course, those other bodies often smelled like old socks and
blood. Vivi Verreau had a scent all her own . . . not pungent
like expensive perfume, not too flowery, not too fruity . . .
just something elusive. He hoped to find out for himself over
dinner.

In the front, Hawk commenced with the mission. Operation Stealth Trap. At least it wasn't something stupid like
Kum Quat. As Jazz jotted down the information, he began to
see how the joint mission was going to take place. Vivi
stayed for another fifteen minutes, then got up to go. She slid
a piece of paper folded in half toward him. He pocketed it
without taking his eyes off the map on the big screen. Her
scent lingered even after she was gone.

* * *

The last time Jazz had argued with Hawk over a woman, they were still officers without any field experience, when they had spent a lot of time hanging out in the officers' lounge and learning about the bad side of being a sailor. That was, he mused, so long ago he couldn't remember exactly what started the fight. The one thing he did remember was her sexy wide mouth and the unspoken promises of what she was going to do to him with those lips.

Then Hawk had arrived and made a beeline for her when Jazz had gone off to the men's room. By the time he had returned, the woman was sucking Hawk's lips like there was no tomorrow. Jazz had blamed his friend immediately, of course, since Hawk's reputation with females was legendary even then, and he had enough alcohol in his system to start some trouble.

"I still have a scar from that kick." Hawk's voice merged with his memories.

Jazz looked up from his notes. The others had gone off after Orders, leaving their commanders alone. "I hate it when you do that," he commented.

"It's tough to share the same brain, isn't it?"

That was how close the two of them were. Their ability to read each other's minds sometimes disconcerted others, although privately Jazz thought Hawk could read him better than the other way round.

"That was a long time ago," Jazz said. "I don't think we should take time-out for a boys' fight over a woman."

Hawk raised an eyebrow mockingly. "I didn't issue any challenge. Besides, that woman with the lips left with someone else while we were busy fighting."

Jazz grinned. "Yeah. Pity."

Hawk grinned back. "I got her weeks later behind your back."

"Fuckhead." Jazz shook his head. "Always got to win."

"It wasn't you, buddy. She was very persistent and I was very young."

"Oh, like you would say no now? You're a tomcat, Hawk."

"I've grown pickier."

"Uh-huh." Jazz stretched his legs out and yawned. He knew how women were with Hawk. "So don't pick her."

"You mean, Vivienne Verreau?" Hawk sat on the table, feet on the chair. "Why not? You interested?"

"Yeah."

"But she hasn't grown warm to your kind of charm yet."

Jazz searched Hawk's eyes. Damn if he couldn't read his mind right now. "I hadn't had the chance."

"You're losing your touch, Jazz. You had all morning."

"And your point is?"

"She agreed to go to dinner with me."

"With me too."

Hawk raised an eyebrow again. "So you want to fight?"

Jazz crossed his ankles. "You're a bore. She'll come to her senses." He didn't feel as confident as his words, but, hell, he wasn't going to fight with Hawk over a woman when he didn't even know what or who Vivi Verreau was. Besides, he thought with some smug satisfaction, she was still wearing his pendant. He added, "Why are you after her anyway?"

"She's intriguing. Smart. And, she's GEM."

"What's GEM?" Jazz was getting more curious about this organization by the second. "Her explanation was evasive, at best."

"Like she said, independent contractors," Hawk told him, giving a small shrug. "I know their women are all well trained in arms and languages, and they all know how to kiss."

The last part was said with a devilish grin. Jazz frowned. He knew for sure Hawk hadn't kissed Vivi yet. "Oh yeah, your cousin's recent romance, the lady the guys kept talking about, the one who wears leather outfits like Cat Woman. Don't tell me you kissed Steve's girlfriend?"

Nothing Hawk did would surprise him, but he had never known Hawk to poach, especially when a woman had committed herself to some other man.

"She kissed me, actually. She thought I was Kisser."

Hawk's cousin, also named Steve McMillan, looked like and had almost the same build as Hawk. They had often been mistaken for brothers but were in fact cousins. But still . . . Jazz gazed at Hawk skeptically . . . they weren't *that* identical.

Hawk's lips quirked. He was reading Jazz's mind again. "It was dark," he offered as an explanation, "and we had our game face on."

With camouflaged faces, one *could* mistake Hawk for Steve. "Okay, so they kiss well. What else do you know about GEM? Why did Mad Dog decide to do a joint mission with an independent? Since when did we become drug busters?"

"For one thing, Dilaver and his drug ring aren't just the regular crime scum. His organization grows stronger every year and he's arming the KLA in Serbia. He has his fingers in illegal arms, sex trade, and drugs, all interdependent when it comes to power in certain regions of the world, as you know." Hawk thumbed at the screen behind him. "You saw the info she gave. He wants to expand but needs the cooperation of the Triads in Asia to make a move. If his gang joins up with the Triads, we have a problem in this part of the world."

Jazz agreed. The region was already unstable, what with different warlords fighting one another and the government. With Dilaver backing one particular group, and selling illegal arms as well as channeling drugs and money laundering, the Triads could grow even more powerful. Could start to control the governing officers the way the KLA was doing now in Europe. But he had more questions that had nothing to do with political repercussions.

"Are GEM operatives female agents who go around saving sex victims?" Jazz asked. "Again, why the joint mission? Besides the fact that Vivienne Verreau speaks many languages."

"From what the admiral told me, there are two outfits that work together—GEM and COS commandos. GEM is independent but COS CO linked up with them for the last two years. When Admiral Madison discovered how all the agencies weren't communicating with each other, he appointed Steve as liaison between them and our STAR Force. They had good resources and an ability to circumvent a lot of the B.S. when it came to real action. They can help us whenever we're in a bind."

"Like when I was in the cage at Interpol," Jazz interjected.

Hawk nodded. "Yeah, that's one on the plus side. And this mission's Intel came from them too. Obviously, their contract is to extract the girls but they checked with the admiral to make sure that we weren't in this area to get Dilaver."

Everything was beginning to make sense. When Admiral Madison had contacted the liaison to get him out, GEM probably grew concerned that his men were here for a mission that might jeopardize their operation.

"Okay. I see the big pic. We hit Dilaver. What about weaponry?"

"It's the beaut part of the deal. No government-issued firepower. They supply it."

Jazz raised his eyebrows. "What do you think about that?"

Hawk gave a lazy grin. "I think we're going to have lots of fun."

So were the others. Nothing like telling a bunch of guys there were many toys to play with in the next week or so. "I'll make a list of what we need."

"Good. I have a dinner date tonight," Hawk said, getting off the table.

In response, Jazz pushed his desk forward, jamming his friend between the tables. Hawk, amusement evident on his face, didn't move out of the way. "Not so fast," Jazz said.

"Sorry, buddy. With someone like Vivienne, I think 'fast' is a must. She's a runner."

Jazz scowled. "Like you know."

"I can spot them a mile away."

"So your strategy is to run faster to catch her?"

Hawk leaned down and pushed the desk back a few inches. Jazz stopped it with one hand. "Maybe I intend to," Hawk told him.

Jazz scowled as he studied his friend for a second. He hadn't seen Hawk this motivated about a woman for a while now. It wasn't a good sign. "I'm going to get her," he announced.

Hawk wasn't at all perturbed by the challenge. "How are you going to do that?"

He kicked the leg of the table lightly. "You're the one who claims we share the same brain. Find out yourself."

He recognized Hawk's confident smirk and lazily grinned back. Usually, Jazz didn't care to join in the chase of an attractive woman, especially when his friend was interested. He much preferred his own company and music. But Vivi Verreau was not a usual woman.

"Better hurry. So what did she say in her note?"

Jazz arched a brow. "Evil twin," he mocked, "do I look stupid?"

Vivi climbed the stairs up to her apartment. Her landlady peered out from the third-floor landing and waved when she saw who it was.

"Late! Your boyfriend mad."

Vivi grinned. She had no boyfriend. Mrs. Lee was always trying to set her up with one of the occupants in the building. A lonely man, she told Vivi, with a smug smile. Ripe for the picking. Never late with rent. Always cook for himself. Good potential husband material. Vivi found Mrs. Lee's persistence humorous and exasperating.

"I have to work," she told the old lady.

"Ah, see? You get him, you don't need to work so hard." Mrs. Lee wagged a finger at her. "Only need some children and then you set for life."

Vivi choked back a laugh as she began to climb the staircase. "I think children are harder work, Mrs. Lee," she called up.

"Ha! Throw them out on the street. Call them home for dinner. What so hard? Beat their behinds if they get in trouble. Make more children. They take care of the young ones."

Vivi pulled her keys out of her purse. She had heard this litany of advice before. Mrs. Lee had six children, all of whom acted older than their age, all of them with a street education beyond their years. Vivi had never pointed out that Mr. Lee was missing from the picture.

As usual, she opted for evasive humor. "I think I'll stick to my fish tank, Mrs. Lee," she said and laughed. "I've only one fish left in there, and I'm still waiting for it to die."

She heard her landlady snort as she shuffled off back to her apartment. Her voice trailed away. "Fish! She thinks fish is better than husband and kids. Something wrong with that girl."

Vivi laughed again as she closed the door behind her. Fish were the best. No need to take them for a walk. No barks, mews, or screeches. And when they died one flush from the toilet took care of everything. No high maintenance. She turned on the light.

"Shit," she said as she stared at her couch.

The figure lounging casually there stretched sinuously, leather-clad long legs in high-heel boots sliding with catlike grace onto the floor. The overhead light reflected the curly blond tresses, the glint of gold jewelry, the metallic gleam of the buttons on her jacket. Talk about something high maintenance . . .

"Shit," Vivi repeated. "You've cut your hair."

"Like it? Shouldn't you be taking a break from wearing those cheek inserts? It isn't good to have them on over a year. The shape of your mouth will change permanently."

Vivi frowned. She resisted the urge to tongue the hidden wire that secured the brace in her mouth that made her upper bite slightly more pronounced. It was a simple little device often used by operatives, and a lot easier than wearing false teeth over her real ones.

She had worn one specially designed for her out of curiosity. Now it was almost a defense mechanism. Sometimes when she looked in the mirror, she kept seeing her old self . . . She quickly shook off the thought.

It was just like her operations chief to put her on the defensive within the first few moments of meeting. Vivi shrugged nonchalantly. "I don't think you've slipped into my apartment to give me beauty tips, T. What's with the surprise visit?"

"You haven't been debriefed for a while now and I was in the neighborhood."

Vivi sniffed in disbelief. "You were busy on assignment in New York, last I heard." She crossed her arms. "I may be living in the boondocks but I do keep in touch with the sisters, you know. They told me you've transferred out of COS Command and were temporarily unavailable to anyone, especially an Alex Diamond."

Tess was studying the rings on her fingers. "The girls talk too much. I'm just taking a break so I can do more one-on-one debriefing in the field."

Vivi had never seen her operations chief backpedaling before. Alex Diamond must be a special man. "I've been sending in my reports. There haven't been any changes."

"There's going to be some soon."

Here we go. T. never did anything without an ulterior motive. "Let me guess," Vivi said dryly. "It has to do with a group of SEALs, a drug kingpin, and some young girls."

"Right in one."

"Tell me why you're in town, T."

"I'm currently residing at the Sofitel."

Vivi raised a brow. "Nice. As?"

"I'm here enjoying a short holiday, darling. Part business, too. I might be negotiating a business deal in town."

T. wasn't just her operations chief. She also undertook some of the toughest assignments that GEM contracted, the kind that required the use of her ability to morph from one personality into another. For the past two years, T. had been in a special joint mission that involved arms dealing with some of the world's most notorious figures. Vivi was sure that her presence in town didn't just accidentally coincide with Dilaver's upcoming arrival.

Vivi walked across the room to turn on the light over her fish tank. "So, I'm curious as to why you asked to be replaced at Center." That was what they called the new HQ for both outfits. She sprinkled a little fish food into the water. "I was surprised when I heard about it. Tell me about Alex Diamond. Isn't he the runaway COS commando whose duties you took over?"

A few years ago, T. had joined the team of covert commandos on a special program called Virus. Part of the reason was to avenge the death of one of their operatives killed by a bomb that had also taken the lives of several COS operatives. GEM had the ability to track worldwide money laundering whereas COS Command Center had the means to bankroll the covert operations. It didn't hurt to have a group of well-trained commandos at one's beck and call, either. The exchange of information had been hugely successful in creating a network to infiltrate international groups running illegal arms.

"You've been underground two years, Viv. Things change."

That hadn't escaped Vivi's notice. From talking with fellow operatives, she had learned that GEM was slowly expanding from contract operations.

T.'s eyes were watchful, although she still lounged in that deceptively lazy manner. "Nothing's changed at my end," Vivi said softly. She hadn't taken a break in two years because she hadn't found what she was looking for, and T. knew how important this contract was to her. She smiled and shrugged. "But I can see it's different at yours. There is this rumor that Alex Diamond, newly returned from the cold COS commando, is looking for you in a very personal way. Could the rumor be true?"

It was fun needling T. for once. She cocked an inquiring brow at her operations chief.

"Rumors have a funny way of being distorted. I don't think a 'very personal way' would be how I'd explain it."

Vivi noted that she hadn't denied the rumor. "Do you think I should take a field position with these commandos you've been working with? If one of them could get under your skin, they must be pretty potent."

In return, T. gave her a challenging smile. "It's not enough you have two SEALs eating out of your hands, now you want my men too? Things have changed if you're after military men, Vivi. I remember your . . . abhorrence of all things uniformed."

As usual, nothing escaped her chief. "You brought up debriefing, yet you already seemed very well informed. Surely, you aren't interrupting your hot romance just to find out about my love life?"

T. laughed as she got off the sofa, crossing the small living room in a few long-legged strides. A tall, striking woman, she had the confident walk of someone used to being the center of attention. One of the few things Vivi liked about her leader was her genuine enjoyment of her own beauty. It was also ironic that even though T. looked gorgeous in her various guises, no one had ever been sure about the real woman. When she had first trained under her, Vivi had often wondered about the many layers that had surfaced then disappeared, had tried to fathom how one could run around without a face of her own.

But that was years ago. She might never rise to T.'s level when it came to multiple identities, but like many of her GEM friends, she had learned to compartmentalize. She was also very aware that T. always prepared her operatives with subtle manipulation, as if she were playing a chess game and Vivi was one of her pieces. She watched warily as T. walked past her to the fish tank, with its one lone occupant.

"Poor little fish, all alone," she said, tapping on the glass. "What's the matter, you can't afford to buy a couple more?"

"I'm waiting for her to die," Vivi explained. "She's obstinate as hell."

"Ah, but loners tend to live a long, long time, darling."

Little hairs of apprehension pricked Vivi's awareness. "Is that right?" She kept her voice light. "I didn't know you're a fish expert now."

T.'s finger traced the movement of the fish. "Self-confinement," she said, darting Vivi a sideways glance, "especially in a controlled environment, makes things very predictable."

"The fish will die eventually," Vivi pointed out, refusing to take the bait.

"Stop feeding it and it'll die quicker."

Vivi canted her brows. "Are you asking me to kill my pet?"

"I was just offering a suggestion. You said you were waiting for it to die."

"I have time on my hands."

"What, another two years?"

"If it takes that long, then I'll be here that long."

"And of course, you'll leave those cheek inserts in till your face is permanently disfigured."

Vivi frowned. Somehow she had been manipulated back into talking about something she didn't care to discuss. She had thought talking about Alex Diamond would get T. off her back. "We're talking about my fish," she said, a little too defensively.

"Artificially controlled environment, regularly fed, mateless, circling around in the same waters looking for something that's not there . . ." T. ran her fingers through her blond tresses. "Of course we're talking about your fish, darling."

"Thanks for your concern about my pet's lonely existence, but really, it's just a fish," Vivi said politely, hoping to sidestep the obvious undercurrent. "Let's go back to the faxed documents with the new orders. Why are we doing a joint mission with SEALs?"

"Why not? We have a contract to extract a shipment of illegal aliens coming into the country, and Admiral Madison has been after Dilaver for a while. It makes sense to plan our operation together—we both get what we want."

Vivi massaged the back of her neck. God, she was suddenly so tired. "We can't win this war, can we? As long as there are men who will buy young girls as sex slaves, there'll always be missing children and victimized kids."

She knew she shouldn't betray too much of herself when it came to T., but it had been a long time since she had someone to talk to. Her daily battle to find a safe house to take in young runaways and underage prostitutes in the city was only part of her own reasons to be there, and lately it seemed that every day was a fruitless battle.

"This is eating you up," T. commented. There was a hint of worry in her eyes. "That's why I'm giving you this new assignment. It'll take your mind away from here for a bit. You're giving up too much of yourself in the situation here."

"And what's wrong with that?" Vivi countered, her voice sounding a little sharper than intended. "These girls have no one to turn to, T. They're either married off or sold to these pimps. Or they run off without knowing what the world has in store for them."

"That isn't why you're here, Viv."

"I know my job. Do you have complaints about that?"

T. shoved her hands into her pockets. The concern in her eyes had disappeared, replaced by a cool flatness. Vivi had seen that look before. T. specialized in a NOPAIN program called mind probe, a skill taught to certain operatives who were trained in interrogation. She had made the mistake of talking too damn much to her chief.

"Let's hear your complaints first," T. suggested as she came closer.

There was usually little escape when T. started one of these sessions. Vivi's chin went up. "Well, I would like more action instead of collecting data on male military men detained and released. I would like to see the local government going after the gangs who kidnap these girls. I would like international laws going after sexual predators. All those would be a good start."

"Do you think you've accomplished none of the above?"

"I haven't seen anything encouraging."

"So just because you don't see it means nothing is being achieved?"

Vivi pointed to herself. "It feels like a losing cause and I don't like it."

"Making it personal can do that to you, darling. You get the urge to feed the hunger all the time." T. surprised her with a light laugh. She pivoted toward the kitchenette. "I think we need some refreshments. This debriefing is turning out to be most enlightening."

Vivi scowled. It was just like T. to go abruptly from subject to subject. She had to be on her toes all the time when T. was around. Fish, drink, makeup, and before one knew it, she'd gotten all of one's little secrets. Vivi should know. She had been trained in NOPAIN herself. The one skill for which many GEM operators were famous—non-physical and innovative negotiation—and the woman checking out the contents of her refrigerator wrote most of the chapters in that book. T. was trying to gauge her weaknesses and probing for secrets.

"What do you mean, feed the hunger?" she asked, joining T., staring inside at the trays of wrapped leftovers on the shelves.

"Something personal always feeds something. Ego. Revenge. Memories." T. pulled out a container, opened it, and sniffed. "Yum. Spicy. That's what I need right now."

"So you're saying I can't feed my hunger, whether it's ego, revenge, or memories?"

"Oh, don't get me wrong. Sometimes it's good to use personal motive to get things done, but once it becomes a personal indulgence . . ." T. shrugged. She pulled some dishes from the cabinet. "It gets in the way of success."

"We aren't just talking about me, are we?" Vivi leaned a

hip against the counter, watching her chief closely. She hadn't seen her for a while, and for the first time noticed the little lines of tension around her mouth. "It's this Alex guy, isn't it? Let's not pussyfoot around anymore. I've heard that you and he weren't getting along at Center now that he's back from the cold, that he pushed you out of your position. Is that true?"

If that was, it would be the first time T. had ever allowed another man to beat her. Vivi had never met any of these commandos, but had heard enough to know they were a different group of men.

T. spooned the food onto the plate and handed it to Vivi. "Needs to be heated, darling. I hate cold, stale food."

Vivi crossed her arms. "Changing the subject, T. darling?" she drawled. This was the second time T. had avoided answering the same question.

"You want me to go personal, darling, you will have to try harder," T. drawled back. "I suppose you aren't going to feed me properly."

Vivi pointed to a microwave oven in the corner. "Quick and easy." She pointed to the oven. "Or slow and tedious. Which way do you want it, T.? Either way, you won't get me to quit till I'm ready."

"Either way, I'll get my food done. And nobody's asking you to quit . . . yet." T. walked to the microwave. "Things are going to heat up really quickly and I want you to be prepared."

"For what?"

"Five minutes ought to do it," T. said, as she pushed some buttons. "How about a drink, hmm? You really are lacking in hosting skills."

Vivi silently handed T. two empty glasses. Sometimes it was just easier to let T. play her mind games. She would reveal what was going on in her own time, and no amount of yelling would yield any difference.

She watched T. pour some iced tea into the glasses, studying the other woman as she moved around her small kitchen. She had lost some weight; her exquisite bone structure seemed more pronounced, emphasizing the hollows in her cheeks and the sensual fullness of her lips. She had always looked at T. closely, taking lessons on how to change her looks from the best in the business. Sometimes the slight changes were chemical-injected, other times it was just a different way of parting hair, but she had a feeling that T.'s physical changes this time weren't self-induced. She waited until T. sat at the little dining table with food and drink ready.

"Not eating?"

Vivi shook her head. Best not to talk about her dinner plans. "I'm not hungry yet. So tell me about D.C." Vivi pulled out a chair. Maybe changing tactics would loosen T.'s tongue. "I heard Operation Foxhole went beautifully. You've spent all these years going after Maximillian Shoggi. It must feel good to know we have him by the balls."

After one of GEM's popular operatives, Emma, along with several covert government commandos, had been killed in a setup, GEM had wanted to catch the culprits. The past few years, T. had done double duty as a contract agent and an avenger, mapping several operations that targeted the individuals involved. With her new promotion and decision-making muscle, T. had been able to make certain changes. One of them was merging part of the GEM sections with COS Center.

The result was Operation Foxhole, a years-long project to undermine Maximillian Shoggi, the main supplier of illegal arms and also the infamous shadow middleman who had caused the deaths. It took a while, but they had slowly squeezed his bank accounts and money flow until he was forced to come out in the open. Vivi had only recently caught up with the news. It wasn't easy to get up-to-date in this part of the world, especially when it had to do with such a complex mission. But T. was here now. And Dilaver was also a very well-known illegal weapons supplier. Very important link here.

"Yes, we have him where we want him," T. said, between

bites. "He has the laptop we sold him and he's a desperate man, running out of money. His main front, Cash Ibrahim, is dead, and Shoggi isn't used to dealing directly. He'll be looking for help to sell that laptop."

"Ah, the meat of the matter," Vivi said dryly.

T.'s eyes twinkled back at her. "Delicious meal, by the way," she said, finishing up the last few spoonfuls. "Spice is good for the soul. You should eat more of it, Viv."

"I eat my share."

T. arched her shapely eyebrows. "Are their names Zola Zeringue and Hawk McMillan?"

"I just got to know them myself. You sent me Lieutenant Zeringue's files, so don't jump to any conclusions," Vivi said, wondering why she sounded so defensive.

"I didn't say anything other than their names," T. came back, amused. "And isn't it interesting that you only brought up one of them?"

Vivi decided to ignore the observation. "I gather this is going to tie in with why you're here and why we're doing a joint mission with the Navy SEALs?"

"Yes."

"Why throw me with them? You can easily do the operations blindfolded, T."

"We have an insider working within the Triads. Everything we know, including the shipment of girls with Dilaver, comes from him. With so many dealers in town, we have to tread carefully here because we don't want any interference with Shoggi's visit and my work. I have a lot on my plate and I know you'd want a piece of the action. Or aren't you interested?"

T. knew very well she would want in. Vivi nodded her answer.

"I thought you would," T. said, drinking down her iced tea. "You're here and I need someone who can handle the girls after the extraction. We can't afford to have our inside man expose himself, and I have my own role to play."

"Can I ask what that is?" A shipment of girls coming in. That was what this place needed, more innocent children traded for sex. Vivi refused to let her frustration show.

"It's not over with Maximillian Shoggi, darling. He still needs to get rid of the laptop. My last attempt at contacting him didn't end so well, especially for his middleman. Without Cash, he'll be desperate to get hold of Dilaver. I mean to make sure Dilaver gets interested in this item."

Vivi absorbed the information, taking a sip from her drink. T., as usual, was going to be in the middle of danger. "Will you let me in on all the details? Who's our insider?"

T. smiled mysteriously. "One thing at a time. First, we have to get the extraction of the girls completed. The admiral's SEALs are perfect decoys."

Vivi frowned. "I hope you aren't going to use the girls we save to lure Dilaver? And, if we use those SEALs as decoys, wouldn't we be jeopardizing their mission?" And safety.

"No, the sea mammals will be fine. With their help, darling, we're going to start a war. A small one . . . but still, a nice bad-guy versus bad-guy war."

Stefan had weighed carefully how to win this battle. He needed help to get to the Triad brother; he needed someone who had the crime lord's ear.

"Are you sure the information is correct?"

"Have I ever been wrong?"

He reclined lazily against the brocade pillows, indolently watching the woman as she tried on the jewelry he had brought for her. The dangling diamonds sparkled in the dim lighting as she swung her head one way and then the other, enjoying her own reflection in the dressing mirror. She put on the necklace with its teardrop diamond pendant, then swung around to face him, eyes glowing with pleasure.

"How do they look?"

"Tempting," he said.

She pouted. "Not my breasts, you insatiable one. The jewelry."

He kept his eyes on her large breasts. "They look good," he said.

He could tell that his answer pleased her, even though she pretended to be a little mad that he wasn't looking at his presents. He didn't care about the baubles; at their price, he knew they would look great on anyone.

She lifted her breasts teasingly, her fingers playing with her large nipples. "How many pills in the shipment?" she asked as she strutted closer to the bed.

He smiled. He wasn't the one who was insatiable. "Give me a good price and I'll tell you more."

Her pout became more pronounced. "Darling, your price is too high. My brother might not want to pay it."

He lay back further against the pillows. His hand reached between his legs as he watched her approach. "Tell him it's my price or nothing. I'm the only one with the map."

Her attention was avidly on what he was doing. "You can't negotiate?"

"I am negotiating," he replied softly, as he leisurely aroused himself.

She climbed onto the bed, her eyes greedy on what he was offering. "Totally unfair," she whispered. "You know I want that. But my brother will never understand this kind of terms."

He pulled on his erection, knowing how much it aroused her that he was in control of himself, of her, of the situation. He never ever forgot that she liked being mastered, even though it was all pretense. She wanted to be the one to have the power to say no. She was playing with him, just as he was playing with her.

It was a dangerous game. She had the power to eliminate him; he was one against an army of bandits. He watched the woman as she climbed onto the bed, sinuously crawling between his legs. The diamond pendant dangled and twinkled like some omen of warning. Her tongue flicked her upper lip, anticipating a feast. He was food. He must always remember that.

He reached out and grabbed the back of her head and pulled her down. Her eager mouth opened and captured him, taking him noisily. He pulled her hair and set the pace he liked. Slow. Faster. Now even faster. She was gasping as she swallowed him over and over.

"Take me deep," he whispered, and he didn't mean what she was doing to him. He reached lower to play with her generous breasts, weighing them in his hands. "Can your brother give you this kind of pleasure? Can he make you swallow every drop?"

She shook her head in answer, as she continued sucking and licking his erection. He allowed her to slow down. He slid out of her mouth and caressed her face with his slick cock. Her eyes were half-closed as she regained her breathing.

"No one ever tempts me the way you do," she whispered hoarsely. "You're addictive, like the drugs we profit from. No one dares make me do the things you do."

That was his ace in this dangerous game. As long as he played it well, he would get something back from her.

"Then show me you trust me," he invited.

She looked up. "I do."

"Take one of those pills you feed the girls," he commanded softly.

Her eyes widened as she jerked up in surprise. "What?"

"Yes. I want you to lie there helplessly, unable to move. I want you to let me do things to you." He opened his palm and showed her the little pill.

"No, no way!" But her eyes gleamed with excitement. Her lips were moist. She stared down at the pill. "You're a devil!"

He moved his hand closer to her mouth. "Don't you want me to be the master? Go on. Trust me. You'll like it."

"No, this is too much!" But she didn't resist as he slipped the pill into her mouth. "I can't do this. You're dangerous!"

Minutes later, he looked down at her lying on the bed,

staring up at him helplessly. Her pupils were dilated. She couldn't move her limbs, although she could see and feel what was going on. She still shook her head, albeit slowly, saying no. Her eyes were beginning to show a little fear as she realized how totally helpless she was. He smiled down at her.

"This is what you give to unwilling virgins the first time," he said as he opened her legs wide for him, positioning a pillow under her hips. "I'm the big bad man come to claim you, my sweet innocent virgin. I'm going to take you any way I want and you can't stop me."

"Oh please," she moaned.

She was wet, excited from what he was promising her. He showed her his erection and slid his hand up and down. He placed a hand between her legs and played with her, until she began to beg. "First," he said. "Negotiations on the deal. Then we play."

"Anything, Stefan, anything!"

He laughed softly, climbing over her. "You'll call your brother and tell him the terms. Tell him these little pills are worth every penny. Tell him how much profit he could make selling them to whoremongers in Europe. Tell him you trust me, sweetheart. You do, don't you? That's why you're lying here in my power, letting me do as I please with your delicious body."

He bit the fleshy part of her breast. She gasped. "I like marking you," he continued. "So whenever you look in the mirror, you'll remember what we've done."

He didn't take her immediately. Instead, he made her watch as he masturbated over her. Then he brought her to the brink of release again and again, only to deny her.

"You aren't acting like a frightened virgin," he chided, his voice amused and bored. "Haven't you noticed—they don't plead; they scream, baby. And they aren't usually wet. What am I going to do with you? You're already a whore; you don't need any little pill to train you into submission, do you, darling?"

He watched her eyes widen as he took a small diamond droplet from a pouch. It was the size of a pea and it wobbled and shivered, its multifaceted surface glittering as he shook it teasingly. "You'll like this, Alissa. It's a toy I picked up that goes with the jewelry," he murmured, dabbing one side of it with an ointment. He showed it to her, his thumb and forefinger squeezing the attaching prongs, and letting her see how the gem moved. "This hangs right on your clit and it also has a heating agent. It makes you hot and tingly as it sways like a crazy pendulum."

He attached the small jewel to her, then admired it for a second. He flicked at it with thumb and forefinger and it immediately began twirling back and forth, up and down, its spring mechanism making the movement continual. The effect was immediate.

"Ohhhhhhhhh . . ." Her shoulders and thighs shook as she struggled to move, to do anything to stop the pleasure-pain given by the constantly swaying movement and the increasing heat from the ointment on her already swollen clitoris.

He didn't pay attention to her pleas as he continued to play with her. She had the wild look of a woman on the brink of ecstasy. He flicked at the diamond gently, making it rotate the other way. She promised to get him the price he had asked for. He rewarded her with another flick of his finger, now moving the jewel to sway back and forth. Her throaty cries filled the room. He would give this another half hour, before he asked for the cell number. He was determined to see this deal done today.

Vivi had picked this particular café because of its dim lighting. She watched as the two men walked into the tiny restaurant. They both arrived exactly two minutes early. They both had shaved and changed into civvies. They both—and she had to admit this reluctantly—looked very good. One light and one dark; both with that look in their eyes that should send all good young women running home.

But there was no hiding the fact that they were still soldiers. They bumped into each other at the entrance, hesitating for a second like gunslingers. Without greeting each other, they walked in with the same cocky stance of men who thought of nothing other than the moment. Eyes searching the room, their gazes landed on hers at the same time. She smiled at them, showing off her new silver tooth among her rotted teeth, and waved her wrinkled hand jauntily. The darkened café should have enough lighting to let them catch sight of its gleam. Her smile grew wider as they approached . . . both pairs of male eyes wary and questioning.

"My boys," Vivi cackled in her old woman accent. "Both mine."

"Grandmamasan," Hawk said. He paused for a second, then smiled. "Nice new tooth."

Vivi gave her wide-mouthed grin. "My present from you,

GI number one." She turned to Jazz, standing a few feet away. He looked very dashing in a white shirt and dark pants, very, very nice. She frowned at him. "There you are, GI number ten. You free, I see. You didn't listen to Mamasan, get in trouble, yes?"

"You were right," Jazz said, shoving a hand in his pocket. He looked around again.

"Still bad boy," Vivi scolded. "Still not paying attention to Grandmamasan. GI number one the good man, always give Grandmamasan time and money."

She preened, showing off her tooth again. Hawk gave a short chuckle, then pulled out a chair at her table.

"I don't think you'll find Miss Verreau in here, man," he said to Jazz. "I think she sent us a representative."

Jazz returned his attention to Vivi. Even in the soft light, his blue eyes had a strange effect on her, sending frissons of awareness down her back. "Did Vivi send you?" he asked, still standing.

"Yes. Vivi busy, said she has to do things and very, very rude to have dinner with two men at same time. She did give a message. She said, eating with Grandmamasan is like eating with her." She smiled again.

"She told you this? Do you live near her?"

Vivi nodded. "Oh, very near. She and I are this close." She pretended to twine her gnarled fingers together, then shook her head at her inability to do so. "She told me to treat you boys good, like you're both mine."

She cackled again, then cocked her head. "Besides, Hawk promised me two kisses from GI number ten. I helped Hawk to get you out, you know. I told Vivi you owed me two kisses and she said she would see to it that you pay."

"Oh, this I want to see," Hawk said, amusement in his voice, as he settled back.

"She said that, huh?" Jazz countered, still standing.

Vivi turned to Hawk. "Is he slow in head? I keep having to explain over and over."

"He's from Louisiana. They're kind of slow there," Hawk explained.

"Where?" Vivi frowned. "They don't like to sit there too? My neck hurts looking up, GI. Sit. Order food. Good food here."

"Yeah, why don't you sit down, Jazz? Kind of rude to make Grandmamasan strain her neck."

Jazz pulled out a chair. "I can't believe she stood me up," he complained.

"Us," corrected Hawk. He sounded amused. "She stood us up, but I told you, she was the running kind."

"Yeah. You're right again. You win."

Vivi tried not to look too interested in the exchange between the two men. Been talking about her, had they? Hmmph. Was she a bet between these two?

A scrawny boy came over, using a towel over his arm to quickly wipe the table down once. "Order? Beer? Tea?"

"Beer. Anything special here to eat, Grandmamasan?" Hawk asked.

"You order the special sandwich. It's very good."

"That's what I'll have, then."

"Me too," Jazz said. "But sweet iced coffee for me, please."

"What about you, Grandmamasan, same thing?" Hawk asked.

Vivi pointed to her mouth. "Can't chew too good, GI, you can't tell?" She looked up at the young boy. "Noodle soup."

There was a short silence after the boy went off. Vivi contented herself with smiling affectionately at the two men as they seemed to be talking to each other with their eyes. Hawk seemed amused and Jazz looked . . . sort of pissed off. She wanted to laugh again.

It was the only way to have dinner with two men at the same time, right? Now that she had been debriefed by T., she didn't need Hawk for details. She had originally planned to use NOPAIN on Hawk to get his cooperation with her plans, but had changed her mind after reading in his file that he knew about NOPAIN.

She did know, however, that she needed something to stop her growing attraction for Jazz Zeringue. At first, the easiest way was to encourage Hawk's interest in her, but again, she had changed her mind after seeing the two men together. She thought of the operation coming up and decided that her disguise was a wise choice. Hawk and Jazz were coleaders and obviously close friends. They worked together closely in a mission. If she had chosen one over the other, they might not be too friendly with each other, and that might affect the battle ahead.

"It's good she didn't choose one of us." Jazz startled Vivi with the comment echoing her thoughts. "I wouldn't want you to be in a bad mood tomorrow."

Hawk looked from behind the glass of beer as he swallowed deeply. He put the glass down. "Why would I be?" he countered calmly.

Jazz raised an eyebrow. "Because you wouldn't be the one having dinner with her."

"You're sure about that?"

"Yeah."

Vivi blew hard on her soup and clanked her spoon noisily as she watched the two men smirking at each other, doing that male communication thing with the eyes again, as if she couldn't read their one-track minds. Jazz had that lazy grin that he'd used on her earlier today; Hawk's crooked smile was infuriatingly arrogant. Okay, time to burst some male egos. She tapped the table, then pointed at the men when they turned to look at her.

"You two funny. How you know Miss Vivienne not has her own man?" Vivi asked, leaning forward a little as she peered at the them, as if she couldn't see them too well. "Maybe she has man and doesn't want you, or especially you, GI number ten."

"See? Grandmamasan thinks you're not worthy," Hawk said.

Jazz bent down toward Vivi, his face dangerously close to hers. She stared back, confident of her disguise in the dim surroundings. Nonetheless, her heart started thudding a little faster anyway as his blue eyes fastened on hers. Nice long eyelashes too, she vaguely noted. "Does she?" He cocked his head. "Have a boyfriend? And why especially not me, Grandmamasan?"

"Miss Vivienne no like you. You sit in jail, yes? So you bad."

"Oh, you know better than that, Grandmamasan. You helped Hawk to get me out, so you know I'm not that bad. But I'm sorry I didn't listen to you when you told me not to go in."

"Ha, too late. GI number ten wants to be GI number nine? You pay me what Hawk says—two kisses." Vivi smacked her lips loudly.

Hawk laughed quietly, taking another swig from his beer. "I think you should bargain, man," he said. "Two kisses should move you to number eight."

"Heck, Grandmamasan, Hawk is very good with kissing. He comes from a family of kissers. One from him ought to move me back to at least number two in your book."

"Oh?" Vivi tilted her head. "You kiss GI number one before?"

Hawk chuckled again at Jazz's expression. "You're losing this argument, buddy. What's wrong—you don't pay your debts?" He turned to Vivi, his eyes a muted glittering amber in the darkened café. "My friend here, Grandmamasan, is a Cajun French. Ladies tell me no one kisses like a Cajun French. He will knock your socks off."

"I don't need you pimping me out, buddy."

"Just pointing out your good features, buddy. Grandmamasan needs to know."

"Kiss my ass."

"In front of Grandmamasan?" Hawk mocked.

Vivi squinted, scowling a little, knowing that deepened the wrinkles on her face. "You two jokers, make fun of old lady. Both bad GIs. What will Vivi say when I tell her you make fun of old lady, show no respect?" She pushed back her chair and slowly got up, mumbling to herself as she did so. "Fine, make fun of old lady. See whether you find it funny when you in trouble next time. This dinner date over. Old lady has plenty of other men to kiss."

Jazz watched the old woman shuffled off painfully, holding to the tops of chairs as she left. "I think you hurt her feelings."

"Hey, you're the one who refused to kiss her." Hawk was still amused. "Do you really want me to kiss her for you?"

"Well, you are my best friend."

Hawk lifted a brow. Then turned to look at the old woman again. She was still mad, gesturing at them as she talked animatedly to the waiter. "In a life-and-death situation, I might kiss her to save your life."

"Thanks, pal. Warms my heart." Jazz shrugged at the waiter, who was showing his palms in a helpless gesture. "Ah, hell. If I don't kiss her, I'll never hear the end of this from you. If I do, I'll never hear the end of this from the guys."

"You don't have to tongue her." Hawk chuckled again and pushed his beer at him. "Here, have some liquid courage."

"I'm going to tell her you're next."

"Hell, you said my family is great at it, so I'll just send Cousin Steve. He's Kisser of the Millennium. He will kiss anything."

Jazz grinned. Hawk's cousin had been voted Kisser of the Millennium in some Navy kook poll. When the guys had heard about it, Hawk had gotten a lot of thrashing for losing out to Steve. Damn McMillans. Ladies' men, all of them. Thank God Steve had gotten himself a wife, but with Jazz's luck, he'd bump into Hawk's still unattached brother some time, and he would want Vivi, too.

Hell, he would just have to think of revenge later. And form some kind of plan to beat Hawk, who was, as usual, sitting there waiting to see what he'd decide to do. As if he didn't already know. They had gone through too much as a team for Hawk not to be able to second-guess his next move.

Jazz was brought up to respect women. His maman had taught him to always pay his debts. He took Hawk's bottle and chugged the beer, then got up and started to walk toward the old lady. "Grandmamasan," he called out.

The little hunched lady peered at him from across the room. "What?" she snapped back. "GI number ten give kiss or not?"

God help him, he was going to kiss some old lady in front of Hawk. Jazz just knew that story was going to make good fodder when the guys were sitting around.

He looked down into the old lady's rheumy eyes. She smiled that ridiculous smile again, that one shiny tooth beckoning among the blackened ones. Hell, even she was having a good time at his expense. Pulling another chair out, he sat down so he could be face level with the hunched-up woman.

"Okay, Grandmamasan. You get one kiss. The other one you have to get from Hawk."

"No bargaining with your elders. You kiss and I think about it."

Jazz couldn't help being amused. She was something else; he'd never met an old woman quite as aggressive as this one. Well, better get it over with. He'd just pretend he was alone in the jungle, focusing on the enemy. He glared at the waiter till he slunk away with that stupid grin. He blocked out Hawk's figure sitting to his left; no doubt he was laughing his head off. He would think of his roots instead. He was Zola Zeringue, grandson to the most famous gator hunter in the deep bayou, son of the fiercest woman with the best prawn gumbo. According to them, he could face anything and never back down.

Jazz tilted his face a little as he kept his focus on Grandmamasan's puckered lips. Oh hell, let's not think about the teeth. Misshapen by old age, her mouth looked dry and crackly, like old glue. They didn't look real in this light. Set together tightly, the wrinkles around her mouth deepened into rivulets of crisscrossing lines. He closed his eyes and aimed his lips.

Vivi hoped she wasn't visibly shaking. Her heart sounded like thunder in her ears, and she could feel her stomach churning as if the soup she'd just eaten wasn't agreeable. Hunched up in her disguise, she was engulfed by Jazz's size. He sat on the chair, rocking it forward as he held her shoulders. She kept her arms limp; tensing them might give away her muscles, but it was tough to keep her concentration as all she could do was stare at that face coming closer to hers.

Why did she always do this? Push people for no other reason than to see how far she could do it? She hadn't wanted Jazz to kiss her "old lady"; she wanted him to kiss *her*—Vivi—but of course, like everything else in her life, the outlet for her yearnings had to be disguised. She understood this about herself and was helpless to stop it.

His lips touched hers. They weren't loverlike, of course, but that didn't stop her heart racing even faster. Thank goodness the back of his chair kept their bodies from touching. He brushed her lips with his and she couldn't help it—she pursed hers in response, delighting in a full second of the male shape of his mouth on hers, his clean scent, and the memory of what that body looked like when he was exercising in the yard. Had it been only that morning?

He pulled back, his eyes a darker blue in the bad lighting, a strange, embarrassed smile on his lips. The thunder in her head receded, and in the background, Vivi heard howls of laughter from the nearby customers, who had no idea why the white man was kissing a dried-up old woman. She, too, pulled back. She grinned, making sure her new silver tooth faced the light. She needed to create as much distraction as possible so he didn't analyze too much. Some of the howlers groaned, apparently disgusted by the sight. Some hooted for Jazz to do it again, this time with tongue.

"Encore! Encore!" they chanted.

"Oi, that is one kiss," Vivi agreed, and was glad her voice

was crackly. She was afraid she would sound squeaky. "GI number ten good!"

"No longer number ten, I hope," Jazz said, a wry expression on his face as he shrugged off the teasing comments around him.

"Oh no, GI so good, I make you number eight!" Vivi told him smugly.

"Why, thank you, Grandmamasan. Just think how you're going to rank Hawk when you get him to kiss you." Jazz said loudly, turning triumphantly in Hawk's direction.

Hawk just waved his new bottle of beer at them. For a fleeting moment, Jazz caught a strange expression on his face. "He isn't afraid of Grandmamasan, not like you," Vivi said.

"You heard that, Hawk?" Jazz called.

"I heard nothing. You're on your own."

"You're going to give her the second kiss."

Vivi turned to Hawk. "If you agree, then I let this GI off. If not, your friend will suffer big dishonor. He will forever owe me one kiss." She smacked her lips. Patted her gray head of hair. She couldn't help it. The idea of Hawk backing off amused her. "Kiss or no kiss?"

"Oh-oh, what about my honor, buddy?" Jazz watched Hawk take a swig from his beer, narrow-eyed, as if the situation was grave and the request impossibly difficult to reply. His friend had saved him in many tight situations. Admittedly, never one involving kissing an old woman. He added, for good measure, "Afraid?"

Hawk's eyebrow raised a notch. *"Moi?"*

Jazz was relieved that the old lady was helping the cause, vigorously nodding her head in agreement with his challenge. He didn't think he should suffer alone in this.

"A soldier always help his friends. One for all and all for one," she said, obviously enjoying herself immensely as the other people raucously cheered her on.

Hawk shook his head and lazily peeled part of the label off the beer bottle. He eyed her thoughtfully. "Grandmamasan, you're too good. Tell you what. I'll kiss you another time."

"Why not now?" she demanded.

"Because I don't want to taste another man's lips on yours so soon," he came back lazily, his eyes glinting. "He may be my best friend but there are some things I'd rather not share."

Jazz laughed. Trust Hawk to slide away with a good argument.

The old hellion considered for a moment and then nodded. "Okay, number one. You gave me money for tooth. You listened to me the other day. You good boy. I'll let you off tonight." She turned to the amused men around them. "What, what, you want to kiss me now? Be off! Or I make you all kiss me one by one! Busybodies! Bad men!"

She moved off, going after a man with a threatening hand. They dispersed, still laughing, and Jazz got up to return to his table. Hawk pushed a bottle in his direction.

"Need to gargle?" he asked, voice tinged with laughter. "How does an old lady taste?"

"You'll find out, won't you?" Jazz countered. "Unless you don't pay your debts for your friends, sailor boy. One for all and all for one."

Hawk grinned. "I'll kiss Grandmamasan for you when the time comes. I just don't intend to do it yet. Maybe I'll do it behind your back."

"That doesn't count."

"Sure it does. Nothing says you have to be around."

"Then how would I know you did it?"

Hawk finished peeling the label off his bottle. "Oh, I'm sure Grandmamasan will let you know. Besides, I'm saving your honor, so quit being so fucking demanding. You ought to be grateful, man."

Jazz's plans for the night were all shot to hell. He wanted to get to know Vivi, not carouse with a bunch of men. She'd made it clear tonight that she didn't intend to do anything just yet. There was also Hawk. He supposed it was small comfort that she didn't choose to be with him, either. He ordered another beer.

"Next time you offer my lips to someone, make it Vivi Verreau, and I might be grateful," Jazz told him. He offered the bottle in a silent toast.

Hawk threw his head back and laughed. He saluted back with his bottle. "Drink up, my friend. Our girl is a good runner."

Vivi slipped out of the café unnoticed. It was easy enough. Who would give an old bag like her a second glance when they were deep in the cups? Especially a group of men talking about women they had kissed.

She walked slowly, giving the café owner a tip on the way out. The night air was sticky, with a feel of rain coming. That wasn't good news. It would mean muddy roads the next few days. She would have to bring this up tomorrow. Of course, those SEAL guys wouldn't appreciate her telling them how to run things.

She hadn't come out just for this little bit of fun, however. There was still one more thing to do. A block away. The sound of music became louder. Turn left. And the street was already crowded. As she had dozens of nights before, she walked into the popular red-light district, shuffling awkwardly down the block of bars with the lights and blaring music, with the girls gathered outside, dressed in micro-minis and high-heel boots, some holding hands, a few standing off by themselves. They didn't pay any heed to the little old woman passing by.

Vivi, I'm scared. I don't want to run away. I don't want you to run away. Vivi, don't go!

Vivi always looked at their faces, wondering whether Sia-Sia had ended up like them. Sometimes she fancied she saw her friend standing there with them, but of course she didn't. If Sia-Sia had walked the street, her days in micro-minis would have been long ago.

Don't go, Vivi, please. I'm not brave like you.

The familiar pang of guilt made each step down the block heavier. Logic told Vivi that she should give up. There was no way she could find anyone from her past, not after so many years. But her promise haunted her. Surely, if she had died, someone would have recorded it at the old nunnery where they had hidden. Surely the nuns would have known.

But the old nuns were dead and the temple had been ransacked by hooligans. They said the first robbers had been after the golden statue of Buddha, had beaten up the women and kidnapped the girls before taking the artifact with them. Not many people would dare to steal a god, even made in gold. It had to be one of the Triad gangs.

Vivi paused to cross the street, dispassionately taking in a nearby scene of a girl calling to another man with suggestive words. Her dress was very low-cut, her push-up bra emphasizing her small breasts outrageously. She beckoned; the man followed.

This was the Triad section. No one messed with their women here.

Vivi had taken this path enough times to memorize the names of the gambling dens and to recognize the faces of the pimps. They seldom paid any attention to her, and she had come in various disguises. In her search and her interrogation of soldiers, she had narrowed it down to the three most likely places young girls might be imprisoned.

She might not find her friend again, but she would find a way to help other girls.

She crossed the small road, then walked into the dark alley behind the hawker. It was a shortcut to her apartment building and she was very familiar with it, having grown used to its smell of refuse. Glimpses of light from the windows above gave her enough illumination.

She was almost home when a shadow cut across her path, silent as an alley cat. She paused, one hand tightly gripping her walking stick. The shadow came forward slowly, holding his hands up, showing that he was unarmed.

The first thing Vivi noticed was his face. It was covered by some dark material, with only tiny holes for the eyes. Without any lighting, she couldn't make them out, except they seemed to be dark, too. He was taller than the average Asian—if he was Asian—wearing dark clothes. He stopped a few feet away.

"I know who you are," he said in English. His voice came out in a gravelly whisper, muffled behind the material. "I have been watching you. I know what you want."

"I'm listening," Vivi said.

"You spent many months asking around. It gets back to certain ears. Since I can go in and out of certain places, I hear quite a bit."

For the first time Vivi straightened a little from her hunched position, enough so she could really look at the stranger in front of her. His disguise merged superbly with the shadows, making it difficult for her to gauge even the shape of his face.

"What have you heard?" she probed, deliberately dropping her accent.

"A name. Sia-Sia."

"And what information do you have?" She pushed away the rush of elation at hearing the name. Lowering her voice, she added, "What is your price?"

"What is it worth to you?"

There was slight mockery in his tone, even though his stance remained the same. His stillness told her more than anything else about what kind of person this man could be. Information around here wasn't that reliable and sources that wore masks weren't very trustworthy. But she had her ways of finding things out. She allowed her training to take over.

She tapped her walking stick on the ground. "You sought me out, young man. You appear to be the one in a hurry to bargain."

There was a short pause. "True. You've been patient for two years. What's two more?"

"Unless you're growing impatient yourself. Unless you want something only I can give."

His mirth was unexpected. The soft laughter didn't sound cynical or mocking. Vivi cocked her head, studying him silently. Very few people could follow her without her knowing, so he must have been waiting here already.

"You think you're so smart, don't you?" he asked, and now there was amusement in his voice. "You forget, I told you I know more about you than you think, *old lady*."

His emphasis on the last two words didn't escape her. "Are you here to blackmail this old lady, then?" she challenged, then smiled. "Bargain, wasn't that your word? And what could I possibly have to bargain, since you know so much about me?"

The masked man lowered his right hand slowly. "I have something tucked under my shirt. Can I take it out?"

"Can I stop you?" Vivi asked, injecting humor in her voice.

He laughed again. "That cane might stop me," he replied in a low voice. "I know what damage it can do."

Vivi nodded, ignoring the last statement. "You can take it out."

His hand reached down and pulled up his black shirt. His bare flesh gleamed for a few moments in the darkness as he pulled out a package. He handed it to her.

"A show of good faith," he said, simply. "Take it with you and consider."

Vivi took a few steps forward, carefully keeping an eye on the other hand, keeping the walking stick in front of her, between them. The small package felt like a folder or some kind of large envelope.

"I'll contact you another time, old lady," he said, backing away. He was very surefooted, each step very secure.

"Wait."

The man stopped.

"What is your price?" Vivi asked.

He reached out, and a rope appeared so suddenly, it almost startled a gasp out of her. She watched as he gracefully swung upward, effortlessly pulling his body weight and bracing his feet against the wall as if he weighed nothing. He finally stopped near a window that had an iron stairway next to it. He dangled, piratelike, and pivoted around, using just his arms and the rope. It was a beautiful sight.

"My freedom," he replied, and swung up onto the stair landing and slipped between the shadows. In a blink of an eye, he was gone.

Vivi tucked the envelope into her loose clothing and continued on her way home. What a day. Sea mammals. And now wild alley cats. Add T. into the mix, and it was a recipe for wild and dangerous times ahead.

CHAPTER
9

Whatever this GEM outfit was, their Intel was impressively detailed. Jazz had spent part of the morning going through the information on the CD Hawk had passed on to him. There were radio intercepts and aerial photographs, suggesting high-tech flyover Intel-gathering techniques. There were also maps tracking similar past movements of the target. Everything had the feel of a smoothly run operation.

His curiosity was piqued. Government-sponsored? Unkoshered? These were familiar words but not familiar territory. As long as he had been out in the field, those terms had belonged to special operations groups, not independent contractors.

Jazz's immediate thoughts turned to his favorite subject, Vivienne Verreau. Being in spec ops, he had learned to expect the unexpected, to deal with the constant change of plans, because war was not only strategy but also the ability to go with the flow. But that woman had truly confounded him.

Icy cold one moment and sultry tease another, she didn't fit the image of an Interpol interrogator, and she damn sure didn't look as if she had ever run a group of operatives. Yet he knew she was the former and she appeared knowledgeable enough to do the latter. Of course, appearing to know how to run a team was very different from actually running it. An unknown factor in an operation was a very risky move on the admiral's part. There had to be more than just a simple extraction operation going on here.

"What do you think of the plan?" Hawk interrupted his thoughts.

Jazz shrugged. "It reads like SOP. We've blown up bridges before." He used the cursor to enlarge a segment of the map. "Look. The territory has plenty of good hiding spots."

"That's advantage and disadvantage."

"Do we need to recon the area first?"

"We can do an insertion of two or three men earlier, set up a hideout at an overwatch location, and have them stay there all day."

"What would that do?"

It was Hawk's turn to shrug. "I don't fully trust Intel that's not ours."

"Agreed. So we watch for . . . ?"

"Dilaver isn't a crime boss for nothing. He could send someone ahead of him to check out the area; who knows? This is new for him, coming to new territory and seeking the Triads. He would be nervous, or at least wary."

Hawk had always been good at analyzing his opponents. Jazz preferred to coordinate the strategy. With combined background in warfare and music, he had always had a unique perspective on how to create and destroy things. His superiors had appreciated it enough to encourage him to take the necessary courses, and he and his team had won many war games that tested strategy.

His new mission was to destroy a bridge at a precise time. Usually that was easy as pie, like any piece of elevator music, but this time they had two oncoming vehicles, one of which he had to leave out of the danger. Timing, as in a complicated music piece, was going to be very, very important here.

Jazz turned. "You said they will provide what we need. Give me the inventory."

"Plenty of C-4." Hawk grinned at Jazz. "You don't have to give me that 'yeah, stupid' look. Blow up a bridge, Jazz. You've done it enough times to do it blindfolded with one hand playing some damn music instrument."

"I'm not that bigheaded. I need both eyes to see what I'm doing," Jazz retorted.

"Conflict resolution, SEAL-style," Hawk said, still grinning. "There's even TNT if you need that. We have Primacord to connect the charges. We have cable. We have sniper rifles. M67 hand grenades, if we feel like tossing some baseballs around."

Jazz lifted an eyebrow. "Happy children, aren't we?"

"What can I say? I like blowing things up." Hawk slapped him on the back. "I'll take care of that. You coordinate the ambush."

Jazz studied the map again. The target point was well chosen. There was a nice sharp bend a little ways after the bridge to keep the "kill zone" out of sight. He and Hawk would be able to control the whole operation from that vantage point, depending on the time of day. That was one of the key unknown factors—when exactly the target would appear.

"Tell me again why we need her along for this?" Jazz asked, knowing he didn't need to give their subject a name.

"Because it's a joint mission ordered by the admiral?" Hawk offered the obvious reply in the form of a question.

"Is that good enough for you? Do we really need her there?"

"Remember the envelopes we exchanged? Besides this particular computer disk with all the Intel on Dilaver, it also contains names of the Triad gang leaders that Dilaver hopes to meet with. GEM's main contract is to stop certain key exchanges between these two groups. They need our muscle. All they want is the cargo. Vivi speaks the languages and she knows the area."

"We're talking jungle here, not city tours," Jazz pointed out. He just couldn't see Vivi running around in the jungle as they had been doing a few nights ago.

Hawk shrugged. "I'm not happy with her there, but to be

honest, I'm intrigued, too. As long as she isn't in the way or jeopardizes the operation, I might even enjoy having her."

Jazz swiveled in his seat and met Hawk's amused gaze. His eyes were glittering with suppressed laughter. "Having her?" Jazz repeated. "Don't count on it."

"This is the first time I've seen you so prickly over a woman, bro. Tell me why and maybe I won't chase her." Hawk paused, then added with quiet emphasis, "Maybe."

"I don't know," Jazz admitted. "She's different."

"Yes, she is," Hawk agreed, "but that isn't a good enough reason to interrupt a session of strategic planning before an ambush. Our heads are in our pants and that's not good."

Actually, they had never been like this, thinking of a woman when they should be sitting down planning every detail of a dangerous operation. In fact, Hawk had never allowed that kind of interference before. Catnip for women he might be, but nothing came between him and battle.

"You're right. We put this aside till after the operation," Jazz said. "You keep your head out of my pants."

Hawk grinned. "I'm not interested in getting my head or any parts of me in your pants."

The electronic alarm signaled the steel door being activated just before it slid open and the men trotted in, most of them carrying their newly cleaned and oiled weapons. They were grimy from outdoor exercises, the heat and dust outside evident on their soaking T-shirts and dirt-streaked faces and arms.

"What I want to know is," Cucumber said, toting his AK-47 on his big shoulders, "why we had to run around the yard like some chickens in search of worms when you two are sitting in the air-conditioned cave drinking iced water?"

The huge SEAL had on a dark green bandana to keep the sweat from his eyes, his jaw darkened by dirt and stubble. He chomped on an unlit cigar as he flapped his sticky T-shirt in an exaggerated fashion with his free hand. Finally he just took it off altogether.

Jazz gestured at the pitchers of water on the nearby table.

"Must have been some tough exercise, since you guys found time to get some cigars."

Cucumber threw a box at Hawk who caught it. "Cuban cigars, man. Vivi's guys gave it to us. A present."

Hawk extracted one and placed it under his nose, taking a long whiff. "Why were they giving out dog turds?"

"Hell, man, there were men hidden all over the whole damn compound," Turner said as he wiped his face with his shirt. "They were watching us."

Jazz leaned back in his chair, shaking his head at the offer of a cigar from Hawk. "Did they cause trouble?" He remembered the hidden weapons under the tables and counters yesterday. Those men had meant business.

"Nah, they were just watching." Cucumber shrugged. "We pulled a couple of them out of the bushes or bellied up behind them and poked them with our weapons. They didn't even seem to mind, just laughed. Then one of them handed us the cigars, saying that he just became a daddy."

Hawk rolled the cigar thoughtfully between his thumb and forefinger. "It sounds like they're testing us."

"Maybe our new Assistant Patrol Leader can tell us something about it," Dirk said, a sly note creeping into his voice as he eyed first Jazz then Hawk. "When will we see her again?"

Jazz refused to be baited. He knew the men were curious about Hawk's and his interest in Vivi. Ignoring Dirk's comment, he just answered, "In fifteen minutes or less."

"Do we have to clean up for her?" Cucumber asked. "Female is female, you know."

"Hell, no," Turner said. "She's coming with us on an ambush and extraction, she'd better be able to take the sight and smell of sweaty men."

"We heard something today, sir," Mink said.

Jazz sighed. He knew what was coming. "What?" Jazz asked, resigned.

"That you kissed a woman last night, and"—Mink paused a dramatic beat, then leaning forward, he added—"and she ain't no spring chicken!"

The men laughed and Jazz shook his head. Hawk's grin was positively evil. "Laugh. You're next."

The men hooted some more at this revelation.

"Playtime's over, boys," Hawk said, putting down his cigar. "We have an op coming up that we need to prepare for, so get your chicken heads back in place. We have Dilaver to deal with, and Miss Verreau will be here soon."

"Yes, sir." One by one the men nodded and echoed Cucumber.

"Our main target is Dilaver, not the extraction, but we are part of the extraction, get it?" Jazz tapped on the open map that he and Hawk had earlier perused. "He isn't your usual drug dealer. He has an army and he's known to sell illegal arms to the KLA in Europe. And," he paused, "there are the young girls he sells for quick cash flow. They're our extraction targets."

"Fucking piece of chicken shit," Mink said.

"I can't wait to take him out," Turner said.

"Hell, for what he's done to those kids, I'll do a reversed Godfather thing—cut his chicken head off and put it next to his horse in bed." Cucumber picked up his newly oiled M16, glaring at the picture of Dilaver that was still on the big screen.

Jazz stood up. Trust Cumber to end with a gory and macabre image. "'Cumber, you got to quit watching those gangster movies, especially if you're going to make weird references. You got the right attitude, men," he said. "Let's—"

The electronic alarm went off again and the sight of Vivi in the screen interrupted Jazz's train of thought. She stared back at the camera, her expression guarded, as she waited outside. He hadn't seen her for a few hours and he had been missing her like crazy. Man, he had it bad.

"Look at that. We have company," Cucumber said, in a singsong voice.

"Hey, Jazz, you look like you just kissed an old lady," someone snickered. Jazz didn't acknowledge the comment as he watched the steel door opening slowly.

"Hey, sir, one last question," Dirk said.

"What?" Jazz murmured as Vivi came into view. Like the mysterious lady in film noir, she walked in, dressed to kill. A black halter-top with some kind of tight stretch pants that emphasized every elegant curve. He immediately noticed his necklace, his pendant tucked into her top, out of sight. But that didn't stop the satisfaction in knowing where it was.

"What did the old lady taste like?"

Jazz strode toward his target. "Like chicken," he said, as he closed the gap.

Vivienne hadn't expected a group of sweaty men waiting for her. She paused just inside the electronic door, taking in the sight. Raw and ready men, handling their weapons with casual familiarity, making jokes about women as they stood next to maps showing their next battle. They had that look in their eyes she had learned to recognize. It was challenge mixed with male appreciation. They didn't want her there, intruding on their male world of guns and sexual prowess.

She caught the gaze of Lieutenant Zola Zeringue. A man. Definitely. And not a simple one. She had witnessed firsthand the contrasting parts of him playing soldier and protector and was drawn to him in spite of her aversion to his profession. There was something gentle about him, in the way he went out of his way to help women, the way he tolerated the kids hanging on to him yesterday, and the way he poked fun at himself the night before. Right now he had a look in his eyes that made her think of the impossible. A lover. The thought sent unexpected shivers down her spine.

"Good afternoon," he greeted, his eyes appearing even bluer than she remembered.

Shoving aside the memory of his lips on hers, she strode into the room. She sniffed and smiled, addressing all the men lightly. "I see you're all ready for combat."

"Yes, ma'am," they answered collectively.

But there was skepticism in their eyes. She didn't belong.

Vivi looked at Hawk at the other side of the room. He hadn't moved since she entered. She had to win her battle one front at a time. "Good afternoon, Monsieur Lieutenant Commander. Have you gone through the material yet?"

He nodded. "Yes. We're ready when you are."

"Any time." Vivi turned to Jazz. The next front. His eyes rested for a moment on his necklace around her neck. Her heart skipped a beat and she avoided looking at him directly. She hadn't been able to explain to herself why she hadn't taken the thing off. "Lieutenant, I hope you find the new facilities a little better than the ones from your previous accommodations?"

"It's an improvement," he said. "But I didn't know we were prisoners."

She frowned. "Prisoners?"

"My men told me they were being watched as they worked out in the compound. And that they found men hiding in the bushes, weapons ready."

Vivi smiled. She had known the SEALs wouldn't like that. She gave the roomful of men an arched look. "You found them anyway, so what's the problem?"

"Did you give those men the order to hide there? And if so, why?" Hawk asked, straightening up for the first time.

Vivi wondered at the intensity of his gaze, trying to gauge whether it was anger or curiosity. She found it difficult to read Hawk. "You have to understand. The men outside have been hearing about SEALs operatives, that they are the elite warriors of the United States. Surely you can see why they decided to have a little fun."

"What if an accident had happened?" Jazz asked. "Someone loses his temper and fires off a shot or two. We could have had a situation here."

She looked around at the group of men. They were all watching closely, studying her response to their leaders' drilling.

"You must understand too, Vivi, that SEALs don't operate with the same rules. We don't trust everything around us, no matter how 'safe' the setup looks." Hawk pointed to the electronic eye with its blinking red light. "There is no observing camera looking on in our world. We don't appreciate being watched and we tend to eliminate things we don't appreciate."

Vivi allowed the tension to stretch as she made eye contact with each of the men. She was quite ready for this. "Displeasure noted, but it isn't my job to make sure I or my men tiptoe around your rules. If I don't push it before our joint mission, how would I know what my limits are? Talk is cheap around here. I prefer to observe the action." She slowly strode past the men toward the front of the room. "I had confidence in your men's ability to judge a war game being played, Lieutenants. No one was injured. Now I ask the same from you all, that you have some confidence in my abilities. I know"—she paused, turned and faced them, the entire front—"when to let men be men and when to bend the rules a little."

She broke into a smile, leaning a hip on the long table in front of the room. "Besides, now that we've gotten my men's curiosity out of the way, we can start work. Ready?"

They appeared to accept her explanation, although it was difficult to tell with Hawk and Jazz. The two of them had exchanged one of those baffling glances. Hawk gave a small nod and the men moved around the room, taking their places.

Her other problem, Lieutenant Jazz Zeringue, didn't seem so understanding. "I would still like to know your reason for giving your men permission to test my team," he said, his expression serious. "First, it doesn't strike confidence in my men and they will be suspicious of a possible ambush in future exercises. Second, it brings up the question as to the need for our team at all, when there are obviously enough hands out there to perform this mission."

Vivi had asked the same question. With T. in the picture, she knew this wasn't a standard operation, and her chief wasn't about to tell her everything. The few times she had been in operations that involved T., she had learned that there were always side deals going on, that nothing was ever as it seemed. But she couldn't tell these men that, could she? They were plenty nervous enough. She could just imagine what they would say if they found out that yet another female operative might be involved. Trust the strategist among them to catch the little details, she noted ruefully.

"Good points, Lieutenant," she said, giving a shrug. "Call it healthy male competitiveness."

"In other words, you aren't going to tell."

Why was Jazz deliberately baiting her? She wondered at this prickly side of him. She canted a brow and shrugged again. When cornered, use NOPAIN. "It won't happen again. As for needing your services, I've been told that SEALs are the best at extraction in unique circumstances. Blowing up a bridge is, of course, not much of a challenge, and sure, my men can do this, but I'm merely following instructions. According to my agency, the admiral's STAR Force SEALs excel in this kind of work, where precision is involved. I cannot afford to have that truckload of girls killed by mistake." Her voice hardened at the thought, and she added, lowering her voice to get their attention. "The men outside aren't trained for that and I can't use Interpol operatives. Your team is here to help me out."

NOPAIN was as simple as it sounded—non-physical and innovative negotiation. Yet it was more complicated than blowing up bridges. She bit back a grin as she looked into Jazz's suspicious eyes. What were they going to do—argue against their own expertise?

She took advantage of the silence and switched on the screen behind her. She had prepared a photo of Dilaver's three-vehicle convoy taken by satellite. Immediately, the men's attention turned away from her. NOPAIN one, SEALs zero.

"A quick run-through. At the speed of travel, the hostiles should be at target point in roughly sixty hours. However, it's been raining, and we have to prepare for delays. You will have to tell me the time the team needs to set up the bridge. The weather will be the main factor."

Hawk spoke up. "Mud," he said. Vivi waited, but he didn't seem to think further explanation was needed.

She nodded in agreement. "Their drivers' experience with muddy terrain comes into question, especially as they get closer to the bridge. The river is overflowing, and there are some soft spots that will slow them down. My men have already made sure the trail on the other side of the bridge will be muddier than usual." She clicked the switch again, and the photo zoomed larger. "The first vehicle will have Dilaver. He will cross first. The second one is the extraction target—the girls are in there. You can tell by the larger back portion of the truck with its sealed bolts. The last one is the guards. We've been watching them. Sometimes they switch with Dilaver's vehicle and they go first, but the target truck is always in the middle."

"How many women?" Jazz asked very quietly.

"At least a dozen," Vivi answered just as quietly. "They are very young, probably kidnapped or runaways. They have been either drugged or starved so they will be very weak."

"Why the need to transport them to the Triads when there are plenty of girls here?"

"Because their business is more than the women," Vivi said. She kept her voice toneless, keeping her anger under control. "The exchange of women is just a goodwill gesture. Nothing like mixing pleasure with business."

Cucumber let out a string of insulting expletives, some of which were very painful to the male anatomy. "Yes, I couldn't agree more," Vivi continued, "and here is the hard part. We have to separate Dilaver's vehicle from the other two. The guards are dispensable, but Dilaver must be allowed to escape. Meanwhile, you have to make sure the truck with our girls stays out of harm's way."

There was silence as the men in the room digested the new piece of information. She knew they had assumed that Dilaver would be either killed or captured, but that wasn't in her orders. She looked at Hawk. He should have similar instructions in his envelope. Obviously he hadn't shared everything with his men yet. Or with Jazz. They were doing that silent communication thing again.

"We let the bastard go?" Cucumber asked, disgusted. "Why the hell would we want to do that? Get that scum now. Better sooner than later, right?"

"That isn't the plan," Hawk confirmed.

"Why the hell not?"

Hawk shrugged. "Orders."

"I can't believe Mad Dog wants scum like Dilaver alive," Dirk said.

"What would happen if he gets killed?" Cucumber asked, playing with the big weapon in front of him. "By mistake, of course."

Vivi heard the underlying threat. The room buzzed with agreement as the men commented on allowing Dilaver to escape. Soldiers. They were always thinking of a kill. For once she agreed; monsters like Dilaver should be canceled right off the bat. But she had learned from experience that sometimes, to achieve the goal, one had to lose a few battles.

"What would you be doing, Miss Verreau?" Jazz interrupted.

Unlike the others, he hadn't voiced his opinion about Dilaver. There was something about the way his mind worked that really intrigued her. Everyone went for the obvious, but he kept bringing up the one important thing that she had been trying to get them to ignore. Her presence.

"I'll be keeping out of your way, of course," she replied smoothly.

His smile held a hint of disbelief but he didn't challenge her. She was beginning to understand another thing about Jazz Zeringue. He was too much of a gentleman.

She smiled back sweetly. Nice guys were easier to be manipulated.

* * *

Stefan wasn't a conventional man, but the sight of Alissa and her brother sitting so close together before him left a bad taste in his mouth. He took a long swallow of rice wine. Although he had suspected that Alissa got where she was through sex, it hadn't occurred to him until now that she would extend her power base in her family with the same method. Being the favorite Triad sister obviously meant more than sibling love.

"My sister must like you very much, Stefan. She doesn't give out my private number to just anyone." His French was very good, without the local accent. "In fact, you're the first."

Alissa's brother cut off a piece of apple. The knife glinted sharply in the dim light as the fruit made its way to his mouth. He tapped the corner of his lips with the blade. When Alissa immediately curled up to him to lick the juice off, he placed a lazy arm around her shoulders, curling his fingers into her hair.

Stefan didn't answer. He knew this man. He was one of the Triad brothers, known for their ruthlessness and power. Unlike Alissa, who had mixed blood, his features were local, with a low, wide forehead; high cheekbones; and small, slanted eyes. There was an angry scar above his wide, thin lips, and it moved whenever he spoke, as if it had a life of its own, reminding those looking that the owner was a violent man.

Right now he appeared to be in a congenial mood. Perhaps the heavy meal of goose and mango rice, with the ever-present filled cup of rice wine, contributed to it. But Stefan was not taking it for granted. He had noticed that the wine had barely any effect on his host as he finished cup after cup, challenging Stefan to match him.

"So tell me, what can a man like you offer me? I have plenty of dealers and information sources. My sister insisted you will be of help, that your information had added to her coffers." His voice was mocking as he added, "And that you had serviced her well."

Alissa looked very comfortable next to her brother, bending over to take a bite from his apple. They obviously had a very close relationship, Stefan noted with quiet sarcasm. Alissa might or might not be a half-sibling, but there was no mistaking the intimacy of the two as being more than brother and sister.

"I heard you're interested in a large shipment of the new drug. I can get that for you," Stefan said.

"I can get that through my usual channels," the other man countered in a bored voice, but his eyes were bright with cunning. "Do you have a better price offer? Or perhaps you have no customers because I own everything around here?"

Stefan waited as the two of them laughed heartily. "I normally don't deal with drugs," he said after they subsided. "This is a favor for a friend, and Alissa was very happy with the pills. Weren't you?"

Alissa smiled coyly as she caressed her brother's hand dangling lazily over her shoulders. "The customers liked the girls who took them, *Yeekohkoh*."

Yeekohkoh was a Chinese familial term that meant second brother. This man was the middle brother of the trio who called themselves Sam Tai Yeh—Three Big Masters—or as the West knew them, the Triads. The second brother had a reputation for ruthless torture, the one who had expanded the gang's power base from prostitution and gambling to more international crimes. Such as drugs.

"Mmm-hmm . . . and I will try a sampling tonight." He bent his head, pulling Alissa closer for a noisy kiss.

Stefan watched dispassionately as the couple took their time. As a middleman, he had talked to many strange characters, some more powerful than others. This deal was a favor to get to bigger things. He could take a few incestuous kisses to get what he wanted.

"Yes, I understand favors. I also understand business, and Alissa tells me you're an excellent businessman." The gangster lazily waved his knife. "Tell me, if I do business with you, what is this favor from which you will profit? And do I get a cut?"

Stefan smiled slowly. He appreciated intelligence, especially in matters of profit and loss. "I'm an expert in international weapons. All things are negotiable if you're willing to share"—he eyed Alissa briefly—"favors."

The knife caressed Alissa's chin, tipping it up. She stared back at her brother unflinchingly, her lips parted. "I live to please my Alissa," the man replied softly. "We're practically family. Won't you call me *Yeekoh*?"

It wasn't just a simple invitation. To call the man across the table "second brother" meant being accepted. Stefan didn't decline the fresh cup of wine from the servant girl. He looked across the table. *"Salute,"* he said, keeping the triumph from his voice.

CHAPTER
10

Vivi looked around the busy restaurant for her superior. As she had done many times before, T. was testing her. Her gaze swept slowly around the many tables, especially those on the patio. It was almost teatime, and many of the customers were dressed casually, some of the sun-pinked faces shaded by wide-brimmed hats.

Vivi smiled at the hostess. "No, it's okay, I'm lunching with a friend," she told her, before walking toward T.

T. looked up from her menu. Her hair was light auburn and pulled back in a chignon. Small stylish glasses perched on her nose, which looked sunburned, as if she had been sitting outside too long the day before. Freckles liberally dotted her cheeks, chest and arms.

"You should really take care of your sensitive skin," Vivi commented dryly as she sat down. It had been almost impossible to recognize T. She looked exactly as she intended—a holidaying European. "A wide-brimmed hat maybe."

"Then how would you know it's me, *chérie*?" T. mocked, sliding the glasses off her nose. Her eyes were a startling green. "You're out of practice. Took you almost five minutes."

It wasn't smugness. It was just T. reminding her there was no room for mistakes. Keeping with protocol, she was wearing something that would be familiar to just the two of them.

Since T. usually did not reveal the item to any of her operatives, Vivi had been wracking her brain all morning, trying to think of all the possible items T. might use. Unless it was during a dangerous and urgent mission, T. always found it amusing to keep everyone on their toes.

Vivi studied the brightly colored fish-shaped hairpin in her friend's hair. "You do know that thing clashes with red hair, don't you?"

T. smiled. "Poor Ma'moiselle Millicent Legaux is sort of color-challenged. As well as a bit clumsy in real life. This is her first real holiday after years and years of slaving on the eighth floor of the library. She isn't used to being outside for such long stretches."

"So I see," Vivi said wryly. "So where is the real Millicent Legaux holidaying?"

T's eyebrows arched mockingly. "She's being taken care of, which brings me to you. You wanted me to take care of something?"

"Yes." Vivi thought of the contents of the package the stranger had given her.

"Does it have to do with those beautiful creatures on tape this morning?" T. fluttered her eyes exaggeratedly. She was referring to the navy SEALs under their protection, of course. "Oh my, all those naked hard abs and steely-eyed testosterone. How did you deal with their macho indignation at being caught without their clothes on?"

Vivi grinned. She knew her commander hadn't been viewing those disks of the men training and their subsequent questions from that morning for eye candy alone. Her grin widened at the memory of how upset they were.

"I have a very good teacher," she replied.

"Oh, you did excellent. Good mental distraction, directing their focus onto relevant things. If it's okay, I've already ordered for us." T. smiled at the waiter who appeared with a jug and glass of water for Vivi.

It amused Vivi to see how quickly that cocky grin had changed into a demure smile. The waiter smiled back and the mousy "librarian" became all gangly and nervous, adjusting her glasses and playing with her napkin. When he leaned over to collect the menus, she dropped her napkin in nervous surprise. He bent down to pick it up at the same time and they banged heads.

T. even blushed realistically. It was amazing to watch, even as the nearby patrons laughed a little. When the waiter stood up, T. pushed her chair back to give him room, bumping into him and causing him to drop the menus and tray he was holding. Her horrified apologies came out in a string of fluent French and Vivi had to hide another grin as T. bent over to help the poor man and her head met his chin again in perfect timing. By the time the waiter went on his way, rubbing his chin and shaking his head, every eye in the restaurant was on their table.

"Was the performance for my benefit?" Vivi asked, after the laughter around them subsided.

T. shook her head, a small smile of satisfaction on her lips. "So tell me." She wasn't even out of breath.

Vivi gave a short summary of her encounter with the mysterious stranger and the envelope. "He claims he has been watching me for a while," she continued, "and there is a high percentage that my disguise has been compromised."

That was potentially serious news. If she was compromised, she could put many operations in jeopardy.

T.'s demeanor didn't change as she sipped her drink. "Love this local sweet stuff," she said, spooning the fruit out of the glass. "What's in the envelope?"

"He said it's a show of good faith. Inside is a picture of Sia-Sia," Vivi said.

"A current photo?"

"No, it's one of her around the age of the last time I saw her."

"So your friend could be dead." T. looked at her thoughtfully. "This man knows who you're looking for but with an old picture, that doesn't mean he has anything new to add. What else did he say?"

"That he has answers for me, but like you said, it could be just bait. When I asked him what he wanted in exchange, he said, 'My freedom,' whatever that means."

"Oh I love a mystery man," T. said, chewing on her straw. With her freckled face and red nose, she didn't look anything like the sophisticated woman from the other night. "Dark and secretive. Spiderman techniques. *Ooh la la*. I would like to test his other . . . abilities."

Vivi cocked her head. "Your hormones are on high these days, T. First running from a man, then it's the group of SEALS, now it's a faceless man. Are you sure you're okay?"

T.'s green eyes were twinkling. "You're the one bumping around with these luscious men and you're asking me whether I'm okay?"

Vivi rolled her eyes. "I'm not bumping!"

"You think not? Well, let's see which of our two guys here will do the bumping."

Before Vivi could ask what she meant, T. jerked unexpectedly and her glass of water toppled over, wetting the tablecloth and dripping all over her clothes. Her shriek sounded very real but Vivi knew better. "*Mon dieu!* This is so careless! I have to go change my clothes, *mon ami* . . . and I'm sorry I'll miss the meal with you and your friend, but here he is!"

Vivi turned around in surprise and could only gape at the sight of Jazz a few feet away, walking toward them with a big white towel. Even from where she was, she could see that his blue eyes were gleaming with laughter.

"Let me help, *mesdemoiselles*," he offered gallantly, wiping excess water on the table.

"Why are you here?" Vivi asked in a low voice, glaring at T., who was busy dabbing at her shirt.

"I was looking for you," he said. "Then I heard everyone laughing at some commotion and naturally, it had to be you, *chouchou*. No one can draw attention like you do. And you too, *mademoiselle*."

T. fluttered her eyes, acting pleased and nervous. Her voice was breathless and stuttering. "I . . . why thank you. Oh . . . my. I'm so glad to meet you but I really have to go back to my room to change out of these sticky things. Please, stay and keep Vivi company. Here, have my seat." She stood up and immediately walked right into Jazz, who had to steady her as she stumbled backward.

Vivi rolled her eyes. She watched, half exasperated and half pissed off, as her chief held on to Jazz's T-shirt for dear life, sliding way too comfortably against his chest. She bit her tongue as T. went off in excited French about good food and wonderful, helpful men, and then somehow tripped over her shopping bag, which of course, brought her even closer to Jazz. He was the absolute gentleman, picking up the bag and offering to carry it for T., and reassuring that she looked fine and could still join them. And all along T. had her hands all over his body.

Vivi caught herself wanting to yell at T. Blinking back her surprise at the unexpected jealousy, she didn't say anything as T. snatched up the package from the table, gave her a parting wink, and went off like a whirlwind, leaving behind a bemused Jazz.

Vivi frowned, glancing around. She didn't see any second man. "Is Hawk here?"

It was Jazz's turn to frown. "I'm beginning to think you have a thing for him," he said, sitting down. "Isn't it enough you talked to him all morning?"

"We were discussing strategy," Vivi said, then stopped. Why the hell did she have to explain anything to him? "Why are you here anyway? How did you know I was here?"

He gave her that wicked smile that seemed to always affect her heart rate. "*Chouchou,* I figure since you couldn't do dinner with me, I'll have you for any meal."

Jazz didn't know why he followed Vivi. Okay, so he had a reason, but he didn't understand the urgency behind it. He just needed to be alone with her for a while, wanted her away from the boys, without any talk about the field operation or

questions about her part in it. He especially wanted her away
from Hawk, and here she was bringing Hawk's name up as
soon as he had sat down. "Quit looking around for Hawk. I
followed you alone."

Vivi frowned. "I didn't see you."

"That's the point, *chouchou*," Jazz replied.

"Damn, I must be losing focus," Vivi muttered. "First him,
now you . . ."

"First him, who?" Jazz hated to sound suspicious. He
looked around too. "Don't tell me Hawk has been sneaking
up on you."

"Hawk?" Vivi's frown deepened. "Why would he need to
follow me? I just talked to him earlier today. *You* were there,
remember?"

The waiter showed up at that moment with the food and
Jazz wondered at Vivi's sigh as she checked the dishes.

"What's the matter? Is the order wrong?" It looked and
smelled delicious enough. He had taken a liking to eating the
local food. "Vivi?"

"Oh, it's nothing," she said, waving the waiter away. "My
girlfriend just knows what to order, that's all."

Jazz looked at the steamy plate of food. "It's some kind of
fish dish," he said.

"Uh-huh."

Well, at least they weren't talking about Hawk anymore.
He smiled. "You don't like fish?" He took a bite. "This is
quite good, even though it looks weird with its head still on.
Really spicy. Don't you like spicy food?"

Vivi's mouth opened and closed, appearing to change her
mind about her answer. She shrugged. "Yes, I do." She
picked up her fork and began poking at the entree. "I love
fish."

"It's already dead, you know," Jazz pointed out dryly after
watching her fiercely attack the thing for a few moments.

"Yes, it is, isn't it? Poor stupid fish, all alone, swimming
there, and then whoosh, it's suddenly curry."

Jazz smiled, amused at himself for even enjoying the sight

of Vivi cutting up a dead fish. She was such a contradiction. All professional this morning, conducting a meeting with all the strategic techno-babble shooting out of that sexy mouth like bullets from a well-oiled weapon. Yet here she was, pouty and a bit mad. His film noir heroine was back, with all her secrets. And he had a sudden urge to kiss her, to see how she would respond.

She looked up sharply. "You're laughing at me," she accused.

"I'm laughing at the poor fish," Jazz said.

"Why? It's dead."

"Precisely. It couldn't be any deader."

She gave an impatient sigh. "Why were you following me?"

Jazz always believed in telling a lady the truth. "Because I wanted to get to know you better. You're always talking to Hawk."

She stared at him. "But we were just discussing the operation."

"I know that but I have to tell you, I don't like the way he looks at you." For the first time in his long friendship with Hawk, he felt jealous and possessive. "So Hawk can update me on strategy. Let's talk about you. About us."

She poked at the fish again, this time concentrating on the fish head. "There is no us. We don't even know each other." Her voice was low.

"That's easily remedied. Here we are, alone, and we can talk about ourselves." Just like the music, there were unknown layers to Vivi that called to him, challenging him to dig deeper. "No more talk about military or strategy, just simple things, Vivi. How about it?"

A small smile appeared on her lips. "You think it's that simple? Talk about us and nothing will intrude? There is always reality intruding, soldier. We can have our moment, then you'll be gone and I'll still be here."

Jazz frowned. "You make it sound so final. It doesn't have to be permanent. I can come back to see you."

"Oh, isn't that the most familiar line around these parts?"

The fish head was mangled to pieces by now. Jazz reached over and took her hand in his. Her gaze finally met his, her hazel eyes searching. "Is that what you're afraid of?" he asked quietly. "Are you putting me in the shoes of some past lover who left you?"

She didn't deny it. And it pissed him off. Instead she tried to pull her hand away, but he held on.

"You don't know me," she insisted. "You don't know what you're talking about."

"*Chouchou*, that's what people who are attracted to one another do—get to know each other."

"You just want to get me into bed."

Jazz dropped her hand. There was a defiant gleam in her eyes, challenging him. He wasn't getting through. He had lived with women all his life, had thought himself familiar with all the jumbled logic and female moodiness, but he couldn't get through to this one. It was frustrating. Every time he thought he had climbed over one wall, he found another barrier.

He pushed back his seat and stood up. Her unflinching gaze followed him as he took the few steps closer to her.

"Yes I do," he told her, "but you have to want it too, Vivi."

She didn't turn her face away when he kissed her. He took his time, uncaring that there were people around. Her lips were soft and willing, even though the owner seemed unmovable as a brick house. He lifted his head and watched her slowly open her eyes. Satisfaction bubbled on top of his frustration. She wasn't as unmoved as she wanted him to believe.

"Not every soldier leaves his girl behind, sweetheart," he said. "Please thank your friend for buying lunch. I'll see you later."

Vivi watched as Jazz stalked off. Her lips were burning and it wasn't from the curry dish. Her heart was still thumping loud and fast from the kiss. The man played havoc on her senses. She felt confused and disappointed, two very unfamiliar feelings.

Her cell rang and she answered absentmindedly. "Vivi here."

"Oh my, is that how you deal with macho testosterone?"

Vivi sighed. She should have known T. was still around somewhere. "You know, life was actually very predictable a few days ago. I get up, sometimes there is a raid or two, I do some paperwork, and then I have some free time to pursue other interesting projects." Like looking for her past, she thought. "Why didn't you tell me he was here? Did you plan all that?"

"Now, now, darling, would I plan something so delicious?"

"You stumbled and created a scene to catch his attention."

"I did it twice, if you want to be specific."

Vivi paused. "Okay, before you left you were hinting about getting two people's attention. Who's the other man?"

"Excellent." T. laughed. "Unlike your Jazz, who was considering whether to surprise you, the other one was just watching. I wanted to test his reaction."

Vivi ignored the comment about Jazz. "Who was it? Our mysterious man?" She was still a bit peeved that two men had been able to follow her without her knowing. She knew T. would bring this up sooner or later, so she might as well do it first. "I didn't even see him."

"They are both very good, but it's the other one who is intriguing."

"Where is he?" She wanted to spot him.

"He doesn't want to introduce himself yet, I guess. He wants to know who you're contacting to show the package. Now he knows."

Vivi frowned. "Is that good or bad?" She wasn't afraid she had led danger to T. T. could take care of herself. However, the more she was learning about this mysterious man, the more she didn't like the way he could compromise her position. "What are we going to do?"

"For now, nothing. He'll contact you when he's ready. He's got what he wanted. Now it's a waiting game."

"I don't understand. What he said he wanted was his freedom."

"Yes, darling, but he wasn't sure how or who he was dealing with, except that you're the one who could give it to him."

"And does he know that now?" Vivi leaned back in her chair and waved to the waiter to collect the dishes. She wasn't hungry anyway.

"Oh, he knows, darling. I made sure he knows."

"Tell me." Vivi opened her purse to get some change for the tip. "I want to know more if he really can help me find Sia-Sia."

There was a slight pause. "One operation at a time. You take care of your job and I'll have some answers for you soon."

T. rang off. Vivi put away her cell, smiling absently at the waiter's thanks as he cleared the table. She hated depending on other people in this matter. It was private, nothing to do with the agency, and she was thankful T. had never questioned the logic behind her quest. There was no easy way to explain about a long-ago promise to a friend.

She trusted T. to handle whatever was necessary to help her. At the same time, she knew T. would somehow do it in a way to persuade her to leave this place and post. And deep in her heart, she knew she would have to, sooner or later. The sights and sounds of so many lost souls were too familiar and painful, and if she couldn't find Sia-Sia, what was the point of staying?

But friendships in those lonesome days were made to last forever. They were blood-bonded, and Vivi felt she owed it to her friend to find out what had happened to her.

"I can't take being alone with these nuns. I'll never make it through that window. I hate the dark. I hate heights. You promise to come for me, Vivi, okay?

Vivi walked out of the restaurant, automatically shielding her eyes from the glaring sun. A school bus stopped close by and schoolgirls jumped out, some chatting, some holding hands. They moved in a group, passing Vivi, as they headed home.

Vivi watched after them for a long moment, then crossed the street. And leaning against her car was Jazz, arms folded, waiting for her.

"A secret weapon? That sounds intriguing."

"Ah, you don't know half of it, *Yeekoh*," Stefan said, his speech slightly slurred. "Every important agency above and below the equator has been after this thing."

"And you're telling me you have it." *Yeekoh*'s voice was disbelieving. He gave a slight, imperceptible nod, and the servant girl appeared to refill Stefan's cup. "How did you do it?"

"I didn't say I have it." Stefan smiled, leaning forward confidentially. "I'm a middleman. I don't handle goods till the right time. Then I exchange for both parties, know what I mean?"

Yeekoh and Alissa exchanged a look. "I see," he said, scraping his chin with his knife. "Tell me more about this weapon."

Stefan looked up from his slumped position, drumming his fingers as if he were considering telling everything. He drank the rest of his wine with slow, deliberate care. *Yeekoh* watched his every move, waiting for him to make up his mind.

He had to be careful how he phrased his answer here. A refusal would be taken as an insult. Too much information would make him sound too eager, asking for suspicion. "All I can say is that it comes from a top dealer. Mad Max, ever heard of him?"

Everyone in the illegal arms dealing trade knew Maximillian Shoggi, nicknamed Mad Max. He was the darling of the elite and a well-known figure in the gray world of politics. The most sophisticated traders went to his parties; the lowliest of the food chain wished to sell to him. By giving *Yeekoh* the name, Stefan knew the man could find out what was in the market through his own sources. It was a business compromise, subtle enough to ensure trust and at the same time, he honored their new "friendship" with some insider news.

Yeekoh nodded slowly, satisfaction seeping into his eyes. "You're tired, my new brother. Let Alissa take care of you. Tomorrow I'll take the shipment of pills off your hands, and we'll be business partners." He stood up and stretched. "Lis, I'm going to test a few of these pink pills tonight. Let me have a pick from your fresh batch."

Alissa lifted an eyebrow. "Just one?"

Yeekoh laughed. "Maybe two. I'm in a celebrative mood." He glanced at Stefan. "Our new brother is a little drunk. You'll have to make sure he remembers our business tomorrow."

"Oh, I never forget business," Stefan assured, then gave Alissa a leer. "Or pleasure."

The men laughed, and *Yeekoh* leaned forward to shake hands. Alissa clapped her hands and another servant girl showed up.

"Take *Yee-siew* downstairs to our special room. No one is to disturb me tonight."

"Yes, madam."

"I'll talk to you soon, *Yeekohkoh.*"

There was a short pause after Alissa's brother disappeared through the door. "Let's go into my private rooms," she invited, walking over and taking him by the hand. "You did well, Stefan. *Yeekohkoh* likes you."

"I'm glad," Stefan said as they entered her room. The air was permeated with scented candles.

He watched Alissa undress. He could tell she was excited; he could see her erect nipples pushing against the thin material of her bra.

"You're drunk," she said, teasing his face with her large breasts, rubbing them against his stubble. "*Yeekohkoh* likes to drink a lot. It's good you didn't pass out. He doesn't respect anyone who can't hold his own against him."

Stefan smiled slowly. "I'm not too drunk," he said very softly, reaching with one hand behind her back and unsnapping her bra with practiced ease. It fell away, and he teased one freed nipple with a lazy finger. A hiss escaped her lips as he trailed the finger slowly to the valley between her breasts, then up the other. "I can still take you, Lis."

Alissa giggled. "That's my plan, sweet. You promised, after all. It wasn't easy getting you a meeting with my brother, so you'd better please me before you go off tonight."

He trailed his finger down her torso and drew suggestive circles on her panties. "I plan to. You deserve to be rewarded for the big favor."

"Big favor. Hmmm. What a lovely image that brings up." Her eyes half closed, she undulated against his finger.

He added another finger, playing with her through the material. He kept his movements slow and easy, dictating her tempo to his will.

"I'm so addicted to you," she whispered. "Kiss me, Stefan. You never kiss me."

Not answering, Stefan took her by surprise, leaning a shoulder into her bare stomach and standing up in one smooth, swift motion. She squealed at being whirled around.

"What are you doing? Where are you taking me?"

"I feel like taking a bath."

He strolled into the lavish bathroom with its ornate sunken tub. It was built for more than hygiene care, of course. The place was a whorehouse, and the private rooms of its mistress had all the amenities for sexual pleasure.

He lowered her into the tub. It was an antique, treasure stolen by the Triad robbers. With its fierce dragon head curling over the huge jewel-inlaid tub, it must have been part of a collection from one of many very wealthy and decadent businessmen who either had been assassinated or had fled the country in the last fifty years. Alissa didn't resist as he secured one hand, then the other, with the golden chains connected to the dragon claws on each side. She laughed in amusement, jangling the bells on the chains.

"Men. They always want to play when they are drunk."
She tugged at the chains. "You're lucky I'm in the mood. I
don't like being tied up."

"Only with me," Stefan mocked as he turned on the water.

Her breath came out in a whoosh. "Oh yes, only . . .
with . . . you," she agreed and watched with wide eyes as he
tore her panties off. "Oh yes, Stefan . . . do it rough tonight."

He wasn't a particularly small man; it was good that the
tub was built with more than two in mind. He unhurriedly
unbuttoned his shirt and shrugged out of it as the bathtub
filled up noisily. All the while Alissa impatiently jangled her
chains.

Her hungry eyes roved over his naked form as he stood beside the tub. "Have I ever told you you're a beautiful man? That
chest . . . that hard stomach . . ." She leaned back as he climbed
in, still standing over her. When he used the liquid soap on his
penis, she sighed. "And such an almost perfect hard cock."

"Almost?" He stopped massaging his growing erection.

"It's off-centered and curves to the left," she said. She
opened her mouth, tempting him.

He accepted the invitation, splashing water to wash away
the soap before sheathing his erection in her mouth. He proceeded to move his hips leisurely, pushing her head back
against the dragon's chest as he angled deeper. Water lapped
back and forth in tiny waves.

"That's what a perfect cock looks like, Lis," he chided, as
he watched his penis slide in and out of her willing mouth.
"It hits the woman's spot just right inside. You should know
that from your orgasms by now. Don't you want it?"

"Oh yes, oh yes." But he had already moved away. "I want
it now."

He smiled wickedly. "I want to clean you . . . but first, you
will take a couple of the pills again." His hand in the water
found her unerringly and he pushed his fingers inside. "For
me, Lis. You're exciting when you're begging, my dear."

"No!"

"No?" He slid his fingers out.

"But Stefan . . ." There was a husky plea in her voice. "You have me tied up already."

"I'll make it better than the last time, love, I promise," he said silkily. "And you'll get some special jewelry I just bought."

She was his to play with when it came to sex, as long as he allowed her to think she led the dance. She opened her mouth willingly as he popped two pills in. She didn't know one was another kind of drug, made to look like the pink ones he had introduced. He watched with a half smile as she swallowed. There was much she was going to tell him tonight.

"Yes, you're all mine. Now, say yes to everything I'm going to do," he commanded softly. This was an essential form of the exercise. The victim had to be taught to say yes, to agree to every one of his orders. It was what his people called brain training, an essential step in sex imprintment. He told her what he was going to do to each part of her body, knowing it excited her that she couldn't stop him. He was going to make her come again and again. He was going to take her so many times she would be begging for him to stop. He was going to torture her little clitoris until she was screaming. She moaned as he started with the washcloth, saying, "Yes, yes, yes" as he asked her whether she would want what he was going to do. "Now, where were we? Oh yes, washing you . . ."

He wanted her clean. Himself, too. It was a dirty business he was in, but he would go through with it to get what he wanted. He dunked his head under, seeking her with his mouth. Her cries were muffled by the sound of water as he captured what he wanted and sucked hard. The pills needed time to start their effect; he could hold his breath for a long time and it was easy enough to whip her into a frenzy. Her thighs squirmed and thrashed as he continued his torture.

When he surfaced, he shook the hair from his face. "No?" he asked her again.

She was gasping, and he could see her mobility slowing. "Yes, yes! Stefan, the things you can do with your tongue!"

He unplugged the tub. The water gurgled as it drained out slowly. "Yes, and with my hands," he said, as he poured bath oil liberally on her. He began rubbing the liquid all over her body, caressing her breasts, stomach, thighs, everywhere except where she wanted.

Her breathing was ragged now, and her eyes had the glazed look he was familiar with. He counted to ten slowly, and her breathing evened out, long and slow. Her expression had changed too, becoming less animated. The pill, a synthetic form of a truth serum, was meant to impede thought only in a willing participant. Alissa had been very willing. It was an experimental drug with which he hadn't had much practice, and he didn't have much time.

"Look at me," he ordered. Obediently, she did so, her blank gaze strangely contrasting with the woman he knew her to be. "Are you going to obey me?"

"Yes."

"Are you going to let me do anything to you?"

"Yes."

"Anything?"

"Yes."

She was definitely ready. "You'll answer my questions truthfully and quickly and when I say the word 'come' you will have no memory of our conversation."

"Yes."

"Tell me about the deal that your brother is offering Dragan Dilaver. Tell me the terms."

He listened and kept a close eye on Alissa's irises and breathing as she answered slowly, unhesitatingly, just as he had programmed her mind. All the while, he kept his slick fingers moving between her legs. Her body was still responding to stimulation and he was careful to slow down when her breathing quickened too rapidly.

"Continue if you want more of this, Alissa," he told her. "Say yes if you want more."

"Yes," she said and gave him the information he sought.

As soon as the telltale flicker of awareness warned that

the drug was losing hold, Stefan put pressure on one slippery finger and softly ordered, "Come."

Alissa's eyes immediately widened, her mind and body taking the command literally. She keened feverishly as her orgasm slammed into her, her drug-frozen muscles straining against the invisible strength of the pink pill. The irises of her eyes were abnormally large still as she panted weakly for him to stop.

"But you don't mean that, do you?" Stefan asked as he unchained her. Her arms dangled uselessly as she lay there waiting for his next assault. "You know you want this."

"Oh yes, I want it." Her voice was hoarse and needy. "I . . . can't get . . . enough."

Stefan carried her back into the room and put her wet body on top of the divan near the bed, another sexual toy. He had her screaming incoherently for a good while, till her limbs began to move, and to make a point, he showed her two more pills in his hand.

"Take them," he said. "And I'll show you why my cock is perfect."

This time she didn't even pretend to say no. She just laughed and licked the pills off his palms, spreading her legs for him as she lay back.

"I don't even care about the present you promised," she whispered. "Give me, give me, give me . . . that!"

She watched as Stefan put on a condom, hissing with delight as he poured oil over his huge erection. He let her fondle him till her hands stopped moving.

She sighed as he climbed on top and started to slow-fuck her. Ten strokes, long and satisfyingly hard, with her saying yes to all his sexy suggestions of different ways he was going to fuck her. Her eyes turned glassy even as she agreed to be obedient.

"Good girl," he whispered back. "Now, say yes to my commands."

"Yes."

His control had always been phenomenal. He didn't pretend that he didn't enjoy the sex. It was dangerous sex, and therein lay the excitement, the sexual stimulation, that he needed. To find that magic button that would get him to perform under these circumstances, he had to ruthlessly take advantage of his own sexual urges and use them so he would win this battle.

His body was rigid from his own need for release. He was a man, after all, and the need to let go was certainly reminding him of that fact. Control. Absolute control. He pulled out.

His erection strained against his stomach and it would be so easy to . . . Bending over, he positioned her to give her the most pleasure. He looked down at himself and gave a self-mocking shake of his head. First, he needed some information for some ladies. He didn't think he would need to give her another dose for tonight. Release was near, he promised.

"You will answer my questions truthfully and quickly, as best as you know and when I say the word 'come' you will have no memory of our conversation. Then you will only remember all the pleasure I gave you and will think of pleasuring me, and nothing else. And I want to be pleasured well, Alissa."

When the session was through Alissa's intense screams of pleasure filled the room.

*There was nothing wrong with acting like a fool once
in a while. It was what a man was good at, anyway.* Maman
always said that to him whenever he apologized for some
silly stuff he had done. *Just remember to apologize to the
lady and never take one's frustration out on her,* Grandpa
Gator always urged when he pushed Jazz or his brother back
home, where they had to set things right with the indignant
women. Of course, while he was thinking about all the best
advice his big family had bestowed on him about being a man
and treating a woman right, he might as well throw in the line
from his only brother. *BYTM, bro. Better you than me.*

Jazz supposed he had done it all today. He had been foolish, following Vivi to the restaurant. But Hawk had disappeared about the same time, too, and, damn it, he wasn't
going to have a good time being alone and thinking they had
a secret rendezvous somewhere. Instead, he had found Vivi
with her girlfriend.

And worse than being foolish, he was a fool to take advantage of the situation and interrupt her lunch, joining her when
he hadn't actually been invited. In battle, impulse could kill a
soldier. He rubbed his nose in self-disgust. In romance, too.
All he had done was make a fool of himself and then commit

the crime Grandpa Gator warned him against—vent his frustration. So apologies were now in order.

His restless gaze settled on the woman crossing the road. There was no doubt in his mind that he could communicate with Miss Vivienne Verreau in bed. That kiss they had shared just now fairly set his socks on fire. She had kissed him back, a little hesitatingly, as if she weren't comfortable with people watching. Well, all he needed was a private place. He could communicate with all the bayou charm in his genes. But where would he find any privacy here and now?

He could hear his brother laughing his ass off in his head. Zippy never apologized about anything; he always said that was what older brothers were for. Besides, as one of his sisters wryly pointed out, who would believe that any apology from two boys named Zola and Zippy Zeringue, with their devilish blue eyes, would be sincere?

"You're the most obstinate man I've ever met," Vivi remarked, stopping in front of him. "Don't you give up?"

"My favorite city is below sea level and its inhabitants are obstinate fools," Jazz said.

"Sort of predisposed to be in special forces, I guess?" She unlocked the passenger door. "Think you can go and live underground, and then strike in the dark."

He took her action as invitation to join her for a ride and slipped into the vehicle before she changed her mind. "You're mixing things up about my city. That's a vampire, not special forces," he told her, amused. He showed her his teeth. "See? No fangs. And it's daylight."

"I suspect your bark is worse than your bite," Vivi said dryly as she started the car up.

"Are you accusing me of being soft?" Jazz threw up his hands in mock horror. "Don't let my men hear you say that."

She smiled. "You're a softie, Jazz. You can't bear to hurt a woman's feelings, and you can't bear to see women get hurt.

Why, you even waited out here in the heat because you felt bad about leaving me in the restaurant."

"It's true. And I wanted to apologize, *chouchou*. That was very rude."

She sighed, turning the AC on higher. "You make it so damn hard. You weren't rude, Jazz. I was."

He shrugged. "That doesn't mean I have to be rude back. Besides, I'm sort of lost, after following you around."

Vivi laughed. "As if. Soldier, you don't lie well, either."

He grinned. "I'm not totally lost, but . . . you did go all over the town, Vivi. For a while I thought you were trying to shake me off."

She had really traveled all over the place before going to the restaurant, going through the red light district and slowing down. He had thought she was trying to lure him out in a place where he would be easily spotted but he had been trained to go unseen in the most unlikely of places. He was pretty confident she hadn't known he was following her. He had merely watched her as she meandered through that part of town, slowing and peering at some of the places. He suspected it had to do with her job, since the location, with its seedy storefronts, wasn't advertising anything that he thought would interest a woman.

She glanced at him briefly, then back at the traffic. "What are you doing out, anyway? I thought you guys always stay together, get your minds set for the job ahead, and all that?"

She was right. Once the Patrol Order was given, focus on the mission was number one. "Hawk gave us fifteen hours."

"To do what, if I may ask? I can't see you boys shopping," she mocked lightly.

Sometimes, when there were two operations close together like this, the men were given some time to "move on," so to speak. The last one, with the child bandits, had left a particularly bitter taste, and the men had looked forward to some down time before this second mission unexpectedly came up. No one had complained; it was the nature of their chosen profession.

"We just came out of one intense situation," Jazz said, keeping his explanation brief and simple. "You take your head out of one fight and put yourself in another. Sometimes, as in this case, we have the luxury of a waiting period. Hawk and I believe in giving the men some time to do whatever they want. It's good for team focus."

"In other words, preparation determines the success of a mission," Vivi said.

"Yeah, but it's also mental preparation, more than anything."

"I see." She was quiet for a bit. "So what do the guys do?"

"It's all in the mindset, Vivi." He realized she was trying to understand life from his viewpoint. He had the feeling that she hadn't cared before. "We're trained to perform under extreme pressure. Every little luxury is enjoyed, is taken advantage of. Sometimes it could be months before we're allowed to surface back to normal, whatever that is. When we find fifteen hours, we don't question what we want to do; we do it. Some go to church or pray; some of us take off just to be alone, away from the brothers."

She turned. "And what do you do?" There was curiosity in her eyes, and something else.

"I like to play music."

"What if you don't have any instruments? No guitar, no piano?"

Jazz tapped his head. "That's the beauty of music, sweetheart. It's all in my head."

She smiled. "You could always sing. I heard you can carry a tune."

Ah, the lady was back to teasing him. "And how would you know?" he asked. "You haven't ever heard me sing."

"I have my sources," she returned airily.

The old lady, of course. He wondered at their relationship, besides the fact that Grandmamasan was working for Interpol. He had to grin at that thought. The idea of that cranky old witch doing covert operations was hard to imagine.

"Are you related to the old lady?" Maybe that was why they worked together.

Her smile widen as she stopped the car in front of the building in which he had been a guest for a couple of days. He had been aware that she hadn't been heading back to the compound, but he hadn't expected to be coming here.

"She and I are close," she said. "Relax, Lieutenant, I'm not locking you up."

"I hope not. I have better ideas for my half a day."

Vivi's smile dimmed a little. "I was about to say I'm sorry that you have to spend your free time this way. I have a few errands to do before I can take you back, so you're stuck with me for a bit. Not much music, I'm afraid."

It was Jazz's turn to grin. He couldn't ask for more right now. He was more than willing to be "stuck" with, and to, Vivi for as long as possible.

"Do whatever you need," he said. "I'll be fine."

Vivi had no idea why she hadn't just driven Jazz back to the compound. This was the first time she had ever taken an interest in talking with a military man. Until now, in her experiences with Interpol and other covert agencies, she had kept a certain distance from those involved. There was no need to understand how or why—she organized foreign teams and played peripheral roles. She was very good at her job. Her training allowed her that distance, and she hadn't felt the need to understand these men whom she secretly disliked.

Okay, maybe not too secretly, since Jazz had pointed this out several times already. She didn't like military machismo; men in uniforms were a necessary evil in her job. She knew her past colored her opinions, but in all the years doing GEM contracts, she hadn't seen anything to change her mind. They came in, destroyed, removed, and then took off, leaving chaos.

His explanation gave her much to think about, and she felt just a bit guilty that she had been rude. She glanced at him, wondering what it was about her that interested him so much that he would want to spend his precious fifteen hours with her. It made her feel . . . special.

"Will I be in the way of your work?" he asked as they walked toward the building. "I don't want to get you in trouble."

"Other than getting me in the gossip headlines in there, you won't be much trouble," Vivi told him with a mischievous smile.

"Is that good or bad?" He opened the door for her. "It's going to be interesting walking through here again."

The front secretary was already dialing her phone as they went by. Vivi didn't say anything as she handed over her security pass. She was going to lose her reputation as the ice queen. She hadn't socialized with her colleagues as foreigners tended to when they lived overseas, and after a while they hadn't included her in any of their functions. It didn't bother her, since she wouldn't have been able to go to any nighttime entertainment anyway. Amusement welled up. Wouldn't they be shocked if they knew she had spent most of her nights wandering through the red-light districts.

She had forgotten her office overlooked the courtyard where he had been working. As luck would have it, the detainees were taking their break at that moment.

Jazz walked over to the window. "Hey, nice view," he commented. "Do you interview every one of them?"

"No, not all of them."

"Only the special ones, huh?"

She glanced up. He had that devilish smile again, the one that put her on guard. "Only the truly bad ones," she drawled. "My turn to be curious . . . what would have happened if I hadn't been around and no one would release you?"

Jazz slipped both his hands into his pants pockets and looked out the window again. "There would have been several options," he replied noncommitally. "Maybe I'd sweet-talk someone from the organization—United Third World something or other."

Vivi chuckled. "That would have been worth it, to see you sweet talk Juliana."

His eyebrows shot up mockingly. "You don't trust my powers of persuasion?"

"Oh, I didn't say that. But Juliana is into . . . numbers . . . and you're worth more to her as a number." She frowned as she read one of the messages. "Damn."

"What is it?"

"Just . . . another headache." The orphanage she had been corresponding with had called with a negative response. She had had high hopes for some open spots, one of which would be for Rose. Another avenue down the tubes. Speaking of which, she had better call to make sure Rose was okay. She kept in touch with Rose as much as she could. She dialed the number. Busy.

"I won't be too long."

"It's okay, Vivi. I'm fine." He strolled to the other wall to look at the paintings by local artists and photos belonging to her coworkers.

She looked through the rest of her messages, trying to ignore her awareness of Jazz's presence. The office was cramped enough as it was, and he made it even smaller. Despite her intentions, she peeked. Why did the man have to look so damn good in a T-shirt, anyhow? The material stretched across the broad expanse of his back, emphasizing the athletic vee-shape tapering to narrow male hips. She had a wonderful view of his backside from her seat. In fact, she could just sit here and stare at it all day.

Tall, broad-shouldered, loose-limbed, he didn't look anything like the filthy soldier she had first glimpsed from the doorway before his arrest. It seemed like eons ago when she heard him singing with his men. Even then she had stopped what she was doing to listen, had peered out from behind the curtain to look for the voice's owner.

She hadn't been able to see him properly until he had come between Rose and the other two soldiers. She remembered how easily he had towered over her, in her bent-up old woman disguise, and yet had impressed her with his soft-spoken politeness, as if he had been brought up to treat women gently. And against her usual rules, she had attempted to stop him from going to the back. Twice.

Vivi smiled ruefully. Not that he had listened. Men, she had discovered in her experience of working with them, rarely paid attention to women when it came to important things. Like communication. They never listened. She had found herself repeating orders several times before they'd realized that she meant business, that she expected them to actually follow what she had told them to do.

She doubted this bunch of he-men SEALs would be any different. Hawk had been very thorough in his briefing with her, and she was impressed that he had actually given her so much leeway as it was. But he was a deep one, that man. She had a feeling that he would pull her back and do things his way when it suited him.

She gave a mental shrug. She had worked around male egos long enough and had done her job without too many problems. She looked at the thoroughly male form standing across the room. Jazz hadn't asked her any questions beyond the safety of his men. Not a single one on what she was going to do while they were popping bullets all over the place. Did he expect her to be sitting prettily behind a rock waiting for them to bring her the girls?

They hadn't asked and she hadn't volunteered the information. Vivi frowned. She knew exactly how they would react if she told them she was going to be in the middle of the—

"You know, it's very bad when a woman starts with a dreamy smile while she stares at your ass and then her expression becomes murderous."

Vivi jerked out of her reverie, her attention returning sharply to Jazz. He hadn't even turned around, so how could he have known how long she had been staring? Damn it, he hadn't been looking at the paintings, as she had thought, but had been looking at her reflection from the mirror hanging on the other wall all this time.

She gazed at his smiling reflection. "I was just thinking about something," she said evasively, shuffling the papers in her hands.

"Uh huh." He turned, and his smile was lazy, looking as if he had found out some deep dark secret about her and he was going to use it to his advantage.

She looked down at the jumbled paperwork. How did he do that? Make her thoughts go haywire as soon as she caught his gaze? "I was thinking about work," she said, clearing her throat. "And how men like you need lots of work."

"Men like me? Are we back to arguing again? I thought we were making headway, just talking like normal everyday folks."

She lifted a brow. "Normal everyday folks?" she repeated and coughed. "I don't think there's anything normal and everyday with what you do."

He sat down in front of her and picked up from her desk one of the small photos belonging to another coworker. "But we're talking about who I am, not what I do," he said. "See, even you have family."

"Those aren't mine." She kept her voice bland.

He looked around the table. "None of these photos belong to you, do they?" he finally asked. When she didn't answer, he murmured to himself. "*Tiens*, now, I understand."

"No, you don't," Vivi countered, quickly. "You don't know anything about me."

She didn't want him to. She didn't need his pity, he of the big Louisiana family with his talk of his maman and sisters. She didn't want to have to explain that she had no concept of what he was talking about.

He gently put down the picture frame. "I didn't mean to upset you, *chouchou*. I didn't know you're sensitive about your family. And my constant talking about mine is inconsiderate."

Vivi raked impatient fingers through her hair. For the first time in a long time, she didn't know how to treat a man. He constantly knocked her off guard with his manners and made her feel as if she was precious to him, which was ridiculous, of course. She barely knew the man.

Yes, she did. She knew so much more than the file T. had faxed to her. Jazz Zeringue was definitely more than some military grunt playing warrior. He made her want . . . things she shouldn't think about. Not. Right. Now.

She shook her head, trying to clear her mind. Let him talk about himself. That ought to reinforce why she couldn't and shouldn't think of forbidden things. "No, no. I'm interested, really. I already know you have a large family and so does Lieutenant McMillan." She sat back. "You're both best friends and I can see why . . . big family and all that."

Jazz frowned. "Yes and no," he said. "Must we always bring Hawk into the picture?"

It was much safer to just think of them all as a unit, she decided. She needed a shield against this attraction she felt for Jazz. "Well, I can't help it. You're best friends."

"So? We aren't Siamese twins. We can function separately, I assure you." His expression turned wry. "We're more like brothers because I have so many sisters and my younger brother is a bit wild. Hawk's family is all men, so naturally I gravitate to his family when I need some male opinions. Our family gatherings are nothing alike. One is an all female celebration and the other is—"

He broke off with a laugh.

"What?" Vivi was interested, in spite of herself.

He shrugged expressively. "You just have to be there. It's an all-male competition at Hawk's family gatherings, and everyone ends up with cuts and bruises."

Vivi frowned. She hadn't imagined family gatherings to be bloody affairs. "They fight?"

His teeth were very white against his tan face. "More or less. You just keep out of the Steves and Stevens and Stevies."

"Huh?"

Jazz paused before he continued. This close Vivi couldn't help but notice the way his blue eyes twinkled with mirth.

"They are all named Steve McMillan, every single one of them."

Her eyes widened. "What do you mean? They can't all be named Steve McMillan."

He shrugged again. "And you think Zola and Zippy would be the weird names in that crowd, right, *chouchou*?"

She tried to gauge whether he was pulling her leg. "You're kidding, right?"

"Nope, all the brothers named their sons after themselves."

She shook her head in disbelief. She had very little contact with family life and she wanted to hear more, but this was a bit too far-fetched. "But . . . why?"

"I asked Hawk's father once and he said, 'Why not? Where do you think George Foreman got his idea to name all his sons George?' I know, you're looking at me like I'm joking, but this is God's honest truth. The McMillans are weird men. So you had better not even think about dating one."

Vivi didn't know what to believe. It was such a ridiculous way to warn her away from Hawk McMillan that she burst out laughing. Jazz joined her.

"I hope I'm not interrupting. Vivi, I need to talk to you."

Vivi reluctantly turned around. Of course it had to be Juliana. Life wouldn't be interesting without a bitch creeping up on you now and then.

CHAPTER
12

Jazz studied the woman. She was tall and blond, mid-thirties, and looking very disapproving at the moment. Vivi didn't appear too ruffled by her hard stare, but her laughter had all but disappeared. He didn't think these two were on friendly terms, not with the tension stretching between them. Damn. They were getting along, finally, and he had thought—

That tanked the moment the woman's voice interrupted them. No more Vivi relaxed and friendly. His prickly and suspicious film noir heroine returned with just a blink of an eye. He felt that earlier frustration returning.

"Of course, Juliana. I'll be right behind you."

Vivi's voice was cool. She didn't make any attempt to introduce Jazz. He recalled her mentioning that name earlier . . . oh yeah, the one who looked at numbers. Maybe that was why she was looking at him that way—like he was vermin or something.

"You're the lieutenant who was released recently," Juliana said, her gaze cold and measuring. "I'm surprised you're still in the country. Usually the soldiers transfer quickly after a little visit here."

And how do you do yourself, ma'am? Jazz smiled easily. "Yes."

Her eyes narrowed. "Just because we couldn't find any hard evidence to keep you, Lieutenant, doesn't mean you aren't guilty in my eyes. If you do what you did again"—her gaze swung back to Vivi—"under different circumstances, you won't get out so easily."

"Thank goodness for corroborating eyewitnesses, then," Vivi countered softly. "We wouldn't want to make any mistakes and put innocent people in jail now, would we?"

Jazz kept his expression shuttered. Although he seemed to be the subject of contention, he had a feeling that this wasn't his battle. The other woman was regarding Vivi with veiled dislike; he could only see Vivi's profile, but her neck and shoulders had tensed slightly when Juliana was talking about his arrest.

"I suppose not. Have you been able to find some placements, Vivienne?"

"No, not yet."

"Well, do you have any idea when you can find some openings? I have a new list already and you're still asking for more funds for the old list. Maybe we need a different approach." Juliana took a few steps into the room, pausing to pour herself a cup of water from the cooler. "You've suggested giving more funds to the different safe houses, yet they remain full. I also know you've been using some of the funds to bribe the parents. You know we don't like that idea. We can't do that forever and you're just training them to be greedy."

"I have no idea where you got the impression that I'm bribing the parents," Vivi said. "I've been helping the safe houses, orphanages, and churches. The cash flow is all accounted for in the paperwork each month."

"I see that, but I'm not stupid, Vivienne." Juliana finished her drink and threw the paper cup away in the litter basket. "I talked to the girls and some of them relate to me incidences when you're giving away cash. Now, what I want to know is, are you doing some fancy bookkeeping, and if that's so, of course I'll have to report that."

Ah, the heart of the matter. Jazz recalled the cash Vivi gave to Mr. Tham the other day, telling him to hold off from sending Rose out to "work."

When Vivi didn't answer immediately, Juliana shrugged and continued, "I'm not against your intentions, Vivienne. They are wonderful and humane but we can't afford it. Some girls can't be saved, no matter how much you want them to be. Pick the youngest—they are the easiest to foster. The oldest ones have to either go out and find a job or . . ." She shrugged again.

"Or what, Juliana?" Vivi's voice was quiet.

"I'm just being realistic. Make some cuts from your list. Our budget gets tighter and we need to show our findings to the UN Council, with high numbers, to get the countries responsible for these crimes to pay more." She looked at Jazz with contempt before adding, "I might also add that it's never good to mix work with pleasure. Not good for our image."

Vivi went to close the door. She didn't need others listening in. She did her usual thing, knowing it irritated the other woman. She circled the room and made her way to the fish tank on one side of the room. She pressed her hand against the glass and watched the fish rush toward it, anticipating food. She could feel Jazz's eyes on her.

"Life isn't all about image, Juliana. Do you have the new list?"

"Of course it's about image. Do you think things just get done willy-nilly? Our organization must look professional so we can achieve our goals. If we want to be accepted as one of the UN-approved organizations, we have to do things a certain way."

Vivi shrugged, teasing the fish. She wasn't part of the organization and perhaps that was what was rankling Juliana, but her job wasn't to appease the woman or anyone in the organization. "Interpol doesn't seem to have a problem with my image." Juliana hated being reminded that Vivi answered to Interpol first, even though her contract was with the organization. It was part of the deal written out by GEM to ensure control and protection from liability issues. "I haven't done anything to create any problems in my work."

"Not yet," Juliana asserted, "but there will be if you keep continuing what you're doing. Do you mind turning around? I find it hard to talk while you play with the fish."

Vivi hid a smile. Turning, she walked back to the desk and sat down. Jazz stayed where he was, silent and watchful. "And the trouble is?"

Juliana heaved out a sigh. "Do I have to spell it out? The cash flow problem. That is part of your volunteer work so I have something to say about it, don't you agree? Your refusal to strike names off the list is creating unnecessary work for the rest of the team. In volunteering, you're part of us and you haven't been a very good team member. And now you're going around with an ex-prisoner. What will people think?"

Vivi sat back too, lacing her hands in her lap. She glanced at Jazz, trying to read what he was thinking. His blue eyes were on Juliana, studying her.

"I don't know. What will they think?" She couldn't care less, anyway, but she knew Juliana was right about the cash flow. She hadn't done anything wrong, since she hadn't used any of the organization's funds for the bribes. "You're the public information officer, so I guess you're more sensitive to these things than I am. As far as I know, I haven't done anything wrong. Jazz hasn't, either, and that's why he was freed, remember?"

"Perception. Everything is that these days. Your giving money to those parents—they see this and they know how to play the game, Vivienne. You want to save everyone and that's very noble, but the reality is, you're hurting the cause. Now, your being seen with this lieutenant—and this is just *my* perception—is in very bad taste. He was recently seen by the people here as a prisoner—"

"Excuse me, *detainee*," Vivi interrupted. She was getting tired of that word. "Lieutenant Zeringue was detained till he was proven to have done nothing wrong. How many times am I supposed to repeat that? Besides, I thought you were accusing me of playing magic number games with the cash logs."

Since the beginning, Juliana had made it clear that Vivi wasn't a suitable volunteer but because of her ability to mix with the locals, the organization had accepted her time and contributions. Today, she obviously thought she had enough information to go to another level in their ongoing battle. Vivi never underestimated Juliana's knowledge of numbers and details; she knew the other woman had been waiting for the right moment before confronting her with what she had been doing.

Juliana came forward and handed over a file. "These are the latest allocations given to our team here. You can see how desperate we are. What you're doing on the side isn't helping the cause." She gave a sideways glance at Jazz again. "I'll use any means necessary to get you to sign off on those names, Vivi. Misuse of funds is a serious charge, you know."

"You would like to see me gone, wouldn't you?" Vivi asked softly. "The others won't argue too much about the lists of names, whether one girl is less important because she's older than another, the numbers will all line up with the detainment report, and *voilà!* a UN stamp of approval faster than you can say 'Au revoir, Vivienne Verreau'."

"I don't see why we couldn't compromise," Juliana said smoothly.

"What do you want me to do?"

Juliana looked surprised. She hadn't expected cooperation yet. "Well, for now," she said slowly, "we have to pare down your old list. This is the newest list of girls who need places to go to. I have already removed the older ones to spare you. The next few weeks are crucial because the second quarter reports are due. If I can show positive results, we will get nominated into the UN-approved associations."

And those were the cards dealt. Make the reports look good and get UN funds. According to people like Juliana, the end justified the means, so a few sacrifices on the way shouldn't hurt one's conscience. And as she had so kindly added, she had already "removed" the older children from the list so Vivi would be "spared" the pain.

Vivi looked down at her lap. Her laced hands had curled into twin fists. As a volunteer, she really had nothing to lose one way or another. But as someone who had been in the shoes of those very same children who were left without hope or help . . .

Vivi, you will come back and take me away from here, won't you? The nuns said we aren't pure, said we are paying for our parents' karma . . .

Hush! The old baldheaded bitches are just jealous. Now, wipe away those tears, hmm? I'll be back, I promise.

She looked up. There was a short silence as she stared at Juliana. She could hear in the background the fish tank filter bubbling merrily. Turning away, she looked at the fish swimming so comfortably in their artificial environment. With stubborn determination, she said softly, "I won't compromise."

There were some things she shouldn't compromise about. Lives, especially those who were innocent, especially those who needed help most. Juliana's eyes flashed with anger as she she turned and left the office. That final look spoke volumes. She was going to show that Vivi's objectivity was compromised when it came to the organization's directive.

Vivi didn't care. She just wasn't going to play God to children's lives. She had made promises and meant to keep them. Her jaw tightened with determination. She finally looked up at Jazz, wondering what he thought of the unexpected meeting.

"I'm sorry you're spending your free time like this, cooped up in an office, listening in on a catfight." She waved at the pile of papers in front of her. "Those are names and places, and most of them are requests for funds or help of some kind. Give them something and they might find an open spot for one girl, or two. And she doesn't think *that*'s bribery? But I can't say anything because this isn't my job. I'm just a volunteer for this."

"Don't worry about my free time. I'm where I want to be, really. This Juliana can't really get you into trouble, can she?"

She shook her head. "I'm the liaison for them with Interpol." She smiled. "I do have some authority, you know. Their organization can't just order Interpol officers around. Interpol recommended GEM as a liaison to help them do their work. It's just that sometimes, the organization is a bit . . . overeager to achieve their goals. It isn't any different from any funded groups who see the result and ignore the way there."

Jazz came to her and leaned over the desk. He touched her cheek. His hand felt warm and tender. "I believe in what you do, Vivi. I know you care about these girls and that they're more than numbers to you."

She smiled back tightly. "Much good caring does, huh? I can't seem to find any permanent solutions. And Miss Numbers wants me to pick and choose. As if—" She bit down on her lower lip.

Jazz felt her helplessness, her inner anger. "We all do what we can to save the world, *chouchou*." Not that his words would help. From what he had just seen and heard, he didn't think much could be done to persuade Juliana Kohl from following up on her threats. But he wanted to comfort Vivi, who seemed all alone in this fight. "One step at a time, that's all we can do. Here, I'll go back to checking out the walls while you finish your paperwork."

"Okay."

Vivi looked up half an hour later, distracted by a strange sound. Jazz was checking out a musical instrument. Her mouth softened at the sight of him plucking out an awkward tune that somewhat resembled "Oh Susannah." She should have known he would be attracted to it once he saw it resting in the corner. It had been so long since she had put it there . . .

"That sounds awful," she said.

He looked up, the frown of concentration still stamping his features. "Its sounds like a banjo. What is it?"

"It isn't a banjo. It's a lute. Here, you hold it like this." She showed him the proper way, with the handle straight up. "It's called a Dan Nhat, a sun lute, because its body is shaped like the sun."

She watched as he positioned it the way she had and couldn't help but marvel at how gentle he was with the instrument. She had easily imagined him with a big heavy weapon, but he held the Dan Nhat as if he'd used it before.

"Is this yours?"

She nodded, then shook her head. "It's sort of mine. I bought it for a friend, but I haven't given it to her yet."

"Do you play it?" he asked.

"Yes, but not well. My friend, though, could play it very well."

"Show me." He handed it back to her.

Vivi hesitated before taking it from him. It had been literally years. She had bought it out of impulse when she saw it in the market, when she had first arrived. It was a symbol, that she would one day find her Sia-Sia and give this to her.

"Well," she said, and laughed nervously, "my mind is blank."

She plucked the strings tentatively, slowly getting used to the tension as she adjusted the chords from memory. Then, smiling at him mischievously, she did a quick rendition of "Oh Susannah" without any mistakes.

"Hey," he said, "you can play pretty well!"

"No, that's just child's play. You should hear a professional sometimes. It's an amazing instrument, sounding between a guitar and a zither depending on the tension and chords."

"Yeah, I'd like that."

They looked at each other and Vivi found herself leaning closer. Jazz didn't move, the blue in his eyes suddenly intense and intimate, the corner of his lips curving up slightly. She could compromise in some things, Vivi thought, as she kissed that tempting mouth.

His lips were warm, gentle even, and he gave her what she

needed—freedom. She had held her emotions inside for so long, it would be so easy to just let go and not think. There was something about him that soothed her, like a mental anodyne, taking away the pain she kept hidden from everyone. She opened her mouth.

He didn't need a second invitation. His tongue crept in, and he was no longer gentle. She felt his hands holding her face still as he explored and tasted with such exquisite demand that the soothing numbness exploded into something more. How could a kiss make her feel this weak? Her whole insides churned as his lips moved across hers. She felt as if he were drinking in those secrets she had never shared.

Vivi responded, allowing the torrent of emotions to push away those decades-old barriers. Oh, it felt so good to let go. Her world seemed to come to a standstill, where nothing mattered but this swirl of passion that had caught her in its web. She was helpless against it as waves of need crashed through her senses.

She murmured throatily, pulling at Jazz's T-shirt, needing him closer. The Dan Nhat was caught between them and its strings jangled strangely, echoing her out-of-tune senses. Unruly. Uncontrolled. Totally letting the moment rule.

Jazz released her lips, and she wanted to protest. His breathing was uneven as he placed soft kisses at the corner of her mouth and up her jaw line.

"This is against everything my body is screaming at me to do, *chouchou,* but we have to stop before I put you on that desk and make love to you."

Vivi felt his lips on her closed eyelids. She didn't want to open them because she knew reality was waiting. Shock rifled through her as she realized how unlike herself she was behaving. Right now, she wouldn't give a damn about being caught in a passionate embrace. If Juliana had walked in with a crowd of her media connections, they could have stood there with their pens and pads taking notes, and she wouldn't have noticed.

All she had wanted to do was continue kissing this man,

with her hand over his heart, feeling it beating faster for her as she responded to his silent demand to let go. Something carnal had reared its head inside, wanting the connection to go further. She allowed him access to the nape of her neck when he nudged at her, then shivered at the first small nibble. His breath was hot against her skin, and his scent tempted her to let this continue.

She opened her eyes, at the same time pushing against his chest. He complied, allowing some space between them, but there was no mistaking the sensual heat in his blue eyes. And that carnal thing inside her responded to that look with the same heat, building and pushing against her as she drowned in that gaze. He looked at her as if he wanted to put his mouth on other parts of her body besides her lips. That thought made those parts clench up in anticipation.

"That isn't the way to play the lute," she said, her voice coming out breathless.

"But we make such good music together, *chouchou*. It gets better with practice. Look how totally cold you were with me our first time when we kissed. I thought you must hate kissing, the length of time it took you to come out of that restaurant."

Vivi frowned at the mention of the first kiss, her heart skipping a beat at the thought that he . . . then she realized he had meant that one earlier in the restaurant, after T. had left. She hadn't responded then because she knew she was being watched. Her walls were still safely protecting her from this man, even though she had to force herself to sit still.

She knew she shouldn't have let her defenses slip where Jazz was concerned. He covered his male determination very well with that easy cajoling charm. He was a SEAL through and through, and when he wanted something, he went after it.

And damn, the man could French-kiss better than any Frenchman. Of course, she had no intention of giving him that piece of information.

"Look how my kiss can leave you speechless," he teased with a smile.

Vivi laughed. She hadn't known a kiss was so tension-relieving. Somehow he had gotten under her skin, and even made her laugh. That was so rare these days. She would have to kiss more often. More often . . . She sighed. "I wish we could continue this exercise but this isn't the time or place." She handed him the Dan Nhat. "Here, you can borrow it, if you want."

"I'd rather do something else." Jazz strummed the lute a couple of times. "See how bad I am with this thing? I'd rather play with you. I promise it'll be better than our kiss."

His wink was wicked as he played with the lute with those long, long fingers. Vivi studied them, imagining them on her body. Without a doubt, it would be an experience to remember. She hadn't wanted to be with a man so badly in a while now. But she had things to do—one of which was to try to find a place for Rose. She was running out of time.

Back to business mode. Back to reality. There was simply no room to think about what Vivi Verreau wanted. She looked at the tall, handsome man who was so out of place in her office. She remembered seeing him without a shirt, remembered the gleaming muscles and flat stomach glistening with perspiration. What sane woman would keep saying no to that body?

"Lieutenant," she said crisply. "Practice makes perfect."

CHAPTER
13

Jazz examined the Dan Nhat in his lap, running his fingers lightly over the instrument. It looked like a guitar but it wasn't. Much like its owner who was also more than she appeared to be. He smiled ruefully.

His mind had been on Vivi Verreau since she'd dropped him back at the compound. She had taken him on some of her "errands," giving him another glimpse of the role she played. She had many, many different sides, and he was more intrigued than ever.

They had driven to a converted old building that served as a safe house for orphans. Vivi had brought boxes of canned food with her. Jazz didn't mind being the center of attention, playing with the kids, while he listened to the conversation between the adults. Vivi had wanted to know when there would be an open spot. From her description of the girl's circumstances, he soon realized that she was talking about Rose, the young girl from the bar. His interest went up another notch.

He recalled her telling Rose that she was having a difficult time finding a spot for her because she wasn't an orphan. Today he was getting to see that what had seemed an unimportant fact at the time now played a big part in state-sponsored environments. How could she just stand there and take all that bureaucratic B.S. so calmly? He couldn't understand what was so difficult about putting up a child in need. Whether she was an orphan or not shouldn't matter.

In the end, Vivi had walked away without securing any kind of promise to get Rose in as soon as possible. He'd sensed her frustration, even though her demeanor hadn't changed.

"I'm sorry, *chouchou*," he'd said and reached for her hand.

She hadn't shaken him off. "I'm used to it, Jazz. Don't worry, I'll find something for Rose. Besides, I still have you to marry her, right?"

He'd grinned at her attempt to tease him. He realized that she rarely wanted to discuss her volunteer job at all. Who could blame her, especially during those times when she couldn't find a way to help?

"I'm sort of taken, but I do have an available brother."

"Interesting. Are you telling me you have a woman in your life back in Louisiana?"

"Well, no, not exactly."

"You're telling me you don't even have one single girl-friend back there?" Her eyes were filled with disbelief. "You have so many sisters. Surely you dated some of their friends."

His grin had widened. Ah, it was good to know she was probing for more information about his life. "Occasional dates, yeah. And yes, I kissed her . . . happy now?"

She had given him a long look before asking, "And what was her name?"

"Karen. But she's happily married now. We're still friends. I helped her landscape her entire backyard the last time I was home."

"Good." That was all she said.

Jazz smiled as he recalled that look Vivi had given him when she had dropped him off. She had wanted to say something but changed her mind, but that look gave him hope. One day, she would tell him what went on in that mind of hers. Like the Dan Nhat, she was just a mystery, but with a little touching, lots of loving, and special coaxing, he intended to make her his. She just didn't know that right now, that was all.

He must have been nuts to stop at just that kiss. She had wanted him; he had felt that. Even now the memory of her response was playing havoc with his concentration. He paused to adjust the tension of the strings.

There was always something restrained about her, as if she was afraid to let go. Maybe some soldier had hurt her in the past and she had never gotten over it. Maybe he had left her and that was why she kept pointing out that he would be gone soon. Jazz understood that he had to listen carefully to what she was telling him if he were to get any closer.

It was like this Dan Nhat. A fine string instrument and tension. Get it right and the notes would come out clear and musical. Get it wrong and the strings would break.

Jazz plucked "Oh Susannah" on the lute slowly, marveling at the different texture of the sounds coming from it. He held it the way she'd shown him, playing with the frets to get the note he had in mind, tuning it one way, then another.

"That is the most godawful sound you're making," Hawk said from the doorway. He strolled in, looking very comfortable in the cotton attire that the locals favored. "What the hell is that thing, some kind of guitar?"

"It's a Dan Nhat." It was almost curfew time. The others were already back. Lockdown toward zero hour was set to start as soon as they had the latest satellite data of the oncoming target. Jazz studied his friend as he strummed on, trying to figure out the frets. "It isn't a guitar, it's a sun lute."

"You need lessons, from what I'm hearing." Hawk paused in the middle of unlacing his shoes. "Where did you get it?"

Jazz didn't say anything, repeating "Oh Susannah." This time he had it in tune.

"Uh-huh, been at Vivi's behind my back," Hawk said, his voice mild, as he pulled off his shoes. "Made any progress?"

"Some."

"Do anything I would have done?"

Jazz narrowed his eyes as he stared at his friend's bland expression. "No. Vivi doesn't like fishing," he said, choosing to be obtuse. Hawk was a fishing enthusiast.

Hawk grinned. "Yeah, but you took the bait. She'll bite, too, from the master."

"Why don't you jerk off?" Jazz countered rudely.

"Nah, too tired. Everyone's accounted for, so I'm going to bed."

"Where did you go?" Jazz asked, changing the subject on purpose.

Hawk slumped back onto the narrow bed, resting his head on his hands. "I was going to say I spent all day having sex with Vivi Verreau but since you said you were with her, I doubt that story would stick." He cocked a brow at Jazz. "But it still pisses you off even when you know what I said didn't have an ounce of truth."

"I don't like it. Can't you go after some other woman?"

"Such as? You have someone in mind for your twin?"

Jazz laid the lute by his pillow and stretched lazily. "I don't know. How about that old grump, Grandmamasan? You two seem to get along. Besides, you owe her a kiss, pal."

Hawk started chuckling, which quickly became loud laughter. His whole body shook with mirth as he looked up at the ceiling. "Turn off the lights, bro," he said, between chuckles. "I'm off to dream about Grandmamasan and me."

"And you find that hilarious?"

The room went dark. Hawk kept laughing, as if he couldn't help himself.

"Yeah," he said. "Extremely."

"Are you going to share this big joke?" The image of Grandmamasan and Hawk was pretty funny, but only from Jazz's perspective. Couldn't be that funny from Hawk's. After making sure the lute was out of the way, Jazz lay down on his bed. "She probably has a thing for you, the way she kept calling you GI number one."

The chuckles quieted down but Jazz could hear the smile

in Hawk's voice. "Nah, she has a thing for you, my friend, or hadn't you noticed?"

"Yeah, uh-huh, keep her away from me, man. I already did my part of that bargain you made with her. Thank God that place was dark. Do you know how hard it was for me to try to get her image out of my mind so I could kiss her? Man, that was tough." Jazz adjusted his pillow. "There's no way I'm going to kiss her for you, too."

Hawk started chuckling. "Oh no, my friend. I always keep my end of the bargain. I'll kiss Grandmamasan. To help you out, remember?"

"That I can't wait to see."

Hawk's laughter filled the darkness again. Jazz listened to the night sounds as they both wound down for the night. It occurred to him before he fell asleep that Hawk never did tell him where he'd disappeared to for most of that day.

"You must be insane to turn down a fine man like that," T. said, as she stood in front of a floor-length mirror, slowly taking out the clips holding up twisted lengths of her hair. "He's a good guy, darling."

"And you know this from what?" Vivi asked as she held the tray for T. to drop the clips in, watching her chief's reflection as she slowly unveiled yet another façade. "From the way you felt him up and down at the restaurant?"

T.'s smile was pure wickedness. She had darkened her light auburn to a rich titian, and as the freed curls slowly untwisted by themselves, the shy librarian she had earlier portrayed slowly morphed into a sensual creature. "That accounts for the fine part," she replied, her voice rich with amusement. "The good guy comes from research. I have read his file, you know, and with that Louisiana gentlemanly charm, so properly trained by all his sisters, you have a winner."

Vivi scowled. "His file doesn't say anything about his family."

"The lieutenant is single, had a poor and simple childhood, brought up by a single mom with six sisters and another brother near Slidell, Louisiana. Despite that horrible name his mother saddled him with, our lieutenant managed to survive high school and BUD/S' ruthless instructors to become part of a group hand-picked by Admiral Jack Madison. His handle, Jazz, comes from his Louisiana roots and love of music. His bank account—"

"Stop." Vivi didn't want to hear about Jazz's bank account or anything intimate about him. T. had always been very thorough when it came to her job, but in this case, it was too much. She didn't want Jazz's portfolio and background being recited to her in facts and numbers. She had enough of that daily. She handed T. a comb. "I don't want to know."

"I want you to see him without his uniform, that's all." T. winked at her as she combed her curls out. "Literally and figuratively."

"Why?"

Vivi *was* curious about Jazz, although she didn't want to dwell on the reason. She immediately regretted asking the question.

"You want to deflect your attraction for the man by keeping a constant image of him in uniform. It's easier to deny your feelings when you can summon up your fears and hatred for that symbol, right?" T.'s eyes met hers in the mirror. "Already you aren't comfortable because you know too much about our lieutenant. He loves talking about his family, which is dominated by women, and his protectiveness toward them is so . . . sexy, don't you agree?"

Vivi stuck her tongue out at T.'s amused reflection. "Stop probing my mind."

"You asked, darling. Now hand me my lenses."

She put down the tray and picked up the contact lens case. She watched as T. popped the new lenses in. The transformation was complete. Unforgettable dark eyes the color of amethyst. A slightly altered nose. Collagen shot in the lower lip to make it poutier. T. flicked back her artificially extended hair, cocked her head as she studied herself, lowered her chin, then blinked; another woman peered up secretively. A wavy length of gleaming hair tumbled seductively over one eye. When she smiled, it was different. Even her stance had changed.

Vivi admired the smoothness of the transformation. Even on her best days, in her now familiar disguises, she had to take more than a blink to get into the right frame of mind, but her chief did it seamlessly. She knew this new "person," having met her several times before. This was T.'s new face for the operation that started a few years back when GEM and COS Command merged forces to find out who had their operatives attacked and slain. Operation Foxhole.

"Hello, Tasha," Vivi greeted softly. "You've been a busy, busy lady lately."

T. pirouetted, fluffing her curls into a glorious disarrayed mass that tumbled down to her waist. "Actually, I haven't. As you know, 'Tasha' was last seen tumbling into the ocean, presumably dead."

She was referring to her last public appearance when "Tasha" was shot at by a certain illegal weapon dealer's right-hand man and his bodyguards. Vivi had gotten a fax about T.'s adventure at sea.

"So now you're back when Maximillian Shoggi is in town. He's bound to see you. And will remember how you're indirectly responsible for his current lack of funds."

By taking out Mad Max's right-hand man and freezing some of his offshore bank accounts, GEM and COS Command had effectively left the infamous arms dealer scrambling to keep his power base. It had been a very lengthy operation, but worth it.

Vivi knew she had to ask. She was too damn curious. "Tell me, does it feel strange to know that Alex Diamond wants to be with Tasha and not you?" According to one of her GEM sisters, there was a blow-up of sorts at COM when Diamond had found out the truth about T. "Is that why you left?"

T.'s eyes narrowed. "Do you have to bring him up now?" Even her voice had changed, a little lower, more modulated.

"You're the one who started the probing session," Vivi

pointed out. She leaned forward to adjust T.'s hair. "I'm in the same position, T. Jazz isn't seeing me, you know."

T.'s expression softened. "You and I aren't in the same boat, darling. You aren't a completely different person with him, except," she said, with a smile, "when you're that nasty old woman, of course. You're Vivi, through and through. Just take out those damn braces."

"You're saying I can't act?" Vivi mocked, not wanting to delve too deeply.

"Don't change the subject. You took the probe challenge, you finish it." T. tapped the bottom of Vivi's chin. "Go on. Give me your best shot."

One didn't ever back down when T. was challenging. It wasn't very often the other woman allowed anyone to test her. "Okay. Tell me, why shouldn't I run like you? You've been running from Alex Diamond for almost five months now, and don't deny it. I've been tracking you since your sudden transfer back to the UN."

T. flopped carelessly onto a nearby loveseat. She examined her newly painted nails. "Darling, you weren't assigned to try to get a man to fall for you. It wasn't in your plan to make him think of somebody special every time he looked into your eyes. In fact, I didn't run. I just refused to compete with a dead woman. What are you competing against, a uniform?"

Ouch. She could get burned playing this game with T. Fire with fire, she supposed. "What's the difference? Your opponent is dead, so why not point this out to him?"

T.'s eyes appeared several shades darker, as if they were projecting her thoughts. "My opponent lives inside a living person's head. Yours live inside yours," she pointed out softly. "You have total control over your behavior. Whether you want to change it or not is up to you. Are you ever going to take out those braces and let go of your past?"

Vivi grimaced. "Okay, you win."

T. smiled, her expression brightening a little. "I always do, darling. When?"

"Soon."

"You won't lodge a protest if I release you from this contract." It wasn't a question. "The survey can go on without you. Besides, they need fresh blood."

Which reminded Vivi. "I need to talk to you about Juliana Kohl." When T. narrowed her eyes, she shrugged. "All right, all right, I won't lodge a protest. But you'll let me see this new element with the masked man through. I want to know what he has."

T. nodded. "I'm not going to pull you out immediately, Vivi. You're still very effective, and besides, there is the joint mission. Plenty to do still, don't worry." She uncrossed her legs and stood up. "Now you need to get going. Can Juliana Kohl wait?"

"Yes, she can wait," Vivi replied. It wasn't an urgent matter yet. "So tomorrow you're going to make sure Maximillian Shoggi sees you. I wish I could be there to see his shock when he realizes that you're alive."

"Oh yes, it will be a very satisfying moment," T. acknowledged with a bitter smile. "We have never officially met, but he watched me behind his two-way mirrors. It had amused him to deny me a meeting while watching me refuse to play with his man."

T. had been dealing with Cash Ibrahim, who was now dead. "Revenge is going to be so sweet for scum like him," Vivi said quietly.

They both looked at each other, remembering their dead friends. "There'll be another greatly satisfying moment in the future," T. promised in a flat voice. "When he finally has no one to turn to, nowhere to go. With Dilaver and the Triads busy with each other, he will have less and less options."

"Don't you think Alex Diamond will be there too? Will you be running away again then?" Vivi had never seen her chief avoid another person like this. She noticed the tension around T.'s eyes and pressed on, "Perhaps he'll let go of his past then, hmm?"

"Perhaps, but we both have one thing in common."

"What's that?"

"Our men don't seem to see us through our disguises."

They both laughed at the uncomfortable truth. Vivi wondered whether Jazz truly saw her. But she didn't have as many layers as T., who had enough personalities to rival a schizo.

"Thank you for the session," Vivi said as she picked up her purse. "It was enlightening."

"For both of us, darling. It isn't very often I give in to a probing, but in this case, the desired results outweigh the discomfort."

Vivi laughed. "I'm afraid to ask what you've manipulated my mind into making me do."

T.'s answering smile was secretive. "Do I ever tell?"

Never. T.'s power of manipulation was like a soldier's well-oiled weapon. She was a mental sniper. Vivi had never seen her miss when it came to NOPAIN.

"Viv? Is he a good kisser?"

"Yeah."

"Then, you know what to do when he's finds out about your disguise. You just start kissing him back and let him know it's you inside."

Vivi laughed again, then sobered. "I know you don't mean me in that old woman's makeup pushing my tongue down his throat."

"Well, that would be something I'd want to see, but you know I meant something else. Look at your real self in the mirror and forgive the past, Viv."

It was an order. Vivi didn't feel the need to argue anymore. Maybe she was just tired. She couldn't seem to find a solution to any of her problems. She knew T. was right. A change of venue and jobs would be good for her. But what about . . . She realized with a start that she was thinking of Jazz in terms of the future, when there probably wouldn't be any.

The drive back allowed her the luxury to dwell on the kiss. He *was* a good kisser. More like fantastic. She had always been able to keep part of herself detached during intimate moments but during that kiss, she couldn't think at all. Everything came in a rush, and she had responded to his lips and caresses eagerly, wonderingly, without a single observation or thought.

Vivi touched her lips with her fingers. She had never felt like that before. It was frightening how just one kiss could churn her insides into such a knot. She had been attracted to men before, of course—charm and attraction were weapons taught at GEM—but she had always been emotionally in control.

The stairwell at the apartment building was silent in the late hour and Vivi was grateful Mrs. Lee wasn't around to chide about her single status again. She didn't feel like going another round about not needing a man.

She locked her apartment door and leaned against it, feeling its hard wood against her back. Because she needed. Right now. It was tough to admit it; it had been so long since she had needed a man. T.'s probing had brought that point home.

Without turning on the light, Vivi walked into her bedroom, unzipping and loosening her clothes carelessly. One could live in the past for only so long, especially when there didn't seem to be anything with which to feed off from. All these years, she had kept wondering what had happened to her old friend, had agonized over a promise she had made, but since her return, she hadn't been able to find any trace of her.

All she had found were painful reminders that nothing had changed in this culture, that it had become worse. She rubbed the crick in her neck as she stepped out of her heels and took off her clothes. She reached for the cotton nightie on top of her bed and froze when her hand touched something that was definitely not made of cloth.

14

Conflict resolution, navy SEALs style. That was the team's private joke when they set out to do utter destruction to bridges, roads, bunker complexes, and other big targets. As Cucumber often said, "There are few troubles that high explosives can't take care of."

The team had traveled by night up the muddy road, driven by a local truck driver, to the observation point that Jazz had targeted on the map. That was the new Point Zero, where all members must return. The truck driver had given them a thumbs-up after they had unloaded the hidden crates of equipment before driving off into the darkness.

The air was damp from the previous day's rain, making the humidity even more oppressive. Within minutes, Jazz's T-shirt was stuck to his body as he and his team moved about silently, unpacking and setting up what they needed.

Hawk had sent out their point man, Turner, the day before to scout the area, making sure the coast was clear and checking the coordinates with the map they had been given. Turner had also returned with a thumbs-up.

From this lookout, Jazz could see the bridge with his night-vision binoculars. Everything was running smoothly. The countdown started the moment they had received the phone call that the satellite had the target within forty-eight hours of reaching the bridge.

That was both good news and bad news. The good news was that it meant the arrival would be around evening time, with enough daylight left so they could make sure which vehicle was which. The bad news was that it would be evening and what they could see, the enemy could, too. Everyone's watch was set to precisely at midnight insertion time. The men would be divided into their usual two groups, one to follow Hawk's orders and one to follow Jazz's. Hawk would run the team from the lookout point first, making sure each team member covered Jazz's team as they went under water to string up the bridge for a special welcome to the visitors.

Then Jazz's team was to move to a safe distance on the other side as Hawk kept watch. Vivi was in charge of communications between HQ and the team. With her calling in to confirm the satellite signals and Hawk's watch of the vehicles' progress from his vantage point, Jazz would be able to time what he had to do to the second. His job wasn't to look up at the bridge but to keep his ears open for Hawk's signal to blow the baby up. His team was to ensure the safety of the vehicle with the women. Hawk's men would take out whoever was left on his side of the bank. Except Dilaver, of course.

"What do you see?" Hawk asked from behind him.

"Just checking the bridge. I like to see what it looks like from afar." Jazz adjusted the binoculars. "The water is high from the rain and the bridge is pretty low. Tricky."

"I'm sure you can handle it."

"Yeah, but another big rain tomorrow and we might not need to blow it down. It looks pretty rickety with the mud banks."

From photos and Vivi's information, it was an old bridge, very seldom used. The locals were aware of its role in the illegal trades and kept out of its way as much as possible. Bribery was the usual currency for access in this region, and

Jazz wasn't surprised to learn that the local government turned a blind eye to the activities in their backyard.

"You just don't want to get mud in your hair."

Jazz grinned as he handed the binoculars over. "Yeah, that too." He patted the haversack next to him. "My guys and I will be able to suffer through this while you guys have it easy up here drinking coffee."

The haversack was loaded with water-resistant explosives, complete with an MC-1 clock, a safety and arming device, and a MK 96 detonator, all designed to provide precision delay and detonation of the main charge. It wouldn't take very long for two swim pairs to attach the explosives. The trick was to apply it where it would blow the bridge down and not up, causing the least damage to the surroundings. They couldn't chance too much shrapnel and chunks of blasted heavy wood flying around.

It was going to be more complex, what with the timing as well as the precision of each blast. Jazz didn't like it when too much depended on Lady Luck. Things could always go wrong, and the need to ensure the safety of a certain vehicle had put even more pressure on the operation. It was tough to leave to chance that none of the female prisoners would be injured.

He hadn't talked to Vivi since their kiss. "Did Vivi say when she will call again?"

"Negative."

"We still don't know her plans. Or did she tell you?"

"Negative."

"I don't think she's just going to call in now and then to update us with satellite feeds."

Hawk finally looked away from the binoculars. "Why not? Somebody has to do that."

Jazz cocked a brow. "I thought you were the expert on these GEM people. Even I can tell they aren't the type to sit back and let things happen. No, they are up to something and not telling us." He couldn't see Hawk's expression in the semidarkness but he knew his friend never liked surprises in a mission. "I know you talked to her more than I did about the operation. Did she give you any hints at all about orders from her side?"

"Negative."

"You're doing that deliberately to goad me, aren't you?" Jazz asked in a mild voice. "What were you doing then?"

"Not puckering lips." Hawk walked away so the men could put up "window dressing," as they called it, camouflaging the opening of the lookout with plants and twigs. "We discussed the weather. Most boring. And she was asking about coordinates and detonation power. I suspect she was concerned about how we're going to get some vehicles and not another."

That made sense. Vivi's top priority would be the girls. "Yeah, that complicates things."

"I mostly asked her about Dilaver and his trip here. Curious about his future plans and why GEM and Admiral Mad Dog didn't want him dead. Dilaver flew from Europe to do some sort of business in South East Asia, then decided to take a road trip in the darkness to meet up with the Triads. Obviously, he couldn't fly again, not with a load of captured women. I wanted to know what he was after."

Jazz shrugged. "Couldn't be anything good. I can imagine a reason why Mad Dog is letting him go. It's a joint mission, so it's easy to assume GEM wants him loose and the admiral obviously agreed to the reasons."

"You've been thinking about this too, huh?"

Jazz heaved the case with the squad communication gear onto a small portable table. "I'd say every man in our team has been thinking about it. It's not everyday we're told to shoot around a big target like Dilaver. They'll obey orders, no questions asked, but they aren't robots. They want to know, believe me."

He handed Hawk the squad radio for testing. Then he pulled out the compact SATCOM radio. They would be communicating until the final moments in case of any changes before the strike time and then everything was to follow as planned. Hopefully.

"Yeah," Hawk said. "The good thing is, they know Mad Dog will tell them sooner or later." Unlike other top brass, Admiral Jack Madison had always been straightforward with his special-designed teams. He had never been one to play fast and loose with the men.

Jazz glanced at his friend briefly. "Are you going to tell me before he does? Is it that big?"

"It's . . . big."

"It's got to be, to involve another group we haven't heard of before. That envelope Vivi gave you, with the instructions. That's a first I've seen a courier between the general and us. What does GEM actually provide, Hawk? They gave us the Intel, I know that, but surely there's more to that."

Hawk smiled. "Maybe if you stop sucking Vivi's lips with your eyes closed, you'll see a lot more."

"Maybe you don't know yourself," Jazz countered.

Hawk chuckled. "She's running a side show," he said quietly.

Jazz went still. "Are you saying she's going to be in the theater out there?" He shook his head. "Not a good idea, Hawk. We don't have any experience with her or her people, and with their penchant for secrecy, things are bound to go awry."

That was something he wasn't going to allow. No one was jumping into the fray without his permission. Not even Vivi.

Hawk's voice lowered, keeping the information for his ears only. "The only thing the admiral would allow me to say is that GEM is going to start a mini-war between the different big dealers and he's all for it. You know we lost four men to Dilaver last year because of the leaks from D.C. Mad Dog isn't forgetting that too soon. With Steve working as liaison between our side and the other agencies, I guess the admiral is comfortable with this joint mission. He knows what's going down and he approves. If the men press for more information, tell them about our fallen comrades. They'll understand then."

Jazz nodded. Leaks had been the killer in their covert operations the last few years. There were too many coincidental ambushes from behind, too many disappearances of targets before their arrival, and with the loss of a whole STAR Force fire squad in a particularly bloody mission that should have been an easy search and destroy, Admiral Madison had vowed to get to the bottom of the leaks. Four dead SEAL brothers. That had pissed off many frogs all over the world, especially when they had heard about the way it had happened. SEALs had long memories and Dilaver's name was etched in their brains.

The admiral had inserted Hawk's cousin, Steve, into the Intel section in D.C. It took a while but he had been successful in finding out one of the big rats in the system. In the course of things, Steve had left STAR Force to be liaison between the admiral and the different agencies. They had learned that many sources were better than just one. GEM must have proven to be very reliable or Mad Dog wouldn't allow a joint mission.

"You still haven't told me much about GEM." He needed to know what Vivi was up to, although he wouldn't bring it up specifically.

"Just think of them like we are—except we're a brotherhood and they are women." Hawk laughed. "And they use gems as their insignia. I've seen Steve's pin. He claimed he got it from one of them."

"Gems?"

"We have mean looking frogs on our patches, man," Hawk pointed out.

"So they have snarling gems on theirs?"

Hawk shook his head. "This is from Steve, so I'd take it with a grain of salt, okay? Marlena's thing is pearls and I think they send it out as gifts, like a call of distress or some kind of code. There's a huge secrecy about what GEM really is. I suspect they are part government, part civilian."

"Interesting." So Vivi had some kind of jewelry symbol of

her own? He had to find out whether that was true when he saw her next.

"Think of it as a very expensive group of Charlie's Angels," Hawk said, his voice rich with amusement. "And I ain't kidding. When I was in D.C., Steve's chick bought the whole squad expensive suits and took us to the opera. We had the best seats. She wore this thing that stuck to her like second skin. The hotel suite they lived in was makeout palace, with butlers and maids. High maintenance."

"No wonder your cousin opted for another job."

"It has its perks."

"So are you telling me all this just to satisfy my curiosity about Vivi or to hint there's something about her I ought to know?" They'd been friends long enough for him to realize that Hawk never parted with information unless he had something up his sleeve. It was the nature of McMillans to compete. "Are you saying Vivi might expect to be maintained like Steve's Marlena?"

"I'm saying there are many sides to these women. I've seen Marlena in that opera fluttering her eyelashes at my poor cousin and he was putty in her hands. And I've seen the same woman take my weapons and calmly mow down enemies with her back to mine while coolly telling me I didn't taste as sweet as her lover and that she was going to kill me for pretending to be Steve." Hawk paused as he adjusted his nylon belt, making sure everything was in place. He looked up at Jazz and added quietly, "You haven't seen the real Vivienne Verreau till you see her in action. Then you make up your mind whether that's the woman you want, buddy. What you see the rest of the time is merely some outer layer. Marlena is reputed to be an assassin. Who knows what Vivi is?"

An assassin. He couldn't picture Vivi as a cold-blooded killer. He was a soldier and understood the essentials of killing as part of his resume, but the mental picture he had built of Vivi didn't include that. But Hawk was right, of course. She was an operative.

"Can you handle it?" Jazz asked as he tucked in his weapon. "Knowing and loving a woman like that?"

Hawk smiled, his teeth gleaming in the dim lighting. "Well, it all depends on whether she likes my kiss."

Jazz thumped the radio against Hawk's chest. "As long as you don't pretend to be me this time, son." He knew he couldn't sound too challenging or Hawk would be even more competitive. He really didn't want Hawk's lips anywhere near Vivi's.

"I can't possibly look as ugly."

Jazz grinned. "Your loss." He checked the watch. "Two hours, forty-five minutes."

Hawk double-checked his watch and nodded. "Here's your earpiece. Don't lose it while trying to beat back the 'squitoes." They were to communicate via the tiny mikes as each team went their separate ways, so it was important to check with everyone so they could hear their channel. It would be pitch black while they worked, and any lost communication pieces might cause a problem.

At exactly midnight, Jazz watched as the men gathered around to listen to Hawk's quiet instructions. Faces smeared with war paint. Backs straight. Toys all ready for play.

"You know what your job is. Keep your eyes alert for women. Those of you who have seen Marlena Maxwell in action will bear in mind that Vivi Verreau is GEM, too. That means you report back anything that catches your attention, do you hear?"

The men rumbled their obedience in one voice. They didn't need to ask any questions. Each of them knew exactly what they had to do and the rest would be training taking over.

Jazz gave his instructions. "Make sure channel four is open for all-way communication. If there is any change of plans while we wait, Hawk and I will use that channel. If you are unable to communicate for whatever reason during the operation, you signal your partner for confirmation. Get the bridge. Get the fuckers. Then get the women. In that order."

"Hooyah!"

They slapped each other quietly on the back before dividing into their separate fire squads. Jazz nodded at Hawk before he and his team merged silently into the darkness. They would be separated from now on, doing what was needed to set up the operation. After that came the tough part—waiting.

Vivi didn't like being manipulated. By T., yeah, she counted on that. T. was always pushing and testing. But this masked stranger was playing with her, and it was pissing her off. Insinuating that he knew all about her background during their first meeting had already made her edgy. Now he had snuck into her apartment and . . .

She swung around, hands on hips. "I'm going to kick his ass," she announced.

T. looked up from the file propped against her thighs. She was seated on the sofa playing with her newly colored hair, twirling a strand around her finger as she took in Vivi's indignation. "If you could find his ass," she said coolly. "He seems to be able to come and go as he pleases. That's pretty good for a nobody masked man, hmm?"

"Well, if he's trying to piss me off, he's succeeded. How's that going to help his cause, whatever the hell it is?"

"You still want to know about your friend's whereabouts, don't you? I'd think he's got the upper hand, darling. I think he's just showing off."

T. was right, of course. The stranger knew that Vivi wouldn't be able to do anything as long as she wanted the information he had. Claimed he had.

"Is that why he's dangling the carrot?" she asked, folding her arms. "Maybe he's setting a trap. I don't like this."

T. closed the file and picked up the other thing that was in the small wooden box left on Vivi's bed the night before. It was a small piece of jewelry, a little anklet local children wore.

"Are you sure this is the real thing?" she asked as she fingered the stones.

Vivi nodded grimly as she approached the desk. "Yes. I have a similar one. Sia-Sia gave me one made of carnelian and I gave her one made of white jade. It's the same make, down to the small cinnabar beads between the stones. One of the beads is different because I repaired it when it broke. I know it's the same one, T. The question is, how did this end up in his hands? Who the hell is he? I'd love to find a way to stop him from shooting two stories into the air."

T. chuckled. "He's just trying to make a point, Viv. A man who can get around like that is an asset." Her now amethyst-colored eyes grew thoughtful. "And he did say he wanted his freedom. I wonder whether we can set up a meeting between Mr. Masked Man and me."

"Oh no, this is my baby. Besides, you have enough on your plate with Maximillian Shoggi. I'm just frustrated. All he has to do is come right out and tell me what he wants and then we start dealing. Why are men so difficult?"

This time T. laughed out loud. "Is that a general question? And did you mean this visitor or another male in your life?"

Vivi chose to ignore the jibe. She had been thinking too much about Jazz the last day and maybe that was why she had been so careless. A man was following her around, breaking into and entering her apartment at will. If she hadn't been so preoccupied with a certain Cajun, she might have noticed something.

"If he knew me at all, he'd know that I won't appreciate his little visit."

"I'm sure he knows that. He wants to demonstrate what he can do, that's all."

"He hasn't done it before. So why now?" Vivi sat down on the love seat across from T.

T. arched an eyebrow. "Exactly."

Vivi's eyes widened with realization. "You mean, he was doing it for you?" At T.'s smile, she sank back against the soft cushion. "Why?"

"He told you he's been watching you. It's fairly obvious that he knows you've been looking for Sia-Sia and also about your role with Interpol. All along, he hasn't lifted a finger to help you when he could have shown you these items—"

"Until you showed up at my apartment," Vivi interrupted. "And then he gave me the first package and told me—"

"—that he wanted his freedom," T. finished. She lifted her arms and stretched lazily. "I'm sorry, darling. This man is interested in me, not you. You're just a means."

"Well, now I'm doubly pissed. He's known all this time about Sia-Sia and didn't think it important until it suited him. Why should I help him? Bastard." She could have had this information earlier. She could have found out about her friend by now. "He can just stick his mask up his rear end. I can find Sia-Sia on my own and he can just find another way to get what he wants."

"Ah, it's too late. He's gotten my interest to help him."

Vivi frowned. "Why? You're supposed to be on my side. Let him rot."

T. stood up, tying the silk sash of her thin wrap. "He knows too much, and it's my job to probe him. A man who wants his freedom. How intriguing, hmm?" She walked toward the bedroom. "You only have time to initiate the meeting, so get going. After that you have to take care of the SEALs." She swung around at the bedroom door and eyed her mischievously. "Unless *you* want to take care of the masked man and let *me* take care of those sexy men up by the river? I must say that would be more fun, especially when Jazz sees me—"

"Not a chance. You're staying here with your glorious red tresses all clean and shiny and in your best bikini by the poolside so you catch the eye of a certain arms dealer, so don't even play your mind games with me." Vivi sighed. "Why do I feel as if time is pressing down on me?"

"Things are moving fast, darling. So far, everything seems to be running on time. The admiral's boys are ready. Our boys are ready. My concern is—are you?"

Vivi frowned. "What do you mean? Of course I'm ready. We're heading out first thing in the morning."

"Why not now?" T. cocked her head. "Why are you still in town, Viv? You did take a few days off your volunteer work, didn't you?"

Vivi sighed again. Nothing escaped T.'s eagle eye. "They need my help."

"That isn't your job," T. said softly.

"I . . . know that." She was reluctant to tell T. the real reason.

"Tell me what Juliana Kohl wanted you to do."

Vivi explained briefly as T. walked into her bedroom suite. She knew her chief would be able to deduce from the information why she had been so busy.

"So you have spent the whole day looking for spaces for these girls that Julie K. wants you to cross off that list," T. said, her voice muffled. "While this is happening, you're staying in touch with Satellite so you can update the SEALs. Not to mention the fact that your mind is on the masked intruder and his little game. What else?"

Vivi bit her lip. She certainly wasn't going to mention that she couldn't get hold of Rose and that she was getting concerned, that she planned to go down to see why she hadn't been answering the phone or returning her calls. A part of her was getting that sickening worried feeling that Rose's father had sent her out to the local bar again. Each time Rose had managed to contact Vivi soon enough that she could set up a raid, but each incident reinforced the fact that Rose's situation was getting more and more precarious.

"Your silence is very telling." T. emerged from the bedroom, dressed in a black cat suit. She carried a light raincoat over one arm. "Tell me the rest of it."

There was really nothing to tell. Vivi knew she was Rose's only hope. End of story. She had to make one quick visit, just to make sure the girl was okay. Then she would go off and—The cell phone's ring interrupted her thoughts. T. picked it. It was the usual time for satellite to call in for the latest update, but her chief's serious expression didn't bode well. Her questions were also out of the ordinary.

"What is it?" Vivi asked when the caller rang off.

"Slight adjustment in plans, darling," T. said. "You need to go to the boys up there ASAP. Call for a satellite meeting."

Jazz peeled off his muddy wet suit. He could see the shadowy outlines of his men as they changed from the protective gear into something dry. The wet suit was a great insulator against hypothermia and mosquitoes but they still had a long wait ahead of them, and a dry wet suit wasn't the most comfortable thing to have on in this heat.

They had spent the last hour doing what they did best, being frogs. In the dark water, they had pulled a haversack loaded with water-resistant explosives to be installed at the target points of the old bridge. They had used a dual-priming technique to ensure that all charges would detonate at the same time.

In the humid gloom of the night, Jazz signaled for his men to take up their positions. One was to keep watch while the others rested. They wanted to be at optimum alert when the time drew closer for the target's arrival. They had done this together dozens of times before; each of them knew how much energy to conserve and how to be alert and relaxed at the same time.

Jazz listened to the night insects chirping loudly around them. They had just applied a thick layer of insect repellent, but even so, now and then some bug would crawl across his face. He was used to it—the waiting, the smells, the soaking wet clothes if it rained.

Once everything was secure for the night, they signaled each other with a small pin light. Nothing to do but wait for morning.

Jazz looked up at the sky. There were a million stars blinking back, like fireflies in a dark bayou. When he was a kid out on a night hunting trip with Grandpa Gator, he would lie in exactly this position, listening to the bullfrogs and the splish-splash of the river current hitting the side of the boat. If he leaned over and looked into the water, now and then he would be able to see the red eyes belonging to the gators staring back at him. During mating season, he would shine a flashlight and he would see some wild stuff out in the deep bayou.

Who knew then that he would be lying in the same position twenty years later, looking into dark waters for wild things? It was strange how life repeated itself in different rhythms. In twenty years, he would probably be an old bayou grandpa looking out into the river and telling stories about wrestling gators. Just like his grandpa did.

Jazz smiled at the thought. He wasn't exactly grandpa material yet. First he had to get himself some woman who would want to be grandma to his grandpa. Vivi came immediately to mind, and his smile turned wry. Funny how her image appeared so easily. He had never thought of a woman growing old with him before.

He was beginning to more than like Vivi. She was a special woman, with strong passions and fierce beliefs. Yet he knew she had an inner layer that was tough as the gator hides he used to help his grandpa dry out. She was obstinate and had kept everyone at arm's length for so long, she didn't know how to share herself. Yet there was something fragile about her that made him want to hold her close and tell her he would be there for her.

He wanted to laugh out loud. Somehow he didn't think Vivi would appreciate being compared to an alligator. But every bayou boy knew how to calm an gator long enough to capture it. One just flipped it over on its back and stroked its belly. His smile widened into a grin at the thought of flipping—

"Jazz, Code Red Alert." Hawk's voice was low and urgent over the open mike.

Jazz sat up, all thoughts focused back to the here and now. "Go ahead, over."

"We have a change in plan. Hang on while I connect with Satellite. You're going to want to hear what they caught sight of from the sky eye."

Jazz radioed Joker, ordering him to continue his position

while he waited for the link with Satellite. "I won't be relieving you yet. There's new four-one-one coming."

"No problem, sir. I'm wide awake," Joker told him.

Minutes later, the patch was through. "What's new, satellite?" Jazz asked.

He imagined the targets experiencing vehicular problems from the mud and rains. Any mission like this was bound to have glitches.

"Bad news, boys," Vivi's voice came over the radio. "Satellite has picked up more than three trucks in the convoy."

15

Special operations was filled with missions on-the-fly. Shit happened and usually at the last minute. Very little could surprise Jazz or his men, not even the announcement of possibly two dozen more hostiles heading their way. Heavily armed hostiles, at that.

Jazz and his squad had to swim back to the lookout point to join Hawk's team. Vivi had sent footage of the satellite feed detailing the two trucks that had joined Dilaver's convoy at the border and they had agreed that they needed a new strategy.

He looked around him. The team had gone through quick plan changes before and their faces reflected their attitude—calm, ready, alert. They had taken the news of a bigger battle ahead—fifty heads to their eight—without a single word.

"Are we waiting for Miss Verreau before the pow-wow?" Cucumber asked the obvious question. The men hadn't heard the tail-end of the conversation between Hawk, Jazz, and Vivi. "This being a joint mission and all."

"She's heading here with reinforcements."

"We don't need a bunch of hooligans to join us, man."

"We can handle the extras, sir."

The team took pride in winning their own battles. Jazz

understood the innate pride of his men when faced with new challenges.

"I know we can but this is a joint mission. They depend on us to do one part of the job while they accomplish theirs," Hawk said. A laptop and a small whiteboard had been set up on the mini table so everyone could gather around. "You all know Miss Verreau is in charge of making sure one vehicle is safely taken out of the area. With these new additional vehicles, her job has just become riskier. Check out the latest Sigint from Satellite."

Everyone paid attention to the small screen as Hawk clicked the footage to start. The tape was sped up for quick reference. Sigint, or signal intelligence, indicated that Dilaver's original three vehicles were stopping for fuel. It was amazing how clear the targets looked, down to the wads of cash Dilaver was seen handing over to bribe the border guards. A sobbing and obviously very young girl was pushed into a small booth, followed by the two men.

"Slime. I'm going to look for him in my crosshairs." Zone was the team sniper. Bad-tempered and rowdy, he was the total antithesis of the cool and collected sniper persona that men of his skill portrayed.

"He's going to be the ex-slime who ate my hot lead," Cucumber promised.

Jazz didn't say anything. His grip on his weapon tightened. He didn't like seeing women being hurt. He wondered what Vivi had been thinking when she had witnessed that part of the tape.

"This isn't the ultimate take-down, men," Hawk said quietly. "We're playing a crucial role for GEM. Our initial mission has been a simple one. Team One across the river and Team Two here. When the bridge goes down, cutting the convoy in half, Team One was to eliminate anyone trying to take the trailer with the women. Team Two was to create enough smokescreen to cause Dilaver to escape. The idea was to make sure he thinks he's being ambushed for the women.

"Now we have double the targets. The extra two vehicles also have a trailer, and it's filled with weapons of some kind. We have no idea what they are but we know it's going to the Triads. So Dilaver now has more firepower than we do, as well as men. Jazz?"

Jazz laid down his weapon and leaned over to change the screen back to show the bridge. "The tactical points haven't changed. We're still going to take this baby down. The timing, however, has to be adjusted. Five vehicles. We need to figure out how fast they are moving and which ones would be left on one side of the bank. The ideal picture is Dilaver's convoy and probably one more vehicle, as well as the two trailers with the weapons and the girls. The others should be over on this side of the bridge so Dilaver is effectively cut off. He might have ample firepower but his men would be trapped on this side."

"Where will we be?" Dirk asked.

"Over here. Teams One and Two will both be here on this side," Hawk replied.

"Who's going to be on the other side with Dilaver then? I know we have to let him escape but what about the women?" Cucumber asked.

"There is a slight disagreement on that point with Miss Verreau," Jazz said, hoping none of his earlier irritation showed in his voice or expression.

"Miss Verreau wants her team on the other side alone while we deal with the bigger trouble here," Hawk asserted.

"That makes sense," Turner said. "We'll take out the muscle. Miss Verreau and her team will get the girls."

"Didn't you hear the part about the new trailer, fool?" Cucumber chimed in. "I bet the disagreement has to do with that. Is she after that, too?"

Jazz shook her head. "No, she wants Dilaver to take off with the weapons."

"That means Dilaver has free rein with whatever it is he has in his trailer," Hawk said.

"And there is a possibility that he might have explosives," Jazz continued.

"And use it on Miss Verreau and her team," Cucumber guessed, his eyes squinting in thoughtful contemplation of the scenario playing in their minds. "Not ideal. What if Miss Verreau and her team fail and then Dilaver takes them hostage?"

"Or cancels her team," Turner noted. He didn't need to add that it would mean Vivi's life would be in danger, too. "No way we can allow that. It would mean the loss of the girls too. Then what good is our taking out a bunch of Dilaver's men over here? The bridge would be gone and it'd be impossible to go across in time to help."

"So what's the alternative?" Dirk asked. "Are we going to wait for Miss Verreau's team before we decide?"

Hawk shook his head. "We come up with the alternatives and we give it to her. We know what we want to do, anyway."

"Yeah, fight like hell," Cucumber growled.

"Hooyah," agreed several of Jazz's team mates.

Jazz hadn't added anything, preferring to hear the others' opinions first. They all appeared to agree on one thing. Leaving Vivi and her team on one side wasn't a good option. If anything went wrong, none of them would be able to lend her a hand. Besides, just thinking of her over there without him . . . he didn't think he could bear it.

His blood had grown cold when she had suggested that during their earlier discussion. Had she any idea how big a battle this could be, with the extra firepower involved? The thought that she was going to be in the middle of it all, trying to wrestle a trailer of women away from armed thugs . . . oh hell, no way. Charlie's Angels, his ass. He didn't care what Hawk said about these women's skills. Her team would just have to deal with some SEALs in the mix.

"I'm going over the other side," Jazz announced quietly. He looked at Hawk. "I can take one of you with me or go alone. I want to set up extra charges to make sure Miss Verreau gets an open road with the trailer. And with extra charges, Dilaver might decide to take off quicker."

"You'll have to make sure our charges don't get the girls' trailer as well. That was Miss Verreau's concern, that a big blast from either us or Dilaver might affect her taking that particular truck out of there."

Jazz nodded in agreement. Of course Vivi hadn't heard this part of the plan yet. He gave Hawk another direct gaze. Maybe she didn't need to hear it. He had a feeling she would disagree. Hell, of course she would disagree. She had been keeping her little operation quiet from the team since day one because she knew none of them would be happy that she was doing the most dangerous part of the mission. Let's face it. The SEALs were just going to shoot and kill. Vivi Verreau had to go into the middle of the firefight and somehow secure a trailer full of hysterical women. All this while Dilaver might be using heaven-knows-what from his cache.

Jazz wasn't going to let his vision of being a grandpa go up in smoke. Vivi Verreau just had to get used to the idea of becoming a grandma with him.

Vivi stood in the back alley of the old warehouse. It was one of those places with lots of ledges and lofts, perfect for moving heavy objects up and down the side of the building. Also perfect for cat burglars. She stared into the darkness. She felt very calm, very ready.

"I followed the instructions in your package," she announced in a bored voice. "You have ten seconds. I don't have time."

"I'm here."

Again, the stranger took her by surprise by his sudden appearance. She had been very sure there was nobody standing where he was when she had looked. Yet there he was now, clad in solid black, his face masked by the black hood. He must be a magician or something. He took a few silent steps forward.

"You've gotten younger, Grandma," he mocked, speaking the local dialect.

"Like I said, I'm in a hurry," Vivi replied in English. He didn't back away as she walked slowly toward him. "It's time you start talking instead of showing off. What do you have on Sia-Sia?"

"I believe your question should be 'What do I have to do for you to get more information about Sia-Sia?'"

Vivi stopped a few feet away. He would know soon enough that she wasn't here to debate. "If you know me at all, you'll know that I don't negotiate that way. Give me what you have and maybe I'll help you."

His laugh was soft, amused. "Your team has a strange way of negotiating, then. I have what you want and not the other way round. I have been very polite so far, giving you the chance to check up on the first package, and not bothering you until you're sure that you really want what I have. Won't you return the courtesy?"

"Courtesy? For home invaders?" Vivi smiled. And attacked.

He blocked her easily and dodged another blow. His head moved left to avoid her right fist but she anticipated his agility and slammed a left kick to his knee. He grunted.

"It isn't polite to be faceless in front of a woman," she said, raising her voice as she continued her attack. He was fast, dodging another kick. She stepped on his foot hard. "It isn't polite to steal into my bedroom and touch my nightie." This time he attacked back and she released his foot and jumped out of his longer reach. She countered his move with a side twist, at the same time jamming an elbow against his solar plexus. Grunting harshly, he reeled back, stunned by the blow. "It isn't polite to fight back when I'm not even hurting you yet. And it definitely isn't polite to think you can use me."

She leaped back several feet, giving him breathing room. She had made her point. For now. "You want me to help you, you'd better start talking straight, mister. If you come onto my property without permission again and leave little knickknacks behind, I'm not going to promise to be nice anymore."

He was silent as he clutched his solar plexus. He was breathing very hard, as if the whole thing surprised him more than it had hurt him. Usually, an elbow in that region would down a man pretty quickly but he didn't seem to be in great pain.

"Perhaps I should wait for another time, when your temper has cooled," he said, after a few moments.

Vivi smiled at the huskiness of his voice. Yeah, he was hurting just a little. He lifted one hand, and she recognized the move from before. "Oh no," she said as she lunged forward. "You aren't going to run off and play hide-and-seek with me again."

He was a few seconds faster as he launched into the air. "I don't fight with women," he said, as the line pulled him several feet above her. "You won't see me again till I'm ready."

Vivi watched as he zipped up toward the balcony. She leaned against the wall, head cocked. Counted to three.

Since Vivi was expecting it, she caught the dark silhouette jumping out from the top of the building just above the masked man. It was silent ballet at its best. The man looked up in his mid-flight through the air, too late to stop the new intruder slamming into him.

That woman, Vivi mused as she watched her chief wrap both of her long legs around the man, was totally fearless. She had to be, to jump off at that height and expect to catch her target rocketing upward at the same time. As the two of them swung from the impact, she saw the glint of metal as it caught some light reflected from the windowpanes. Then the two bodies tumbled onto the balcony nearby. Several seconds of scuffling. Silence.

"That sounds painful," she called up. "Do you need any help?"

T. leaned over. "Nope. You get going to your next little adventure, darling. Mr. Masked Man will be sleeping this off for a while. He isn't going to be happy when he wakes up and finds out he's been set up."

Jazz and Cucumber unzipped their waterproof haversacks. Vivi hadn't called back yet and Hawk had decided they couldn't wait any longer. Jazz needed the time to set up shop and Cucumber wanted upfront action. He hoped Vivi would call soon.

He wiped his hands dry so he could better handle the second set of explosives. C-4 looked, felt, and acted like putty. Earlier, he had made a ribbonlike device out of it to wrap around the steel girder of the bridge. Now he was going to shape the stuff differently to create craters at strategic points of the dirt road.

He pulled the white material from its box, giving it to Cucumber. Then he took out the TNT and set it on the ground. From his sack, Cucumber pulled out the Primacord, which would connect the fuses, and handed it to him. Their plan was to make a set of little charges go off at the same time about fifteen meters in front of the bridge as well as prime the ditches alongside the kill zone.

Jazz took the block of TNT and started to carefully adjust the blasting cap to the threaded receptacle on the ends while Cucumber used a tiny flashlight. This was the trickiest part since the blasting cap could go off if handled carelessly.

"Fuse," he said softly. Cucumber handed him a section of the coil. He cut six inches off the end and discarded it. Quickly, he cut a section about six feet long. Then he lit it and timed the delay to make sure it was proper.

Timing was very important. It usually took about four minutes before the small flash of fire at the end of the fuse. That meant forty seconds per foot of fuse. He cut a healthy length, enough for a five- or six-minute delay. He repeated the procedure, making sure Cucumber's was the same length so both blasts would go off simultaneously.

"Blasting cap." Taking one end of the det cord, he gently slipped it as well as an end of the primer fuse through to connect the ignition charge of the blasting cap before inserting it into the TNT block. He reached for the crimpers in his pouch. Cucumber and he worked quickly and silently as they prepared the needed number of blocks, and when they were finished, they gave each other the thumbs-up.

Jazz wiped the sweat from his brow with the back of his hand. Adjusting his mike, he said quietly, "We're ready, over."

"What's the delay time before detonation, over?" Hawk asked from the lookout point.

"Five minutes." He would light the fuse only when Hawk gave the signal. "Has she called yet?"

"Negative, over."

He needed to talk to her. Where the hell was she? He had the whole thing orchestrated and he needed everyone to be exactly where he wanted them so they could "play off the same sheet of music," as covert operatives would say.

"We have hours yet. Quit worrying," Hawk continued.

"You're pretty confident about someone you never worked with and a team you never saw, bud." It was totally unlike Hawk.

"The admiral assured me she has run teams before and I'll take the big man's word. And being that she has run teams, she would know to communicate her plans to me. It's a tough call. I know it, you know it. She knows it."

Jazz understood the meaning behind Hawk's words. It was because she was a female. There had never been a woman in the teams. Neither he nor his teammates had ever worked with one during a battle before. As coleader, he had to express any discomfort by his team, even if it was against the woman in whom he was interested. And he knew his guys were concerned, more so than Hawk's men. The latter had, as Hawk had pointed out earlier, seen another GEM operative in action a couple of months ago.

"Jazz, I've already said the same things you're thinking of. You can tell your guys over the mike what Mad Dog said to me."

"What's that?" Jazz knew his men would accept Admiral Madison's instructions unconditionally. Each of them had been hand-picked by the admiral to be in the STAR Force black operations SEAL teams. Every one of them would lay their lives down for their hero and role model.

"When he had told me that a woman was going to be in joint mission with us *and* running a team, I said, 'I'll believe that when I see it.'"

"That sounds like you," Jazz agreed. "And?"

"And Mad Dog said, 'You'll see it when you believe it.'" There was total silence before Hawk continued, "Well, shit, that was exactly how I reacted."

"What were you hoping for—some snide remark?" Jazz countered wryly.

"To the admiral? Nope. I just said, 'Yes, sir,' but hey, now that I've met our Vivi, I think she can handle it."

"You think? And what do you mean *our* Vivi?"

Hawk chuckled. "You're so fucking easy, you know that?"

"Boys, do you know all your channels are pretty much accessible to Satellite's controls?" Vivi's voice suddenly popped up. "Please click on channel three so we can have a private conversation, hmm?"

Ah shit. Jazz scratched his stubble. He clicked on the secured channel. "How long were you there listening in, Satellite?"

"Long enough, Lieutenant," she said noncommittally. "Let's do a quick run through of what your team is planning to do, shall we?"

"Where are you now?" Jazz asked.

"On the way, of course. Not soon enough to sit around and catch up. It's best we conference while I'm traveling towards you." She didn't interrupt as Hawk laid out what they had planned. Jazz noted that his present location had been omitted by his friend. When Hawk finished, Vivi continued, "We're in luck. From satellite reviews, we can see that Dilaver is in the third truck with the weapons trailer and the one with the girls is the fourth. He hasn't changed trucks more than twice and when he did, he prefers those two trucks, protected from any attack that way. So if things stay the course, the first two convoys are all yours."

"How many on your team, Vivi?" Jazz asked. He wanted to know how many would be on that one side of the river.

"My men are the ones you saw in the compound."

"That's about a dozen," Hawk asserted.

A dozen. With his set charges and the surprise element, her dozen might be able to take out twenty, maybe thirty men. But there was still the trailer with the women. "How are you going to secure the women?" Jazz asked.

There was a very slight pause. "I can't risk Dilaver or any of his men to take off with the girls, so my main concern will be their safety. You won't detonate the bridge until I signal Hawk and Hawk signals you."

"What are you planning to do?"

"You need a certain amount of distance between the first group of vehicles and the second. The longer the better so you can bring that bridge down and not have the girls' trailer too close to the explosives, right?"

"Yes," Jazz said.

"My team will make sure there is enough of a distance."

"Are you initiating the first attack?"

"Just look for my signal as the convoy appears. This mike is coming in clear, isn't it?"

"Vivi, don't change the subject." Jazz wished he could say more but Hawk was listening and he didn't want to make it too personal. "I need to know how far away your team is going to be in the kill zone."

"We'll be right smack in the middle of it, Jazz. There's no other way."

He had a few choice words to say about that plan. "Stay out of the ditches," he advised instead. "They're rigged."

"Anywhere else?" She was cool and businesslike whereas he was sweating bullets at the thought of her out there. She was driving him nuts and she didn't even know it. "Give me the coordinates. I'll make sure my men know this."

Jazz had no choice. He did so curtly and still left out the part about his current location. If she needed backup, he would be there. That was all there was to it.

"Ten-four. Got it all. Thank you, Lieutenants. Hawk?"

"Yes, ma'am?"

"It's a matter of faith. If you wait till you see before you believe, then there is no faith."

"Ah. NOPAIN shit from the admiral. I should have known."

Jazz didn't understand what the hell they were talking about. But before he could ask, Vivi said his name softly. His whole body responded to that one word.

"Jazz?"

"Yes?" he said. She had called him by his name. Did she know that?

"Be careful out there." She had lowered her voice.

"Yeah." He wanted to say so much more. "You, too."

She clicked off so quickly, he wasn't sure she heard him.

Jazz wanted to slam his fist on something hard to vent his frustration. He waited for a moment before asking, "What's NOPAIN, Hawk?"

"NOPAIN is what she did with that last sentence. She made you think of something else, didn't she? It's a GEM thing and I ain't talking anymore with her listening in. Hell, next she'll ask whether Cumber's finished jerking off. Will reconnect in zero-five hundred hours."

"Yeah." Jazz leaned back, a smile forming in the dark. She had called him by his name. That meant she did care. If that was NOPAIN or whatever, then she had succeeded.

Tomorrow they were going to face a small army. It wasn't going to be the cake walk they had originally planned. But as they like to say at BUD/S: The only easy day was yesterday.

CHAPTER
16

The distant low rumble of vehicles was heard first.
Jazz raised his head.

"Target sighted."

"All operatives acknowledge positions."

"Aye, aye, sir!"

"Here, sir!"

"Five vehicles, distance apart thirty meters, maybe forty. Jazz?"

"I'm ready. Distance between first group and second group of targets?" That was the key element to the first part of their operation.

"Stand by for confirmation. Unclear for now. Stand by."

"Confirm stand by."

"Men, we don't need to be selective if Dilaver remains on the other side of the bridge. All targets are expendable on our side."

"Aye, aye, sir!"

"Give or take, fifteen minutes. Lock and load."

Jazz didn't need to be there to know what Hawk and the other members of his team were doing. They were in the trees, the bushes, behind a log, bellying the ground. They had their weapons on, in front of, and beside them. Their eyes were focused ahead on the curiously silent bridge while their ears were alert for the patrol leader's signal. Six SEALs carried a *lot* of firepower, and he had every confidence that they could take care of two or three dozen hostiles on their side of the river.

On this side of the bridge, they had watched Vivi's men arriving the night before and had made note of where they were situated. He didn't want to think about Vivi out there, too.

He signaled to Cucumber, the big operator who had chosen to cross over here with him. They had the big task of timing. Timing was everything. One second too early and the targets might get warned; one too late and the wrong people might be targeted.

Cucumber gave the thumbs-up and started to belly-crawl up the muddy banks, slithering like one big snake that just happened to have a massive weapon. Jazz moved to his position, ready for the signal to blast the bridge down. They had chosen a higher place to hide out so they could see where the targets scattered at the first explosion. Easier to pick them off.

"Oh hell."

"What is it, Joker?"

"Nine o'clock, over the bridge. What the fuck is that?" It took a lot to surprise Joker. Jazz turned in that direction.

"Do you see what I see?"

"Jazz? Confirm sighting. Nine o'clock, about one hundred meters—"

"I see her, Hawk." He squinted his eyes. Her hair color was darker, but he would recognize that walk anywhere. "She's not alone."

"I believe that's the cavalry for your side, Team One."

"Yeah, but what the fuck is she doing strolling her way toward us?" Cucumber chimed in from his end. "With goats."

There were several repetitions to confirm that last observation.

"Goats?"

"With what?"

"I see goats. Lots of goats."

"Oh hell. That's the cavalry?"

"Lock and load, men," Hawk repeated quietly.

Jazz clicked on channel three. "What's she up to, Hawk? Over."

"We continue as planned. I'm waiting for her comm signal. She'll notify me when it's time. Wait for my signal, over."

"She's going to walk into the kill zone with goats." He was going to kill her, if she survived.

"Got to admit it's a good distraction, buddy. Her team is out there somewhere." There was a pause. "I'm checking with the viewfinder. At her speed, she will make it here just in time for the convoy's arrival. Our girl has good timing."

Jazz ignored the admiration in his friend's voice. "Our girl won't have a neck left when I'm done with her. She didn't say goats last night."

"You didn't say where you were last night either. Are you ready, Jazz?"

His mind was on a woman walking into a trap he had set up. Of course he was ready. He had a job to do and he had better get it done right. He smacked at the channel buttons.

"Cumber! Lock and load."

"Waiting for signal for my side of the ditch, sir. By the way, tell Vivi, nice outfit."

Jazz snuck a glance with his scope. The woman was . . . he shook his head. She was close enough to be seen by anyone within firing range, she and her damn goats, moving up from the banks of the river as if they were coming back from their usual watering hole. And her bright flowery top stuck to her body as if she had just taken a bath—like all the local women in the countryside tended to do—right in the river.

"First target vehicle rounding the bend."

"Second target vehicle sighted."

The "girl" and her goats moved up the dirt road, seemingly oblivious to the danger ahead, busy with her stick and her dogs, herding the noisy animals. The first vehicle slowed and passed her. She didn't pay any attention, yelling at the animals to move out of the way.

"First target moving toward bridge, over. I can see the driver on his cell or walkie-talkie," Hawk informed over the mike. "He might be saying something about our girl because I can see the hostile on the passenger side glancing back."

Dust kicked up from the first vehicle obscured Vivi for a moment and Jazz's hand tightened around the scope as he watched her cough. The second vehicle passed by, swerving awfully close to her as she tried to keep control of her herd. She looked up, as if suddenly realizing that there was yet another truck heading her way and that she wouldn't be able to dodge dust and keep her animals safe for too long.

"First vehicle on bridge. Second vehicle moving toward bridge. Definitely talking about our girl and her goats. Stand by for signal, Team Two."

"Standing and Ready," Jazz said, giving the STAR Force motto. Everything and everyone seemed to be holding its collective breath, just waiting for that one moment in time when hell let loose. Vivi's colorful blouse stood out against the dirty browns around her and he knew that all eyes—the men in the trucks and those hidden—were on her, as she had planned.

"Third vehicle sighted. Second vehicle still heading toward bridge. I can see the targets looking out of the trucks, sir."

"Wait for diversion. Stand by for signal, repeat, stand by."

The third vehicle closed in on the girl. By now the goats were wandering out into its way and she threw her stick at the oncoming truck in frustration, putting up her hand in the universal gesture for it to halt. The stick landed right on the hood and bounced against the windshield. When the truck didn't stop, she defiantly stood in its path, hands on her hip, glaring at the truck.

"Jaysus!"

Jazz ignored the mutters coming through his helmet intercom as he held his breath. If Dilaver didn't stop . . . for the first time in his career, he was considering leaving his post here and instead picking up his weapon and aiming . . .

"Target two right at bridge. Stand by for signal, Team Two."

"Standing and Ready," Jazz's reply was automatic, spoken through gritted teeth, even though he was still staring at the oncoming third vehicle. His thoughts whizzed in his head with the speed of a fastball. Everything else, however, was freeze-framed. The sound of the vehicles rumbling on the planks and steel of the old bridge. The stupid goats milling all over the dusty pathway. The huge truck and the tiny woman. It was mere seconds, done in slow motion.

Jazz's breath hissed out in relief as the vehicle grounded to a halt in front of Vivi, barely missing one of her goats. She screamed in panic, running after the bleating animal, tripping over in her haste. The truck door opened and some-one who looked like Dilaver stepped out. The driver also did the same. The weapons in their hands finally clued the "girl" to the fact that she was in danger and she started to back away.

Jazz had killed people before. In the dark, on the run, or in an ambush, like this one. It wasn't something he was espe-cially proud of, nor had he ever made it personal. Most of the time he compartmentalized—he switched off emotions so he could just focus on getting his job done.

He had never felt as he did at that moment and he would never forget it as long as he lived. Watching Dilaver and his men manhandling a woman as she finally realized they weren't stopping for her and her goats to cross safely, then watching *Vivi* helpless in their hands, being dragged and slammed against the side of the truck, the rage that burst from his gut almost blinded him. He wanted to go after Dilaver with his bare hands right there and then and rip him limb from limb.

Every cell in him was screaming. He could feel the rage reaching boiling point as he watched the big thug run his hand over Vivi's blouse, touching her intimately. Even from here, he could see the dark tanned hand against her bared flesh.

It was startling to hear her calm voice through the intercom as he witnessed the whole scenario. She was over there, acting up a distracting storm, and her disembodied voice in his head was composed as could be. "Activate the fuse."

"That's it. Activate, Team Two."

It was training that moved his limbs because Jazz couldn't have walked away from the sight of Dilaver manhandling Vivi. Looking down, he noticed his hands had curled into tight fists and he had to mentally relax them. He turned away to execute his mission. Vivi had succeeded in delaying the third vehicle for him to do *his* job.

The first set of charges was linked together closely. Like rolling thunder the bridge roared to life, collapsing inward from one end to the other. Another roar sliced the air, this time followed by the frenzied sounds of battle reverberating from both sides of the river as all the hidden men started the ambush.

Jazz turned his attention back to his side, signaling to Cucumber. The big guy clambered quickly over the bank. Their next target was the ditches.

Mass confusion in the kill zone. There were suddenly men everywhere. Dilaver and his men were on their bellies, their faces mirroring their shock as they shouted at each other. The air vibrated from all the firepower. Vivi's team was shooting, moving in from their hiding places. Dilaver's men were firing back. And too many damn bleating goats were in everyone's way. Vivi was nowhere to be seen.

The fourth vehicle and its trailer stopped in its tracks and Dilaver's men jumped out to help their boss. Some of the first surviving hostiles dove into the nearby ditches for cover. Jazz twisted the handle of the blasting machine, signaling to Cucumber. Soon, the det cords they had laid the night before exploded in sequence. Screams of pain. Men scrambling in different directions. Vivi's men picked them off.

Jazz watched the far-off figure of Dilaver running back toward his truck. He had a few men with him, dragging weapons and carrying a few wounded away from the kill zone. At almost the same time, the fifth vehicle sped into view, its occupants firing at their attackers. That one didn't have any trailers hitched to it. The hidden explosives he had wired earlier went off not too far in front of the vehicle and it careened wildly as it swerved to avoid the craters. He ducked as some wildly aimed bullets hit close by and then started heading down to the smoking and dusty kill zone. Something bright and flashy caught his eye. Vivi's blouse.

Vivi screamed and struggled, as any young country girl would, when she realized the newcomers were Caucasian men carrying weapons. Dilaver was strong, much stronger than she had anticipated, as she allowed him to overpower her.

"What is she saying?" he asked the driver in a Slavic dialect, amusement and irritation etched in his voice. "Look at all these damn goats."

The driver was obviously the interpreter so Dilaver could communicate with the Triads. "She just called you a 'devil.' That's what they call white folks around here."

Vivi kicked Dilaver in the shin to make another universal point, screaming in a panic.

"Ow, the young thing's got sharp toes," Dilaver said and some of his men hanging out of the side of the truck laughed as he held her closer and ran his hand over the front of her blouse. "Not too young. Devil, huh? Ow! Damn girl's got sharp teeth too!"

He slammed Vivi hard against the side of the truck. She gasped out in pain. "Ha, I bet you fucking understand this. And this." He crudely groped her. "I think I'm going to keep you for a while." He dodged as Vivi tried to claw at his eyes. "What is she screeching about now? Tell her I'm going to take care of this nice blouse for her."

He tore the front of it and Vivi kicked at him again. It wasn't easy pretending to be afraid when all she really wanted to do was show the brute how she could dismember him with one blow. The slam against the truck had taken the breath out of her and ridiculous as it was, the pain helped her to remember to hang on to her cool. Just one more minute, she told herself, one more minute. She went for an ineffective attempt to escape those horrible hands as the men around her leered and laughed.

"She sure knows a lot of big bad words for a little girl, boss," the translator told Dilaver with a laugh. *"Binchy-san buku diep. Kontet kolong-doh."*

Vivi turned to the other man and spat in his direction, struggling to go after him. Dilaver laughed at her stream of invectives. "What did you say to her? Look at the spitfire! Man, she's going to be something in bed."

"I told her she's a pretty lady and that we want to put our pricks in her pretty pussy." The men roared. Minute almost up. Time to plant the seed of suspicion. Vivi's sharp warning had the interpreter chuckling. "She said, 'Fuck you and she hopes the Triads kick your ass for going into their territory.' I guess we have reached the right place, boss."

Dilaver laughed and reached for the rest of Vivi's clothes. "Let's get you out of this thing and see whether you can really fuck m—" His hold loosened as the earth shook with the first explosion. "What the hell—"

Vivi didn't wait as she tore away from Dilaver, leaving most of her blouse in his hands as she slipped under the truck. Shots erupted. The ground trembled from explosions and weapon fire. Game time.

Where the hell was she? Jazz darted from shrub to bush to rock, moving at a steady rate into the midst of the firefight, his eyes sizing up the situation as quickly as possible. The bedlam of the initial surprise attack was slowing down into a deliberate duel between sides. Many of the enemy lay dead or wounded from the first blast and surprise attack. Vivi's men had taken out most of the men that were looking out of the truck. The few that had dived into the ditches had a big surprise from Cucumber's and his det cord. From what he could gather, most of the surviving hostiles were from the fourth and fifth trucks.

The rat-tat-tat of submachine guns sallied from different directions and he had to be careful not to be caught in the crossfire as he moved toward the truck with the trailer. Smells from gunfire mixed with smoke and dust permeated the air.

Where was she? He cast glances in different directions, worry gnawing at his guts. Vivi's team, for some reason, was dressed in black, making the men unbelievably easy to spot. What the hell was that all about? Two of them lay injured, howling and moaning, fifteen or so meters away from the third vehicle with the trailer. Even with the sounds of gunfire, he could hear the screams coming from inside. He hoped to God none of the girls was injured.

Vivi's blouse. It lay on the ground by where she was last seen. Dilaver had been all over her. The bastard couldn't have dragged her with him, could he?

Jazz squinted through the hazy air to look farther up the dusty trail. He could see figures running toward the last truck. He had a bad feeling about this.

He knew Cucumber had been following him as he had made his way closer and he signaled to him to move forward. The big SEAL appeared at his side in moments, a satisfied grin in his face.

"I forgot to say, 'Look out!' when they jumped into the ditch. Ooops." He indicated his side of the ditch where Jazz could clearly see the bloody effect of his handiwork.

"Cover me," Jazz said. "I'm heading down there to find Vivi. See that blouse?"

Cucumber glanced at where he pointed, registered the article of clothing on the ground, and his smile disappeared. He looked back at Jazz. "Go," he said grimly. "I got your six."

Jazz nodded. He checked his weapon and sped off toward

the kill zone. A lone wandering goat bleated as it zigzagged through the bushes.

Well, it was good she was still wearing a bra. She hadn't quite anticipated Dilaver throwing her over his shoulder as he headed down toward the other trailer. She had thought that as he realized he was being surrounded, he would drop everything and opt to escape. She had also assumed the first thing on his mind would be the weaponry in the other trailer. Not *her*. But the arms dealer seemed determined to have a woman even in the midst of an ambush.

Her mind on taking over the rapidly emptying truck, Vivi had been taken by surprise when he had gone after her. The cries of alarm coming from the trailer were heart-rending, and she had to ignore the urge to run back there to reassure the girls. But she needed to get them out of harm's way as quickly as possible. She had to crawl out from under the truck to get into the cab. Her focus was on the possibility of anyone still inside the truck. The butt of Dilaver's weapon had glanced off her head hard enough to make her see stars for several seconds, and before she realized what was happening, she was hanging upside down and seeing the object of her operation growing smaller and smaller as Dilaver ran off with a few of his men. He was in good shape, she vaguely noted, as she shook off the pain.

Of course, none of her men would dare to intervene. They had strict instructions to let Dilaver escape. They did, however, manage to pick off two of her captors. That left—she tried to count upside down as her head smacked against Dilaver's back—six. Maybe. She couldn't see very well with the blood rushing to her head and making her headache worse.

She had split seconds to decide her next course of action. Right now, Plan B had been, if she was killed, and thus failed to secure the girls' trailer, one of her commanders would take over the responsibility. But she was still alive. She strained her neck trying to see whether anyone was running toward the trailer. She hoped the two figures in black on the ground weren't dead. Please, let someone succeed at getting to the trailer before the girls were all shot.

"Get the truck with the weapons! We need the weapons!" She heard Dilaver shout to the few men rushing back toward the trucks. "We're going to get those bastards!"

She was shoved into the cab and Dilaver and two others squeezed in amid sounds of men scurrying into the back, shouting at one another. She peered over the dashboard. The last truck that had sped past them was blocking much of her view, locked in battle with some of her team. She could see dead or injured bodies hanging over the canvas railings. She grimly noted some of those on the ground wore black. Those were her men.

If Dilaver decided to stay and fight with his weapons, more of her men might fall. Not willing to sacrifice any more lives, she started to point and shout, then curled into a ball in panic.

"Shut her the fuck up."

"She's saying 'Triads,' boss. Those fuckers are Triad men. Seems like that put the fear of death into the villagers. Look at her."

Dilaver turned and raked her with his eyes. "Ask her how the fuck she knows. Hold the truck from going in after our guys."

"Yes, boss."

Covering her bosom with one hand, Vivi backed away as far as she could from Dilaver in fear; she gestured animatedly with the other hand. The interpreter grabbed her by the neck, demanding answers. She pointed again, using all the local euphemisms for the Triads.

"She's calling them, I think, second brother's enforcers. Sam Tai Yeh is the standard clan name for the Triads in this area. I believe we're in the second brother's territory."

"Of course we are, you fucking idiot. We're supposed to meet him! Why the hell are his men ambushing mine?"

Dilaver slammed his hand on the dashboard. "I thought we had a deal!"

"Maybe he wanted the weapons free, boss. Those damn slant-eyes are pirates at heart. They don't like doing business with foreigners, traditionally. They don't understand business our way."

"Money is fucking business-understandable!"

"Look up there, boss! One of them is driving our trailer away."

"I think they believe they have our weapons, boss."

"Let's go get the bastards, show them what we have here. Chase down our trailer. We aren't going to let them take it."

Dilaver drummed his fingers on the dashboard. "Start the truck," he ordered. "Those back there! Let's use the big stuff!"

Vivi had been silent as she listened to their exchange. Grimly, she watched the truck rolled forward. Dilaver might be another arms dealer in most spooks' books, but she knew better. He armed the KLA in Serbia and was known to have taken part in several very brutal battles. He knew how to conduct a thorough massacre. She wasn't going to let him expend his energy against her people. Later. Against the Triads. That she had no objection to.

"I'm heading up further out of the kill zone," Jazz informed the team through his helmet intercom. He hoped Hawk was picking up. "No time to coordinate. I think they have Vivi."

There was a pause. He imagined they were still busy over the other side of the river. Watching from his end, he could see Dilaver's men were determined fighters. He aimed his weapon and fired off a few rounds. Needed to go very quickly now.

Hawk's voice suddenly crackled through. "Cumber?"

"He'll take my six then go back when this is over to report. I'm going in pursuit, over. This is just for me, over." He had no intention of jeopardizing any of his teammates because of his whims.

"Don't kill Dilaver, Jazz."

"Sorry, can't hear ya, bad connection," Jazz said. He wasn't promising anything. Not if killing Dilaver meant getting Vivi back alive. He signaled to Cumber, who signaled back. He was going after those running off. Alone.

"You realize if you die out there, I'll have to tell your mother and sisters that you were drunk and drowned accidentally?" Hawk piped in again.

Not answering. Standard answer to all family members asking about dead relatives who were killed in covert military maneuvers. Accidental training death.

"So you son of a bitch better get back here alive. I'm too busy back here to get over there to save your ass."

Not answering.

"You sure?" Cucumber asked, pulling up alongside again.

"Yeah." He pointed to the final truck blocking his path. "That one has the most live fire. We need to take that down, although Vivi's team is doing a good job. They are taking down too many of her men trying to secure the truck with the trailer. Let's intervene."

"Affirmative."

"Go!"

They ran like hell, firing their weapons toward the truck. They hoped Vivi's team would know who they were and not shoot at them. It was a damn risky move but they did it anyway. Jazz was counting on Vivi's men recognizing them. It dawned on them that maybe that was why those men were watching and "playing" with them during the SEALs' morning training sessions. Had they been familiarizing themselves with his team? Jazz and Cumber jumped into the ditch.

Jazz ignored the dead men close by. Heart pounding, he worked two grenades out of his harness. Then he changed his mind and handed them to Cucumber instead. The other man took them from him, surprise on his face.

"You get the men when they scatter out," Jazz explained. "I'm heading in myself first, then flashbang them out with gas. You got your mask?"

"Yeah."

"Well, you're gonna need it." He pulled his from his back harness. Looking around, he tore off the front of the black uniform of an injured operative and draped it to the front of his. "Sorry, buddy, got to borrow this. Medic will come and take care of you soon, okay? Cumber, I'll take the truck and go after Dilaver with it. Hopefully, wearing this black T will make Vivi's men know I'm on their side and they won't decide to go after me in a mask."

"How are you going to get Vivi with that truck? They'll know you're behind them."

"No fucking clue."

"That's a great fucking idea." Cucumber pulled out his mask. "Go!"

"On the count of three!" They readied themselves. "One, two, three!"

"Look in the back and see what they pulled out from the trailer."

The man sitting closest to the window leaned out to look at the back of the truck. "They have grenades, some of the submachines, and the RPG."

Dilaver nodded, eyes trained on the trucks ahead. "Tell them to get the grenade launcher ready. No fucking way I'm going to allow them to take anything of mine so easily. Launch one at the trailer with the girls."

"Our truck there is in the way, boss."

"Fuck the truck. Drive close enough so we can pick up whoever is still around it and blow the truck out of our way. I want that trailer taken down. They aren't getting their hands on my girls."

Vivi sat there, stunned. The scumbag was willing to blow everyone to bits, including young girls, just to get back at his "enemy." A rocket propelled grenade launcher meant no survivors to any truck or tank it hit.

She came to a quick decision. To make sure her men had a fighting chance of getting the girls out of the area, she would have to expose herself. Take out the driver and Dilaver before the truck got too close. The probability of her surviving that was . . . She looked ahead, catching the tail end of the all-important trailer. If Dilaver reached his men in the truck ahead, there would be too many of them against her team trying to extract the girls, especially if they were going to use explosives. The RPG would kill all the girls and her men, too.

She couldn't allow for this operation to fail, not now, when so many lives were involved. Her shoes had been equipped with blades that were meant for emergencies. She moved her feet into position, her eyes on the scene ahead, watching the truck and the men getting bigger and bigger.

"Shit, boss, look at that guy gassing our men!"

Vivi frowned. She could see one of her men in a gas mask. She couldn't remember any of them with any. He had thrown something into the truck. A grenade? No. All the occupants were jumping out, holding their faces and throats. CS gas.

Dilaver's expression was grim as he noted how his men were slowly picked off as they escaped willy-nilly, blinded by the gas, uncaring about their safety as they sought to escape the burning sensation. A bunch of hardened killers brought to their knees, gasping and holding their throats. They were close enough that Vivi could see the bloody splatters appearing on their shirts as her men took the dozen or so thugs out. With a small shudder, she looked away for a moment. This was more than she was used to seeing.

"Stop."

The driver applied the brakes hard and Vivi pushed against the dashboard to stop from going into the windshield. That should teach her to look away again. She had to concentrate on what was happening. This wasn't the time to be grossed out. She returned her gaze to the sights ahead with dogged determination, trying to figure out what was happening.

"Turn around," Dilaver ordered. "Keep firing the weapons

so they can't come at us. We can't go in. They have gas and we don't have any masks. We'll just end up like the others. Back up."

"Yes, boss."

"We'll figure out a plan in the woods. Take out the map."

The truck shook and its tires squealed and rumbled as the driver obeyed Dilaver. A few bullets hit the truck, and Vivi could hear the screams from the injured men. A few who were hanging out fell off onto the ground. One body rolled down the front of the windshield and landed with a thud over the large hood, blood smearing the glass. Vivi remembered to scream. She pulled her foot away from the driver, changing her mind about stopping him. Maybe her time to die wasn't quite now.

A bullet suddenly cracked the side mirror. "Blow that truck up. That should keep them from using it to chase us down."

Vivi couldn't see anything as the truck turned from the chaos but she could hear someone climbing above the cab. As they pulled away, there was a loud whistling *whoosh* and the truck shook from the ensuing blast. She glanced at the smashed side mirror as they took off down the road. The other truck was on fire. Her heart sank at the thought of the dead men, especially the one in the gas mask. He couldn't have survived an RPG blast. He had saved her life. She had been about to sacrifice hers when he did what he did. Her eyes welled up in tears for the anonymous man who had taken her place. At least the girls were safe now.

A hand groped her thigh, and she glanced at Dilaver. He was as cool and dangerous as an unused stick of dynamite, a small smile on his lips.

"Poor little girl. Not such a spitfire anymore, are you? I'll wipe those tears off later, I promise."

She wasn't supposed to understand what he was saying but his roving hand was quite specific. She pushed his hand away, her skin crawling from his touch. There wasn't much room to move, squashed as she was against the men in the front. She crossed her arms in front of her as she stared back at him unblinkingly, her chin jutting up in defiance.

Dilaver stared back for a moment, then shrugged. "Bring out the maps," he ordered.

Vivi hugged herself tightly as she listened to the men figuring out their next move. She was in a dangerous situation, among men who put very little value on lives. She had just witnessed exactly how little when they had sent their own men to their deaths to ensure their escape. As a young goat-herdess, she was pretty much valueless. But as a GEM operative, she still had a weapon or two up her proverbial sleeve. She would wait for the right moment, give herself a chance to escape without getting killed. She owed that at least to the man who had died for her.

The road was dusty and filled with potholes, and
every bounce and groan of the truck jarred Vivi's bones. Her
captors ignored her as they reworked their plans, pointing to
various sections of their maps.

She listened quietly, gauging the enemies' intellect.
Dilaver's orders were crisp and decisive. He was a good
strategist, albeit a bloodthirsty one. He wanted revenge in a
big way and told the interpreter that he wanted him to go
into town to pay for informants. The man had just lost four
trucks, men and a trailer of "goods" to someone he had
thought would be a new business partner. He didn't want to
leave without letting the other side know that they had made
an enemy for life.

From his earlier actions and his current demeanor, she
could see that the man was a mercenary at heart, someone
who liked the taste of battle, who had little regard for morals
or human lives. On a whim, right in the middle of an ambush, he had decided to take her despite the danger to himself and his men. In one split second, to make his escape, he
had totally wiped out a whole truckload of his men with an
RPG launcher. But Vivi understood that his thoughts hadn't
been on rescuing or avenging his men. Everything was focused on someone having tricked him, won the battle, and

then taken away something belonging to him. He had wanted to destroy the trailer of women rather than "lose" them to the other side. And now he wanted one final show-down, a tit for tat.

Vivi didn't care if Dilaver destroyed anything that belonged to the Triads, as long as innocent lives weren't involved. That was GEM's game plan, anyhow. Admiral Madison's, too, she supposed. GEM wanted Dilaver and the Triads out of the way while they were dealing with Maximillian Shoggi's secret rendezvous in town.

And now she saw exactly why. Dilaver wasn't a bottom-feeder. He would find out that Mad Max was in the area quickly enough, and every gun-running counterpart, from shady to the shadiest, knew who Maximillian Shoggi was and what had happened to Cash Ibrahim. If they were to meet, Mad Max would see Dilaver as a good replacement of his dead right-hand man and, in all likelihood, make an alliance with the man. No, that would mean a setback for GEM and COS Command. They wanted to keep Mad Max as weak as possible so they could use him to further their agenda. Then they would take him down once and for all. Of course, that would also make Admiral Madison happy; he had probably lost some men to people like Mad Max and Dilaver.

Vivi changed the direction of her thoughts from the admiral to his SEAL team. Vivi wondered how they were doing on the other side of the bank, with their ambush of the first couple of trucks. Eight men against at least two dozen targets. Dilaver hadn't traveled unprepared. She hoped that everything was under control back there. And that no one was hurt.

Jazz. She hadn't been able to talk to him privately, not with so many listening in. She had wanted to say more than "be careful." But what could she have added? They were all heading for battle and . . . She almost laughed out loud. She, Vivi Verreau, the woman who hated men in uniforms, was actually in the middle of a real firefight with them; was, in fact, worried about their being injured. The irony of it was laughable, except after witnessing the gory battle, there was nothing funny at which to laugh.

We do what we can to save the world, chouchou. Jazz's words echoed in her head as she stared into the growing darkness outside. How would he react when he found out that she was missing? She badly needed to see him, to reassure herself that he was okay. She half regretted expressing her harsh views about soldiers to him. He had been exemplary toward her; in fact, toward all women that he had met. She knew now it wasn't just an act. From the moment she had watched his chivalry while she was in disguise, to the other day when he had accompanied her in her rounds to deliver food and aid to the orphanages, he had shown nothing but respect. And, she acknowledged with an inward smile, he had exuded enough sexy charm to win over everyone except maybe Juliana Kohl.

Those men, the SEALs on one side and her men on the other, were willing to lay down their lives to extract a trailer full of young women. She had seen their anger and heard their disgust when she had briefed them about Dilaver's side gift to the Triads. When she had first seen that satellite feed of how young that one girl was, and how brutally she had been treated by Dilaver's men, something had died inside. She couldn't save that poor soul, now in the hands of those nameless border guards. She peered at the bastard dozing beside her. She wanted to kill him. And she knew now, so did those men who had been fighting on her side.

She had been taught to always look at the big picture, to realize that some sacrifices were necessary. She bit her lip, thinking of how many had sacrificed themselves to get to the trailer, for people they hadn't ever met. And she bowed her head in grief at the man with the gas mask, who had died. He hadn't known it, but were it not for his sacrifice, she would have given up her life to ensure that Dilaver didn't reach the girls. Using CS gas had been a brilliant idea. Dilaver couldn't go through that without any protective masks, no matter how well armed his group was.

When she made it back, she would make sure to find out who this man was and visit his grave. *If* she made it back.

Vivi knew she would probably be killed or sold off once these men were done with her. She could take a few of them down but it was highly unlikely that they wouldn't shoot and torture her once they found out she had more skills than the average country girl.

She looked outside the window. The truck was climbing higher up into the hills, heading for the deep forests where many a group of guerrillas had found sanctuary. Even if she managed to escape, she had to find her way out of the wilderness so that a chopper could pick her up. She gave a slight shake of her head. If she managed to escape, Dilaver would surely be looking for her and a chopper would pinpoint her location. And of course, he had that handy RPG. No chopper till she hiked a ways off.

She needed another strategy. Again, her thoughts veered back to Jazz. He was his team's strategist, and she admired the way he could see a straight line through a maze of problems. What would he have done, she wondered, if he were on her side of the river? She bet the SEALS had been cursing their heads off when she and her goats showed up at the scene. She would give anything to have seen their expressions, especially Jazz's. What would he have thought of that strategy?

No doubt she probably would have gotten an earful had she had her headset on. Maybe not. She had never heard Jazz curse or seen him angry. Even when he was rescuing Rose, he had used strategy over emotion, paying for the girl and avoiding direct confrontation with the drunken soldiers. No, she imagined Jazz would probably be strategizing now, trying to figure out where Dilaver was heading. She could see him, getting the news from her commander that she had been taken, standing there in his camouflage—

Oh my God.

Vivi sat straight up, eyes widening in startled realization. *Oh my God, oh my God.* The man with the gas mask. His pants. His pants were camies. They weren't the Triad black that her men had been wearing. She had caught sight of the black shirt and assumed—*oh my God*. Her mind raced as she tried to remember. She was very certain she saw camouflaged pants because her eyes were trained on the figure as he ran.

Vivi felt sick to her stomach. If that was a SEAL, she knew who would insist on being on her side of the riverbank. It wouldn't be Hawk who had to direct the action as Patrol Leader. It had to be Jazz.

Her guts clenched as a cry of denial caught in her throat. Jazz couldn't have survived that blast. Dilaver had killed him when he ordered the RPG to be used on that truck.

She had to live, but she was dying inside. Not Jazz. Please, not him. She was going to find a way to get back alive. She was going to see this whole thing through and then personally finish off Dilaver herself.

"We'll stop here for the night," Dilaver ordered. "I need to take a piss anyway. No one is following us."

At the welcome news, Vivi opened her eyes. They had been traveling for hours, reaching the hills as the darkness descended. At one point earlier, Dilaver had decided that riding in the dark with a woman in front might be dangerous, so he had tied her hands together just before the sunlight disappeared. Not that she could have escaped them. She was waiting for open air, where there was a chance to escape and hide in the cover of darkness.

When they hadn't stopped, she had become resigned to the fact that it might be a while before she could actually do that. She had been trained in escape-and-evasion skills in case she was ever held hostage.

Vivi flexed her tied wrists. Well, time to put those rusty skills into practice. When the time came, she needed another diversion. Dark humor popped up in her head. She supposed goats wouldn't work this time.

From listening to them, she knew they had followed the dirt

road closest to the river that wound up the hill. It was smart—less likely to get lost and plenty of water, if they needed to hide out.

Dilaver opened the door and jumped out. The driver and guide exited from the other side. Vivi remained where she was.

Dilaver paused to look at her. "Out," he ordered. "You don't need any interpreter for that word."

When Vivi shook her head, he reached in and pulled her out by her tied wrists, and she tumbled from the huge truck onto the ground. Not letting go of her wrists, he dragged her along, uncaring as her body slid against the rocky ground.

"I'm going off to the bushes," he said as he casually continued while his prisoner struggled to get on her feet. "Which direction is the river so I get my bearings when I am done?"

Vivi's mind worked furiously as she winced from the rocks and weeds cutting her bare skin. Maybe she didn't need a diversion. The bastard was something else. He was taking her to the bushes before he even had a chance to stretch his legs after a long trip. There was something about him that told her that the gunrunner was very used to living on the go.

She heard the water from the river. This high up, it moved quickly, tumbling down toward the muddier banks in the lower areas. Dilaver kept walking. She turned to look behind her. His men were stretching and setting up camp. They didn't seem to be worried about their leader going off alone. Okay, one thing going right for once. Dilaver alone.

He tethered her to some low-lying branch, using the length of rope dangling from her wrists. It was dark but she could see parts of his face in the moonlight.

"I think you know what I want, spitfire. You don't need to speak the same language for what I have in mind, but maybe you speak French? I speak a little Francais." Vivi heard him unzipping his fly. His next sentence was spoken in hesitant French. "It's hard to piss with a hard-on, baby."

Vivi screamed and let out a stream of words in the local

mixture of several languages, calling Dilaver every name she could think of. She wanted the men setting up camp to think that their boss was having a good time. She could hear their laughter as her shrieks reached their ears.

Dilaver laughed. "Hang on, let me finish here. Then you can scream all you want."

As she listened to the sounds of him pissing, she positioned her feet, ready to attack. It had to be done right. If she didn't knock out Dilaver quickly, he could call for help; tied up like this, she needed at least a few minutes to cut the ropes. She tensed up, waiting for the right moment.

Dilaver gave the usual male grunt as he answered nature's call. He turned back to Vivi, his shadow looming menacingly. Leaning close, he untethered the loose end of the rope. He was just close enough. Screaming to surprise as well as cover any sounds from him, Vivi leaped and wrapped her legs around his waist, using her tied fists to smash into his Adam's apple, his most vulnerable point at that moment.

Stunned by the unexpected blow, his breath expelling in a big *whoosh*, Dilaver went backward from her sudden weight, but even in pain, his reflexes were incredibly fast. As he stumbled, his hands came up almost immediately, pulling her head back by her hair. Wincing at the pain, Vivi grabbed his thick neck, pressing her thumbs viciously against his windpipe to cut off his air. They both panted as he weaved around like a mad man, still clutching her hair fiercely. When he recovered his footing, he raised one fist, at the same time shaking his head hard, trying to dislodge her hands. She held on obstinately.

Just as Dilaver's fist swung down, a shadow jumped out of nowhere and an arm blocked it from landing on Vivi's face. Both Vivi and Dilaver froze for an instant in their struggle as they turned to look at the intruder. The instant was what the newcomer needed. There was a loud smack and this time Dilaver crumpled to the ground.

Her legs still wrapped around her captor tightly and too surprised by the new twist to jump off, Vivi fell on top of the big man. It wasn't a bad move since it muffled Dilaver's cries enough to make them less suspicious to his men.

But Dilaver was a big man. His instincts were that of a man who would fight while he still had strength. He rolled, trying to disengage her. In doing so, he exposed his back to the other person on the scene. Vivi looked up and saw a karate chop coming down at the base of the thug's skull. There was another painful-sounding crack and her captor suddenly went limp, his weight trapping her against the ground.

This time he didn't move and his dead weight crushed her breath from her for a few seconds before it was suddenly removed. Before she could gulp in fresh air, she was unceremoniously lifted onto her toes. The man held her face as he gave her a swift and thorough kiss. Hard. Bruising.

Her heart seemed to leap into her mouth as Vivi could only breathe his name into his mouth, "Jazz . . ." Still silent, he set her gently back on her feet and immediately knelt down beside Dilaver.

Vivi understood. No time right now. They had to secure Dilaver long enough to make an escape. But she couldn't stop the smile trembling on her lips as she quickly cut the ropes so they could use them to tie the unconscious man. Jazz cuffed him quickly and efficiently, then did the same to his feet. Then he took out a handkerchief to gag him.

"Wait," she whispered. She ran her fingers along her carnelian bracelet, looking for the fake bead. It was big enough to hide a tiny vial. "I need water, liquid of any kind."

Without questioning the reason, Jazz stood up and disappeared for a minute or two. "Here," he whispered back, handing her a soggy wet cloth. "No container, sorry."

"This is fine." She broke the vial with a fingernail and poured the liquid and pellet into wet material. Then she placed the whole concoction over Dilaver's mouth and nose.

"That should put him out for a while," she observed quietly.

"Ether," Jazz said, his voice low, recognizing the smell. "Do you carry chloroform pellets on you all the time?"

"Doesn't everyone?" Vivi countered as she gagged the man tightly.

"Ready? I'm going to get us out of here."

Vivi smiled in the darkness. She couldn't believe he was here—alive and going alpha on her. She put her hand in his and allowed him to lead her into the shadows.

Jazz wanted to stop and hold Vivi in his arms. He wanted to yell at her. Then kiss the woman mindless. He had never been so angry. And fearful. It had taken all his control not to kill Dilaver. If the bastard had hurt Vivi, he would have done so without hesitation.

But they needed to get as far away as possible before the unconscious thug woke up or his men came looking for him. There was no way they could find him and Vivi, of course, even if they tried. But he wanted Vivi away from those men and their weapons. He wanted her somewhere safe where he could use his flashlight to look at her.

He tightened his hold on her hand as she followed him silently through the thick undergrowth toward the river. He paced himself, making sure he wasn't too fast for her. As soon as possible, he would stop.

He glanced at her but she still hadn't said anything since leaving Dilaver, moving alongside of him with a quiet grace that was both surprising and yet not. She was braver than any woman he had ever known, using herself as a distraction to get a mission completed. Her screams of fear had taken years off his life until he realized that they couldn't be real since she wasn't doing it in English. She was still playing a part.

When they reached the river, he stopped, looking around quickly. There were some bushes nearby, large enough to screen them for a while. He tugged at her hand and she followed.

The instant they went behind the brush, she turned and pushed him against a shrub. His lower back slapped against one of its branches. Hands moved all over his chest, as if she was making sure he was real. Her lips forced his apart and her tongue slid into his mouth, not giving him a chance to say anything.

Heat exploded, adding fuel to his already adrenaline-filled psyche. He responded to her silent plea, kissing her back. She went wild, tearing at his clothes, trying to find flesh. He breathed in her scent, tasted her desire, and something else. Blood. He tasted blood. He had forgotten that she might be injured, she had been so quiet. He tried to lift his head but she refused to let him go.

Her hands found an opening. Slid inside. And molded his flesh. Jazz groaned into her mouth as her seeking hands went lower. She couldn't be too injured, he thought faintly.

He broke free of her questing mouth. "Vivi—" he said, and paused as she nibbled down his neck, her hands unfastening the Velcro on his pants.

Her assault was insistent, pushing away the hindering clothing. His lower body jerked forward as her hand brushed against the hot hard length of his erection, urging it to escape its confines. He felt the coolness of the air before her hand encircled his naked flesh tightly. At the same time, she was kissing her way down the open front of his shirt, and Jazz found himself backing helplessly against the branch for support, letting her have her way with him.

The moon had gone behind the clouds and he stared up into the darkened sky with a million stars as her mouth found him. Sweet God Almighty. He was thankful for the branch's support as his knees buckled at this new onslaught. He could feel her tongue licking the top of his penis, making him harder. He groped down and tangled his fingers in her thick hair as she took him into his mouth. She was like a woman on a quest, as if his sexual excitement proved something to her, and she refused to let up, taking him deeper and deeper into that sweet wet mouth.

Jazz stroked her hair mindlessly as he continued looking at the beauty of the sky above. He vaguely noted that his breathing sounded rapid and uneven. He resisted the urgent need to release even as her mouth teased him to the point of intolerable madness. This was insane. Totally not the place for a . . . This was—the stars blinked back at him—heaven.

And he wanted to share heaven with his woman. The next time she released him, he pulled her onto her feet in spite of her muted protests.

"Vivi," he began again.

"Shut up," she told him in a fierce voice. "Lift me up, you idiot. Shut up."

It wasn't the most romantic line to say in heaven but Jazz followed orders and lifted Vivi by the waist. Her legs felt strong and sure as they curled around his waist.

She leaned down and kissed his lips and face, quick hard kisses. "I thought you were dead. I thought he blew you up." Her words tumbled out as she reached down and took hold of his eagerly waiting erection again. "I thought you were dead."

She was feverish, commanding, and totally irresistible. "I think you can tell I'm very alive, sweetheart," was all Jazz could manage to say as she nudged him against her own very heated and wet flesh. When did she lose her underwear? That question got lost somewhere with a million other logic cells as she slowly took him inside her.

Heaven. She was so ready he slid in all the way.

She moved. Oh definitely heaven. *Sur la terre comme au Ciel.* And so much more.

Jazz gave in. Desire and need swamped his senses. He kissed her roughly as she controlled the pace. Her response was equally as rough as she gave in to her own sensual pleasure.

He released one hand from her waist, slipping it where they were joined, seeking to add to her excitement. She was slick with need as she shuddered against his massaging fingers.

Vivi bit back a cry at his intimate touch. He moved his fingers in a leisurely fashion that contrasted with her urgency. She rode him hard, demanding a quick release, and he deliberately slowed down even more, driving her pleasure into an intense need. Everything centered on what his fingers were doing to her.

"Please, Jazz," she finally whispered against his mouth.

"*Regarde, chouchou.* Heaven. Look at the stars. It feels better if you look up."

Confused, she did so and stared in wonder at the night sky lit up with twinkling jewels. Her hips slowed. It seemed as if the whole universe was glowing. His questing thumb continued its sensual rubbing, sliding up as she came down on him, and going slowly back down as she pulled up off his hard length. That felt . . . so . . . out of this world.

"*C'est comme ca pour moi, chouchou.* You bring heaven to me."

Vivi trembled at the beauty of his words. He was right. The need to feel him inside, the desire to celebrate his being alive, was magnified by the silence and beauty above. This world was theirs, watching them, making them a part of it.

She had never felt so close to anyone in her life. To be connected this way, mind and body, staring up at the incredible vista above them . . . It was an experience she couldn't compare to anything she had ever gone through. And she wanted it to last forever, even though each intimate stroke brought her closer to completion.

He built her pleasure to an incredible slow tight ball of nova heat, whispering sexy words as he urged her to come for him. She began to move faster again and there was no stopping the tumbling fireball about to explode inside her. She finally paused in mid-stroke, a whimper of pleasure caught in her throat.

Jazz swallowed her cries, his hips surging up eagerly and taking over, and finally, unable to hang on to his control, he pushed her down one final hard time. He pushed in as deep as he could, needing to reach inside and give all he had to this woman.

A thousand mini explosions. He had never climaxed this hard and this long. He imagined a shooting star streaking across the sky. Hell, a hundred shooting stars as his release kept surging his hips against Vivi over and over, as if he wanted to merge with her all the way.

"Heaven," she whispered into his ear, already sensitized by her kisses, "is finding someone you thought you've lost forever."

Jazz couldn't agree more.

CHAPTER
18

Vivi looked at Jazz's face in the dark. He was still inside her. He was breathing hard and she could feel the rapid beating of his heart under her hand. He held her securely by her hips, hugging her tightly, arching his back as if he were still climaxing. He felt so good. He turned around and pushed her against something hard. A branch. Using that to brace himself, he let go of her, and it took her a few seconds before she realized he was fumbling with his loosened pants. His movements teased her as he kept pushing deeper while kicking his camies aside. She could only cling to him, her legs around him, loving the feel of him. The branch behind her creaked slightly at their combined weight.

When he was ready, he held her again and turned in the darkness, surefooted as a cat. He kept walking, and each stride had her gasping as she felt him growing big and hard against her womb. He refused to let her move, his hands insistent as he kept her firmly lodged. A whimper escaped her lips.

"Do you think you were the only person who thought you lost someone? God, Vivi . . . when I saw your blouse on the ground, *I* thought . . ."

Jazz didn't finish. He found what he was looking for, a flat area where he could go on his knees, with her under him.

Vaguely, she noted that he was still wearing his shirt, but all thoughts fled as he pulled the cup of her bra to one side and began to suckle her breast.

She arched into his mouth and gasped as one hand found her other breast, pulling the cup away so his fingers could stroke her nipple. She could see the whole span of the night sky above him now, and his mouth was so hot in contrast to the cool mountain air.

He rose up above her. "Your appearance scared the day-lights out of me, *chouchou. That* wasn't the distraction I had in mind for us. What the hell were you thinking, don't you know being in a crossfire can get you killed?" His hands traveled over her face. "Did he hurt you? Did he do anything?"

"I'm okay," she told him, cutting into his string of questions.

He kissed her fiercely, possessively. "Do you know I lost half my life, clinging to the back of that damn trailer, wondering whether you were okay? Are you sure he didn't touch you? Your blouse . . ."

The man had clung to the back of the trailer all this time, just to rescue her. Vivi's eyes filled with tears. It hadn't crossed her mind that anyone would ever care for her that much to risk his life like that. His lips kissed away her tears.

"He didn't, Jazz. I wouldn't have let it go that far," she assured him.

"Baby, there were at least a dozen men in that truck. Not letting isn't going to stop them." He laid his stubbly cheek against hers. "You're too damn independent."

Vivi choked back a laugh. This was Jazz being his most alpha yet. "Too independent? What, I'm supposed to have your approval about my life?"

"Damn right. Too strong for your own good."

"You're being silly."

He slid out of her. His lips traveled down her stomach. Lower. She tensed her stomach, waiting for his kiss, wanting it, but he teased her, nibbling at her upper thighs instead until she burned with need.

"Silly, huh?" he murmured. She shook her head restlessly

as she waited. "I want you weak for me. I want you to think about what you'd do to me if you get hurt. I want you to depend on me enough, *chouchou*, so you feel you have to come back to me safely. That should stop you from putting yourself in danger like that. What's so silly about that?"

Finally, to make his point, his hot tongue touched Vivi where she wanted it most. She had plenty to say about those macho lines he'd just thrown at her, but right now . . . all she could do was writhe under his onslaught. The surrounding darkness of the shrubs and the inky night sky, the hidden moon with its sliver of light that allowed Vivi to catch glimpses of the man making love to her, the scent of their bonding, the insistent pressure of his clever tongue—if there was such a thing as the edge of consciousness in the throes of pleasure, Vivi knew this must be it. She could only lie there, floating and tumbling through a swirl of sensation, as she relinquished ownership of her body.

He was different. It was as if the soldier in him had disappeared and those compartmentalized emotions he had held within were freed. All his rage and fear. The part of him that was under control while he was getting things done was shoved aside. In its place was a determined male, needing reassurance that he had what he was after, wanting to punish her for making him so angry, so afraid.

His tongue was exactly that. Punishing. Taking. Uncompromisingly insistent on her giving in to him. He knew how to weaken her. Not with words. He weakened her with desire, with the need for him to continue staking a claim with his mouth. She could hardly breathe as he stoked her desire to a peak and kept her there, his tongue holding her independence a willing prisoner. Then she felt his fingers. Another punishing weapon of desire. Sliding inside her willing flesh and mounting pressure upon more pressure.

She bit down on her lower lip to stop a moan. There was something very earthy and sexy about letting a man take a woman on a journey like this in the wilderness. He was totally in charge in this setting. Man claiming woman as his own, using his natural-born magic to make her his. He didn't have to utter a word or beat his chest. He kissed her where it was the most intimate, where her essence primed her for his taking. And his fingers kept her very primed, stroking her until she shook from pleasure.

Vivi understood his mood. She had been desperate in her need for reassurance that Jazz was really there. She had taken him; now it was his turn. She understood that he was doing the same. And she wanted him.

He was tortuously thorough, driving her mad as he found and paid attention to the hidden nub over and over. He didn't tease. He went after what he wanted—her capitulation, her desire, her acknowledgment . . . everything. She trembled helplessly as he built dark pleasure stroke by silken stroke, as he stoked that sensual fire into another nova about to explode. All the while, she played with his hair with restless hands. Desire was a sensuous flow of white-hot need, slowly taking over every part of her body, until she was weak from it. Just the way Jazz wanted her. She needed. She wanted. Depended on him to give her back her strength. She whimpered in protest when he stopped.

Climbing on top, he slowly entered her again. She sighed. Oh God, that felt so good. Her legs eagerly curled around him, and she pushed him with the back of her legs, but this time it was he who set the pace. He pushed deep into her and stayed there, unmoving.

Vivi used her thighs and calves to urge him to move. Instead, he kissed her ear and whispered, "Do you need me now? Do you want me to continue?"

Of course she did. He was buried deep and his pubic bone rubbed against her clitoris as he flexed. "Move, Jazz," she whispered back. "It feels so good when you move."

He flexed and she could feel the flanks of his buttocks tightening against her thighs and the tension grew fiercer as he pushed even deeper. She could feel him rubbing inside.

"Clench around me, *chouchou*," he ordered. "Hold me tightly."

She did so, flexing her internal muscles to give him that extra incentive to move. But Jazz had other ideas. He flexed with her, his hips moving, even though he didn't come out of her. She shuddered again as a wave of pleasure hit her unexpectedly. Testing, she tightened the walls of her vagina again, holding him, and he rewarded her with the same upward plunge, flexing deep, yet not moving. The sensation was even stronger as she clenched longer the second time.

She loosened and he relaxed. She tightened and he flexed. And then he started to pull out with deliberate care the next time she let go. It felt as if he controlled her pleasure. Her orgasm gushed out in one long release, as he unplugged the sexual tension by withdrawing ever so slowly, and she jerked uncontrollably, her contractions ferocious and prolonged, as he began to move in and out of her in measured strokes. Every slide in had her wanting more. Every slide out made her even wetter.

Trying not to scream enhanced the pleasure even further. She gasped, taking in deep breaths, as she clung to Jazz. He was in a world of his own, his whole concentration on her body and its reaction to his taking. He listened to her body the way only a musician would, fine-tuning her pleasure to please himself, playing with her need until he created what he wanted. And he wanted her. And he wanted her pleasure.

Vivi gave him both willingly. Here, in the most unexpected of places, unplanned and in danger of discovery, in a country with which she had always associated pain and loss of innocence, she found the most unexpected, most unplanned, and most dangerous thing of all—a man who seemed intent on replacing the sense of loss that had always lingered inside her. And if she let him in, was she ready to let go of the past?

CHAPTER 19

Vivi opened her eyes slowly. She'd just had the most marvelous dream. She had been flying, floating higher and higher. She could still smell the sweetness in the air as she flew toward some unknown destination. Everything was light and joyful, and a smile fluttered the corner of her lips as she sleepily enjoyed the last vestiges of her dream. Light and joyful. She hadn't felt that in a long time, and wondered where she had been heading in her . . .

Dream. Her mind came alive with a start and she jerked up and found a heavy vise wrapped around torso. Her hand reached up automatically and felt the warm muscular arm keeping her against a very warm body.

"Go back to sleep." His voice was low.

"Have you been awake all this time?" She couldn't believe she had dozed off like that. They were still far from safe, for God's sake. What had she been thinking, attacking the man like a sex maniac while in the middle of an operation? Then she remembered what they had done—what *he* had done to her—and heat suffused her entire body.

"Mmm-hmm," he murmured.

She couldn't think of anything to say. "You go to sleep now. My turn to keep watch."

"I'm fine. I like listening to you snore."

"I do not snore." She poked him with her elbow when he chuckled sleepily.

"I'm only teasing, *chouchou*."

She felt him kiss the top of her head. "Thanks for coming to my rescue," she said.

"I like the way you thanked me. Ouch."

She gave him another poke to the ribs. "Are you teasing me?" She felt very comfortable lying here in the dark. The man was a marvelous lover, just as she had known he would be. She guessed it had been inevitable that they would end up naked but she hadn't thought it would be in the middle of nowhere. "Seriously, I can't believe you came after me."

His caress paused. "Did you think I'd just leave you on your own?" He sounded incredulous. "With Dilaver?"

She smiled in the dark. No need to start a fight after such wonderful sex. "I didn't know anyone saw me. Everything happened so fast," she replied soothingly.

He gave a disbelieving snort. "*Chouchou,* after watching your antics with the goats, I'm having a hard time believing that you were unaware that half your men watched your being taken prisoner and didn't lift a finger to go after Dilaver. They were following orders, no doubt."

Vivi shrugged. "They knew what was more important—the girls."

His arm tightened around her. "Not to me." His voice had turned edgy. "If I hadn't been there . . . You shouldn't take such risks."

Vivi sighed. She really didn't want to discuss this right now, not when she wanted to savor the last couple of hours.

"It's my job," she said, repeating T.'s usual line. Well, at least now she understood why T. used it. It was the easiest way to answer any question on which she didn't want to expand.

"I know. Part of me accepts it. But I don't have to like it."

She thought about it a moment. Fair enough. "Okay."

"You should have told me about your crazy plan."

"Sweetheart, I don't have the energy to lead my group of men *and* mollify a group of SEALs who aren't used to GEM activities. I know how you guys would have been. All of you would have insisted on changing the original plan."

"What's wrong with a little input?" He had resumed his caressing. "A joint mission is about teamwork, isn't it?"

"Yes. I'm also aware our groups had two different goals and I was only trying to make sure both got accomplished. Let's face it, Jazz, had your men known, they would have gotten all protective of me. I really appreciate it but I don't need all your eyes on me while I do my job. As it is, the mission goals have been accomplished."

"You've rescued the girls. We've gotten Dilaver stranded. And . . ." Jazz pulled her closer. "I got you naked. Mission goals accomplished."

Hearing the amused note in his voice, Vivi relaxed again. One thing about this man she really liked—as long as she had an explanation, he always accepted her as she was. She suddenly felt the need to give a personal one. He had freely spoken about his family, giving glimpses of his childhood. Perhaps if she shared a little, he would understand.

"Are you awake?" she asked.

"Yeah. I won't sleep. I want you to rest, though. We have a long way to go tomorrow."

His concern for her touched her more than anything else. Physical attraction was just chemistry, but personal sacrifice and a willingness to shoulder responsibilities, even pain, were choices that spoke volumes to her. They were important lessons she had learned from the past and she admired those qualities in others. Jazz had all these, and more. She leaned back against his heat, giving a soft sigh. So maybe this was what being wanted felt like.

"When I was very young," she began, softly, "I fantasized about who my father was. He had strange hair like mine and weird colored eyes, and for a small child, it sounded as if her father had been from outer space. The fairy tales in my culture always had gods and goddesses coming down to earth and doing magic and fighting bad evil spirits, so in my mind, my father was from heaven and he came down to do battle with bad men, and one day would come to take me."

She paused. What a stupid way to start an explanation. She hadn't ever told him she was brought up here—how would he understand if she didn't tell him? Maybe she should stop. She felt Jazz's arm tighten around her, as if he had read her thoughts.

"Go on," he urged.

She gathered her memories and tried to gloss over the emotional parts. "He was going to be tall and strong. Big as an ox. And he'd come back and beat up on those horrid people who called me names, who said kids like me were unwanted and useless." She paused again. "Back then, being mixed-blooded was a sign that the mother was probably unmarried and so the child was a bastard. Basically, my whole future was ruined, and being a woman made it worse. I didn't know that, of course. I only knew I looked different."

"You were like those children we saw in the slums that first day," Jazz interrupted. "You said they were orphans but they weren't really, were they?"

"No. They were abandoned by their mothers. Or told to stay away from home till nighttime. Or their mothers probably ran away and left them in the care of relatives, which was even worse. But yeah, I was one of them, Jazz." She closed her eyes, and once again she was the grimy child of the past, fighting bullies, stealing food, and trying to survive. "I had relatives but they didn't really want me."

Jazz removed his arm and turned her around to face him. Vivi opened her eyes but could see only the dark outline of his face. His hand was very tender, his knuckles tracing her jaw, then her lips. "I'm sorry," he said.

Vivi kissed his fingers. "It's okay, you don't have to comfort me now. I'm one of the lucky ones who got out. There were many who weren't as fortunate." She smoothed a hand over his chest. It was solid and strong. She closed her eyes again. She had never shared her childhood memories this intimately. The version she always gave to people was less personal, with a lot of the details left out. "Anyway, where was I? I wanted to show them I was better than the names they called me, that my father was a god, like the ones depicted on the temple doors—very strong-looking, fierce, in battle gear and holding some big weapon, guarding the place against evil." She smiled bitterly. "Of course, when I was old enough to dare tell others about this, I was laughed at by the adults. I was so humiliated. I hated their laughter."

Your father is a what? A god? You're a slut's daughter, that's what you are. Here, here, take a look at your father. Over there, those men that just came to town in the Jeep.

"One day, I saw some soldiers in town. Their hair was light-colored, like mine. One of them had blue eyes. And they were all in uniform, with big shiny weapons. They looked so handsome. Big and strong and . . . well fed." She laughed. "I was very hungry, so well fed was kind of attractive, you know? I quickly learned why the older girls were always around these soldiers. I learned that they weren't gods very, very quickly."

"You didn't—"

Vivi shook her head. "No, I didn't. There was a nice young man who gave me chocolate all the time. He taught me quite a bit of English while he was stationed here, and I think he saved me from his buddies who were less discriminating about the differences between a woman and a child. He was different from some of the other soldiers."

You stay away from my friends, you understand? Don't take their chocolate. Say no and run away if you see them drunk, okay? You're too damn young. You just stay away, especially at night, okay?

"I get why you're so hostile against anyone in uniform now," Jazz told her softly. "Growing up in that kind of environment . . . my God, Vivi. How did you get out of there?"

"I discovered that I could pick up languages easily. Pretty soon I was speaking English and French well enough and was running errands for the soldiers who wanted to buy stuff in town. They gave me food and change; I got to ride in their Jeeps and show off. One day, my friend said good-bye because he had to leave. I was very sad but didn't think much of it till he was gone. Then I realized how much he had been a buffer for me. He had always sent me off on errands or away from the place when the soldiers were rowdy, and I'd never asked why. With him gone, I saw everything, Jazz. Every disgusting thing that they did. It was a shock to see my heroes doing those things to girls. I knew it was wrong because some of the girls would be crying and saying no, but that never stopped the men when they were drunk. I was very afraid then because I knew this was my fate, that I would end up like . . . my mother."

Jazz gathered her closer, and his tender kisses pushed away the pain of reliving the humiliation. She let the minutes drift by, grateful for the comfort given. She didn't want to admit it but today's events had hit too close to her heart. She understood adrenaline played a big part in the cathartic release of emotions, that different people reacted to danger differently.

She released a cleansing breath. Today had been more than role-playing. Then all those hours thinking Jazz was dead had been agony. Emotionally, she had been put through a wringer. No wonder she had attacked the man when they had found somewhere to hide. And now it felt right that he be told about her background.

"How did you run away?" he asked, after a long satisfying kiss.

Vivi laid her head against his breast and listened to his heartbeat for a while. "I had a best friend. She was going to be given to this ugly old man. So we decided to run away."

Vivi, I'm so scared. Where are we going to go? What if we get lost?

Everything is going to be all right, Sia-Sia. We'll hide out in the temple for a bit.

"We hid in a temple but one of the nuns locked us in the

upper room one night. Said that it was for our own good. I tried to convince my friend to escape with me but the window was too small and she was afraid of the height and dark. I knew I had to go, so I went off on my own. Somehow I made my way through the woods and village paths and survived. I don't remember how long it took, except that I was hungry and tired all the time. Some missionaries mistook me for an orphan and put me in a refugee camp. I must have been very close to the border or something because there were many foreign visitors coming in and out constantly. One day, a woman told me I was adopted and that my new home would be in America."

She didn't elaborate about the guilt of leaving her friend behind. She was the stronger of the two and she had promised Sia-Sia she would return for her. She never did. She had carried the guilt all these years, wondering what had happened to her childhood friend.

I hate the dark. When you come back, you'll bring me something nice, okay?

What do you want?

A new Dan Nhat would be nice. Mine's all out of tune.

All Jazz wanted to do was to hold Vivi like this and take away all that painful past. He understood how difficult it was for her to tell him about it. His mother was the same way, always telling him and his siblings stories about their dead dad. Whenever they had gone to her about their pain of losing him, she had focused on how strong and brave he had been and that they should be too, and had never once betrayed her own feelings.

As Jazz grew up, he had realized that it was a defense mechanism. His mother was the strongest woman he had ever known. She had been determined to bring up all her children without crying for help and although they had started out dirt poor, she had learned to run a small laundry business.

His mother's strength had been his moral compass all his

life. As a kid, he had helped out with the work and had learned how much a woman would sacrifice for her children. In his job he had seen so many abandoned children that only emphasized how much he owed what he was today to his mother.

Vivi had nobody. And yet she, too, had the strength to overcome her obstacles. She didn't tell him all that she had gone through but he got the picture. Watching his mother had given him plenty of insight at how some people responded to personal pain and loss.

Vivi had been determined to rise above her lot, and she had succeeded. And she was so alone. From her story, he knew this. She had done everything alone for so long that he knew that sharing her story was something she didn't do with anyone. In her own way, she was reaching out for his understanding of her past. He was also beginning to realize that he had fallen in love with this remarkable woman.

"It has a happy ending," he said.

"But not for others." Her voice cracked a little. "Not for too many girls."

"You can't save the whole world, sweetheart. You saved those girls today, and that's enough for today." It was a soldier's philosophy. If one kept imagining the entire bloody war, one would go crazy. Somehow he needed to instill this in her. "Dwell on the positive, Vivi."

"You don't understand. I failed so many times. I can't find homes for them . . . no solutions. I'm just a total—"

"Sweetheart," he interrupted because he couldn't bear to listen to her denigrating herself. "Don't do this. I understand. Hey, how many times have I told you about my maman and my sisters? Believe me, I take it to heart when I see so many women and children suffering during my tours. You're not a failure, okay? You are strong and brave, and you are doing something to help. Good things always come to one who works hard."

There was a silence as Vivi absorbed his words. She snuggled closer, inserting one leg between his thighs. He smiled sleepily in the dark. Strong and brave *and* sexy as hell.

"Is that what your maman taught you?" Her voice was muffled against his chest, her lips teasing his nipple.

"Something like that." Right now, his maman should stay away from his mind. His thoughts were starting to get a little too disrespectful.

"I can't imagine a family, especially one with so many sisters. But they have made you special, do you know that?"

He didn't want to think about his sisters right now, either. Not when a woman's tongue was licking his chest. But if she thought he was special because of his sisters, he should talk more about them, he guessed.

"They . . . tried their best to make me special," he acknowledged, hissing slightly as sharp little teeth nibbled. "Gave me a sense of humor about women, anyway."

"Really? I never had that. I wish I had a bunch of sisters to joke around with." Her sigh was a breath of hot air against his sensitive skin. She moved even closer. "My mother didn't have a sense of humor at all. Jazz, you're so lucky to have so many sisters."

Right now he felt like the luckiest bastard in the whole world, not because he had a bunch of sisters who would rag his ass for talking about them while a woman's hand was traveling down his body. The topic of conversation was at odds with what was going on in his head, but Vivi needed comfort and reassurance, and he wanted to help her forget. He tried to ignore his body's growing response to her exploration.

"Do you have a brother?"

Jazz didn't want to talk about his damn brother. He wanted the hand to go lower, actually. "No."

"You're lying. I read your file, you know. What, don't you think I remember you told me your brother's name is Zippy? Zippy and Zola . . . tell me why your mother gave you guys those names." She wiggled her leg that was between his thighs. "Pins and needles."

Jazz hadn't realized how tightly he had clenched his thighs together. He forced himself to relax, allowing her to shift her leg. There was no way to hide his arousal poking into her stomach, of course.

"So, tell me about your brother. Is he like you?"

Zippy was nothing like him right now. And if he had a dick bursting with need against a woman's body, Jazz didn't want to know, hear, or think about it, thank you very much. He let out a frustrated sigh. All this talk about his family was wilting his desire in spades.

"I like it that you're telling me so much about your family. It makes me feel better for some reason." Vivi sighed again, stretching her body as she relaxed against him. "Is your brother a gentleman like you? Polite and kind to women and children?"

His erection wasn't acting like a gentleman at all as it happily nudged the soft skin it was touching. Her stretching and moving around wasn't helping either, but he didn't want her to stop. She was unconsciously drawing circles with slow, sexy strokes of her finger and definitely moving in the right direction. Lower. Yeah. His dick nodded with eager agreement.

"Zippy's name came from an accident."

"What do you mean?" She yawned, stretching again.

Jazz really didn't want to think about Zippy's accident. Or talk about it. It wasn't conducive to keeping a happy penis hard and ready. "Let's just say that it was a traumatic childhood experience and he never wears zipped pants again."

"Oh my God. A man's nightmare! It hurts just to imagine the pain!" Vivi chuckled softly and yawned again. "You know what?"

"What?" He prayed that she wasn't falling asleep, even though he had wanted her to earlier. If he could just stop her from bringing up his mother and brother while he was contemplating sexier images, everything would be perfect.

"I suddenly remember my mother had a saying similar to

yours. You know, the one about good things coming to one who works hard?"

"What's that?" Okay, better to talk about her mother than his mother. Less sacrilegious. It was just not right to talk about his mother when all he wanted to was put his . . .

His breath came out in a hiss as a hand encircled his arousal tightly. "She told me, 'Good things come to one who is hard.' "

It took several seconds before he realized he had been had. It took that long because his hard dick was too busy enjoying something good. The little minx had done all that on purpose. Sisters and mothers. Gentlemanly behavior. His brother's dick, for God's sake.

Jazz growled and pushed Vivi onto her back. Her hand remained busy as her laughter filled the night air.

"Come on," she urged, between chuckles. "You still haven't explained about Zola. Tell me more about your family."

He sighed happily as he settled between her parted legs. "Spanking," he threatened. "We do that a lot."

CHAPTER
20

"This is very unprofessional, you know," Vivi commented as she looked around. She sat up as soon as the first streak of dawn broke the sky. Jazz stirred, then he, too, sat up, using a tree trunk as a back rest. Vivi leaned back, enjoying his body heat too much to move away. "If Dilaver and his men had found us last night . . ."

She gestured at the clothing scattered around. "Really unprofessional," she repeated.

"I still have my boots on. We could run," Jazz offered lazily.

Vivi chuckled. "Well, I don't have my shoes on," she pointed out.

"I'd have carried you, no problem."

She had a feeling Jazz could do that and more. After all, the man had determinedly hung on to the back of a trailer for hours, intent on saving her. He kissed the side of her neck, distracting her.

"What are you thinking?" he asked.

"Our next course of action."

"I was thinking the same thing."

"You're such a liar," she said, smiling, as she reluctantly got on her feet. Jazz remained where he was, watching her as she retrieved articles of clothing. "Well? Are you going to sit there all day?"

"Just enjoying the view," he replied. In the morning light, she could see the streaks of dirt and camouflage on his face. He smiled, revealing startling white teeth. "Bend over again."

She shook her head. "You know that isn't going to get us out of here quickly."

"I thought we were on our next course of action." He stretched his legs out lazily.

"The next *course* is not going to be me again," Vivi stressed, ignoring the way her heart skipped a beat at the sight of Jazz naked. He was totally at ease with his . . . She looked up and caught the amusement in his eyes. She frowned with mock anger.

"Tell him that," he suggested as he touched his erection.

"Lieutenant Zola Zeringue." Hands on hips, she drew satisfaction at his wince. "Are you paying attention to the fact that we're still in danger?"

"I'm giving you my fullest attention, *chouchou*." The man was totally shameless as he opened his legs wider. "Come here and let me show you."

"I suggest someone take a cold morning bath in the river pronto," she suggested.

Jazz heaved an exaggerated sigh before getting up. Sunlight emerged in the dawn sky. His masculine beauty took Vivi's breath away, from the broad shoulders to the well-defined abdominal muscles to the powerful flanks of his legs. There wasn't an extra ounce of fat on the man. And standing in the wilderness, he looked . . . absolutely gorgeous.

She had to turn away. She had never acted so irresponsibly before and although she didn't regret it, she mustn't let her feelings take the place of more important things. They had to get back to HQ so the rest of the mission could continue smoothly.

She heard him moving about. "How long will it take you to get ready, sweetheart?"

"Not as long as you. I had on less clothing," she pointed out, hooking the bra with her forefinger and pulling it off a small bush.

"Here's my shirt. Don't think you can fit my shoes, but I have another pair of socks."

Frowning, Vivi turned, just in time to see his cute butt disappear back into his camies. The man didn't wear underwear. Another thing that was going to keep her distracted. "You don't have any underwear but you have an extra pair of socks," she said in disbelief. "Extra ammo, small weapons, and *socks*?"

He turned. "*You* had ether in some pellet on your necklace!" He picked up the heavy belt and proceeded to check the pouches.

She shrugged. "I'm GEM. And ether is a weapon."

He looked at her briefly. "I'm a SEAL. Everything is a weapon." He threw her a tight ball, which she caught. It was encased in Saran Wrap. "Trust me, *chouchou*, when you've been in situations in which you're wet for a long time, you learn to have certain things available whenever possible."

Vivi peeled off the wrap. It was a wadded pair of socks. "I'm off to the restroom," she said, pointing to the river.

"I'll keep watch, but stick close to the bushes. We don't know whether Dilaver is still looking for us."

"He isn't stupid. He won't wander too far away when he's not sure of his territory."

Jazz nodded in agreement. "Yeah, but he can still follow the river."

"Point taken. I'll be careful."

She knew he would be watching as she made her way out of the screened clearing. She took a minute or two to survey the area. There were clumps of trees and shrubs near the bank of the river, similar to the one they had used as protection. She quickly mapped out a path.

He was in love.

Jazz kept watch as Vivi made her way to the river. The

morning light was good enough to cast a bluish and greenish tint to the surroundings. She was good at blending in with the shadows, he noted.

There was so much still unsaid between them, but she was right. Better wait till they were in a safer place. She was a fine-looking woman, totally unaware of the sexy image she was projecting. Walking half-naked here in the wilds, she looked like some wood sprite. He had thought her hair was darker yesterday; he had been right. She must have dyed it. And when she was standing just now, he had noticed she seemed a bit shorter without her boots.

There was still so much he didn't know about the woman. Yet she had opened up to him last night and had shown him the passion and warmth that he had always known were there. He watched her disappear into a clump of trees. Good girl. She might be in charge of paperwork at the liaison office, interrogating military personnel in custody as well as working to help young girls find homes, but Vivi Verreau was certainly a lot more than some paper pusher. Yesterday she had displayed some of those skills—a mesh of spook antics like disguises and acting and some really good fight moves.

When they got back, he would ask her more about her past. He had a suspicion that she had purposely distracted him last night from asking questions. She had told her story in a way that didn't reveal much about her own feelings, what she had gone through when she was alone and heading for the border. What had she left out?

Vivi reappeared from the other side of the shrub, retracing her steps to him. When she reached him, he saw that her hair was wet.

"Cold water. You're going to love it," she said with a grin. "Your turn."

"Okay." He handed her his shirt. "Put this on. There are some scratches on your back. Did I do that?"

She shook her head. "No."

He recalled her being dragged on the ground the night before. "I'm going to kill him someday," he promised in a low voice.

"I'm okay," she said. "It was just part of the job. Now give me some weapon so I can watch your back, too. I'm sorry, but I haven't killed anyone with a pair of socks lately."

Her humor blunted the edge of his temper. He knew she did that on purpose, too. "Be back in a minute, *chouchou*. Next time, I'll take you swimming frog-style."

When he returned, Vivi already had put on the large black shirt. Her hair had been pulled back and braided. Except for her face and feet, she was protected from the elements.

Jazz pointed to the river. "We're heading downstream. It's going to be quite a hike back, so whenever you need to stop, let me know. At the rate the truck was going, it will take us a good twelve hours."

Vivi shook her head. "I never walk into danger unprepared, Jazz. I have a locator unit on me. Once activated, my superior can pinpoint our exact location."

He cocked his head. "And when were you going to activate it?"

"Not now. We're too close to where Dilaver is, and if activated, I'm afraid T. would send in a chopper. Dilaver and his men would be able to see that."

"True. Who's T.?"

"She's my chief."

Another woman. "Do you all work in teams like we do?" Jazz asked.

Vivi shook her head. "Not the same way. We infiltrate, so it's best to do that alone."

"Where is this locator now?" He hadn't seen anything on her other than her underwear. Where would she hide something like that?

She grinned. "It's in my bra lining. It's a really tiny piece of wire, actually."

His interest perked up instantly. "Show it to me."

She smacked at his fingers reaching out for the buttons on her shirt. "Uh-uh. As if I don't know what that hand will be up to, soldier. We'll hike downstream till we're sure we aren't being followed. Then maybe I'll let you play with my . . . bra."

"Fair enough." Jazz gave the clearing one last look-over. He would always remember this as a special place. He reached behind him and pulled out a small knife.

"What are you doing?" She came closer as she watched him.

"Getting a souvenir."

He smiled down tenderly at her. She smiled back.

"Where have you been? Didn't you get my messages?"

As soon as Stefan walked into the back room of the Cha Cha Club, he could tell Alissa wasn't very happy with him. First, he had been asked to meet her at one of the businesses in town, and not at her private training place. Second, she hadn't come up to him and demanded a kiss, as was her habit of greeting. There was an anxious urgency in her voice that didn't go with the low-cut top she was wearing that nearly exposed her entire cleavage.

She walked hurriedly toward the back, her familiar sexy sway missing, and opened a door that had a "Private" plaque hung outside. He followed, noting the very businesslike atmosphere of the office, with its computers, electronic equipment, and file cabinets, a direct contrast to the sensual trappings of the outside rooms, in which flesh and sex were the decor.

"I came as soon as I could."

"That's not what I want to hear." Her gaze was direct, hard.

"What is it, Lis? I'm a busy man." He sat down in one of the plush office chairs, laced his fingers on his lap, and cocked his brow expectantly.

Alissa leaned back against the gleaming cherry oak desk. Dressed in a red micro-mini that barely covered her thighs, with sharp stiletto heels, she looked ludicrous against the background of books and files.

"You're so damn arrogant, Stefan. If you want to work for *Yeekohkoh*, you have to bend a little. You're no longer an independent once you join us."

Stefan allowed a small smile. "I don't think that's an option. I have no desire to be less independent. And," he settled back comfortably, "I didn't say I wanted to work for *Yeekoh*."

"We agreed to take the shipment of pills off your hands." Alissa crossed her arms. "That's a favor we did for you."

"Exactly. But I don't work for you, Alissa my sweet, or any of the Triad brothers. I can work with you, if you like. This is a give-and-take business, and for your brother's favor, I owe him one."

Her beautifully plucked eyebrows shot up. "You," she said slowly, "are very, very brave. If my brother heard your words, you might not be walking out of here alive."

Stefan shrugged. "It's a way of life. I'm a middleman, and a middleman must always be independent." He purposefully glanced at the clock on the wall. "If this is about business, your time is almost up."

Alissa slowly pushed off the desk. She approached him with that practiced sexy sway she used whenever she wanted to seduce him. She stopped a couple of feet away, standing close enough that he could see that she wasn't wearing anything under the thin material of her outfit. She placed her hands on her hips, a pose calculated to bring attention to her ample bosom.

"And if it's not about business?"

Her perfume wafted toward him. She moved her hands lower on her hips, her pose growing more suggestive.

Stefan's smile widened. "This is a place of business, so whatever it is you or *Yeekoh* want must be very important. You'll just have to convince me that you're worth it, like every woman here."

He insulted her on purpose, of course. There was a perverse streak in her that liked it when he did that. He knew she wouldn't take it from anyone else, but he had carefully cultivated this relationship between them in such a way. He excited her because he treated her differently. He crossed his legs, relaxing even more. Now was the time to test whether he had succeeded in pleasing her. He beckoned with one hand.

"What can I do for you, Alissa? And what will you give me in return?"

"But I already did you a favor." Her voice grew softer. "Many favors."

"But this one is different. You ordered me here, to this office. At your place of work."

"This is urgent business." She took a step closer.

"Something I can take care of for you."

"Easily."

Stefan pulled out his cell phone. "In that case, don't you think I deserve a reward?"

Alissa laughed. "Your street reputation stands." She fingered the front buttons of her tight blouse. "You drive a hard bargain. I . . . like it."

"Being in this office brings out the businessman in me. While the men outside guard the place, we might as well conduct business properly."

Alissa threw back her head and laughed again. "Fine, my love. We'll do it your way. I always like doing things your way."

Stefan nodded and gestured with his hand again. "Pour us some business drinks. Then . . . let's hear your proposal."

She sauntered off to a cabinet nearby. Soft music suddenly came on. She returned with two filled wineglasses. She deliberately leaned forward as she put them on the table next to him. Then she returned to stand in front of him again. She raised an eyebrow, indicating that she was ready. He nodded.

She started unbuttoning her top slowly, in a teasing, practiced manner. "Our first problem is a missing business acquaintance named Dilaver. I'm sure you have heard of him. If you agree to find out what happened to him," she said as she peeled off the soft material, "you get this."

"Agreed," Stefan said lazily. Alissa knew of only one way to persuade a man and it never seemed to occur to her that he already got what she was offering.

Moving forward and swaying her hips suggestively, she rolled the micro-mini down her hips. "Our second problem is finding the gang who attacked Dilaver. We heard they took a trailer of weapons that should have been ours. If you find out who these people are, you get this."

She released the bunched-up skirt, then touched herself intimately. Every move was calculated to excite the male eye, as if she had done it many times before. She smoothed her hands sensuously up her body, arching her body as she squeezed her breasts together, then up the back of her neck, fluffing her hair languorously.

"Very nice. Come closer." Stefan uncrossed his legs.

Still in her stilettos and wearing only her garters and fishnet stockings, she stepped out of her skirt and moved in between his thighs. "Do you like the proposal?"

He pretended to study her seriously. She really was an attractive woman, one who knew how to use her beauty to get things done. In this corner of the world, she had grown successful using the only means she had—her body. A woman like her was an asset for the Triad brothers. He wondered whether she had any feelings beyond those of greed and sexual gratification.

He picked up the cell phone he had set down on the arm of the chair and hit a button. He watched the smile of triumph spread on her face. Then she dropped on her knees between his legs. He sank deeper into the chair and conducted business, watching with hooded eyes as the woman unbuttoned and reached inside his pants. His eyes narrowed thoughtfully as he looked at the computer on the desk. He finished his instructions and slid the cell back into his breast pocket. Alissa continued to fondle him, but he didn't doubt she had been listening to the conversation. Laying his hand over the drink next to him, he surreptitiously dropped the pill he had palmed.

"Let's drink to the success of our new business," he said.

She looked up, her lipstick smeared. "You're interrupting a transaction," she said.

He sipped his drink, then pushed the other glass to her lips. "Every good business meeting ends in a drink, don't you know?"

She obediently drank as he watched. He finished his.

"Now," he continued, reaching out to settle his hand on her breast, bouncing its weight as his thumb rubbed her nipple. Her lips parted with a sigh. "Let's move onto the desk and see the rest of the contract, shall we? Let me see whether you will give me what I truly want."

What he wanted was a password.

CHAPTER
21

Jazz had never hiked with a woman this long before.
He had to admit it, he had had doubts about Vivi's stamina, but she had once again proven him wrong. They had traveled at a fast clip the past four hours and she had stopped only once, to take off the soggy and muddy socks he had given her.

"I'd rather go barefoot," she'd told him.

"You might cut yourself," he'd warned.

"I'll take the risk. Besides, we're far away enough to signal T."

It was getting very muggy again. He watched Vivi wipe away perspiration on his sleeve, leaving a smear of dirt on her cheek. He offered her a drink from his small canteen, then pointed at the canopy of trees nearby.

"As soon as we've activated your locator, we'll head over to the shade and wait."

"Sounds like a brilliant idea." She smiled. "If I weren't so tired, I'd race you over there. Besides it isn't fair that you have shoes."

Most women would complain about the heat, but Vivi had not only kept up with him, she had injected humor into the situation. He grinned at the sight of her blackened feet.

"I offered to carry you," he reminded her.

"For four hours? You wouldn't be quite this perky," she lightly mocked back as she handed back the canteen.

He made a face. "Please. SEALs aren't perky."

She grinned, then eyed a specific area of his body. "If you say so," she said. Without warning, she started taking off the black shirt. She unhooked the front of her bra and worked a finger inside the cup, giving him glimpses of her nipple. When she looked up, her eyes had a definite twinkle. "It's getting perky again."

Jazz's lips quirked. "That's my personal locator," he informed her.

She laughed. "Do you think, while we wait, Perky can help me find something?"

Oh yeah. Definitely.

Whoever T. was, she was remarkably quick. Within an hour, the unmistakable thumping drone of a helicopter was heard in the distance. Jazz reluctantly lifted his head.

"You know, we should have activated that thing in your bra a little later," he complained, half meaning it. Part of him wanted to spend more time here, talking with and touching each other. It had given him a chance to get to know Vivi better, and he didn't want it to stop.

"Ummm," Vivi agreed. "Do that again."

"Babe, the copter will be here any second now." The thumps were getting louder. "We need to signal them."

"Okay."

They ran to the clearing where they had planted the locator. Vivi shaded her eyes and pointed toward one direction. Jazz pulled her behind a tree. Just in case. One never knew. The bird flew fast and low over the trees, casting its shadow, first over the trees, then on the bare earth as it approached them. It seemed to know exactly where to land. Within minutes it set itself down and a man appeared in the doorway and waved.

"It's Cumber. Let's go," Jazz shouted over the noise, holding out a hand. Vivi placed hers in his and they ran together toward the waiting helicopter.

Vivi climbed in first, with Cucumber's help, then Jazz followed. He gave the big guy a thumbs-up.

"Up and away, buddy!" Cucumber shouted to the pilot. "Everything all right, sir?"

"A-OK. How did you get on this bird?"

"Orders. All we were told was that Miss Verreau had been located. I was sent just in case you were with her since I was the only one who saw you running off toward the truck. All of us assumed that you and Miss Verreau were together."

"How's our team?"

Cucumber gave another thumbs-up. It was too noisy to go into detail, but it was good to know his unit was intact. The big man handed them bottled water.

After a long gulp of refreshment, Jazz looked down at the landscape. From up here, the view was spectacular, showing miles and miles of pristine forest. Yet one never knew what could be hiding in there, especially near the river.

He turned when Vivi touched his arm. She moved closer and shouted into his ear.

"Thank you for saving me."

He nodded. "My pleasure," he said, and winked.

The chopper landed at a private landing strip Vivi recognized as belonging to a former asset. She told Jazz all she knew about the owner. He was now retired, and his rules were simple. No questions asked. "Rentals" were payable in cash wired to a dummy offshore account. In return, the well-equipped and tightly guarded compound was highly prized among certain circles. Two cars, with tinted windows, were waiting when they got off the helicopter.

"Why aren't we going together?" Jazz asked, making the right assumption.

"I have to meet with my chief first. Besides, I need a bath." She wrinkled her nose. "You, too."

His smile did funny things to her insides. "I didn't hear any complaints earlier."

"That's because I'm too much of a lady," she teased. She noticed Cucumber's growing interest in their conversation and coughed delicately. "I'll see you very soon, Lieutenant. Thank you once again for coming to my aid."

She turned away before she succumbed to the temptation of kissing him goodbye and briskly walked toward the car that drove up slowly, indicating that it was for her. The back door clicked open, and she slid inside. The air-conditioned interior brought immediate relief.

"Everything okay?" T. asked, sitting at the far end. "You look terrible. Did Dilaver hurt you? If he did, I hope that absolutely gorgeous naked torso out there canceled the bastard."

Vivi cocked an eyebrow. "You sound worried, Chief." She was going to ignore the comment about Jazz's body.

"Your kidnapping was an unexpected turn of events."

"You did calculate the off chance of it happening, though, or you wouldn't have given me the locator," Vivi pointed out. T. sometimes seemed psychic when it came to preparation for the unexpected. "So why the worry, Chief?"

"You're a friend, Viv. And I know Dilaver." T. tapped the divider between the front seat and the back, letting the driver know they were ready to go. "I was glad when I heard Lieutenant Zeringue had gone off after you. Here, have a drink, darling."

Vivi turned to catch the last sight of Jazz talking to Cucumber as the car turned. "Dilaver caught me by surprise," she admitted. She only did it because this was her chief; she hated acknowledging any weaknesses to anyone, but it would have come up during debriefing anyway. "The situation was sticky but I got out of it without killing him. It would have ended our operation if Jazz had canceled him."

"Not necessarily. I have contingency plans."

That didn't surprise her. "But it would have been problematic," Vivi said.

T. smiled slightly. "One less Dilaver in this world . . ." She shrugged offhandedly.

Vivi relaxed against the leather seat of the car, wincing slightly. The skin on her back felt dry and stretched, and the scratches were beginning to sting. "You have taught me that a known enemy is better than an unknown one. A new Dilaver would be less predictable in our calculations, if there is such a thing as a predictable killer."

"What happened to your back?"

Vivi sighed. She had hoped T. wouldn't notice. "I fell and the ground was rocky," she said carefully. Maybe changing the subject would help. "Update me on the operation—how are the girls? Tell me about Masked Man."

T. studied her for a long moment, then as if she was satisfied that Vivi wasn't really injured, she nodded. "I'm sending a Medic to check on you before debriefing. The operation was a success. None of the girls was injured and they are now in a safe house. As for our prisoner, there's quite a bit to tell, the most interesting of which is his identity."

"Who is he?"

"Our man claims to be one of the Triad brothers. Not the big three, but one of them, anyhow. He gave me a lot of interesting information that I still need to verify but he wouldn't disclose anything about Sia-Sia till you return. He can be an asset to us."

"Do you really believe what he's telling us?" Curiosity filled Vivi. Why was he so adamant about keeping that information from her when he could have told her all this time? "He's still playing games."

"Of course. That's why I kind of like him. Fearlessness is good for an asset, yes? And a warped sense of humor." T. lightly touched Vivi's arm. "I just want to keep you prepared, darling. Just in case Sia-Sia is already dead. That would explain why he chose not to contact you until I showed up. Right now he might just be having a last bit of revenge for your setting up that trap."

Vivi silently agreed. Sia-Sia could very well be dead all these years. But at least she would know for sure.

"I can't wait to talk to Masked Man," she told her chief. "Does he have a name?"

"He calls himself Armando Chang."

At a GEM safe house at the edge of town, T. gave Vivi the keys to the upstairs apartment. Hot shower. Glorious sudsy soap. A thick fluffy bathrobe. T. sent up some food with a medic, who efficiently cleaned the deeper scratches with iodine to prevent infection. As expected, the shower relaxed Vivi even more, and she splashed her face with cold water.

She studied herself in the mirror. There were shadows under her eyes. Her lips looked and felt bruised. She hoped T. wouldn't notice *that*. T.'s ability to probe everything out of someone was downright uncomfortable, and if Vivi could help it, she would rather leave out certain events from the night before.

She stifled a yawn. She would probably be less tired if she hadn't had marathon sex. No rest for the wicked, she told her reflection in the bathroom, and frowned severely. That stupid dreamy smile popping up on her lips had to go. This wasn't the time to think about—she sighed—how her man didn't wear any underwear.

A knock at the door jolted Vivi out of her daydreaming. She briskly wiped her hands on the towel, determinedly pushing wayward thoughts out of her mind.

"Come on in," she called.

T. handed her some clothes. "I guess you won't mind if we burn whatever that's left of your jungle clothing," she said dryly. "It was very nice of Jazz to give you his shirt."

Vivi avoided meeting T.'s keen eyes as she pretended interest in the jeans and shirt. "Yes," she said, keeping her answer short for now.

"He must really care about you. It isn't easy to run after a speeding truck and hang on to the back for hours."

Vivi mumbled something as she pulled the shirt over her head.

"So did he help you get over your abhorrence of military men?" T. drawled.

Keeping her face bland, Vivi lifted her hair out of the shirt. T.'s eyes glimmered with suppressed laughter, daring her to tell a direct lie. "He's different," Vivi finally admitted. Then she shrugged. "But he's still leaving after the operation."

"Darling, don't be so negative." T. headed for the door. "Let's meet Mr. Chang downstairs."

The thought of Jazz leaving was painful. Vivi shook her head. What was the matter with her? She was in the middle of an assignment. And she was also this close to finding Sia-Sia—maybe. To distract herself, she purposely brought up the list of things that needed her attention. Dealing with the Masked Man. Debriefing. Then tomorrow she had to deal with Juliana's cut-off list. There was so much to do.

"Is he violent?" Vivi asked when they paused outside a room.

"No. In fact, I left the door unlocked today." T. knocked.

"Don't you think that might encourage him to escape?" Vivi asked.

"Come in," a voice said from inside.

T. smiled at Vivi. "Having seen his remarkable disappearing skills, I had a hunch he could have escaped whenever he wanted."

She followed T. into the room. Armando Chang was lounging on the sofa watching television without the sound on. He had the remote in one hand, clicking it rapidly.

"Hello, Tess," he greeted. His smile disappeared. "Hello again, Vivienne."

Vivi didn't hide her surprise. "You're the waiter at the hotel!"

He was younger than she had thought, too—probably mid-twenties. He nodded. "Yes."

She turned to T. "Did you know?"

"Yes."

"That very day? When we were lunching?"

"Well, I tested him when I first bumped into him—it was before your arrival, darling—and he refused to trip. So I tested him again at the table. He was a pretty good actor but his reflexes were a bit faster than normal." T. smiled at him. "That's meant as a compliment."

Armando Chang's lips quirked. Like Vivi, he was of mixed blood, his features an exotic mixture of East and West. He had deep-set black eyes, with a strong nose and jawline. His high cheekbones accentuated his masculine yet sensual lips. He appeared quite at home on the sofa as if he hadn't been thoroughly vetted by T. That in itself was noteworthy because T. didn't just interrogate. She could, if she chose, exhaust a mind.

"How long have you known about me?" Vivi asked.

He directed those intense dark eyes at her. "No apologies for kicking me in the groin?" he countered, mockery in his voice.

She arched a brow. "I don't like people walking in and out of my apartment without my permission. All these little hints that you keep throwing at me—my patience is wearing thin."

Armando turned to T. "She isn't like you, Tess," he remarked. "She gets personal."

T. sat down at the far corner of the room. "Careful there," she warned lightly. "She's one of my best students."

"In that case, my apologies," he said smoothly, not sounding the least bit sorry. He turned back to Vivi. "Please be patient with me. I've been watching and waiting for so long that sometimes I forget to be more direct. I do have information for you."

Vivi crossed her arms. "For a price, of course."

"No need to be cynical," Armando chided. "Everything and everyone has a price, sooner or later."

"And you call me cynical?" Vivi decided she didn't like the man. Or trust him. She didn't like people that set prices on themselves. "What's yours?"

"I already told you."

She frowned. "T., are you going to tell me what is it Mr. Chang wants? I'm too tired right now to play guessing games."

T. sat back, looking as if she were about to enjoy some spectator sport. "Armando claims to be one of many Triad siblings," she told her. "The three main brothers that we know about are full-blooded relatives. However, it appears that their father's other wives have given them many half siblings. Armando is the son of the youngest wife. He gave me a name to check up and I'm still on it. His offer to GEM is quite generous. He'll tell us as much as he knows about the Triads, from the drug dealer rings to piracy on the high seas. Being the youngest half-brother, he has limited power and is privy to very little of the family trade secrets, but while his father was alive, he had been given a Western education and groomed for certain overseas operations, Or so he claims."

Vivi studied the man in front of her. Youngest half-sibling. His mother was probably Caucasian. T.'s words suggested that his father was no longer alive. The possible scenario of an internal power struggle came to mind. So perhaps Armando Chang lost out. But that didn't explain his appearance now.

"Why did you show up now?" she asked. "Or is it recently that you've decided to betray your kind?"

Armando's shoulders stiffened, for the first time showing something other than quiet mockery. He didn't like her accusing him of betrayal. Another interesting reaction, Vivi noted. A drug-dealing young gangster with a sense of honor. Well, not much, since he was here, spilling his guts about his beloved brothers. Probably petty jealousy and revenge.

"I suppose I deserve that," he conceded, after a slight pause. "Being related to the Triad brothers brings a certain taint. However, I believe you'll approve of my betrayal in this case."

"Well, I'm here now. T. tells me you won't talk about the girl I've been looking for. So tell me what it is exactly you want and why you came to me about her at this time."

"I didn't see the need till now." He nodded toward T., who was quietly listening. "I've been watching you for a long time, Miss Verreau, and from your various disguises and work with Interpol commandos, figured you were more than the regular social worker you appeared to be, but I couldn't figure out who exactly you worked for because you were also asking personal questions. Out of curiosity, I made it my business to look into your mission. I can be very thorough when I want to be. I finally found proof of what you're looking for, but . . ." He shrugged. "It seemed more interesting to watch your progress."

"Until you found out about Tess," Vivi guessed.

"Yes. I heard about a big thing happening in town, a major weapons dealers' convention, so to speak, and seeing Tess with you finally gave me a clue about your background. I realized then that our paths were going to cross one way or another. I also saw it as my way out."

"You keep saying that phrase. Out of what?"

Armando abruptly clicked the remote, turning off the television. "In exchange for information about the Triads, I want your agency to get me out of this country, away from this life. I believe your people can give me a new identity . . . seeing that both of you have so many." He swung an arm over the back of the sofa, pinning a hard gaze on Vivi. For an instant, her training helped form a mental picture of a young man used to wealth. It was in the way he sat, the polite, stilted language he used that betrayed a childhood among older people. "In exchange for information about the missing Sia-Sia, I want something personal in return. You have to help someone equally important to me."

"Who?"

"My real sister. She's being held against her will."

Vivi looked at T. for confirmation. Her chief shrugged. "I'm still verifying the former. As for the latter, that's your deal to make."

"No," Armando said, a steeliness in his voice, "both deals

are contingent on getting my sister to safety. If Miss Verreau doesn't agree, then I'll be forced to think of other ways. Like maybe betraying your insider."

Vivi gave T. a questioning glance. How much did he know? T. looked back serenely at them both, apparently unperturbed by the threat.

"Why are your brothers holding your sister prisoner?" Vivi asked.

"Because I refused to do certain things while I was overseas." His lips twisted. "As long as they have her, they have a hold on me. They made me come home so they could keep a closer eye on me but since I'm Western educated, my usable skills are now limited to dealings with Westerners here and certain accounts. I prefer that to . . . other things, shall we say?"

Vivi could imagine what those other things were. The Triads had their fingers in the United States underworld dealings with slavery and drugs. If Armando Chang was telling the truth, he had been subjected to emotional blackmail by his stepbrothers.

"How do I know this isn't a trap?" she asked.

"I believe Tess can verify this. Right?"

"Yes," T. acknowledged. She seemed amused at his acting so familiar with her.

"How?" Vivi asked.

"As Armando pointed out, we have someone on the inside who can confirm his and his sister's existence, but that's the least important factor," T. said, her voice subtly turning neutral. "Everything else depends on you. The question is, do you truly think the information he has on Sia-Sia is worth it? What he's asking for ups the risk percentage significantly because now you're asking our insider to look for someone in his environment, extract her to safety, and still finish his mission."

Vivi wouldn't ask that of anyone, and T. knew it. "If what Mr. Chang says is true," she said, "he would be used to being spoilt by servants and all the trappings of wealth. Why would such a man give that up, want a new identity, and go somewhere else? We can still save your sister, regardless, so the question is, why are you putting yourself in the equation? Why ask *me*?"

Armando stood up and walked to the window, turning his back to them. Vivi suspected that he didn't want them to see his expression, that asking for help was something he hated. She recognized the gesture in herself; she disliked explaining herself to anyone and if she had to do it, she usually created distance either verbally or physically.

His back was very straight. "Because you'll understand how I feel. My sister is very dear to me and I promised to keep her safe. I haven't done a good job because I don't know where she is. All I have is some videos showing her confined in a small room somewhere. My brother assures me she's fine but . . ." He finally turned and his eyes flashed with emotion for the first time. "Let's just say I have seen how my family treats women. I don't want my sister missing like your friend, who, I believe, is like a sister to you. I do empathize with your loss, Miss Verreau, but your search had nothing to do with mine until I was sure you could help me."

He had watched her long enough to know what was important to her. Sia-Sia. Young girls victimized by circumstance. He was pulling on her emotional strings.

"You still haven't answered the main question," she pointed out. "Why do *you* choose to leave what you have?"

"Yes, I can always escape without your help. But I don't trust you to take care of my sister, nor can I ensure her safety without me close by. The Triads are a big family and you can't exactly assure me that they won't find her again someday." His voice lowered. "I don't like my life. I don't want to live on money that came from women and children. I wasn't able to save my mother. Find my sister for me. Please."

"You have a lot of confidence that Vivi will agree to help you, Armando," T. said.

Armando smiled humorlessly. "I'm counting on her need to see the truth for herself. I can lead her to Sia-Sia. She's alive. You see, she's one of my stepsisters."

After Cucumber gave him the *Reader's Digest* version of events, Jazz napped during the ride back to the compound. His team was okay, except for minor injuries to Turner. Vivi's team had suffered most of the damage, Cucumber told him, especially those on the other side of the river where the two of them had been. The big man told him how some of them had been hit when they had tried to take the trailer with the girls.

"Where are the girls now?"

"I gather they are in some safe place," Cucumber said with a shrug. "Screaming girls aren't my cup of tea."

Vivi was probably going to be busy for a while. That was his last thought before he had drifted off. He opened his eyes the moment the car's engine cut off. It was dark.

"Underground parking," explained Cucumber.

Jazz rubbed the back of his neck, working the crick out. "We're under the compound?"

"Yeah. Pretty cool way to go in and out the place unseen, don't you agree?"

The compound sure hid a lot of things. Kind of like Vivi. She had so many different sides and he loved every one of them. The snotty Interpol officer. The sultry team task force leader. The brave operative who put her life in jeopardy to save young girls. And last night . . . he loved the woman he had made love to the most. So honest with her emotions. So generous with body, mind, and spirit.

A couple of flights of stairs later, he grinned at the sight of Hawk and the rest of the team. They were in what they now called the mess hall, doing what SEALs do best during down time—playing with their toys. Hawk looked up from sharpening his knives.

"Well, look what the wind blew in."

His team greeted him raucously, asking questions and making comments about his appearance. His shirtlessness didn't escape their notice.

"Beg your pardon, sir, but you have on your chicken lips again," Mink said, with a knowing smirk.

"I think he graduated to goats," Hawk observed. The others snickered. "How's Vivi?"

One couldn't hide much from his fellow frogs. They knew. "She wasn't hurt," Jazz answered the unvoiced concern. "How's Turner?"

"Hurt one of his knees." Joker handed a tray to Mink, who passed it Cucumber.

"Yeah, his weenie," Cucumber said, stressing on the "wee" as he gave the tray to Jazz. "We saved some of the leftover feast for ya."

"Thanks," Jazz said, looking at all the different small containers. "Very nice. You guys went to a Tupperware party while I was gone."

"Eat, clean, debrief," Hawk told him.

"With all respect, sir, he looks like he's already been debriefed," Dirk said, wiping hands blackened from gun oil with a cloth, "several times, last night."

"Yeah, I want to read his After Actions Report."

"Top Secret, I bet."

"Yeah, well, dude, I just want to get to the bottom, which would be the more interesting part, ya understand?"

His team's easy camaraderie was their way of telling him they were happy he was in one piece. But for the first time, Jazz didn't want to exchange the usual male locker-room humor and easy banter. His night with Vivi—or at least, certain parts of it—was off limits.

"I'll see you all in an hour," he told them, as he headed toward Hawk's and his quarters.

"What the hell is wrong with him?" he heard Mink ask as he walked out of the hall.

"Sensitive and broody, isn't he? He doesn't look well at all."

Jazz shook his head. The Stooges—Mink, Cumber, and Dirk—were deliberately needling him in loud whispers. He paused long enough to hear the punch line.

"Yeah, he's got Coxic Shock Syndrome."

Everyone in the room was a fucking clown. Jazz slammed the door shut to their laughter.

Back in the room, he peeled off his torn and filthy clothes and threw them in a small pile near the door. He opened one of the containers and snatched up some kind of rice snack. He was starving and if he didn't clean up now, he was going to sit here and eat and eat. Hitching the towel around his hips, he headed off again, this time to the community bath facility down the hall.

As the water beat on him, he looked at the water draining at his feet. He definitely needed the shower. Keeping clean was a luxury that SEALs didn't usually have during an operation. He had been in situations where traveling with farm animals was the only option in or out of a region, and after a few weeks, the animals around probably thought the men hunkered among them were their brothers. He grinned at the fleeting memory. Life was never boring.

But it was time to think about wanting more. He loved his country and his job, and hadn't given serious thought about his future. He wanted Vivi to be a part of it. Maybe if he had something more to offer her, she would see something in him, too.

Back in his quarters, he found Hawk in the room, writing something on a notepad. He didn't look up as Jazz went over to the dresser and pulled out the top drawer. There was the same kind of loose-fitting local garment that Hawk had worn before. He pulled on the pants. They were too short for his long legs but it would have to do for now.

"Is Vivi really all right? Why isn't she here?" Hawk asked.

"She went off in another vehicle, probably needed to be debriefed," Jazz said. He paused in the middle of buttoning his shirt. "And I don't want to hear another debriefing joke. "What are you writing?"

Hawk shrugged. "A shopping list. A letter. A will."

Jazz frowned. That wasn't quite Hawk's usual thing. "Why now?"

"I was going to wait till after the admiral talk to tell you—"

"Mad Dog is going to talk to us?" Jazz interrupted.

"Yes, video link. It'll be in two parts, one a private meeting with just our team and then with the joint mission."

Admiral Madison always took time to congratulate his teams after a mission. It would be interesting to hear him address the joint mission panel. After watching Vivi at work, Jazz's admiration for the independent contractors had grown in leaps.

But something wasn't right. He could sense Hawk's restlessness, even though his friend hadn't shown any sign of it. "What were you going to tell me?"

Hawk's expression was closed. "I'm probably going to miss Christmas. The shopping list is for you to pick up a couple of things for me and send them in my name so folks back home think I'm okay. The letter for you to keep just in case . . . you need to explain anything. The will . . . well, that's self-explanatory."

"You care to give me a fuller explanation of what's happening?" Christmas was months away, so why was Hawk preparing a list now? And his words seemed to mean that he wasn't going to be with the team during that time.

"Remember when I went to help my cousin extract his girl in D.C.? I told you about Project X-S-BOT."

Jazz nodded. "I remember. Some files in the laptop stolen from the Naval Lab. That was why Marlena was in D.C., you said—to find out who was trying to sell it."

"Yes, and that's how she and Steve met."

Hawk's cousin had been sent to D.C. to find the mole at the agency responsible for providing information that had led to several members of the admiral's SEAL teams being killed. With Marlena's and GEM's help, Steve had uncovered the traitor. Through his own snatches of conversation with family members, Jazz heard there was a big scandal happening in D.C. right now. It had been reported that the same traitor had been selling national secrets for the last decade. He had tuned out most of the stuff his sister had told him about security councils, public outrage, and all the political shenanigans happening back home. News never made sense, anyhow, when one was living it. However, this incident with Steve and Marlena had been of interest to the teams because they had wanted to catch the man who had sold out their brothers.

Hawk handed him a piece of paper, indicating a need for secrecy. Jazz read the small and neat handwriting. "Recently, we have found proof of the traitors selling our high-tech weaponry secrets to arms dealers. Mad Dog made a deal with GEM. Their top operatives have been working to infiltrate several very well-known arms dealers the last few years. Marlena Maxwell in D.C. was Phase Two. Our side wants the location of where the latest cache of weapons was dropped. It has to do with X-S-BOT. I've been ordered to do Phase Three and GEM will facilitate my new role. I'll be in deep cover for probably up to six months, infiltrating Dilaver's network."

"Alone." It wasn't a question. Jazz already understood that it was a lone assignment. One clearly couldn't access Dilaver's network with a team of SEALs. His statement was meant to underline the danger of the job of working as a double agent. "What's the assignment?"

"Find out his U.S. contacts and where he hides the 'extra' weapons sent by our traitors. Break down his army in zones. But most important of all, destroy the latest shipment. Then run like hell." Hawk cracked a small smile. "With the knowledge in my head, they'll be hunting me down. I have to pass it along to another contact just in case they capture me."

Jesus. The KLA had, among various factions, a formidable army of gangsters. They and other Dilaver gang members would find Hawk and kill him, if they had to go house to house. His friend was foreseeing the possibility of being exterminated before he could escape, thus the shopping list, the letter, and the will.

They eyed each other for a full, sobering minute. Hawk and he had made an agreement a long time ago. If one didn't make it, the other would take care of personal things. If by chance, one went missing, the other was to somehow do the impossible—find out whether he was dead or alive so family members could be told one day.

"You'd better come home in one piece, buddy, or I'd have to tell all those Steves and Stevens you got drunk and drowned during training," Jazz said quietly. "They won't believe me and I don't feel like beating up a bunch of your relatives when they attack me for lying to them."

Hawk grinned. "I'll try my best to save your pretty face from my family."

"And I need you back in case I need a best man," Jazz added.

Hawk played with the pen, studying him thoughtfully. "Sure she's the one?"

Jazz nodded. "It'll take time to get her to come around to thinking about being with me." He hesitated, then added, "Okay, so I don't really know how I'm going to accomplish that."

Not when they hadn't actually talked about the future. So far, he had just found out about her past.

"Find out her real name," Hawk advised.

"What do you mean?"

"Do you know that opera called *Turandot*?"

Jazz walked over to the small table where he had set all the food containers. "I need food. My twin is talking Puccini with me," he addressed no one in particular.

"I saw the opera with Steve and Marlena in D.C."

Now he remembered. Cucumber, Dirk, and Mink had talked about that particular night not long after their big shootout. Of course, their version had nothing to do with the opera. In fact, he recalled hearing that Cucumber had slept through the whole show.

"Okay, let's talk *Turandot*," Jazz said as he sniffed at an orange-colored concoction.

"It's about a beautiful princess who won't marry you unless you answer three riddles correctly. If you fail, she orders your execution." Hawk used his pen to demonstrate a mock beheading. "Pretty cold lady."

"So, are you trying to tell me I'm going to fail or that I'm going to win Vivi's hand? This mango rice is delicious, by the way."

Hawk stood up and went to join him at the table. He scooped up some of the rice with his hand. "I'm betting on you to get all those riddles right, buddy."

"Oh, good. You're on my side. I thought you were interested in the princess and were wishing me to be the unfortunate dead suitor."

Hawk reached for more rice. "What, you want competition? Isn't that a bit tough when I'm not around to win?"

Jazz pushed the container out of the way. "My food. I can't win what's mine."

A smile tugged at his friend's lips. "Touché," he said. "Just remember one thing, and I'm telling you because I'm your best-est friend who wants to see you win your girl."

"You're getting soft and sentimental."

"I'm going away for a while. Who's going to give you all that girly advice while I'm gone? Are you letting your sisters do your work for you?"

Jazz shuddered. He could just see all his sisters around Vivi. They loved him fiercely and would probably scare Vivi to death with instructions and questions. "Fine. Tell me what to do, Dear Abby."

"The princess has a riddle, man. Answer it."

Jazz chewed for several seconds. "You're kidding right? You're asking me to follow an opera's storyline. That's your girly advice?"

"Yeah."

"Well, it sucks."

"Think it over tonight while you jerk off."

"I'd rather think of Vivi, thank you."

They bantered lightheartedly for a few minutes before Hawk went back to his desk. They had to go to debriefing soon. Jazz ate quietly, watching his friend write. It was sort of macabre to eat and observe Hawk taking measures against an uncertain future. Just in case.

Time was so precious in this world. He wanted Vivi in it. In a perfect future, he would wish for his best friend to be there for his wedding.

"It'd be a pleasure to get to kiss such a beautiful princess bride," Hawk murmured without looking up, uncannily reading his mind as usual.

"I might even let you, my friend."

A riddle, huh? He'd better brush up on his *Turandot* story.

CHAPTER
22

In spite of her aversion to military talk and political tactics, Vivi had to admit that Admiral Madison cut a very commanding and captivating figure on the big screen. He must be very impressive in person. He certainly had a way with words, cutting to the chase without any frills or pompous references. She could see his men looked at him as a role model; every time he spoke, it was as if Moses was handing down the Commandments.

She had always been cynical about the top brass—they were up there, looking down, and usually never knew what was truly happening. Admiral Madison struck her as someone who actually did care about his men and their lives. He was strong and authoritative, yet took the time to listen to Hawk and Jazz when they had something to say, and he certainly gave a lot of weight to T.'s advice. It wasn't a show he put on, like some higher-ups did when there were female figures around. He was neither condescending nor smarmy, and Vivi found herself actually paying attention to everything he said.

GEM was in a covert war within a covert war, and she played a tiny part in it now, like it or not. Her current contract had to do with women and children, but now that she had agreed to help Armando Chang, she would have to insert herself into Phase Three. She hadn't planned to before, but Armando's desperation had touched her. He was looking for a missing sister. Even if he hadn't baited her with Sia-Sia, she might have taken up his cause.

She bit back a wry smile. Or maybe not. She was still mad at his underhanded tactic but a part of her was grudgingly acknowledging his skill at having gone undetected by her. She was very good at what she did; she usually knew when someone was following her around, but Armando Chang had successfully evaded her. She knew that had caught her chief's attention.

Kosovo. KLA. Arms dealing and drugs. Macedonian cartels. Those contracts had never interested her before. Her focus had always been on more immediate things, like tracking female slavery and child abuse. Those were important causes to her.

Yet T. and Admiral Madison had given her a new view of how everything was connected in this horror. And how tangled the web of political intrigue was. The different wars in Kosovo had given too many factions reasons to abuse power.

"I know sometimes we don't see the big picture," the admiral addressed them quietly. "If you ask the average person on the street, they can't tell you anything about the battles going on that our young men are fighting. They will say the general things—the war against terrorism, against despots, against injustices. You who fight in the trenches know these things are just faceless banners. They don't mean a damn thing. Whether it's the heat of the jungle or desert or anywhere on this earth, each of us battles small pockets that sometimes don't even make sense.

"The newspapers give a lot of attention to the public battles. I also know you could care less what the papers report while you're sweating your asses off knee-deep in mud and blood. There is no glory in what we do, men. And ladies, too, pardon me, T. and Miss Verreau. We are in a covert war that grows more urgent everyday because our enemies—the real ones—play shadow games. Our troops are fighting battles with the enemies' foot soldiers. That is all very well and important. It's essential to destroy our enemies' weapons—human and nonhuman.

"But let's be clear among ourselves about the invisible front—we who stand in the crossfire. I have come to realize that we must also win the war behind the war. That's the job of special ops units such as ours in this room. Both our worlds must work together for optimum success. One is our world of dirty fighting, going right at the source, those damn cartels and factions that run all the illegal activities that finance terrorism. The other is infiltration and covert subversion, which the COS commandos and GEM operatives do. Our battles are different—we SEALs favor quick injection of violence, in and out, with maximum destruction of potential enemy networks; they, on the other hand, specialize in going in deep and working among our enemies for long periods to gain insight and knowledge. But we are also alike in many ways. We lurk in the shadows to find the real enemy. We do a lot of the dirty work behind the scenes because it's necessary. We are in the crossfire because we're the invisible warriors. If anything goes wrong, the average Joe on the street will never know the real story."

The admiral paused, and even across the miles, his blue eyes were direct and steady. Vivi found herself holding her breath, waiting for him to continue. She had never seen the big picture the way he had described it. He made sense out of a lot of confusion. At one point, she caught T.'s eyes on her, studying her reaction to what was a pep talk for a group of soldiers. T. understood her discomfort with the talk of war and battles. To her, soldiers had always done the destruction, created the problems; her job dealt with the aftermath. But Admiral Madison's speech gave a new spin.

"I'm here in D.C. because of this shadow war. State secrets and high technology are being sold by traitors within our borders to illegal cartels merging like Wall Street corporations. There are countries eager to buy this information. Intel. Arms dealing. Sex trade. Drugs. They all combine to finance power. We just caught one of these traitors recently, but not before he had done untold damage to our nation. Not only did some of our SEAL brothers die because of this scum, but probably many other covert operatives have been sacrificed.

"The latest discovery—not told to the public, of course— is some dropped shipments of high tech weapons not meant for the KLA or any foreign troops. From our investigations here, we know Dilaver either knows where they are or has them. We need to find and destroy these shipments or risk bigger and more expensive wars. I'm sending in a lone infiltrator, just like GEM and COS Command has already done. This man will work with their man. He will go back to Kosovo with Dilaver—alone.

"There will be one more joint mission that will give our man the opportunity to insert himself as Dilaver's helper. The specifics of the operation will be given to you by Tess Montgomery, a very capable strategist in her own right. You—and I mean everyone in this room—are an invisible warrior, a soldier who is in the crossfire taking all the risks while avoiding being caught. Know this. You are the big picture. Get the job done and come back home safely, men."

The whole speech was spoken without any drama. Admiral Madison's approach was simpler—he was sincere and direct and he didn't mince his words. Vivi, seldom impressed by military trappings, felt the tingle down her spine, the kind that made one feel proud and good about oneself. This, she thought in private amazement, was NOPAIN at its best. The admiral must either be a natural or had a hell of an instructor. Again, she caught T.'s gaze and thought she saw the tiniest gleam from those amethyst eyes.

Yet, she couldn't dispute the truth of what Admiral Madison outlined. The sex trade was just the tip of the iceberg. And the drugs. She gave a mental shake of disgust. This drug that made its victims helpless . . . she shuddered inwardly. The information her superiors had given was grim. From GEM's view, sex trade plus drugs equals finance for arms dealing. From Admiral Madison's side, the arms dealers weren't just dealing with illegal weapons floating around from obsolete Soviet countries, but they are also vying for power in an unstable region. The endgame was simple. The faction with the biggest weapon to sell to the highest bidder would win.

She felt somebody tap her shoulder and turned. Jazz's blue eyes smiled down at her. There was an intimacy in his gaze, even though his expression remained solemn. She smiled, unsure of what to say. The admiral had also pressed home a point that she had never considered. Funny. And totally ironic. She was a soldier.

Jazz knew that it was going to be impossible to be alone with Vivi for the rest of the day. She was talking to her chief, Tess Montgomery, whom Mad Dog had introduced briefly. There was something different about the new GEM operative who had joined them. It wasn't just because the woman looked more like a movie star than an operations chief. Tall, long-legged, with flowing reddish hair that floated loosely to her hips, she wasn't dressed like any operations chief about to conduct official business. It was the effect she had on his team. In fact, he could have sworn when she winked at his team as she passed them, some of them shuffled their feet. That certainly wasn't the usual attitude he knew his team had when it came to beautiful women. He caught the Stooges giving each other secret signals.

He frowned. Hawk was talking to Tess with an easy familiarity that suggested he'd met her before. He noticed that Vivi was also watching and frowning, as if she, too, was thinking the same thing.

This was the woman he had to spend time with to go over strategy about what his team needed to do to insert Hawk. Instinct told him that she was more than she appeared to be, that the glamour she projected was an illusion. She looked vaguely familiar, but he was sure they hadn't met before. No one could possibly forget those Elizabeth Taylor eyes. Vivi looked over and gestured to him to join them.

"Lieutenant Zeringue, this is my chief, T.," she said. "She's been involved in all the phases of the operation, and that's why she's here today to brief you."

There was a dry note to Vivi's voice, as if she was absolutely aware of how her chief affected men in general.

"Nice to meet you, ma'am."

"T.," she said easily, shaking his hand. "That way you won't get confused when people call me by other names later."

"T." he agreed. Other names?

"I heard you're pretty proficient with the piano, Lieutenant. I gather, from your handle, that you favor jazz and blues?" She had a beautiful speaking voice, the kind that advertisers go after. His musician ears appreciated the different inflections she placed on words.

"Yes, being from Louisiana . . ." He shrugged.

"You have to play me something one of these days, when we aren't so busy. I have a particular blues song that is my favorite."

"Sure. What is it?"

Her beautiful eyes had a gleam in them as she flashed a breathtaking smile at him. "Oh, it's about the usual blues thing. Masquerade and masks, things to do with the heart."

Vivi was frowning. "T. . . ." Jazz caught a hint of a warning in her tone of voice. "I believe we don't have much time to talk about music."

"There's a lot of choreography in music and war, darling. Don't you agree, Hawk?"

He was right about his earlier impression. T. and Hawk were on a first-name basis. His frown deepened. When did they meet? Hawk had never mentioned her—just Marlena Maxwell and Vivi—whenever they had talked about GEM.

"Yes, although Jazz would tell you that they are opposites. One is creation and the other is destruction," Hawk said.

"Interesting point. And Lieutenant Zeringue is skilled in both." T. arched an eyebrow.

Jazz lifted a shoulder. He hadn't thought about it that way. "I'm good at arranging things in sequence," he said mildly.

"It's all sight and sound, isn't it? Things can be created for destruction and vice versa, hmm? And sometimes what you can't see can turn out either way, right?"

Jazz frowned. He had no idea what the woman was talking about. He hoped she didn't speak in those terms when she gave him the information about the Triads' bunker or he was going to have a hell of a time figuring things out. "I suppose," he hedged cautiously.

"T., stop messing with his mind," Vivi interrupted at that moment, her voice low. "We don't have time for this."

Tess Montgomery gave him a cryptic smile. "Timing— very important in music and explosives," she told him, then abruptly turned back to Hawk. "Introduce me to your men, Hawk. I've heard such good things about them."

Hawk flashed Jazz a quick grin, amusement stamped on his face, before going off with the GEM operative. Jazz knew that expression well. It meant his friend knew things that he wasn't going to share yet. He turned to Vivi.

"How's your back? Did you do something about the scratches?" he asked.

She looked surprised, as if his concern was unexpected. Did she think he wouldn't remember the scratches? "I'm okay," she said. "I'll probably feel it more tomorrow."

"Tired?"

She eyed him suspiciously. "Are you suggesting that I can't keep up with you?"

He widened his eyes innocently. "I was going to suggest that I continue to keep up with you. But only if you aren't too tired, of course."

She kept her expression severe even though a small smile tugged at the corner of her lips. "I knew it," she mocked. "I knew I shouldn't have slept with you. Now all you're going to think about is me naked in the woods, tearing your clothes off, pushing you to the ground, climbing on top of your naked body and having my way with you."

Jazz groaned at the instant reaction the description brought up. "You win," he said, ruefully hoping no one would notice his condition.

Vivi snickered. "Men are so easy."

"I wish we were alone again. Then I could show you how easy I can be."

She hesitated. "I . . . wish that too."

He hid his satisfaction. He understood how difficult it was for her to admit that. He had to be very careful with how he worded his next few sentences. "I don't know how tight the schedule will be, *chouchou*, but I'd like to have dinner with you. I know it's going to be very busy for both of us the next few days and without a way of contacting you, I'm at a disadvantage." He took a step closer. "Call me?"

"And if I don't?"

He cautioned himself again. "You'll hurt my feelings. I'll feel used and abused," he deadpanned. "You'll feel guilty about how you've hurt me for the rest of your life. And it'll be your fault if I play 'Oh Susannah' mournfully on the Dan Nhat like some lovesick puppy, dying from unrequited love. Believe me, you don't want that to happen."

His attempt to keep it as lighthearted as possible worked. Amusement chased away the hesitation in her eyes. She shook her head. "I believe you. I heard your first attempt," she said wryly. "I'll call."

"Soon," he pressed. He wasn't quite *that* patient.

"Soon," she agreed. She looked away for a second. "I have to go now. Got the other job to catch up on. T.'s going to sort of take over my role for the next phase."

"I get the feeling she's more into the illegal weapons division of your agency. Will you be involved in this operation at all?" He was fishing for information, selfishly wishing for her to be close by. "Miss Montgomery doesn't have the same . . . touch as you, *chouchou*."

"Don't challenge T.," she said, but she looked somewhat

pleased that he wanted her to work with him. "I probably won't have any direct involvement now that we have gotten the girls out of Dilaver's and the Triads' clutches, but I'll be busy, too. Like you, I need to be briefed about certain details that we've just gotten."

"Okay." He could appreciate keeping their jobs separate. He would definitely have a heart attack if he watched her "at work" again. He frowned. Not that it would be any better not seeing or knowing. Damn, this was harder than he'd thought. So this was how Maman felt every time he had been deliberately vague about his job. "Just be careful."

He wanted to kiss her but of course he didn't. She licked those tempting lips, as if the same thought crossed her mind. At least he hoped so. He wanted her to think about him.

"You, too," she said.

He watched her walk off, enjoying the sway of her hips. One day, he would tell her that her walk turned him on. He joined Hawk and the rest of the team in the conference room. T. was the center of attention, with his team sitting and standing in a semicircle around her. She must have made a joke of some sort; they were laughing. Loudly. He frowned, walking closer to Hawk, who was leaning against the back wall.

"I see the session hasn't started," Jazz commented softly.

"I believe it has," Hawk told him in an equally soft tone.

"Twin, you're keeping something from me. I can feel it."

Hawk glanced at him briefly before returning his attention to T. and the others. "What makes you say that?"

"For one thing, you didn't tell me you had met Tess Montgomery. You also seemed quite prepared to leave the team for a while, as if you've known about it. There's also the mention just now of training. Lastly, look at that." Jazz jerked his chin at the sight in front of him. "Our team doesn't react like that, no matter how beautiful the woman."

"You notice too, huh?" Hawk turned to him again, quizzical expression in his eyes.

"They are laughing with her, for God's sake. How can I

not notice that?" Jazz asked. A sudden thought occurred. "It isn't more of that NOPAIN shit you told me about, is it?"

"Some of it," Hawk said, "but more lethal, I think."

"You think?" Jazz studied the group again. T. was talking and his team—men he had fought and lived with for years, whom he knew would never react this way—was giving her the kind of focus they usually had when they were receiving orders. "What the hell is going on, Hawk? Is she doing something to them?"

"It's something to do with mind control. I've only heard of it. You know Steve has met her. He told me that she can do certain things with her voice. And that she is the one who teaches NOPAIN to most of the GEM operatives."

Jazz went on instant alert. Mind control? That was the kind of gook myths and experiments the frogs laughed about. "What do you mean, her voice? You've talked to her before. Did you laugh and joke along with her like that?"

Hawk shook his head. "Negative. She didn't seem to have it turned on like now. I've heard she's a mistress of disguises, that she's really not this person we're watching. But then that's sort of a GEM trademark, isn't it? Steve told me to pay attention to her voice. He didn't mention that she has the sort of beauty that keeps one's eyes trained on her, though."

Jazz looked at her closely again. She was really a stunning woman. There was something almost untouchable about her, though. Celtic music. He preferred Vivi's warmer beauty. "Here's another GEM operative you can get interested in," he said, injecting a hopeful note in his voice.

Hawk grinned. "Hell no. This one's lethal, man. I think she can kill with her voice."

"You aren't serious, right? That woman is not a mind-controlling seductress. Our guys are just horny from being locked away from female company."

Hawk's grin widened and he shrugged. "You're probably right. Let's join them."

Half an hour later, Jazz was convinced Hawk had been half

serious after all. T., as she seemed to prefer to call herself, had given the men all they needed to know about the next operation without one of them asking any questions. Hell, they were so absorbed in her that they seemed surprised when she addressed him.

"I'll get in touch with you after you've rested, Lieutenant Zeringue. We have to go over all the logistics."

"What you said earlier to me, about what one can't see turning out to be either destructive or creative," Jazz began, and when she arched a brow, he continued, "How about subliminal messages in music?"

T. smiled cryptically and left without actually answering him. It suddenly felt as if energy had been sucked out of the room. There was a moment of silence.

Mink took a deep breath. Then another. "Wow." He looked around and headed for the flask of water on the table.

"Yeah, wow. Hawk and Miss T. I think some people have all the damn luck," Cucumber commented as he too joined Mink. "I think she's fabulous."

Jazz exchanged glances with Hawk. T. had used that to describe things several times.

"Fabulous? What kind of asinine word is that for a man?" Dirk asked.

"That's ass and nine and a half to you, scum."

The guys snickered. Okay, that sounded more like the Cumber Jazz knew.

"Her ass and your—"

"Men, we're talking about a friend of the admiral's. Watch the language," Hawk said.

"Yes, sir."

"We have to coordinate this very carefully because it is more than our usual sneak and attack operation." Hawk looked around at the men. "As you know, I won't join you on the trip home. As soon as I disappear, Jazz will take over and you are to get out of there even if you see me in any trouble with Dilaver. No exceptions."

The team sobered up as realization dawned that this was

probably the last mission they would see Hawk on for a while. They had bonded in a way that few men had—blind faith in one another's abilities to keep each other safe. They had always gotten the job done as a team, even when they went off in pairs. This time, their commander was going to go at it alone.

CHAPTER
23

Vivi burst into Juliana's office without knocking,
barely containing her fury, as she headed straight toward the
woman sitting at the desk talking on the phone. She leaned
over and disconnected the call.

"Why did you have all my calls transferred to you without
my permission?" she asked, in the most civil tone she could
manage.

Juliana replaced the receiver on the phone. "You weren't
here to take the calls," she replied dulcetly.

"First, you have no right to do that without asking me.
Second, you have no right to act upon any calls placed to me
without knowing the situation or checking with me." This
time Vivi didn't bother to lower her voice. "What did you do
to Rose?"

Juliana widened her eyes. "You're a volunteer. I can see
that you were busy and had a backlog of work on your
schedule. Judging from the calls, it appeared you have been
unable to keep up with it and I decided—"

"*You* decided? How dare you cut off my communications
and tell the operator that you're in charge of my cases?" Vivi
leaned even closer, eye to eye with the other woman. "I
checked with the logs and there were three calls to me from

Rose. I want to know exactly what you said to her because I can't get hold of her now."

Juliana pushed away from the desk, keeping some distance from Vivi. "I needed the numbers down. You were unable to cut them as requested. I did your job for you." Her smile was small, malicious. "You think just because you're an outside contractor, I can't touch you? But I can certainly help out with your responsibilities when you're away doing other things, like dating a certain GI that you just happened to release. I told you I can be a bitch."

The insinuation was there to serve as warning but Vivi didn't care right now. She was worried about Rose. She had called her house repeatedly since last night but had gotten no reply. An awful feeling had sunk into her gut when she had discovered the messages. Instead of transferring the calls to her private message line, the secretary had forwarded them to Juliana. When she had finally gotten through, a woman had whispered that Rose didn't live there any more.

"What did Rose tell you? Damn it, Juliana, she isn't a number."

"You were giving her father cash. He ran through it like water and he wanted more, so he dangled his daughter at you again. I told you that was against organization policy. Rose is old enough to go out and find a job and that's what I told her, that you can't help her any longer. I've also reported your actions to the department for reevaluation and replacement." Juliana picked up the receiver again. "Now, if that's all you want to know, I have my job to do, too. You interrupted a very important media interview about—"

Vivi rudely jerked the phone off the desk. "What I do with my money is none of your business. Yes, it's my money that I've been using to stave off a child—a child, Juliana, not someone you can just shove off because she is suddenly a cut-off number—from being forced by her father to live the kind of lifestyle you and the organization are fighting against. Remember *that* policy? Ethical treatment of women and children? Or is that now amended to ethical treatment of women and children below the cut-off number?"

"How dare you insinuate that I care any less than you? I have to make the numbers work so you can get the funds to keep the safe houses going. You think it's easy for me to pick and choose? I've been here longer than you and have given myself fully to this organization's work, endlessly raising the needed funds. And we are so close to getting the UN required recommendations for approval, I am *not* going to let some outside contractor destroy our chances to get those funds. You owe me an apology. You owe the organization *and* your agency an apology. How dare *you* talk about keeping children safe when you're out like some loose woman with a military officer accused of molesting a child? The very same child you're looking out for?" Juliana took in a deep breath, then released it slowly. "There are always some sacrifices in any cause. You're blinded by your emotions. I believe it'd be better if you're released from volunteering and just focus on your real job with Interpol. You have to admit, you work better with men."

Vivi straightened up. She wasn't blinded by emotions, as Juliana had suggested. She had just been so busy with running another operation that she hadn't seen this coming. She had felt the tension in the air, had known from the last confrontation between them that a big one wasn't too far away, but had ignored the warning signals because of the events around her.

She had sacrificed Rose with her consuming desire to save that trailer of girls. That didn't sit very well right now.

"Do you know who's blind? You are." The heat of anger had gone. Her heart fisted, holding all her emotions in. "You sit here with your numbers, playing with lives. You make excuses that the ends justify the means, so you say some of these 'numbers' can be slotted off because they don't fit your columns. You ignore the fact that these kids are forced into that system you're fighting against and they end up pregnant and their kids repeat the cycle. Voilà! You need more funds. You can continue with your cause. There will always be victims. Hitting too close to home, Juliana? I believe you just turned a tad white. And I know you want bigger things. All that media coverage and fund-raising galas—very nice to get all dressed up and be around the important people, isn't it?"

"You have no idea what you're talking about. What I do will benefit the kids—"

Vivi shrugged. "Yes, you're concerned about the children but you love these side things a little more, don't you? There's even more access to the spotlight if you can only get UN approval and UN funds. International foundation sounds so much more glamorous than a small organization of women without enough money. You're addicted to being associated with the people and its cause but not its work."

"Shut up."

"I will for now. But don't think I'll just quietly go away. You think I don't know what I'm talking about? I didn't volunteer to help out. I did it because I was one of these kids here a long time ago and I know exactly which ones could be saved if given the chance or the push. People like you . . ." Vivi shook her head. "An apology? My going out with a military man— you're going to use that as an excuse to remove me? And here I thought there were higher priorities and problems. I'm going to find Rose and if anything has happened to her, Miss Jung, I'll personally make your life such a living hell that you will wish you weren't that bitch you so proudly proclaim to be."

"I don't like your threatening tone, Vivienne. If you can't discuss this in a more businesslike way, please leave my office." There was a tightness around Juliana's lips. She pulled on the cord, retrieving the fallen phone from the carpet. "I have a meeting to schedule and as you point out, fund-raisers to attend. You might not think that's important, but the people who matter see things my way, not yours. To them—to us—you're trouble to this business. It's out of my hands. Discuss your views with the board and see whether they will side with me or you. Personally, I'd be happy if there is a new liaison replacement."

There were many people like Juliana Kohl. They wanted to belong to an organization and the running of it. After a while, the cause became secondary.

"This isn't business. Business uses people to promote and propagate itself." Vivi turned and walked to the door. She felt sick. That these people would do this to a group of women and children—people they were supposed to protect—how different were they from those who sell them as a trade? She glanced back and softly added, "When it's a girl's life you're destroying, it's personal. Will you please stop thinking of them as your precious numbers for once? My liaison isn't with you, by the way. It's between the organization and Interpol. You might not have me as a volunteer, but I'll still be around in this office."

"We'll see about that."

She was going to give this woman something to see and think about. "One more thing. Getting your numbers right might get you the funds you want, but I've checked the breakdown of actual allocated funds. What would the public say when they see how expensive certain personal perks like vehicles and residences for public information officers are? Especially when the pat answer is it's for *media* functions?"

"How—" Juliana bit her lower lip, turning red as she realized she had betrayed herself.

"I have my own sources, Juliana. Do you think it'd escape my notice that you hold functions that government officials attend? It gets in the papers, you know . . . your name, officials' names. Does anyone on the board know that Minister Nguyen Onn has been known to frequent brothels?" The minister had been a strong supporter of women's rights lately and had come to the functions to voice his opinions as well as get publicity. He had contributed some big checks to the cause, but Vivi and every local person knew about his hobby. She had wondered whether Juliana did, too. The other woman's now pale face told Vivi she did. "I know you're going to feed me some crap about money being money and that it's all for the organization."

Juliana's expression hardened with defiance. "I suggest you'd better be ready with facts and numbers if you're thinking of doing battle with me about my paperwork," she said angrily. "As for your insinuations, I'll make damn sure it'll appear I didn't know anything about the minister. His contribution will be seen as just that—contribution. The board can choose to do whatever they want with it. I'm just a collector, nothing else."

Vivi raised her eyebrows. "Just a collector? Is that how you see yourself? Not the helper of young women in trouble, as you've stated in your pamphlet? Or that newspaper article that quoted you saying that 'no young girls will be denied help'?"

The other woman leaned forward. "This meeting is over. I'm going to destroy your credibility. Who would believe anyone who sluts around with one of the offenders? I'll make sure the board get letters of complaint. Try denying that. You walked in here with him."

"Petty, Juliana, really petty, but then it doesn't surprise me."

The other woman shrugged. "The letters will be anonymously written, of course. The board will have plenty of reason to replace you. I told you I won't let you hurt the cause."

Vivi shook her head. "You're under some delusion that you're promoting a cause when all you're doing is destroying yourself and those around you. How can you sit there on your ass calmly telling a desperate young girl being beaten by her father to go find a job?" She acted out a scene. "'Hello? My father wants me to be a prostitute. Please help me.' 'Oh go find a job, dear, and everything will be fine.'"

Juliana answered her with a frozen stare. Vivi knew she was going to send those anonymous complaints that very afternoon. The woman hated her guts because Vivi saw through her. Turning to leave, Vivi added, "You're a zealot, Juliana, you and those like you. While you say you're for the cause, you won't admit to the fact that it's the side trappings and accoutrements of being associated to wealth and power that you love. Try visiting the red light district sometime.

Look at the faces of the girls working there. You will see Rose staring back at you, Juliana. And I truly hope you don't think their being there is just a job for them."

The walk out of the building was less strident, as she tried to figure out where to find Rose. She had planned to spend the day catching up with paperwork and calling Interpol for reports but that had to wait—the missing young girl weighed heavily on her mind.

She knew exactly where to find Mr. Tham. Rose had often pointed out the gambling den hidden in the street corner. That was where the small-time gamblers went but they were all the same—Triad sanctioned nests filled with thugs and addicted men playing with dice and cards.

There wasn't any time to dress up as Grandmamasan, and she knew she couldn't walk into that place all by herself. The only option she could think of was to wait outside until Rose's father stumbled out. That could be hours. She slammed her car door in frustration. She didn't have time. Damn Juliana Kohl. Damn her own inability to find a safe place for Rose. Damn everything.

This was a personal war and she knew she couldn't drag T. or her agency into it. They had a job to do. This wasn't a covert operation. It was something that Vivi knew how to do if she only had the damn man outside alone—put the fear of God into a bully.

For once in her life, she couldn't let her pride keep her from asking for help. Rose was missing and—

Vivi flipped open her cell. She waited impatiently as her request ran through the chain of human messengers. God, she needed to teach some people to keep a cell phone on them.

"This is Jazz."

His voice sounded so good. He was exactly what she needed. Muscle. And a big heart who would understand her pain.

"I need your help. Rose is missing and I can't walk into a gambling den without causing a lot of unwanted attention.

Can you get away for a few hours?" She kicked herself mentally. She could have at least started the conversation by asking how he was.

"Hang on." There was a short pause as she heard conversation in the background. "Come pick me up now, Vivi."

"Thank you," she said. "Jazz? I don't mean to just be calling you for help."

"I know, *chouchou*. I'd rather you don't walk into that place without telling me, anyway. You don't have a few dozen goats with you, do you?"

That sexy drawl of his, laced with his brand of Cajun humor, was exactly what she needed to restore a semblance of calm. She didn't even mind being called that stupid pet name he always used. She massaged the crick of her neck to release some tension.

"Your presence will be able to do the same work my goats did," she told him lightly.

"Ouch, *chouchou*. I'll wait for you in that underground garage they have here."

Stefan climbed the stairs slowly, aware of the eyes on him and his companion. During the drive out of town, he had briefed him about Dilaver and what to expect. Room 212. He rapped three times. The door opened immediately.

"You're late." The man's accent was heavy. "I don't like people who are late."

Stefan took a couple of steps into the room, keeping his hands by his sides. There were four other men in the room, armed and ready. He signaled for his man to follow and waited patiently as two of the guards searched them. They took away the few weapons they could find.

"These will be returned to you when the meeting is over," one of them told him.

Stefan nodded, keeping his eyes on the one sitting at the table, drinking beer. "I'm a busy man. There are many people in town who are in need of my services right now." He stood where he was, letting the other man decide what he wanted him to do. He could feel the tension. Someone was in a very bad mood, and from the bottles on the floor, alcohol wasn't helping rid him of it. "It would have been easier for me if you had made this meeting there instead of here."

"You brought only one man. You're either confident or stupid."

"He's my interpreter. I'm a middleman in Southeast Asia. Since you're from the former Yugoslavia, I wasn't sure whether you could speak English or any of the local dialects well enough and misunderstandings in this region can be deadly." He purposely did not let Dilaver know where he came from and why he was there.

"So now you're saying you came here alone. Again, either confident or stupid."

They studied each other, gauging strengths and weaknesses. Stefan was used to it. Trust wasn't exactly a strong commodity in this business. When engaging with a potential new associate, especially one new to the territory, one had to figure out quickly whether his word could be trusted. This individual was discovering that, too.

"I've heard a lot about you," the man said, as he opened three bottles of beer. "You have different names. Over in Kosovo, you're known as Ice. Here, I suppose they don't think that's a tough name, what with it being so damn hot and sticky all the time. Ice easily melts, doesn't give the connotation of how cool you are under fire. Over here, *my* interpreter says they call you Ghost Lightning. That is so . . . scary."

The others followed their leader's snort of laughter. Stefan still hadn't moved from where he was standing. He was being challenged. What he said next could either make or break whatever deal was in his opponent's head.

"I've also heard a lot about you, Dragan Dilaver," Stefan said. "You were just an underling KLA thug when I left Europe. You've done well since the war."

Dilaver shrugged. "Sit down. Beer? I'm afraid these

are"—he gestured, looking for the words—"American shit-water. No one around here eats or drinks right."

Stefan joined Dilaver at the table. His man remained by the door. "He doesn't drink while he's working," he explained to Dilaver easily.

"Good man." Dilaver took a swig. "I don't trust any of these slant-eyes anymore, not after what happened. That's why I chose you."

Stefan nodded. "I understand the comfort level."

"You know your way around here. You speak their language."

"It's a plus."

Dilaver took another swig. "My first mistake. I thought an interpreter and I could do this, but I need someone in this area, who knows the ins and outs, who understands whatever the fucking rules are around here."

"There aren't any." Stefan took a drink from his bottle. "The Triads rule these parts. Or at least the second brother."

"But there's something going on in town. My man told me there are some big names meeting up. How is it that the Triads allow them there?"

Stefan cocked a brow. "You're full of questions, Dilaver. Your man told me you have a business deal to discuss with me and I came without any questions. Suppose you tell me why you need me."

It was the other man's turn to raise his brows. "Need? That is a weak word."

Stefan shrugged. "You need me because the Triads are looking for you. That little bit of news is no secret. They have men looking for you everywhere."

"They reneged on a business deal. Like I said, there are these big names in town, people who deal in Europe. Arithmetic is still the same in this part of the world, isn't it? Two and two makes the Triads wanting my weapons to do business with the visitors. My question is—why? I took a lot of trouble working out this deal with them, took a long trip to come here for a vacation, and it's been hell so far." Dilaver finished his beer and carelessly threw the empty bottle on the floor. He barked something in Slavic at one of the men. He picked up another bottle. "I'll make this simple for you. You're the middleman. Cash. American dollars."

The man came back with a small briefcase and laid it on the table. He snapped it open. Stefan looked at the greenbacks stacked neatly inside.

"In case you didn't know, the Triads are in the business of women and drugs. The eldest brother deals with piracy and smuggling. He's known for international slavery. The Southeast Asian oceans are filled with his thugs." Stefan gestured at his interpreter with his beer. "Another brother lives in the States. My man here deals with him and reports to me. Same things—gambling, women, drugs. The brother here—the one you were meeting—is small-time. He is regional and has been working to expand his power base." He was the weakest link and that was why Stefan had chosen to come here. "He allows any activities in his territories as long as you give him coffee money."

"Coffee money?" Dilaver looked at his interpreter for explanation.

Stefan's man answered first. "Bribery, payments, rents . . . permission money. You pay the Triads for the right to do business in their territory."

The Slavic thug nodded, thoughtfully eyeing the man at the door. "I don't hear anything about weapons. This brother wanted weapons."

"Perfect timing," Stefan said. "He had accepted the coffee money to let a group of arms dealers in town to do business. He can't have a foothold in the industry unless he has some weapons to move himself. He buys it from you and shows up at the meeting. Like I said, he wants more power. Sibling competition is also common around here."

"He owes me a big sum of delivery money. I intend to collect it," Dilaver said, his voice deadly.

"You claim he attacked you."

"I have lost . . . enough about what I lost. I'm sure you know the details already. I'm leaving this damn place with a loss."

"I've heard about the incident at the bridge," Stefan acknowledged. "I deal with arms. I have had no dealings with the Triad drug business so if you want their drugs, I can't help you."

"I don't need you to do that for me. I just need some information in exchange for that cash. My second mistake was to want to start international arms dealing with a slant-eye. I got bored of politics back home and thought a few days with some Asian females . . ." Dilaver shrugged and drank down his beer. "I suppose it's the same in any business. A few days of pleasure and make some deals. I obviously dealt with the wrong brother. Maybe I should talk to your man over there. He's got the right contacts."

Stefan smiled humorlessly. "Is that what you asked me here for?"

"No. This cash is for you for one thing and one thing only. And, I intend to have enough leftover weapons for you to play middleman for me at this meeting. I can't go, not with the Triads looking for me and my weapons, but you can." Dilaver raised his beer bottle. *"Salute."*

Stefan looked at the crisp new cash in the suitcase. "Fifty percent. You keep the weapons till I make the deal. The money will be electronically transferred to a Kosovo account of your choice."

"Thirty percent. I have already taken a hit."

"Forty. And the information for the cash."

"Thirty-five. All I want to know is how to have personal contact with the brother here."

"You intend to do a double-cross?"

Dilaver set down his bottle. "He tried to get my weapons for free. Someone told me his clan members wear black clothing and the people who attacked us had black clothing on. But I'm interested in meeting this brother. I might even offer him some of my weapons to see how much he is willing to pay me. But I also intend to keep a lot of it for my own profit through you. So, are you in or out?"

"Thirty-eight, and I set up the meeting."

"Done."

Much later, driving back into town, Stefan turned to his interpreter. "That weapon he showed us—that's proof that the United States is supplying him too much firepower. He's using the sales to fund his own businesses."

"Which is going to make the U.S. look like the bunch of idiots that they are."

Stefan ignored that statement. Political opinions had nothing to do with his job. "You know what you have to do. I have to go set up this meeting with the Triads. Everything will be happening really quickly."

"Yes."

"Be ready for anything. I don't trust Dilaver."

"Is there anyone you can trust in this business?"

Stefan cracked a ghostly smile. "It's a matter of what kind of trust. Do you trust them to not take your life when they feel like it? Never. Do you trust them to deliver what they promise? Most of the times, yes. I always deliver what I promise. Mr. Dilaver will meet with the Triad brother. I didn't promise that the meeting will go well."

CHAPTER
24

Jazz glanced at Vivi several times as he drove. She hadn't said a word when he asked for the keys. After giving him directions to her address, she had been silent since questioning Rose's father. He could tell her mind was far away; in fact, he doubted whether she cared if he was going the right direction.

He felt bad for her. He had gone into that gambling den with the cash she'd given him to use as "coffee money," as she called it, and had done exactly as she had instructed, talking to the head thug and slipping him that envelope. Then, after being pointed the way, he had hauled that son of a bitch out of there without any trouble at all. Everyone had left him alone as Tham yelled and kicked.

Jazz grimly recalled Vivi's demeanor. This was yet another side of her. As he had tightened his hold on the struggling little man, she had surprised both of them when she suddenly clamped a hand around Tham's neck. A little telling squeeze and the man had gone limp with fear. Cold and calm, she had told Rose's father exactly which points of his body she was going to hurt if he didn't tell her what he had done to his daughter.

He couldn't understand what the poor bastard said after that. Fear had robbed him of whatever broken English he had, and the words that poured out were fast and frightened, pleading in tone. And as he watched, Vivi's face turned pale. She had pursed her lips tightly, reining in her control even as he noted her clenched fist at her side.

"I would have broken his face, Vivi," he said quietly.

She sighed. Her eyes stared blankly ahead. "What good would it have done? She's gone and there's nothing I can do about it."

The slight catch in her voice tugged at his emotions. She hadn't been just holding in her anger and frustration. His girl's heart was broken, and she was trying so hard not to show it. He had never felt so helpless. Nothing he could say was going to help her.

"We've reached your place . . . where do I park?"

"Behind the building. Jazz?" She finally turned, and the pain in her eyes almost did him in. "Can you stay with me tonight? I can get T. to take you back to the compound or get someone to give you a ride. I just can't—"

"Shhhhh . . ." He reached out and gently fingered her lips. "*Tais-toi, chouchou*, I'll stay. The team knows where I am and there's no lockdown yet."

She nodded and sat back in her seat again. Jazz looked at her for a moment, then turned back to drive the car to the rear of the building. She got out and waited as he locked up. She then took his hand in hers. He followed quietly, letting her lead him wherever she wanted. He sensed her need to get into her apartment before she allowed herself to fall apart. Rose's disappearance had really hit her very hard. His Vivi wasn't one to easily break and she was very close to the edge right now.

Her apartment was small. She didn't pause to turn on the lights and he didn't really have time to look around casually anyway, his mind registering just the size, the way the furniture was laid out, the small kitchen to the left, as she pulled him toward the only place he was interested in. She pushed open the door, and the silken darkness reminded him of the other night in the woods when she was also taking him by the hand like this.

Just the thought of her jumping his bones again had him hard. But he was torn. On the one hand, she needed him now. On the other, he didn't want to be just comfort sex. He wanted so much more. He could walk with her to that bed over there right now and they would be tangled between the sheets in no time, and he knew she just wanted to go somewhere that would take away the pain she was going through.

That last thought dissolved all hesitation. Vivi in pain was unacceptable. He would figure out a way to get through to her. But right now, she needed him just to be here.

He turned her to him and slowly undid the buttons of her top, using his hands in the dark to give her the reassurance she was seeking. He kissed her softly as he slid her bra off her shoulders. She didn't move, but her response was wild, almost desperate. Her pants fell to the floor, and, still kissing her, he nudged her toward the bed until she fell backward onto it.

She remained that way as he quickly shucked his clothes. His eyes had gotten used to the dark and he could see her soft outline on the pale sheets. When he came to her, he felt her legs wrapped around his waist, pulling him forward.

He touched her and found her dry. She didn't seem to care, her thighs clamping onto him insistently. She didn't reach out with her arms or say anything, just silently imploring him.

Jazz shook his head in the dark. Her pain was his, even if she wasn't going to share it. She wanted the intimacy but not the emotions that went with it, and no, cold comfort wasn't what he was willing to give.

He leaned forward and gave her another kiss, this time harder, trying to get through. He reached down between her legs again, using his arousal to stimulate her. She shook her head—or tried to—as her hands finally came alive, sliding down his sides and joining his. She wanted him inside. Now.

But she still wasn't ready. He slipped one finger inside her and she jerked against him in protest. She said something against his lips but he continued kissing her, his tongue tangling with hers. He slid another finger inside her, sliding deep inside and cupping her.

"Nnnnn . . ." she moaned as he felt the first slide of moisture. Her legs dropped and she tried to twist away.

He worked the moisture out and slid his wet fingers to another area to get more but her hands trapped his, refusing to let him continue. It didn't matter, he was already familiar enough with her body to know all her erogenous spots. He released her lips and went to kiss her neck, right under her ear. Right there, where her pulse thrummed against his lips. Her head rolled back to allow him access, and as if she suddenly realized what she was doing, she stopped herself and tried to turn the opposite way.

But he already found where he wanted to nibble and he knew he had her from the way her hands couldn't hold on tightly any longer. He bit a little harder and ran his tongue down the side of her neck. A helpless gurgle escaped her lips, and this time she didn't stop him as his hand moved higher. He parted her and found her other, more sensitive, spot.

"No . . . Jazz . . . I . . ."

He kissed her neck and whispered in her ear, "Yes, *chouchou*. I know you're hurt but you can't lock yourself in. You can't lock me out and have me use you. Let me love you like you deserve, honey. I'm here for you—all of me."

She shook her head. "No! I don't want . . ." and she moaned even as she tried to get away from his roving fingers. He could feel her wet and ready but she was still fighting herself and him. "Oh God, no, don't want to feel this . . . good."

"There's nothing wrong with feeling good." Jazz nudged against her heat and slid in slowly, using more pressure with his fingers. She might be protesting but her body rewarded him with that silken dampness he wanted. "I can't give you what you want, Vivi, not that way. It has to have pleasure, love, lots of pleasure . . . it comes with the territory. Don't hold back, please don't hold back. *Donne-moi tous.*"

She gasped as he went deep. He could feel her squeezing him, the faint contraction inside her starting. Yet she still twisted to get away. She gasped again as he cupped her, moving his hand in tandem with the rhythm of his body. He went for her neck again, nibbling and tenderly sucking her sweet flesh.

"No . . ."

Her body went limp as he shaped her growing pleasure, using every part of him to push her over. His need for her was almost boiling over and he had to force himself not to move any faster. Just as he was about to lose control, he felt her climax starting even as she pounded against his shoulders.

"No . . . no . . . I . . . don't want to feel . . ."

And she went over, her body bucking under his. Only then did Jazz allow himself to go too. She was hot and wet now, her internal muscles milking him as she came. Her arms reached up and wrapped around his body. With a grunt, he gave one final thrust and let her pleasure tip him over. His careful control produced a fierce orgasm, and his whole soul seemed to vibrate with the different layers of pleasure.

He finally pulled out and turned over to lie beside her. They lay quietly, catching their breath. Now and then his body shuddered involuntarily, still reacting to the blast of pleasure minutes before. Vivi moved first. She turned, and so did he. She hid her face against his chest.

"I broke my promise to her, Jazz. I lost her. Oh God, I broke my promise again."

And she started to weep.

Vivi hadn't cried in a long time, not like this. Jazz gathered her in his arms, murmuring softly into her hair, and she couldn't stop the torrent of tears. She had never felt so helpless and hopeless. Rose had depended on her, and she had failed the girl. She hadn't even been there to return her calls for help. What could have gone through the kid's mind when Juliana told her none was coming?

"Don't blame yourself, *chouchou*," Jazz said gently, after listening to her half-sobbed explanation. *"C'est pas ta faute."*

"If I had taken care of the situation, found some place for Rose . . ."

"Listen, sweetheart, it would have been another girl, and you would still be feeling the way you do. Now that you've told me about your friend Sia-Sia, I see why this is so important to you. You promised Rose the same thing you promised Sia-Sia, and both times, you feel you have failed them." He kissed her forehead. "Don't beat up yourself like this, *chouchou*. In between those two promises, you have done many good things, helped out many young girls. I've seen the way you work. You're generous with your time and money, and you give away so much of yourself to others, Vivi. You haven't failed, not by a long shot."

He made things sound so simple. All day, she had walked around with a painful knot in her stomach that had gone tighter and tighter. She hadn't been able to stand it any longer after hearing Rose's father admit that he had sold his daughter to pay off his gambling debts. The little ray of hope she had held out, that Rose had somehow escaped, had extinguished, and all she could think about was how the young girl must have felt abandoned and what she was going through now. And her own promise to Rose—that she would come back for her—had mocked her like a sharp slap.

She had never had anyone in whom to confide her fears before. Every time she saw a girl like Rose, all the past feelings of hopelessness returned. No one to turn to. No place to go. Jazz was the first man she had ever sought out for help. Before it had always been her own strength, her own wiles against a man's world. But it hadn't been enough this time.

"You know what Admiral Madison said about being in a crossfire? That's how I feel," she said, her voice hoarse and tired. "I volunteered to help because I felt I could make a difference. Because I have been there before. Because I thought I could offer solutions. But I find myself fighting the organization. In its quest to solicit funds, some of the people in it also have begun seeing these kids as numbers. Rose called for help and what did that Juliana do? She ignored the human being, thinking only of that magic number on paper to show the media. And you know what? Many people would agree with her, that what she does is more help than someone like me running around crying foul over a few kids left on the wayside. But Jazz, I was one of those kids . . . I know what it's like when you're too old to be considered cute and too young to know right from wrong. It's so easy to step off the edge and join the kids in tight skirts and low-cut blouses, waving dollar bills men slip down their push-up bras. I can't bear the idea of Rose . . ."

She started crying again. She was thinking of Sia-Sia now.

"Why didn't you do it?"

She looked up in the dark. "What do you mean?"

"Why didn't you end up like them? It's easy to step off, like you said. Hunger. Pain. Threats from relatives. Yet you chose to run away. And you made it as a person. Why?"

"I . . ." She paused, unsure of how to answer.

"It isn't that story about your dad being a warrior god coming down to take you away. It isn't about you abandoning your friend. You saw an open window into the night and you chose to slip out of it. Your friend didn't—couldn't, whatever—but you did, in spite of the fear of being alone out there by yourself. Why, Vivi?" His hand caressed the side of her face, wiping away the fallen tears. "I know you have heard hundreds of times about how brave and strong you were, that you dug yourself out of a hole, or any number of other things. But have you ever thought why *you* didn't end up being sold?"

"Lucky, I guess," she told him.

"There's always a little bit of luck in anything we do, sweetheart. I'm lucky to be alive in the job I do. But it also takes perseverance and choices." There was a pause. Jazz's voice was low, distant. "I grew up very poor, *chouchou*. It was just my maman, and she had eight young mouths to feed. Eight kids, and no man in the family. Like you, there were few options for a woman like her in those days, even in the States. My grandfather did the best he could but he was a rascally old man and didn't change his ways much. He disappeared a lot, but when he came home, he always took care of whatever repairs the house needed before taking off again. Maman refused to give up. She chose to keep us together, even though it had meant a lot of sacrifices. She did it all herself—one lone woman—and we grew up relatively happy. Poor, but happy. And luck played only a bit part, *chouchou*. It was mostly what she made of life. Like you did. She saw a window and went through it."

Vivi rubbed her face against Jazz's rough palm, imagining him as a child. She had this picture of him and all his sisters and brother, happily skipping to school and doing what families do. It was just a fantasy on her part. His background wasn't that much different from hers. It wasn't just poverty. It was the way they had both grown up knowing there was more out there than what was being offered. It was that knowledge that had spurred her to escape that night so long ago.

As if he heard her thoughts, Jazz continued, "Many thought my maman couldn't make it, told her to give her kids away, told her she could then move into town and look for a man there. But she refused to see things the way others did. And if you think about it, Vivi, so did you. And you can't blame yourself that others didn't. Your friend. Even Rose. You can only protect them as much as you can, but sooner or later, they have to survive on their own. And Sia-Sia did survive, as you just recently found out."

"That's the soldier talking," she told him. "You can't give a kid a weapon and tell him to jump into battle."

Jazz sighed. "Tell that to the two kids my men were assigned to take out in the jungle not too long ago. It was a shock to see them, sitting there in the dark, using their weapons like any grown men. They were probably only nine or ten, yet they had a whole group of grown ups at their beck and call. Life is what you make it, *chouchou*. I choose this life. I cannot go around thinking of those kids as just kids . . . because they aren't. What I'm saying is—there are different options to survive. Look at you again, hmm? When you were alone, all by yourself, and really, really hungry and frightened, and you had no one to turn to, not that mythical daddy or even your best friend, and you were tempted, desperately tempted, at the idea of joining those girls with the pushed-up bras, standing outside those strip joints, why didn't you?"

Vivi remembered that feeling of hunger very well. In the woods all alone. Then in strange towns as she made her way toward the border. The hunger pangs were never far behind. And each town, with its women sitting on the stools outside the bars, with the money she saw exchanging hands, had tempted her.

"A man," she said, frowning in sudden recollection of a distant memory, "came up to me one day while I was standing in the shadows staring at the bright lights and the smells of food coming toward me. He said, 'Are you hungry?' I told him yes and that I was going to walk into that place any second now. I think I was probably half dreaming when I said that. I was so damn tired of everything. But he tapped me hard on the shoulder, and made me turn around. 'No, no, you don't want to do that, little girl,' he'd said. 'Here, take this money and go get yourself some food. And go on, get out of this place.' I did. And somehow made my way close to the border."

Vivi shrugged. There had been kind people who had helped her. This man—his words somehow had stuck in her brain. Little girl, he had called her. And she had repeated it to herself that night when she had taken shelter under a stairway. Little girl.

"It's a sane voice in the dark, *chouchou*. I have heard it once or twice myself, someone who said something that registered, that pulled me back from a bad idea. That man did you a favor but he didn't physically stop you, did he?"

"No."

"And so it's the same way with you and every one you help out. You can be just a voice, among many, and if they choose to listen, what you're saying will register."

Vivi shifted and lifted her head. "You won't get a big head if I say you're a pretty wise man, will you? Who taught you all that stuff?"

He chuckled sleepily. "It's like music, *chouchou*. You have to listen closely to different instruments, especially in jazz. Every sound is unique and some of them stand out. Like yours. Do you know you have the sweetest music following you around?"

"Oh yes, of course, big cymbals and grinding electric guitar," Vivi teased. The man was a musician. He would always see things differently from her. But she liked the world viewed through his eyes.

"No, that's only you when you have a few dozen goats around you." He paused. "I don't suppose you will bring in any animals with you and this Armando guy during your operation? I don't trust him. Are you sure his saying Sia-Sia is alive is true?"

He was trying so hard not to show his worry. Vivi found herself smiling. Somehow, he had made her feel better, in spite of all that had happened. It was her turn to reassure him.

"I agreed to do this only because T. checked him out thoroughly. Getting his sister out and seeing Sia-Sia . . . he assured me she's okay." Armando hadn't offered any more information. She suspected he didn't want to share all the details because something bad had happened to her friend. It didn't matter. She would find out soon enough. "I'll be okay, Jazz. I've done extractions before."

He gathered her in his arms again. This time, his hug was tightly possessive.

"I don't want anything to happen to you, that's all," he said.

He cares about me. She was touched. Remembering all he

had done since they met, it warmed her to know how much he cared. And she also realized that she had begun to care for him too. For the first time she felt ready to take a step into the future, that maybe she could share it with this man.

"I hear us making some sexy music," she told him, moving suggestively against him.

"I always obey a voice in the dark," he said.

It was late by the time Stefan reached *Yeekoh*'s place. He knew that the man didn't like to be kept waiting but it couldn't be helped. He needed that extra hour to plot out the newest strategy. It was always risky when unexpected new elements appeared. He would have to be extra careful. He followed the guard into a large living room.

"Dilaver has expressed a desire to meet with you, *Yeekoh*, to straighten things out. He doesn't seem too trusting right now and I don't blame him. After all, he lost a number of his men recently. He thinks it's you."

The youngest Triad brother didn't look at Stefan. He was engrossed in watching a porno movie on the big screen television. "What do you think of this?" he asked, nodding toward the show, as he flicked cigarette ash onto the floor.

Stefan sat down on the sofa, his back to the screen. "Kids don't interest me, *Yeekoh*."

"You should expand your smuggling activities. There is big money in kiddie porn, especially with Westerners coming here to get their little excitement, huh?" *Yeekoh* laughed at his own wit. "They can't get it where they're at, so they fly over here. I have a whole travel agency working over in the States through my brother, you know. We book tours for those with special interests."

"I have no interest in pedophiles either," Stefan said quietly.

The other man finally looked up, his eyes assessing. "You're already in an illegal business, my brother. There is no need to start calling our clients names."

Stefan returned the gaze steadily. "I don't make excuses for what I do, *Yeekoh*. Women and children appear to be your specialty, let's leave it at that." And drugs and gambling. But he wasn't here to discuss these things with the Triad brother. He was only interested in getting him to make a move about Dilaver and his weapons. "Dilaver still has the weapons. You have told me that you want to diversify. Since these are the same weapons you wanted in the first place, are you still interested? You're going to need to renegotiate with him."

But *Yeekoh* appeared to be in the mood to talk about other things. "Speaking of want, are you interested in my sister? Alissa is a very attractive woman, don't you agree?"

"Alissa is a very beautiful and smart woman," Stefan said noncommittally.

Yeekoh smiled, showing yellowing teeth. "Yes, my father was very fond of her, too. Her ability to communicate in English attracts many clients on the Internet. And she does look quite beautiful naked. A bit too voluptuous, especially as she begins to get older. I sometimes miss her younger body, when she was less . . . developed. She does have a knack at training the young ones we get in, though." He looked at the screen again. His voice became faraway, almost dreamy. "You should watch her at it sometimes. So . . . stimulating. That's why we let her run this side of the business. She brings in money." He paused to take a drag from his cigarette. Exhaling a plume of smoke, he added softly, "She had gotten quite fond of you, Stefan. I like to make my sister happy, and since you make her happy, I want to make you an offer."

Stefan didn't say anything. There was a minute of silence broken only by the moans coming from the TV.

Yeekoh's brows shot up. "Not interested?"

"You haven't offered anything yet."

"Ah, a careful man. That's why I like you, Stefan. I just want to be sure of your intentions, since she is so precious to us here. She has this illusion that you want her for yourself, set her up as your mistress or something. Is this true?"

Stefan studied the other man for a few moments. "It hasn't crossed my mind," he replied. "Besides, she is *Yeekoh*'s sister, a family member of the Triads."

It went without saying that one didn't just set up a member of the Triads as one's mistress. Stefan knew playing with one of the favored female siblings' affections was a risk but he had targeted Alissa precisely because of her background and her connection to the brother.

"I was going to offer her to you for marriage, Stefan. You can be part of the family and be in charge of the gunrunning for us. That way, my sister will also be happy and won't decide to move off with you somewhere. What do you say?"

The glint in *Yeekoh*'s eyes betrayed his cunning. Stefan knew the other man was trying to corner him. His sources and connections would be very valuable to this brother trying to gain more power among his brothers. If he agreed to the proposition, it would mean working for *Yeekoh* and no one else, essentially cutting off his freedom to do business with any rival clans, or moving in and out among others without them knowing that he owed his allegiance to the Triads. To say no would be an insult. The Triads didn't take insults lightly.

Stefan smiled. He had a few days to make the next move in this game yet, and he had no intention of losing his freedom. When this was over, he would be gone from the region.

"An offer so well thought out should be honored by an equally thought-out response," he said. "I like doing one business at a time. When you agreed to take that shipment of drugs off my hands, I owed you a favor, which I intend to first accomplish. You wanted to find out where Dilaver is. I have him and he has the weapons. I can set up a meeting between you and you can get this unfinished business out of the way. You'll need me for an interpreter—I don't trust the one he's using. Once that's done, we're even, aren't we, *Yeekoh*? Then I can pay proper attention to this new business proposition you just made."

Yeekoh's answer was a satisfied smile. He nodded. He snuffed out his cigarette and cracked his fingers, ordering one of his men to turn the television volume down. "Very well. I shall tell Alissa the good news. Now, let's talk about

Dilaver. Why is he behaving like an idiot? I thought he and I could do business, but one little attack and he's in hiding. These Europeans aren't used to gang wars, I suppose. Did you reassure him that it wasn't my men?"

"He wants to meet you, doesn't he?"

CHAPTER
25

"Come on," Hawk said. **"Let's go."**

Jazz looked up from the Dan Nhat. "Where to?"

"You're killing me with that damn awful twanging and that lovelorn worried look on your face. We'll kill two birds with one stone. Since Vivienne is at the same place on assignment, we'll go scope it out for ours, too, while you can keep a general eye on what's happening. I'll get some of the men so we have a better feel about the target area. We'll get miked so we can test different positions. Maybe you'll even see your girl in action again."

Jazz put down the lute. "Done."

An hour later, they reached town. Hawk gave the truck driver a thumbs-up before they slipped out and headed to the Cha Cha Club.

Jazz sniffed the air. Each night mission was different, with its set of colors and smells. When they were in the jungle fighting the child warlords and their men, everything was dark and shadowy, with the smell of jungle mold and the sounds of crickets and night frogs that had gone strangely silent as the gun battle became more intense.

The night by the bridge was filled with the wet dankness of mud and the sounds of lapping water and chirping night birds. Tonight the smells of the town permeated the air. He could distinguish the scents of spicy food and incense, mixed with the distant sound of a night bazaar. The lights made everything brighter, making it harder to hide in the shadows. But his team had had training in urban warfare; they knew how to blend into different types of darkness.

Each one of them had already studied the map. All they needed now was to pinpoint their physical location and set up shop. Cucumber, Dirk, and Mink would be in front. Zone, Joker, and Jazz would take the rear. Hawk, an excellent shot, wouldn't be with them, of course. He would be in the theater itself. He had finally let them know that he had gone in and out of the building before, and that the thugs in there would recognize him. That was Hawk's way of telling them that he had been undercover for a while now, that he had known what was coming up way before they did. Jazz was curious, and he was sure the team was, too, but like him, they kept their questions to themselves. For now.

They moved silently, using prearranged hand signals and occasionally communicating with the intercom. From years of training, they knew exactly how far apart they should be from their targets without being too close.

The people walking about and around the target area helped screen their presence as they scouted the location, checking out the size of the building and alleys nearby. The meeting would take place in the rear, where the informant had given a map of the key exits from the building. It would be even more extensively guarded at that time, of course. There was one more instruction added into their orders. Their informant wanted the contents in a certain room near the exit to be destroyed. C-4 would do nicely. That would be Jazz's business.

"I see Vivienne."

Jazz saw her, too. She was standing across the street, holding a bag. She was dressed in a light-colored top and casual pants, her hair tied back in a ponytail. She ignored the people passing by, staring at the building intently. She didn't show it but he knew she was trying to contain her excitement. She was finally going to see her long-lost friend.

Vivi had opened up more about her past the other night. He hadn't realized how much guilt she carried inside her about leaving her friend behind. He could understand it by thinking about it in the context of leaving any of his men in a dire situation. But her friend had chosen not to go with her.

He had tried to press that point home. She seemed to think that if she hadn't left, her friend might not have suffered such a horrible fate. He had tried to show Vivi that she would probably have ended up in the same boat if she hadn't left.

"I know. But that doesn't make me feel any better. Does that make sense?"

Yes. Survivor's guilt was common among soldiers. All he could do was to hold her in his arms and try to prepare her for the coming shock. After all, her friend would be a very different person from the last time she'd seen her. No matter how prepared Vivi was, the coming meeting had to be traumatic. After years of being a prostitute, her friend might not be quite so friendly. Actually, he doubted that it could be her. He didn't like this Armando person's story one bit. Something didn't sound right. And that was why he had been worrying.

"She's talking to someone," Jazz buzzed him again.

"To that guy Armando, I bet. She's probably miked like us."

"You said she's just going to walk in there with the coffee money and try to bribe her way to see Sia-Sia. I don't think it's going to work."

"I didn't say it was money," Jazz reminded Hawk.

But he was worried just the same. He was already thinking of alternate ways to intervene if those men strong-armed her.

"They are going to be curious about you and won't pay attention to me walking in. And if you succeed in getting to see Sia-Sia, they won't see me slipping inside the secured area. I know what to do when I'm in there."

Even through the mike, Vivi could feel Armando's confidence. With his ability to tail her without her knowing, she knew he would be able to get to his sister once he got inside, especially when the guards were busy with her. "Okay. Which one is the head thug again?" From her shadowy corner, she checked out the tough man standing at the far end of the doorway. "That one with the red pants?"

"Yes. He's a martial arts expert. Be very careful with him."

She smiled without humor. "Oh, now you're worried about my safety."

"No, just mine. I don't think your SEAL boyfriend will be happy if you get hurt."

Did she have no secrets from anyone anymore? Vivi shook her head. Boyfriend. When did that happen?

"Don't worry, Vivi. I'll try my best to rescue you too, just like your boyfriend did." This time he was back to his mocking self.

"I don't think so, buster," Vivi retorted. Certainly not the way she was remembering. "Okay, going to start the show now. Are you sure he will recognize Sia-Sia's picture?"

There were many women working in there. How could she stand out to these men who didn't even see them as persons? That picture was of a younger Sia-Sia, after all. She crossed the street, holding the bag tightly.

"Trust me, Vivi. Sia-Sia is still a favorite after all these years and when you mention that you're her sister and show him the bracelet, he will at least give you some time to explain."

Still a favorite—Vivi didn't want to think about the connotations behind that phrase. "What if she isn't working tonight?"

"She's there. And Vivi . . . I haven't thanked you for doing this."

She looked up at the three-story building, wondering which room Sia-Sia was working in. "I still haven't kicked your ass for keeping this from me for so long." She couldn't see Armando among the people walking in and out but she knew he was nearby. "She's been in there all this time."

"I have my reasons."

"Selfish ones."

"Yes."

Vivi took a deep breath. Water under the bridge. She was going to see Sia-Sia now. "Okay, ready to roll."

While Jazz listened to Hawk's instructions to the others, he kept his eyes trained on Vivi. She was careful not to appear to be talking to somebody, moving around, checking her bag now and then. He could tell she was preparing herself.

"Copy," he said, replying to Hawk's question.

"We'll move on to the back of the building as soon as your gal goes in there, buddy."

"Affirmative."

He watched Vivi cross the street slowly. She was looking at one of the two entrances. Two men stood outside, casually greeting some of the people going in. She walked straight to the one with the red pants. A woman approaching one of the Triad guards—that ought to generate a big buzz.

"What's she showing him?"

Vivi had given him some details about her plans. "An old picture. She's going to tell him she's been looking for her sister and that the local authorities have sent her to them."

"Shit, Jazz, there's no way that asshole is going to listen to her story," Cucumber chimed in. "What's going to stop him from pulling her in there and imprisoning her?"

"Look, she's giving him a wad of money, too."

"She knows what she's doing, men," Jazz said, half reassuring himself.

"Look at them laughing at her. Come on, we can't go to case the back. We've got to rescue her," Dirk said.

"I can blow the guy away, Jazz. Say the word." That was from Joker, who never had much to say.

Jazz's team had become very protective where Vivi was

concerned. She had gained their respect from what they had seen of her work in the last assignment.

"They're laughing at her, men, except the one in the red pants. Whatever Vivi is saying to him is making him think," Hawk said.

"I just don't like the way he's grabbing her at the elbow," Cucumber muttered.

Nor did Jazz. He wanted to go over there and—

"Jazz, three o'clock."

Jazz turned in that direction. Someone else was watching Vivi. It was Dilaver.

Vivi forced herself to look around. She hated these places. She had been inside a couple of them before and after each time, she had spent days trying to forget the sights and sounds of debauchery. Gambling at the lowliest caliber, without the trappings of well-dressed wealth or the hushed professionalism of uniformed card dealers and cashiers. Here there was nothing to hide the addiction. Men gathered around in a circle over there, talking loudly as they wagered against cockerels in a pit. Groups at tables playing dominoes and cards, shouting above the clatter. There were no chips, just cash exchanging hands. And the girls on the couches . . .

Vivi had to look away. There were some things she refused to let her senses register. Those girls were the same ones sitting outside the bars on the stools, hiking up their already short skirts for all to see what they weren't wearing. In here, some of them were already half naked and totally drugged out—the reward for bringing in a client. She didn't want to see what was happening on the couches.

Thankfully, the thug in the red pants was shoving her toward the back rooms. Not that the acts back there would be any less nauseating. The authorities seldom, if ever, raided the whorehouses here; the Triads were too powerful a group. But she had interviewed many victims over the last two years who knew the horrors that went on for those who had initially resisted their lot. They were usually freed after their relative had paid their debts. Freed . . . until the next time. Some of them had sought help from the United Third World organization.

Chained to beds. Starved. Drugged. And for those who were too young to even understand what was happening . . .

"I'm in," Armando interrupted her thoughts. "I'll let you know when I get my sister out."

The back was painted in red, with traditional music playing. The Triads had put some money into the place—there were mirrors and even carpeting, a luxury in these parts in what looked like a waiting room of some sort. The huge vase of fresh flowers in the middle of the room was an obscenity to what was going on here, and Vivi had to bite back a scathing remark.

Now wasn't the time. She would take notes now. She'd find a way later to help these women somehow.

Jazz swallowed a curse. He should have done more than knock out that son of a bitch the other night, kept him off his feet for a few days. He wished he was close enough right now to do exactly that. Dilaver had caught sight of Vivi. That didn't bode well.

"What do you think he's doing?"

"He is smart—he's casing the place, like we are," Hawk said. "He's out for revenge and he doesn't seem like the type to sit on his ass and wait for others to do all the action."

Jazz watched Dilaver signaling his men. One joined him and they started staggering toward the entrance, acting drunk and rowdy. It was like watching a play within a play, seeing two different stories happening at the same time. Jazz didn't like how the plot was moving.

"That's his interpreter with him. Dilaver needs him like a crutch."

"You sound like you've been up close and personal with him, Hawk." It was just a guess. His friend had been too damn closemouthed about this lone assignment. "Tell me you didn't know about this appearance."

"I didn't," Hawk said. "Listen up, men, I want you all to proceed with our plan."

"Yes, sir."

"I'm walking in there, I'll check out what's happening. Jazz, you're in charge."

Hawk going in there alleviated his fear for Vivi's safety. "Is it going to be a problem to appear suddenly? Won't the thugs be suspicious?"

"No."

Hawk didn't bother to explain. Jazz looked in the direction where he knew Hawk was. His friend's shadow suddenly emerged. He was adjusting his clothes. Probably making sure his weapons weren't too visible. Then he watched Hawk walk to the guards at the door and greet them by their names.

"All right," Jazz said, moving toward the alley leading to the back. "We'll get into position like we'd planned, but you keep in contact."

"Sir." Zone's voice was urgent. He had been the first to head down the alley to the back.

"What is it?"

"I think Hawk should come back out. From my view, it looks like Dilaver's men are wiring the damn place with charges. They are going to blow it up."

26

"Get out!"

Stefan stood up to leave. He hadn't expected Alissa to say anything else. He had hurt her woman's pride, after all, rejecting her proposal.

"I came to you first because I didn't want to discuss you with your brother," he told her. He also meant to keep her distracted. "Wouldn't you rather hear it from me than from *Yeekoh*?"

"You . . . bastard!" Alissa looked around, then picked up her glass of wine and threw it at Stefan. She screeched in anger when he caught it in mid-air. "You think you can use me and throw me away, just like that? I brought you in. I can take you out!"

She rushed at Stefan, pummeling him with her fists, yelling obscenities. Stefan stood there and let her. Much as he abhorred the woman's way of life, he had used her for his own ends. He wasn't one who saw things in black and white, and neither was Alissa. She, too, had chosen this life to suit her ends, and he knew she understood, even though she was too angry to admit it right now. He didn't flinch when she slapped him.

She started crying. "I know now why you never kiss me."

Stefan didn't say anything. He never kissed anyone he

didn't care for. He had seen the way she kissed other men, especially her half-brother, and he had no desire to join the list. Sex was just part of the job.

"Don't you care about me? Just a little?"

"Would it hurt a little less?" he asked gently.

Alissa glared at him, her cheeks wet from her tears. "Pity? I don't need any pity from anyone. I have everything I need."

"Then you don't need me."

"But . . ." She turned away. "I do. A woman needs a man sometimes."

"Lis, you have all the men you want," Stefan pointed out. "And marriage . . . that was just a fantasy in your head. We knew from the start there'd be no future for us. I made it clear what I wanted." Very clear. She had been intrigued when he'd told her he would pleasure her like no one ever had. "But you're mixing business with pleasure."

She swung around fiercely. "What's wrong with that? I want you as mine. Besides, I'm getting older and you don't seem the type to mind having a woman like me as your woman."

Stefan shrugged. "You label yourself. You are what you are."

"Oh, don't tell me you want some pious sweet virgin for a wife. Or a normal woman. What kind of woman would fit a gunrunner? An illegal arms dealer?" She wrapped her arms around herself. "We'd be perfect, Stefan. Me. You. The sex's great. I speak perfect English and can go anywhere with you. You even have my brother's power behind you. What's wrong with the picture? It's a business deal, too."

Maybe she didn't get it. Even if he had wanted her, he would never ever share her with her brother or anyone. Maybe she would never get it. He chose not to waste time explaining. "I work alone. I don't need your brother. And I don't need marriage as a business deal." He walked to the door. "Goodbye, Alissa."

"Fucker!" she screamed and started throwing the remaining glasses at him. "You'll come back! When you need my brother to help you out with another favor, you'll come back to me!"

Stefan turned to open the door. She would find out soon enough that *Yeekoh* would be too busy trying to rebuild his power base to do anything for a while. Especially when he discovered that someone had gotten their passwords and emptied all their overseas accounts. That all his warehouses had been "discovered" and raided by the authorities. *Yeekoh* would be needing his other brothers' help, and they wouldn't be too pleased with him. Mission completed.

He opened the door. And frowned. Almost completed.

Hawk had turned off his communicator. Jazz hoped he had heard the last part about the explosives.

"As long as Dilaver is still in there, the building isn't going to blow up," Jazz said, assuming command. He was worried about Vivi now. Dilaver's following her inside could only mean that the brute was after her again. He wished he were inside the casino instead of Hawk.

"What should we do next?" Joker asked.

Jazz thought for a moment. "This is turning out to be the real thing, boys. We've lost the luxury of practice. How much ammo did we bring along?"

"Not much, sir. We certainly didn't bring our own explosives. Not that we need any, looking at these fuckers."

They had to move quickly. If they had timers on the explosives, he needed to get to them before they were discharged. "We live to improvise, so this is now Plan B. Assume positions."

"Let's meet up first," Joker said. They had all memorized the map. "Point one."

"Ten-four."

Jazz pulled out his cell phone. He punched the numbers, waited for the rings before punching in the code. An electronic voice at the other end politely asked for a verbal password.

The line clicked several seconds after he did so. "What is it, Jazz?" T. asked.

Red Pants was about to knock when the door flew open. A stream of obscenities came through, along with some glassware. Vivi ducked from the flying objects. She looked up curiously when the thug at her side nervously greeted the man standing there. Whoever he was, he had instilled a certain fear in her guard. He didn't seem to be bothered by the noise behind him, either. Red Pants' head was bowed, as if he didn't want to meet his eyes.

So Vivi did. If eyes could change body temperature, then this man's could freeze blood flow. Killer eyes. The color of lightning. They narrowed a fraction at the sight of her.

"I think you have a guest, Lis," he said to the other unseen screaming occupant.

He was soft-spoken, with the slightest lyrical accent that Vivi couldn't place. She waited for him to open the door wider but he didn't. His eyes continued to hold her prisoner and she found herself staring back.

"I don't want to see anyone! I gave specific instructions not to be bothered when you're around. Why is everyone not doing what I want tonight?" More objects thudded against the back of the door, one of which missing the man's head by inches. He didn't flinch away.

"I believe it's urgent, Lis." The stranger shifted his attention to Red Pants, changing languages with ease. "Go in first. You'd better have a good explanation why you're disturbing her. I'd watch out for flying objects."

Red Pants nodded, still avoiding his eyes, and taking Vivi's bag with him, he slipped in when the door opened wider. Vivi didn't follow. Despite her excitement, something was very, very wrong with this picture. Was the woman Sia-Sia or not? And if so, why would Red Pants be so afraid?

"I found her, Vivi. It'll take some time to disarm her guards," Armando chose that moment to remind her that there were other things going on. Since she wasn't alone, she couldn't answer him, or ask him what the hell he kept secret about Sia-Sia.

The man at the door continued studying her, his strange eyes unreadable. His face looked like it'd been carved, it was so still. He appeared perfectly content to stay silent even as the muffled screaming behind him continued, this time berating Red Pants. She stared back defiantly. Whoever he was, he was still scum for being in what could be Sia-Sia's room.

"No!" Vivi heard the woman in the room exclaim.

"She isn't going to be happy with the news," the man finally spoke.

Vivi frowned. "How would you know?" she challenged.

"Because she was already furious when I was about to leave just now. I didn't know you were coming here."

Her frown deepened. There was a slight emphasis when he said "here," as if he knew more than he was saying. "It isn't your business what you know or don't, Mr . . . ?" She cocked her head inquiringly. She had this urge to know more about the stranger.

"Just call me Stefan."

Shock reeled through her at the name. Her own gaze searched his. He was Stefan? Their insider? But he was supposed to be distracting the—

The door suddenly swung wide open. A barely dressed woman stood beside Stefan, her hair disheveled, her makeup streaked and eyes red from crying. She was holding the old picture of Sia-Sia that Armando had given Vivi in one hand. The other held Vivi's carnelian bracelet. She looked at Vivi up and down, disbelief in her eyes.

"Vi . . . Vi? Vivi?"

Vivi stared back. Dear God. Stefan had told them he would distract the Triad boss in charge while she and Armando did their extraction. She had assumed the Triad boss was the second brother. Not . . .

"Sia-Sia?" Vivi whispered.

* * *

Jazz gave the hand signals. There was no time to waste. This was supposed to happen tomorrow night, a controlled ambush to make sure both the Triad second brother's and Dilaver's men thought they were killing each other. Dilaver, however, appeared to have an alternate plan. Jazz wasn't sure, but he could make a guess. The arms dealer wanted revenge and had taken steps to make sure that, unlike the last time, he would be the one doing the surprise attack.

Damn it. Vivi was inside the building. He needed to get her out. Why hadn't Hawk responded to his signal yet? He took a deep breath and exhaled. He needed to clear his mind and concentrate. Right now, the most important thing was to stop Dilaver's men from finishing their tasks. He had to leave it to T. to help Vivi out.

Quietly, he instructed his men. Each of them was to take care of the hostiles as quietly as possible. The best way for that was with knives. A couple of them had brought their silencers, and he nodded, indicating the furthest hostiles for them to take out. They would keep their big weapons until necessary. Right now, they had the element of surprise through stealth.

It was difficult to ascertain how many men Dilaver had brought along. Jazz kept his eyes glued on the moving shadows. He had to find out which one was the main man; that was the one he wanted for himself.

"Go," he murmured into his mike.

They streaked off at different targets, weapons ready, moving efficiently. Jazz sped toward his man, the one he hoped was in charge out here. A sudden smothered groan from one of the hostiles split the dark silence, alerting his target that something was wrong. He swung around just as Jazz reached him.

Jazz swiftly kicked at the weapon in the other man's hand and it landed with a thud somewhere in the darkness. His opponent pulled out a knife and crouched low. Jazz did the same. Around him, he was aware of the sounds of fighting. Fortunately, Dilaver's men appeared to have orders to be quiet too because no one shouted; everyone just fought furiously.

Jazz's man pounced, weapon glinting where it caught light. Jazz jumped out of the way and lashed back. The other man was quick with the knife but he wasn't used to fighting in the shadows. There was hesitancy in each lunge, as if he wasn't sure of his footing.

Jazz used his height to force the man back farther into the shadows, giving him no chance to escape. Darkness was a SEAL's friend. He had been trained to do almost everything in the dark for survival. He could smell his opponent's fear now as the latter realized his own mistake.

Too late for him. Jazz easily avoided the next desperate move, tripping the man as he lunged forward. The thug fell to his knees and gasped in pain when Jazz karate-chopped the back of his neck. His knife clattered to the ground.

Jazz quickly secured the stunned man. Then he gave him a hard smack across the face to wake him up. The man groaned loudly.

He needed quick answers. There was no time for niceties. Vivi's and Hawk's lives were in danger. Without qualm, he drew blood with his sharp knife. "Answer quickly and I'll spare you," he grimly told his prisoner. He didn't speak the Slavic dialect he had heard during his rescue of Vivi. He'd try English first, but he hoped the man understood some other European languages, like French or German. If not, pain is a universal patois. "Where are the explosives? How many? Show me."

Stefan stood at the bottom of the stairs, surveying the people in the casino. He found the person he was looking for and nodded at him. In a world with no rules, he was a man used to sudden changes of plans. Things appeared to have sped up.

His cell phone buzzed twice, then stopped. He pulled it out to read the code, then clicked to redial.

"You didn't say anything about her coming in with a second assignment," he chided gently. "I only okayed the first. Isn't she supposed to be getting Chang's sister now?"

"There isn't time to explain, darling. There are multiple things happening right now."

"T., isn't it always that way with you? Tell me." From where he was, he could already guess the turn of events. He knew the kind of man Dilaver was. He listened without interrupting, his mind already dissecting the different scenarios that could take place within the hour. "So at least I don't have to worry about Chang."

"He's on his way out with his sister. Admiral Madison's team are taking care of Dilaver's men at the back, so it's possible that nothing will happen. Nothing that goes boom, anyway."

Stefan quirked his lips in amusement. "You don't seem too worried about Vivi."

"But I am. You too. Get her out of there."

"And what would I get in return for this favor?" he asked mockingly, eyes still following the men in the casino. "After all, you transferred out and left me in charge of some very unhappy men."

T. laughed throatily. "Don't be mean to me, Stefan. I'm under a lot of stress."

"Then I'll make sure I send Diamond to help you out after I'm done here."

There was a beat of silence. "Don't do it," T. warned. "I can take care of my assignment without him."

"Payback, T. I have to do a lot of stressful work tonight. So we'll be even the next time we meet. Besides, you can't keep running from him forever. The game is fine as long as it doesn't interfere with my job. I foresee such a possibility in the near future. I need you back in the fold, T."

"The hell I—"

Stefan cut the connection. He would have to get hold of Diamond later and—his lips twitched—tell him about T.'s new prodigy, Armando Chang. Putting away his cell, he headed toward his targets. They looked up in midconversation.

"I was hoping you weren't here," Dilaver said. "Take my advice. Get out of this place now, Stefan."

"What do you plan to do?" Stefan asked calmly. If nothing else, Dilaver was a very succinct man.

"Revenge. He took my girls. My man here found out where the fuckers keep theirs, so I'm going to hurt him where he hurt me." Dilaver looked around. "And more. I don't like double-crossers. Our deal is still on, if you're wondering, only it's without any Asian bastard as my partner. I'll expect you to wire the money as soon as I release the weapons, as we've agreed. Contact me for a new time and place to meet."

"Of course. And now, gentlemen, I guess I'd better gather my people and leave."

"You do that." Dilaver smiled coldly. "I'm going to have some fun with a certain bitch tonight. I knew there was something about her the moment I laid my eyes on her the other day. Wait till I get my hands on her."

Vivi had spent almost her entire adult life dreaming of this moment—finding her lost friend. Her whole life had changed that pivotal moment when she had decided to leave Sia-Sia. They had always done everything together, dreamed about their future together, but during the darkest time of their lives, Vivi had taken off when her friend wouldn't.

She had known deep down that Sia-Sia might have suffered, even been sold off. She had hoped to prove herself wrong, endlessly making up scenarios in her head of finding Sia-Sia a happy housewife with kids, living with someone who loved her.

However, Sia-Sia—Alissa—now stood before her, giving her the same silent perusal. Vivi recognized the girl in the woman's face—the same heart shape, with the small lips that tilted at the corners. She was almost naked, her bustier showing off a beautiful figure, and she looked extremely comfortable, as if she walked like that on high heels all the time.

It wasn't an image Vivi had of her long-lost friend. The last time she saw Sia-Sia, she was a frightened young girl, clinging to her fiercely, very unsure of what they had chosen to do. Vivi had been the one who had been confident, the one who felt responsible for the both of them. Now she studied Sia-Sia as the other woman sat at her dressing table.

The tables had turned. It was Vivi who felt uncomfortable in this place, unsure of her next move. Another thing. Stefan being here in this room had meant one thing—Alissa was his connection to the Triads. The latter had looked at him with a mixture of anger and yearning before he left the room; Vivi realized now that she had just interrupted Stefan's assignment. Alissa was her agency's filter to the inside.

There was no way around the truth, that she and Sia-Sia had literally grown worlds apart. "I've been looking for you for a long time."

Something hard flashed across Sia-Sia's face. She turned away to check herself in the mirror. "Looking for me?" She shrugged. "I've been right here."

She was right. She had been here all along, right under Vivi's nose. "Everyone in the village said you ran off with your mother. No one knew where you were," Vivi said.

"Of course not. Why do I care whether they know where I am or not?" Sia-Sia—Alissa—wiped her face with a tissue. "It's been . . . eight or ten years? You look good, all tall and sexy. I wouldn't have recognized you. What've you been up to? As you can tell, I've been doing very well for myself."

Vivi bit her lower lip. This wasn't how she'd envisioned the reunion at all. No hugs. No joy. Instead, a tension stretched between them. It was magnified by the way they were dressed—the contradiction of her casual clothing with Sia-Sia's tightly laced red bustier and fishnet stockings. Now that she had time to look around, the room, with its silk screens of nude couples and the huge bed that dominated it, only emphasized their differences more.

What did one say to a woman who was living the lifestyle she opposed with every ounce of energy? "I have thought of that last night often," Vivi finally said. "I wondered whether you were okay. I never thought—"

Alissa laughed. "That look on your face says it all. You don't approve. You're shocked and horrified that I'm a madam. Is it because you remembered those childish talks we had about sex and how bad men were with their private parts, that we would never let them use their thing on us?" She looked mockingly at Vivi's reflection.

"You're right, I don't approve," Vivi said, "but I'm not here tonight to judge you. After a long search, someone led me here, and I wanted to make sure it was really you."

"So you bribed and threatened my men. Sister." Alissa laughed humorlessly. She put on fresh lipstick, rubbing her lips to smudge the bright smear of red. She turned. "You've always been very brave, Vivi. That was what has driven me since the night you left, you know. Be brave, you always said. Then I decided I would have a new motto. You want to know what it is? Be smart. Be very, very smart. My mother had my new stepfather as a protector. She was treated like a queen. So I knew what to do. I needed to get one of my stepbrothers to be mine. It isn't something you would do, is it? You're dressed like one of those office workers, so I don't think you're in the same business I am."

Her expression was mocking, her smile brittle. She stood up and ran her hands down her figure, as if she enjoyed making Vivi uncomfortable. She sauntered forward. "You really caught me at the wrong time, you know. I'm in such a horrible mood. The man I've set my heart on just told me he didn't give a fuck about me but he still liked this body just the same. Do you remember how we always compared ours? How we loved to dance? Well, I still do that, except I think it's a bit racier than what we did. What do you think?"

Vivi watched as Alissa started to hum an old tune they used to sing and gyrate sexually to emphasize the beat. The other woman was mocking her with her sexuality. Vivi understood that it was her weapon in life, since she had used it to get where she was now. She thought about the Dan Nhat that she had bought for her friend. Somehow, she knew she would never give it to Alissa.

"When I think about you, Sia-Sia, I think about our friendship. I felt bad leaving you that night and when I was in a position to look for you, it became my goal." Vivi took a deep breath. "I made the mistake of not thinking how you would think of me through the years."

Alissa laughed and continued her dancing. "Of course I think about you now and then. In fact, I can sum up my thoughts through the years. Look at me, Vivi, I know these things." Her body swayed rhythmically to each punctuated beat. "Look at me, I'm powerful. Look at me, I can make a man melt in my arms." She stopped, a frown forming. "Except him. I can't get him, no matter how much I pleasure him. He wouldn't even kiss me. Do you know what it's like to have a man who doesn't want you back?"

"No."

"I have my pick of men and yet, I want him. Are you married?"

"No."

"Do you have a lover?" She looked at Vivi curiously. "Many lovers? Do you have one you want for your own?"

Vivi thought of Jazz but she didn't answer any of Sia-Sia's questions. She suddenly realized that she had to let go of her past, that this would take her nowhere at all, but she couldn't leave without some sort of closure.

"What are you doing here, exactly?" Sia-Sia continued. "You can't tell me you're all alone here searching for me. I'm not that naive kid anymore, you know. You aren't here to ask me for a job, are you? Because I'm too busy right now. I do have some girls who might teach you how to dress better. I can even teach you different ways to pleasure a man."

"Alissa." She couldn't call this person Sia-Sia, not when she was telling her about her bordellos. "I volunteer for a women's group that helps women and children in trouble, sort of the way we were. We find them safe houses. If there

had been these places in the past, we would have gone together, found sanctuary somehow."

Alissa stared at her, then shrugged. Her smile was catlike.
"Somehow I don't think you're going to like the things I
teach my girls. I buy them now, my dear old friend. I buy
them and I teach them myself. They all learn in the end."
She laughed again. "And if they don't, a little drugs can be
persuasive."

This time, Vivi didn't hide her disgust. She didn't want to
stay here any longer. Sadness welled up inside her. "You'll
always be my special friend," she said in a low voice, patting
her heart, "in here. But you stand for everything I work
against, Alissa. So I have to say goodbye and if we meet
again, I won't let our past friendship stand in the way of saving those girls you lock up."

"You and who against my brothers?" Alissa asked. "Who
are you to judge what I do? My girls are saved from hunger
and begging on the streets. Your stupid organization can't
take them all in, anyway. And if they are smart like me, their
lives aren't that bad. Come by anytime you want to learn
something, Vivi. I can teach you how to be powerful."

"That's not the kind of power I want."

"Here, you'd better take these things with you. I don't
need them. I made my choices a long time ago."

Vivi took the old picture of Sia-Sia and her bracelet from
Alissa. For an instant their fingers touched and their eyes
met. Emotion tightened her chest. She had found her friend
and lost her all the same.

"Goodbye," she said. Tomorrow she would be going after
the Triads more than ever. "Stay . . . safe."

"Goodbye," Alissa said. Her chin went up. "I would never
have survived the dark jungles with you. I have a better life
this way and don't regret it. Not one bit."

"By destroying other girls' lives? You're living off some
other children's future."

Alissa dropped her hand, her gaze turning cold and ruthless. "Ah well. What can I say. A girl has got to survive the best she can. So, go. The next time my men won't be this friendly with you, old *friend*."

Vivi turned. The door behind them opened at the same time. It was Stefan.

"A fire has been started downstairs. It's time to leave," he said. He looked at Vivi with those strange eyes, as if he could see right into her. "Now."

"We can't tell whether this is all there are," Zone said. "All the other hostiles are down."

Disgusted, Jazz turned away to look at the prisoner they had tied up next to the building. "Listen, I'm going to leave you here and if there are any charges left, you'll blow up with it."

"No, no, please! Please get me out of here."

That alone told Jazz that there was something still missing. "Where is the timer?"

"Dilaver. Dilaver has gone inside. He paid to find out where the girls are and he's going to make sure the Triads lose them. Revenge, he said."

Vivi. Jazz was about to charge to the front of the building but found himself blocked by Cucumber and Dirk.

"Sorry, sir, can't let you go in there when it's about to explode. Hawk's already inside."

"Precisely," Jazz said coldly. "We have to go in and find Dilaver and stop him."

"One of us will do that. You have to be out here."

"You're kidding me, right?"

"No, sir. Protocol. You can see the targets from out here and direct the rest of Plan B," Dirk said firmly.

"There isn't going to be any fucking Plan B if everyone

gets blown away," Jazz pointed out. He didn't push forward. He had learned to listen to his teammates during times when his emotions were involved. Vivi was inside. Everything in his heart was urgently commanding him to rush in there and get her out.

"What are your orders, sir?"

Think, Zeringue. Jazz took a deep breath. He pulled out his cell again. "I'll let T. know what's happening. Dirk, keep an eye on the front, and the moment Dilaver or Hawk shows up, let me know. The bastard would give himself some time to get away. Joker and Zone, get in position to take out Dilaver's sidekicks for Hawk. Cucumber and Mink, come with me. We'll check out that back way and see whether we can get in through there."

"What about the prisoner, sir?"

"Secure and gag. Keep him out of sight. T.? It's me. Any news from inside?" A little of the tension eased as he listened. Someone was with Vivi and getting her out. He told T. what Dilaver's plans were. "The sick son of a bitch just wanted to do a tit-for-tat. I don't think he really cares about attending any peacemaking meeting tomorrow."

"Not likely, when he found someone else for his weapons," T. said. "Jazz, I'm communicating with Armando right now. I'll alert him about the girls in the back. Hang on."

Jazz had been wondering how on earth the man was going to escape with his sister. But he was a Triad sibling, Vivi had said, so he must know all the different exit points.

"Jazz, he said someone has started a fire. It's his chance to get behind the guards and release all the girls. The guards will be running out the back door with them."

"Affirmative. We'll take out the guards, make them think it's Dilaver."

"Good. And Jazz? I know Vivi will get out safely. The person I sent will do his job."

"I hope so, T. And for the record, you didn't make me trust you with your voice thing, did you?"

There was a slight pause. "Darling, despite the rumors, I

can't make people do what they don't want to do, or some males I know would be less pigheaded. Now go."

"Sir!" Dirk's voice was urgent. "People are rushing out in panic out front."

"Any sign of Dilaver or Hawk?"

"Not yet."

"Okay. I think our side started the fire and Dilaver's caught by surprise. Stand by and be ready. Plan B is about to play out, men."

"Standing and Ready!"

"Hooyah!"

Jazz checked his weapon one final time. No need to be so stealthy anymore. All he needed was Vivi out of there. Now. Damn it. There was no time to call T. back and warn her. Whoever was with Vivi had better haul her over his shoulders. By now he knew how the woman he loved thought. She was going to try to save the girls, of course.

Vivi could hear the melee downstairs. The sounds of yelling and stomping feet were strangely muffled through the walls.

"It can't be fire. I don't see any of the guards," Alissa said. "Stefan, what's going on?"

"I saw Dilaver downstairs. Not too long after that, I heard the first shouts."

"Dilaver?" Alissa stopped at the top of the stairs. "But . . . tomorrow . . . I have to call *Yeekoh*! He should be here."

"Alissa, we have to go down now," Stefan said.

"My cash! And jewelry! Help me while I call—"

"Alissa," Vivi interrupted, sensing urgency in the air, "there's no time. Let's go."

Alissa pushed away Vivi's hand. "No one's getting my cash and jewelry," she said angrily. She looked back, her mind on her belongings. "You go. I can get away on my own."

All around them, doors were opening and closing as news of the fire reached the girls upstairs. They came running out of their rooms, some half-dressed, some pulling their drunken customers by the hand, and tried to rush down the stairway. In their panic, they pushed whoever was in the way. Vivi found herself separated from Alissa. A horrible thought occurred.

"Alissa! Sia-Sia!"

Alissa turned around impatiently. "What?"

"The girls that are locked up downstairs—you have to let them out!"

Alissa shook her head. "Who cares? Stefan! Come with me." She ran against the wall of bodies. She turned and realized Stefan wasn't beside her. "Stefan? Stefan!"

Vivi saw him halfway down the stairs already, helping some of the girls who had fallen. He looked up and beckoned. She glanced back at Alissa. But her friend was barely paying attention, calling out Stefan's name as she slowly moved farther and farther out of hearing distance. Vivi squeezed her way forward until she reached Stefan.

"You'll have to get Alissa. I'm going down to the locked rooms."

"You don't know where those rooms are," he pointed out. When Vivi looked back up the stairs, he leaned forward so she could hear him amid the noise, and said, "You have to make a choice. Go back upstairs or save the girls? You can only do one thing."

Vivi glanced up sharply. His face was a mask, except for those strange light eyes. He didn't seem in a big hurry, as if he was willing to wait for her decision. But of course they were in a hurry—there was a fire. His presence was just oddly calming, even when everyone around them was getting hysterical. A part of her noted that he didn't offer to go upstairs to get Sia-Sia.

"Downstairs," she said. Those girls had to be freed.

He nodded. "Alissa can take care of herself." He took her by the arm and put her in front of him. It took her a second to realize that this made it easier for him to talk into her ear as they moved forward. "The building has been wired with explosives. I told one of my men to start a distraction to get people out. I guess a fire is the best scenario."

Vivi stumbled as someone elbowed her out of the way. She found herself pulled back against Stefan's chest, his arms around her. She was confused. Had Jazz wired the building?

But there was no time to ask anything right now. She smelled the acridness of smoke in the air. They had reached downstairs, and the place was definitely in exit mode. She stood there, trying to place herself before she continued. Before she could gather her thoughts, someone grabbed her roughly. Her world suddenly exploded into stars.

All the air in her lungs seemed to have left her body. She fell backward even as she vaguely realized someone had punched her out. Someone held on to her.

"She's mine!" she heard someone yelling. He sounded very familiar. She tried to shake off the stars buzzing in her head. "I'm taking her with me. You coming, Stefan?"

"I'll be right behind you. Don't hit her again." There was a pause. "You'll have to carry her out. She isn't going to make it on her own."

"Don't worry. I won't let her escape me again. Better get out. Fast. You haven't much time once I'm outside. I don't wait for anyone. I'll see you tomorrow, Stefan."

Vivi felt herself swung around and then hung upside down. Oh shit. Dilaver. She could hear him yelling for his men but it was difficult to understand what he said with all the noise. She seemed to be hearing muffled echoes in her left ear. Lifting her hand, she touched the side of her face. It burned. The brute had certainly given her a wallop. Grimly, she counted the voices. Okay, Dilaver and maybe three . . . four men? She couldn't hear Stefan among them.

She forced herself to ignore the blood rushing to her head, adding to her dizziness. As long as Dilaver was moving, she had time to think and come up with a plan. He was probably the one who had wired the building with explosives. Somehow he had caught sight of and gone after her. She recalled her earlier conversation with T. and how she had agreed that this mission was personal and that she mustn't jeopardize their insider's work.

When Dilaver snatched her up, Stefan obviously couldn't just rescue her without revealing himself. Besides, the girls in the back—they needed rescuing more than she did. She had handled the thug once before; she could handle him again. If only she didn't feel as if she was headless.

Jazz couldn't believe it. He had been staring at the entrance, watching desperately for Vivi among the hordes of seemingly naked girls. The last thing he had expected was seeing Dilaver and Hawk coming out of the building with Vivi over Dilaver's shoulder. Hawk was talking, gesturing. There were two others with them. The interpreter and a bodyguard.

"Are you getting Hawk's signals, Cumber and Joker?" he spoke into the mike quietly.

"Affirmative. He wants those two with Dilaver put out. The one on the right not a problem from my angle," Joker replied.

"I can take out the other hostile from my angle, sir."

"Good. Stand by for clearance." The screams were louder now as thick smoke whirled out of the windows. "What's happening in the back, men?"

"Situation under control. As expected, the guards are running out through the secret exits, leaving the doors wide open. We got them. We made sure those who fought and escaped think they were being shot at by Dilaver's men. There were a couple who had taken off with a dead hostile, sir. I think they're going to show the body to their boss."

"Good."

"We have women running out too but they need help. Stumbling and acting funny, sir."

"Help them. They're the locked-up ones Armando freed, probably drugged." Jazz heard the sirens of the fire department in the background. "You have to stay out of sight as soon as the authorities arrive. Do you hear them?"

"Affirmative. Ten-four."

Hawk was signaling again. Jazz froze. His friend had a message just for him, using signals that only he would understand. He wanted two shots in his direction. One to hit him in the arm, the other for Dilaver. He wanted Jazz to shoot both of them. As if Hawk was aware of the thoughts running in his friend's head, he looked up at their direction, his gaze direct, fierce.

"What's Hawk saying?" Cucumber asked quietly. He knew about their secret language.

"He wants me to nick his arm first, and then get Dilaver." He had no problem with the latter. But shooting Hawk . . .

"Shit. Why wouldn't it be better just to get that bastard the way we had planned? I thought he was going to help Dilaver when he's down. Why shoot him too?"

"Because . . ." Jazz swallowed. "Vivi's in the way. When Hawk reacts to being shot, Dilaver will turn toward him and that'll give us a clear shot at him without risking Vivi."

And he had to be the one. His best friend trusted his aim.

"We have to get away fast. I hear the fire engines. That means the authorities won't be far behind."

Vivi frowned. Her hearing must be playing tricks with her. That sounded like Hawk speaking another language. She peered to the left. Dilaver shifted her like a sack of potatoes and she winced as everything whirled in her head.

"You should just leave the girl."

"No! She's probably working with them. That's why she was at the bridge. She has a lot of questions to answer." Dilaver cursed rapidly. "Where the hell are the others?"

"We can't wait, boss." That was somebody else . . . not Hawk. Maybe she heard wrong.

This time she managed to slowly turn her head without becoming dizzy. She craned her neck to glimpse the man next to Dilaver. It *was* Hawk. She frowned. Wasn't Jazz's team going to be here tomorrow, too?

"Well, where is your boss?" Dilaver was asking the man who looked like Hawk.

"He's probably gone already. He doesn't stand around waiting for trouble. I'm going to—" Hawk groaned in pain, fell on one knee, holding on to his arm. Vivi could see blood streaming between Hawk's fingers. He had been shot.

"What's the matter?" Dilaver quickly turned toward Hawk and this time Vivi closed her eyes to avoid being dizzy again. When she opened them, she was facing the other way.

"Fuck!"

"Who—" Vivi heard a thud and Dilaver's body jerked under her. He shouted in surprised pain and toppled forward.

With all the screaming and yelling around them, they hadn't heard any gunshot. The sirens sounded closer and closer. Vivi tried to move but her legs were trapped by Dilaver's weight. He moaned as she groped and grabbed at clothing and limbs, wrenching herself free. Someone pushed at her back until she was finally able to crawl away from the fallen man on her own. She turned around. All of Dilaver's men were down—dead. Dilaver—no, he was alive, howling in pain. She caught sight of Hawk beside him. It must have been him pushing her just now. He was looking in the direction of the trees behind her and signaling. Then he looked down at Vivi and winked.

"Dilaver, are you all right?" he shouted as he got on his feet, still holding on to his arm. "We have to get out of here. Come on! We're being shot at. The Triads are after us."

Vivi watched Hawk haul the injured big thug up on his feet. He urged him to put a hand over his shoulder, helping him along. "Let's go, come on, man. The police are almost here." As they passed her, Hawk winked again and dropped a small piece of paper next to her.

Jazz rushed toward the scene, his eyes glued on Hawk. His shot had hit him exactly where he had intended, but it was still tough to see his friend go down. He pushed people out of the way as he hurried forward but Hawk was already back on his feet and helping Dilaver up. He was on his way out of there. His mission had started. Just before he disappeared into the crowd, he paused and half turned. Dilaver appeared to double over in pain. Hawk took that moment to signal. Two taps to his heart.

"Jazz!" Vivi called out.

Jazz went down on his haunches, shocked at her puffy face. Blood streaked all over her hands. He pulled her into his arms, relieved that she was alive and free. He looked up again. Hawk and Dilaver were gone.

"Are you okay?" He pulled back to examine Vivi's face again. A fierce anger replaced concern as he saw the damage. "Son of a bitch. I wish I could kill him for doing this to you, *chouchou.*"

Vivi shook her head. "I'm fine, just . . . a tad . . . swollen. Jazz, why are you here?"

Jazz stood up with Vivi in his arms. "Later. The fire engines are here."

"Okay." She seemed content to lay her head against his shoulder as he walked quickly toward the back of the building to join the rest of team. "Hawk's gone, isn't he?"

"Yeah." Using a weapon on his own friend had been the toughest thing he had ever done.

"Are you okay?"

He smiled tenderly. She was worried about him even when she was injured. "Yeah. Just a bit lost. I've always known where Hawk was and how to contact him, but now . . ."

He didn't know how to explain what he was feeling. Hawk was his best friend and they had been together in the navy for over a decade. They had grown up together, had watched each other's back in their missions together. He was no longer able to do that.

"I know. I lost a friend tonight, too," Vivi said softly. "I saw her, Jazz, but . . . she's no longer Sia-Sia."

The others had already returned to the agreed meeting

point. Someone brought out lanterns and flares and he could see spectators and helpers gathering in the melee. Without needing an order, the men merged into the shadows of the nearby trees and buildings.

Dirk gave a quick update. "The live prisoner is ready for transport. You should've seen the number of young girls who escaped through the back exits after we'd gotten the guards—I lost count, there were so many. Somebody apparently unlocked their cells before the fire reached the back. One of them said some man pointed them the way out. We made sure the weaker ones are together where the firemen will easily see them. No explosions . . . yet."

"Good. Let's get ready to go then."

"Is Vivienne okay?"

"I'm fine."

"No, she isn't. Dilaver punched her or something."

"Fucker!"

Jazz quickly did a head count. Everyone was there, except for . . . "Did you all see Hawk signaling our team sign?"

"Yeah," Cucumber said. "The shot was good, sir. He's okay."

"I signaled back but I doubt he saw me," Joker said.

"That was strange, how everything worked out, even though—"

"Jazz! Put me down!" Vivi, who had been quietly listening, tapped Jazz's arm excitedly.

"Whoa, sweetheart. Wait." She wriggled impatiently till he sat her on her feet. She took a step and stumbled. "Where are you going off to now?"

"Look! Look!"

A man was walking slowly through the gathering groups of people, making his way toward the alley where the fire engines were parked. He had a girl in his arms.

"What? Who's he?"

"That's Stefan. But look at the girl in his arms! That's Rose. I'm sure that's Rose! Let's go over there!"

Stefan. That must be the insider T. was telling him about.

"No, sweetheart, we can't afford to be seen right now. I'll get Stefan to come here instead."

It did look like Rose. They watched as Dirk sprinted over. They exchanged a few lines and Stefan nodded, changing direction.

Vivi turned and hugged Jazz. "Oh God. It *is* Rose, Jazz. I can't believe he found her!"

Jazz smiled. There were no words to describe how much he loved this woman who cared so much about the well-being of others. He knew that had she been able, she wouldn't have hesitated to risk her life to save any of those women inside. He tightened his hold on her. He owed Stefan and Hawk a big thank you for getting her out for him.

CHAPTER
28

The room back at the compound wasn't really that small, but two attending medics, T., Armando Chang, as well as six SEALs sitting around her bed, took up a lot of space. Rose was resting in another room. Vivi wanted to be with her but no one appeared to think she could walk on her own two feet. She had never been carried around by so many men in one night.

Stefan hadn't stayed once he deposited Rose into Cucumber's arms. He studied them for a second, then he touched the injured side of Vivi's face gently. "I'm sorry I couldn't stop him. But your friend's bullet should hurt like hell by now." He nodded to Jazz. "Good shot. Tell T. I'll call." With that, he went back into the crowd and disappeared.

Back at the compound, Vivi had learned what had happened earlier and how the timetable had gone down the tubes the moment the team saw Dilaver scouring the place. Everyone's adrenaline was still high from the night's unexpected adventure; a low-key tension wove around the room as each member of the group related his or her little part. Even T. had been an important player, directing offstage, the glue that held the action together. Without her, no one from all the different groups would have any idea what was happening inside or outside the Triad den.

"We're lucky we decided to do a little checking," Jazz said quietly. "Dilaver had planned to bring the place down. If he had succeeded, there would have been many more casualties."

"Yes," T. said. "As it is, the authorities are suspecting gang war, since the dead are mainly Triad members and some unknown foreigners they will discover are part of an arms-dealing gang."

"Courtesy of GEM?" Jazz asked, cocking a brow.

T. smiled. "The governing authority here might be under the Triad thumb, Jazz, but there are still some who celebrate Triad deaths. They'll pass news on to everyone that the second brother has suffered a serious loss. We've emptied all their accounts and will be sending information and coffee money to certain people concerning Triad secret drug locations."

"Good." Vivi found herself relaxing against the pillow. The medics had given her something for the pain, which reminded her . . . She shuddered at the sudden image of Rose lying in some locked room, unable to move, at the mercy of those people. How could her father do this to her? "I hope we find all those damn pills and destroy them."

"Stefan has already taken care of the batch we used as bait," T. reassured her.

"How? That man couldn't have had time," Vivi said.

"I don't know the details, darling. I just know it from the brief status report he sent. But if he said he destroyed them, he did."

"Who's he, T.?" Vivi asked curiously. "Is his name really Stefan? I have never heard of him through the channels. Is he GEM?"

There were male operatives in GEM but Vivi had never heard of a Stefan. The standard operating procedure for two newly met operatives was to send or communicate to each other a gift or symbol of their GEM insignia for quick identification and later references in their own debriefing. He hadn't done so.

"Not exactly." T. wasn't very forthcoming. "He's involved in a few GEM contracts."

"I would like to meet him some day to thank him," Jazz said. He was looking at Vivi. "He was very quick-thinking, what with so much happening inside. And still got his job of putting Hawk and Dilaver together done."

"The insertion was more complicated than our planned one," T. agreed, "but Stefan always finds a way to finish his job."

"What's his job? I know he's one of the COS commandos, T. He isn't Alex Diamond, is he?" Vivi stifled a yawn.

T. looked startled for an instant, then her expression turned to amusement. "No. Alex's job is more like"—she watched Jazz readjust the cold compress Vivi had on her face—"Lieutenant Zeringue's. A lot of strategy. He initiates the operation. Stefan usually takes over near the end of one."

That made sense. Vivi understood Phase Two was in the final stages and that Phase Three began with Hawk. She was getting more and more interested in GEM's new partnership with COS Command.

"I'd like to thank him for Rose."

It was a sneaky attempt to find information and of course T. didn't fall for it. Her chief's eyes were filled with secret amusement as she shook her head. But hey, a girl could try.

"Since all of us, except for Armando, have been briefed about Phase Two, I'll confirm that he's one of the COS commandos," T. acknowledged. "And no, his name isn't Stefan. I think he chose it to attract Hawk's attention at the beginning."

"That makes sense, since there are so many Steves in Hawk's family. Ladies, you have to tell me what COS stands for. The admiral used it and I didn't have a chance to ask Hawk," Jazz said. "I'd like to know what outfit my friend is working with right now."

T. hesitated. There were, after all, quite a number of people present. "Covert Subversive commandos. They are an infiltration system that destroys organizations from within."

"The guards inside knew and feared him," Vivi said. "I heard the one in the red pants call him Ghost Lightning or something like that. I can see why too."

"Why?" Jazz asked.

Vivi put down the compress and touched the side of her face. She couldn't feel a thing there as her fingertips pressed on cold, numbed flesh. "It's his eyes. I bet he scared the hell out of the locals with that strange color. Like lightning. I noticed those thugs didn't dare look too long into his eyes. And he had this stillness about him. You should've seen him when everyone was running around inside that awful place, Jazz." She didn't mention how she'd found him with Alissa, that the latter had obviously been his assignment. There was no black or white in their cloak-and-dagger world, and she didn't harbor any feelings against Stefan for using her former friend. She looked around the room with her one good eye. She realized suddenly that she had lost much but she'd also gained a lot, too. "Of course, you were all doing just as good a job as he did. Thank you, every one of you. I've decided you guys aren't too shabby after all. I'm going to make you my honorary goats."

She grinned at the sudden explosion of machismo in the room. It was also her way to distract the men from asking any more questions about COS Command or Alissa. She knew T. would take the ball and run with it. She was right.

"I think you should rest now, darling. Plenty of time tomorrow to debrief and get everything in order. Rose will be fine. I'll check on her later. Jazz, you make sure she stays in bed. She probably has concussion. Every one of you, except Jazz, follow me. I have this strong desire for some food."

Vivi rolled her eyes as T. winked at all the men around her. She was out of the room in seconds. The men, except for Armando, jumped to their feet.

"Yes, ma'am!"

"Food! Did she mention food?"

"I can eat a whole cow."

"Move, man, you're such a freaking sloth. Can't you tell Jazz wants us gone?"

"Do sloths eat? Besides jerk off?"

They filed out noisily. Vivi tilted her head, using her good eye to glare at Armando.

"I'm sorry," he said. "I didn't know how to tell you."

"I know you unlocked those doors and helped save many of those girls tonight," Vivi told him, "but I'm still going to kick your ass for keeping Sia-Sia's identity from me."

Armando smiled. "Then we'll be even."

She gave him a solemn stare and then smiled slightly. "Then we'll be," she agreed. "I'm glad you found your sister. How's she?"

Armando's expression hardened. "Not good. They'll pay for what they did to her. But I'll let you rest now. Good night."

The door closed behind him. Vivi scooted to one side of the bed. "Are you going to let me rest all alone?"

Jazz smiled and moved to join her there. "You're going to be asleep soon after taking that medication anyway. You're trying not to yawn already."

"But you'll stay?"

"Yes, *chouchou*, I'll be here when you wake up."

She sighed, resting her cheek against his shoulder. "Oh, wait." She stretched one arm out, patting the night table by her. Sitting up again, she stifled another yawn as she handed over Hawk's note. "Here, Hawk dropped this. I think it's for you. I can't read it anyway."

Jazz unfolded the crumpled paper. Vivi leaned back. She could barely keep her eyes open now.

"Strange, but totally Hawk."

"What does it say?" she asked sleepily.

"It says, 'Remember, twin, I'll always be GI number one.' What the hell did he bring that up for?"

Vivi chuckled sleepily. "Jazz . . . ?"

"Hmm?"

"Don't be mad, okay?"

"About what, sweetheart?"

She yawned again. She couldn't even form the thoughts to explain what Hawk's note meant as she fought to keep her eyes open. Needed . . . to . . . do this. She put a finger into her mouth pushing up inside her cheek. She used her thumb to scrape at the tiny wire that held the disguise in place. Thank God for the painkillers or the task would have been impossible for one side of her face. Slowly pulling out the inserts that changed the upper palate of her mouth, Vivi said, in her grandma accent, "You're my Number Ten GI. But I love you anyway."

There was silence. She sighed as she closed her eyes. She was in so much trouble.

"You . . . what . . . don't you fall asleep on me! You're Grandmamasan? You're . . . wait, wait . . . what did you say after that? Vivi!"

But Vivi could only smile as the drugs took over. Her last thought was how sweet her lover's frustrated yelling was.

New Orleans
Four months later

It was supposed to be a happy day. Jazz looked around him. Everyone was waiting expectantly for his speech. He had it all planned, too.

He was going to tell how incredible the last four months had been, running back and forth between two continents, trying to make a relationship work out. He was going to outline all the funny things that had happened between Vivi and him. How they had first met, without some classified details, of course. How he had finally proposed while playing a melody on the Da Nhat in front of a bunch of laughing locals and had played "Oh Susannah" mournfully till she had finally agreed. How she had transferred out of her GEM assignment with Interpol. So many things to celebrate. Most of all, today he was going to talk about the love of his life in front of all his friends who had shown up for his engagement party.

Vivi, the woman he adored. And how capable and wonderful she was. He smiled, as he always did, when he thought about her.

She had finally flown home to the States and met with his

mother and sisters in Slidell. She had been nervous. His maman, bless her heart, had taken one look at Vivi and hugged her.

"You're perfect for my Zola," she had exclaimed. "Come and tell me everything."

Everything had gone so well. Even his brother, Zippy, appeared to be on his best behavior around Vivi. He had actually shown up in a shirt—a rare thing for his wild and unruly brother when there was a strange woman around. Jazz had no doubt Vivi would have handled Zippy, but he was glad he didn't have to deal with his brother's outrageous sense of humor. She was already a little overwhelmed by all the sisters—all of whom took her out on an all-girl pow-wow—but she hadn't run off, not even when his mother kept introducing her as the future Mrs. Zola Zeringue.

Maman had insisted on an engagement party and Jazz, as usual, let the woman steamroll over him. What began as a simple affair had bloomed into an extravaganza that would have had him hiding in the bayou in the old days. But this was his engagement party and he had seen the light in his Vivi's eyes; she was happy and that was what he wanted. This was new to her, he realized that now, this attention to her. She had always focused on others and now she deserved this. His wise maman had known this.

Then an hour before the party, Admiral Madison called. Jazz hadn't expected the admiral to show up anyway, so he had thought the call was just to congratulate him and Vivi. But his commander had tagged on another piece of news after a pause.

"It's Hawk," he'd said. "I have to tell you while the others in the team are there, Lieutenant. We lost him. Our source reported that Dilaver found out he was a plant. There's another report of a body found with Hawk's description but no confirmation as of yet. I'll keep in touch."

Hawk could be dead. Or in deep shit somewhere. Jazz felt that it wasn't right to be celebrating his own engagement while Hawk was missing. But everyone had arrived, including his own team. They sat in shocked silence in a corner of the huge hall as they absorbed the news.

"He would want you to continue, sir," Cucumber finally said. "It's your day today."

"Nothing's confirmed yet so I refuse to believe he's dead anyway," Mink said.

"We'll take it one day at a time." Joker gave him the microphone. "Go make the speech. Vivi's waiting for you over there."

Jazz took the mike and looked at Vivi, standing on the dais. She looked so beautiful, dressed in a soft green dress. She had told him she would support anything he decided, that they were in this together.

Together. This was a special day for Vivi. She had given him her trust and love, overcoming her fear of being abandoned. She had even gotten to like uniformed men now. He couldn't go up there and put this off. She belonged to him, just as he belonged to her. He made his way to the dais. She was wearing the pendant he gave her when they'd met. Her eyes told him all he needed to know. He bent and softly kissed her. The guests cheered lustily.

"Hey! Speech first!" someone yelled.

"We want to hear this big news you wanted us to fly here for!" another person added.

Yes, the big news. Jazz looked out into the crowd, very aware that his family, his team, and Vivi's own friends knew of his fear for Hawk, knowing that they would support him in whatever he chose to do. Friends were that way.

"It's okay," Vivi whispered. "I'm with you a hundred percent. I love you, my darling GI number ten, no matter if it's now or later."

That was now her nickname for him. In retaliation, Jazz called her Grandmamasan. All this only served to remind him of Hawk.

"Love you too," he said.

"Speeeeeech!" one of his sisters called up.

Jazz put up his hand and everyone shushed. He pulled Vivi closer to him. Her hand caressed his back.

"I can't start celebrating love without first talking about friendship. It's friendship that brought Vivi and me together, and it's also friendship that brought all of you here. But someone who should be here isn't. He's my best friend and I wanted him to be my best man. Right now, it doesn't seem possible. I'd like to have him here in spirit at my engagement to Vivi." Jazz paused, trying to gather his thoughts. "I believe in miracles. In my job, little miracles happen every day. Like meeting Vivi, my love. I also believe that music is everywhere, that one could celebrate and mourn with a song. Hopefully, Hawk, wherever he is, will hear this song and know that he's in our thoughts." He turned and picked up his brother's guitar. Strumming a few chords, he added, "This is a song by the Fab Four."

The choice of song had just come, like all his music usually did. It was written with a simple, haunting melody, conveying layers of emotions. Jazz kept his eyes on Vivi as he sang the lyrics. It started about places he remembered and he knew she was thinking about the woods where they had made love. About how these places had their moments. And he thought of Hawk and him during their times together.

Of friends and lovers. The room was so silent as he sang the part where "some are dead" that he could hear the squeaky strings of the guitar. He played the beginning chords again, this time adding a touch of energy to it, giving the tune a more hopeful beat as he tapped on the guitar. He smiled at Vivi.

Of all the friends and lovers. Vivi smiled back, her eyes bright with tears, as she realized the rest of the song was about her. That she was everything to him. That he loved her more than anything in this life.

"In my life, Vivi, I love you more," he ended and put down his guitar.

There was a pause. Then Vivi let out a small sob and

stepped into his arms. The room came alive as everyone cheered.

"I love you, Zola Zeringue," she yelled out above the pandemonium. "But I'm still going to kick your ass for making me cry in public."

Jazz laughed. Their lives would always have worries and obstacles, what with his job and her constant need to save young girls. But now they had each other.

Roses are red, violets are blue,
but these books are much more fun than flowers!
Coming to you in February from Avon Romance . . .

Something About Emmaline by Elizabeth Boyle

An Avon Romantic Treasure

Alexander Denford, Baron Sedgwick is a gentleman much envied for his indulgent and oft-absent wife, Emmaline—who is in fact a mere figment meant to keep the *ton* mamas at bay. But one day Alexander starts receiving bills from London for ball gowns in his imaginary bride's name, and he realizes a real Emmaline is about to present herself, whether he likes it or not!

Hidden Secrets by Cait London

An Avon Contemporary Romance

A missing boy, an unsolved murder, the feeling of impending danger. Marlo cannot figure out how they are connected—until she finds and develops an old roll of film that unlocks the past. But as she gets closer to the truth of the missing boy, she must choose between two men for protection. And if she makes one wrong move, it will be her last . . .

In the Night by Kathryn Smith

An Avon Romance

A life of crime is not what Wynthrope Ryland wanted for himself, but he will do what he must—if only to protect his dearest brother, North. Moira Tyndale, a stately viscountess, is to be the victim of this ill-timed theft, but she is also the one woman who can tempt him . . . or perhaps, somehow, set his wrongs to rights.

Stealing Sophie by Sarah Gabriel

An Avon Romance

Connor MacPherson, a Highland laird turned outlaw, must find a bride—or steal one. Intending to snatch infamously wanton Kate MacCarran, he mistakenly abducts her sister, Sophie—recently returned from a French convent. Quickly wedded, passionately bedded, Sophie cannot escape, and cannot be rescued—but perhaps this is not such a bad thing after all!

REL 0105